PORTION

of the

SEA

Books by
CHRISTINE LEMMON

Portion of the Sea

Sanibel Scribbles

Sand in My Eyes

Whisper from the Ocean

PORTION
of the
SEA

A novel

CHRISTINE LEMMON

Penmark Publishing
Ft. Myers, Florida

ISBN-10: 0-9712874-6-5
EAN: 978-0-9712874-6-4

Penmark Publishing, LLC
www.penmarkpublishing.com

First Trade Printing: July 2010

Cover by Julie Metz. Book design by Carla Rozman.
Editorial production by Jeffrey Davis, Center to Page.

Printed in Canada

| 10 | 9 | 8 | 7 | 6 |
| 5 | 4 | 3 | 2 | 1 |

To John

"You hurled me into the deep,
into the very heart of the seas,
and the currents swirled about me;
all your waves and breakers swept over me.

I said, 'I have been banished from your site;
yet I will look again toward your holy temple.'

The engulfing waters threatened me, the deep surrounded me;
seaweed was wrapped around my head. To the roots of the
mountains I sank down; the earth beneath barred me in forever.
But you brought my life up from the pit, O Lord my God."

—JONAH 2: 3-6

AUTHOR'S NOTE

THIS IS A WORK OF FICTION. I wrote it while living on Sanibel, and my love for the area has inspired the writing. It has always fascinated me how generation after generation of families who could vacation anywhere in the world continue returning to Sanibel. My grandparents were the first in our family to fall in love with the area and move to the island.

They passed their passion on to my parents who began vacationing there from the Midwest. I was two years old when I first walked the white beaches in search of seashells, and I continued doing so all the way through college, spending spring breaks with Grandma on Sanibel. I like to think of my love for the area as being inherited.

My husband and I did most of our dating on Sanibel and later held our wedding reception there. A portion of my heart stayed even as the tides of our careers carried us geographically near and far from Florida over and over again throughout the years. John and I have lived all over the country. But just as two songbirds travel to far-off places seasonally only to return to the same nest year after year, so too did we find ourselves returning to Sanibel, this time to live. Living here has inspired the writing of *Portion of the Sea*.

The history of the island has always interested me; however, in this story I did not intend nor attempt to portray real people or real-life experiences of any of Sanibel's historical residents or visitors. For information on the history of Sanibel, I recommend a visit to the Sanibel Historical

Village & Museum. I created this story and its characters from my imagination; however, I did read historical books, and they were valuable to me. I recommend them. They include the following:

Dormer, Elinore M. *The Sea Shell Islands*. Tallahassee, Fl: Rose Printing Company, 1987. (A History of Sanibel and Captiva)

LeBuff, Charles. *Sanybel Light*. Sanibel, Fl: Amber Publishing, 1998. (An Historical Autobiography)

O'Keefe, Timothy M. *Seasonal Guide to the Natural Year*. Golden, CO, Fulcrum Publishing, 1996. (A Month by Month Guide to Natural Events)

Oppel, Frank and Meisel, Tony, eds. *Tales of Old Florida*. Secaucus, NJ, Castle, 1987.

I

SANIBEL ISLAND

1953

Lydia

There is a time in every woman's life when pink is her favorite color, when anything is believable and the lines separating the possible and the impossible are blurred. It was that time for me when I first met Marlena, and the colors of my world changed forever.

There are many reasons why women tell their stories. I'll tell mine for one reason only—I never want to forget the girl I was and the dreams I had.

IT WAS SPRING IN Florida, and I was as much a part of the spring day as the roseate spoonbills flying overhead and the hot pink periwinkles covering the ground and the pale pink coquina shells burying themselves beneath the sand. I was shy, too, like those coquina shells.

I was sitting on a blanket spread out across the white powdery sand of Sanibel Island, with the late afternoon sun beaming down upon me when I opened my diary and began to write. This crescent-shaped island located in Southwest Florida and extending into the Gulf of Mexico, my father had told me when we arrived two days ago, was my place of conception. Ever since he shared that news with me, I had been trying to squeeze from him more juicy details regarding my conception, but I quickly learned it was one of those "hush hush" topics, the kind that makes fathers who hate any form of dancing look like they're about to do the jitterbug.

"So you and my mother were vacationing here when my conception occurred?" I had asked him over breakfast.

"We were."

"Define the word *conception* for me, Daddy."

I was good at vocabulary, and my father was proud of me for this. But when I asked him to define that word for me, he looked nervous as a school- boy on stage before an audience and judges. And then he choked on his grapefruit juice. I waited until he recovered, and then I repeated the word.

"Conception," I said. "What is the definition of conception?"

He walked over to the bookshelf and picked up the wildlife book he had been reading the night before. "Most of the year the heads and necks of brown pelicans are white," he explained. "But during breeding season, the heads of the pelicans turn a distinctive yellow color, and the sides and back of the necks a dark reddish brown."

"Daddy," I said, rolling my eyes, "you're speaking to the state of Illinois vocabulary champion. You think I'm going to accept a definition like that? I'm not."

He closed the book and tried once more. "Much like the pelicans, there are also changes that must take place in the body of a man and woman right before conception." He was looking back and forth at the bowl of fruit and me. "Let's just say, after 'courtship' is over, the neck and heads of the pelicans return to white. I know it's a lot to think about. Conception—it's all so detailed."

"One more thing," I said. "Where exactly on the island did my conception take place? Was it in a bungalow or on the beach?"

"Lydia!" he said, and I knew I had rattled his cage. "There are things a girl shouldn't ask, nor know, nor think about. Enough! Understood?"

"Sorry, sir. But I am growing up."

"You're only fifteen."

"Almost sixteen."

"You could be thirty and I'd still say you're too young to know those sorts of things about . . . about courtship."

"Conception," I corrected. "The word in question was 'conception.'"

"Whatever," he said. "I regret mentioning that word in the first place. It's time to move on now. How about you start making me lunch."

I stopped writing about it all and looked up from my pink-poodle diary, wondering whether the details of my conception meant anything at all. I did have hair as white as the Sanibel sand I was now digging my toes into, and eyes which were most days blue but on occasion green like the Gulf of Mexico. Then again my mother was a fair-skinned Irish woman with green eyes. I could probably credit her for the way I look more than my place of conception.

I often watched mothers and daughters as they shopped, drank sodas, walked in the park together, and now strolled by me on the beach, and I could always match which girls belonged to which mothers. Usually it was their hand gestures flapping about in a synchronized manner like wings of birds, or their smiles, identical to those of dolphins. Sometimes it was less obvious, and I had to match their eyes or the shapes of their hips and butts. And there were the girls who gave it away the moment they opened their mouths, sounding sarcastic, critical, uppity, or sweet like their mothers— similar to parrots repeating whatever they'd heard over and over again.

As the warm, comforting air wrapped itself around me, I tried not to feel sorry for myself, a parrot alone in its cage with no one to mimic, no one to teach me about certain words and things I wanted to know. My mother died when I was an infant, leaving me her smile, her hair, and on some days, if I wore green and stood under the right lighting, the color of her eyes. I loved to look at pictures of her, but all they told me was what she looked like.

One day I had asked my father to tell me more about her, about things she loved. And when he told me there was an island off the coast of Florida that the two of them had visited once, and that my mother had fallen madly in love with, I had to go there, to see it for myself. And if she were sitting here beside me now, I would turn to her and say, "You and I are a lot alike. I agree with you that this place is utopia." And just as my father said that my mother never wanted to leave the island and return to the Midwest, neither did I. But after a one-week vacation here they did leave, and nine months later I was born. This was the first time my father had been back since her death nearly fifteen years ago, and we were here for a week.

It was also the first vacation he had ever taken me on. He didn't like vacations. He had accumulated a treasure chest of wealth and money but didn't know what to do with it, nor did he care. It wasn't the money he liked but the acquiring of it. He was a man who lived to work, and earning salaries that rose higher each year was pure recreation to him. Vacations, vocabulary competitions, and me in general, only got in the way.

I'm sure wives know as much or more about their husbands than daughters do about their fathers; so, my mother must have known this about him, which is why she put it into writing, that sometime around my sweet sixteenth birthday my father must take me here to see the place she loved. They found this request of hers in a letter she wrote the same morning they found her on the bedroom floor.

I turned to the front of my diary, to where I had first started entering all the information I had gathered about my mother. And now the book was like a precious seashell to me, with a living creature inside. As I flipped my thumb through its pages, I swore I heard her laughing, whispering, and crying out loud.

I clasped my hands together tightly, closed my eyes, and whispered to my mother. I only talked to her every so often and didn't know whether or not she could hear me. "Thank you for insisting that I see this island. I love it. If loving a place is an inherited trait, then I got it from you. We are alike in many ways, I think." I stopped only to wipe a tear from my face and then continued. "But I hope we're different. Please tell me we're different. I want to be different from you, too."

I opened my eyes and listened, thinking I heard and felt someone or thing hovering behind me. Maybe it was the seagulls, for great numbers of them had been stalking my box of crackers. Or maybe it was my mother's spirit. But then I twisted around and looked up to find a woman standing behind me holding a plastic bucket.

"Did I interrupt?" she asked, soaring over me, wearing a white bathing cap decorated with brightly bold circles. She looked like a movie star.

"No. Interrupt what?"

She shrugged her shoulders. "I thought maybe you were praying, so I waited to hear an 'Amen.' "

"No, I was talking to my mother," I said, and then regretted telling her that. I should have said I was talking to myself or, better yet, said nothing at all.

But she didn't look at me like I was crazy and instead turned her focus toward some shells in her bucket and nonchalantly picked a few up and tossed them back to the beach. I had to stare. She was glamorous, wearing one of those two-piece bathing suits, the kind my father would never allow me to wear, and the kind I had never seen anyone other than a mannequin at Marshal Fields wearing. I pulled my eyes up off her belly—a good quarter of it was showing—and placed them back onto her face.

And that's when I noticed she wasn't looking into her bucket at all, but rather her eyes were stretching all the way down to my diary, lying open on the blanket beside me. The woman was trying to read what I had written, so I nudged it over a few inches to be sure, and then she cocked her head to the side and continued reading with the fervor of a gull feasting on its prey. As I did with the cracker box earlier, I slammed it shut, not wanting some stranger to peek any further inside at the essence of my mother captured in a book. Then I jumped up from the sand, ready to "shoo" her away, to fling my arms and possibly kick, but I didn't know her next move and feared she might take off down the beach with the seagulls, my diary and the words depicting my mother dropping from her mouth.

"Hi. I'm Marlena," she said in the most elegant of voices, turning her eyes back at me. "Marlena DiPluma. Are you here on vacation?"

"Yes," I said as quick and snappy as one might say the word "yes."

"Aren't you going to introduce yourself?"

"Lydia," I said. "Lydia Isleworth."

"And your mother?"

I made a face at her and then remembered it was me who said in the first place that I was talking to my mother who clearly wasn't here. "She died when I was an infant."

"I'm horribly sorry to hear that."

"It's fine," I said, sitting back down again. "I've written everything my father has told me about her in my diary. And it's private. Diaries are private, you know."

She laughed and started swinging her pail back and forth like a child as she looked up at the clouds. There were only two clouds in the entire sky, and they weren't shaped like anything fascinating so soon she stopped swinging the pail and bent down eye-level with me. "I respect journal keepers more than you could know," she said. "And I am a firm believer that the words a woman writes in her journal are like bits and pieces of her heart, soul, and mind."

I loved words, vocabulary words, but I never thought about words as bits and pieces of anyone's heart, soul, or mind. I wanted to ponder what she had said, but I also wanted to know why she wore a scarf wrapped around her head, covering her nose. Back home we wore our scarves as belts or halter-tops, or tied around a ponytail like mine was now, but never around our faces to cover our noses, like she wore hers. It was a pretty scarf, brightly colored chiffon.

"I don't mean to pry," she said, standing back up again. "But is your father remarried?"

"No," I snapped.

"So you've been raised by a man?"

"No," I said again. "I've got nannies, housekeepers, and tutors, and they're all women."

"I see. So, where are you visiting from?"

"Chicago."

"Do you come here often?"

"No. It's the first time I've been back."

"Since when?"

"My conception."

She raised an eyebrow at me. "Really? Not many people know that sort of information."

"My father regrets telling me."

"Where's your father now?"

I reached for my pink saddle shoes and my socks. She was nosy, and I wanted to leave.

"Maybe you could introduce me."

"No," I said. "He bumped into an acquaintance, and now they're having a business meeting. He's always working."

"And where do you want to work when you grow up?"

It was my turn to raise an eyebrow at her. "Work? What do you mean?"

"A job, a profession. What do you want to be?"

"A wife and a mother." I started to back up, sweeping the sand off my feet with my hands while looking up at her.

"I see," she said, her dark eyes peering at me like a bird digesting its meal.

"So what is your most favorite thing to do?"

"Write," I answered without hesitation. "In my diary."

"You love it?"

I nodded.

"You love it more than . . ." She scratched her chin. "I don't know. It's been a while since I was young like you . . . more than Hopscotch and Hula Hoop and dancing?"

"More than anything."

"Then why not apply it to a profession one day? You sound like an intelligent young lady."

"I am," I said. "My father says I'll be able to keep up with my husband in conversation and educate my sons one day." I couldn't get all the sand out from between my toes, so I tossed my shoes in my bag instead of putting them on and then stood up and tugged the blanket out from under her foot. "I've got to get going," I said as I lightly shook the blanket.

"If that's what you want to do, fine," she said. "I won't keep you. I just think it's a shame that in addition to being a wife and mother your father has you thinking there is nothing else in life a girl can do. What about one day when your kids grow up and your husband works all day? What will you do then?"

"I don't have to worry about any of that. I'm only fifteen."

"Oh, I think all girls around your age should be challenged to look ahead and ponder who it is they want to be and what sort of life they'd one day like for themselves. But people don't give it any thought until they're grown up and disliking their lives and then they don't know what to do. If only they could think back to when they were around your age and remember what sorts of things they loved to do, things they were good at and things that made them happy."

"Interesting," I said. "But I've got to go." I started to walk.

"It was nice meeting you, Lydia," she called after me. "But don't forget how much you love writing. I do think you could be a writer one day, perhaps a famous one."

I stopped and turned my head. "How do you know?"

"I don't for sure. I said 'perhaps.' You were the one who said you loved to write more than anything in the world."

"Yeah, but only in my diary."

"Well, we all start somewhere. You just remember that, darling. If a successful writer is what you see for yourself, then by all means, you'll become it. I believe in you."

I turned fully around and walked a few steps back toward her. "You do?"

"Yes. It was a pleasure talking with you." She blew me a kiss in a movie star sort of way, and then turned as if, this time, she was the one ready to leave.

"Wait," I said. "I'll let you read a little of my journal, if you like. You can tell me if it's good or not."

She laughed. "I'm honored. Let's go sit down." She walked over to an enormous piece of driftwood shaped like a bench and sat down as if to perch. I followed and pulled my journal out from my bag and handed it to her, hoping I wasn't handing my mind over to the claws of some bird of prey. But I never thought of my writing as being good or bad. I only thought of it as something I loved to do, so maybe I could use some objective feedback. I watched as she flipped randomly to the front of the book and her eyes began to skim.

"An ever-serving, obedient and domestic wife," she read aloud. "Thrilled and thankful for being born a woman, destined to become a wife and mother," she continued. "A woman envied by all her neighbors for having the most meticulous kitchen floor and dinner on the table by five o'clock nearly 365 days a year." She stopped and looked up at me. "Mature words coming from a girl your age."

"They're my father's words, not mine."

"Yes, I assumed that much." She rolled her eyes.

"They're things he has told me about my mother. I can't write creatively. I can only write about things that have happened or things people have said. I'm not at all good at making stuff up."

"Then you're a nonfiction writer," she said. "That's what most journal writing is. That's fine. Maybe you're in the making to become a journalist."

"Of course not," I said. "I'm just a girl."

"Yeah and Sanibel was just a sandbar once. Look at it now!" She glanced from east to west. "And Thomas Edison was just a boy. Did you know his mother schooled him at home because he drove his teacher nuts with so many questions in the classroom?"

"No." I laughed.

"It's true. What would this modern fifties world be like had he never gone on to become more than just a boy? What if he didn't pursue his interests?

We'd be living in a rather dark place, I think." I thought about it a moment. "But what would Edison have done had his own mother not been there for him? His mother deserves credit," I said. "She had a very important job. Every mother does."

"Yes," she said. "I suppose you're right."

"If you ask me, anyone with a mother is fortunate."

She handed back my diary. "True, dear, but we need to look at what we do have and not what we don't have. You, for instance, have a desire to write. I do believe you will be a successful journalist one day, famous maybe. If that's what you want to be."

She read a little more, this time to herself and I thought about whether I should bolt from this stranger, the strangest stranger I had ever encountered and that was pretty strange. Living in Chicago gave me daily opportunities to pass by, say hello, exchange eye contact with, or walk right by strangers, and sometimes they'd mumble something my way, and once it was about the end of the world coming, but none of them ever told me anything like this. Not even anyone I knew ever told me I could be and do anything that I wanted, and I wondered whether or not I should believe her. Believing her would bring options and possibilities to my life that I never knew I had, but then again, she was only a stranger, and it would be stupid of me to listen to what some stranger had to say.

"I don't believe what you're telling me," I said, standing up from the driftwood. "I don't believe anything you've said." I walked a few steps away, knowing I should keep going, that my father would go ape if I didn't return soon.

"Then what do you believe?" she asked.

I shrugged my shoulders. I believed one day I would get married and have babies and those were my only options. I never believed anything other than that. I never gave it any thought.

"Do you believe you can build a snowman here on the beach?"

I turned and laughed. "You're crazy," I said.

"Oh, no. I'm not. I've been called many things—dramatic, eccentric, fun, but crazy I am certainly not."

"How can anyone build a snowman here on a beach in Florida? It's impossible. There's no snow."

"If you believe, you can achieve," she said, jumping up from the driftwood. "Now get down and help me build a snowman." She dropped to her knees and started digging in the sand. A moment later she looked up and said, "C'mon, join me, and I'll show you."

I didn't want to get my new pink sailor dress dirty, but there was something inside me that wanted to believe; so, I joined her on my knees and started scraping my hands through the shell-fragmented sand, and she started humming. We were close enough to the shore that the sand was damp, and it packed nicely into a mound. I noticed her fingernails, long and beautiful, painted in mauve, and I felt the pressure of sand building behind my own nails, short in comparison. Her humming grew louder, and I dug harder until broken miniature shell pieces pricked the tips of my fingers. I no longer needed my sunglasses, so I took them off and tossed them aside.

"What are you humming?" I asked.

"A lullaby my mama used to hum."

"Oh." We dug and packed some more, and when I looked at her, I noticed the scarf around her face loosening and falling to the ground. There were white bandage-like wraps covering her nose, and she caught me staring.

"I was born with the long, curved beak of a White Ibis and wanted the nose of a woman," she said, stopping to retie it. "I always imagined how beautiful I might look with a more womanly nose; so, I just recently got a nose job."

"Oh."

"I blame it all on my great, great grandmother. I got my nose from her."

I smiled, wondering whom I got my nose from and also what a nose job was. I hadn't ever heard of that kind of a job before and assumed it meant she got paid to smell stuff like food or cologne. Or maybe a nose job meant she worked as a nose model. Hers was perfect enough. And maybe it's why she wrapped that scarf and gauze around it, to protect it from the sun and air and from catching a cold and becoming red and runny, I thought as I dug in the sand until my stomach growled, reminding me it was almost dinner time and my father would be upset if I wasn't there.

"Why don't you start making the middle ball now?" she said standing up, leaving me to dig alone.

I scooped two handfuls of sand and smacked them atop the first ball, but it all crumbled down the side. I hoped the erosion might remind her we're on a beach with sand, not snow.

"Oh, come on! You can do it," she said.

I raised my eyebrows at her. "I don't think so."

"You still don't get it. You still don't believe that anything is possible, do you?"

"Realistic things are possible," I said. "But one can't build a snowman in the sand."

"You can do it," she reassured, then stooped over and helped me pack sand atop the first ball. Once more, it all slipped down. "This is why we must be flexible," she said, scratching her long dark hair with her sandy hands. "You've got to change your mindset. Make him lying down. Who says snowmen have to stand up? Keep going," she said. "I'm sick and tired of the world teaching a girl she 'can't' do this, she 'must' do that. She should do this and she shouldn't do that. Can't, must, should, shouldn't! What is it that you want in life, Lydia?"

I couldn't think of anything. My father got me everything I ever wanted, which is like eating before getting hungry and never knowing what a hunger pain feels like. We owned three sixteen-inch black-and-white televisions. I had been the first of all my friends to get a Hula Hoop and Silly Putty. When the bridal dolly had come out, my father went to every store in Chicago until he found one for me.

My father, Lloyd Isleworth, was gone most of the time, but I was never alone. He employed an entire staff of females to handle our housework, shop, prepare our meals, tutor me in reading, writing and arithmetic, teach me piano, and so on. And when they all went home to their own families, the television went on, and it kept me good company.

Lloyd had told me this would be our first no-work-allowed vacation, but then he bumped into that man. The man was a developer and had all kinds of things he wanted to develop, and my father, a banker, had all kinds of money he wanted to lend. He gave me a new dress, and I felt better.

"A new pink dress—that's what I want," I finally said. "This one was new, but look at it now."

"Dig, dig deeper!" she chanted. "Think hard about all that you want from your life. You've got to dig to find the real answers, to discover what you want. It's easy to live on the surface, so dig! Dig harder! What else might you want?"

Curves. I wanted curves, but they were something my father couldn't buy me. As I felt the sand working its way deep into my girdle, itching me horribly, I knew how ridiculous it was to wear a hot, uncomfortable item in Florida. Still, a girl never knows when she might bump into the man of her dreams, and curves are essential to getting the all-important husband and insuring one's economic future. Money, thanks to Daddy, I would never lack, but alluring curves, I had no idea why they weren't yet showing up on me. I wanted them badly. I wanted to look as curvaceous as Marlena. Her hips were wide and the same size as her bust, and her waist was tiny like the necks of the birds trekking along the shore.

"Why are you grinning?" she asked.

"I think trying to build a snowman in the sand is funny," I said, using my arm to rub sand out of my eyes.

"My dear. Then stop thinking and keep moving. There are times when thinking hinders us from achieving the impossible," she said as she stood with her arms stretched overhead. She began swaying as we do in art class when our teacher tells us to act like trees, feel like trees, then paint those trees. "You are in the spring of your life, child, when possibilities are blooming as profusely as Florida's wildflowers." She leaned to the left, then to the right again. "It's looking so much like a snowman," I heard her say. "You're about there. Now let me rephrase my question to you. What is it that you dream of for your life, Lydia?"

Her words suddenly reached me as if she were a fairy godmother and was tapping me on the shoulder with her magic wand and the world was growing pinker by the moment, probably from the setting sun. And then I spotted a group of motionless bright pink birds, more beautiful than any bird I could ever imagine. I knew of flamingoes, but these weren't flamingoes! It was sometime after I saw these birds that the white silken sand of Sanibel transformed itself into glistening snow within my own hands and I knew then that anything was indeed possible. I knew then that I would one day become a wife, a mother, and, if I wanted, a journalist!

"I've done it," I announced, jumping up from the sand with my arms in the air. "I've built a snowman . . ."

"Snowwoman!" she corrected. "Let's call it a snowwoman. Who says snowmen must be men?"

I laughed. "Then I've built a snowwoman on Sanibel."

"You have, Lydia. Do you believe now that you can do anything?"

"Yes!" I shouted. "I do." I gazed over to see if those pink birds were still around, and just as I spotted them, one of them raised and lowered its beak, and the flock took off. The pink was gone.

"Your snowwoman needs facial features. Go and gather up seashells," Marlena said.

I rushed to the water and stooped over in search of eyes, a nose, and a mouth in the clear water below.

"Be kind," Marlena called out to me as she tied her chiffon scarf around the snowwoman's neck. "Be especially kind in choosing a nose."

I returned moments later with my hands filled with shells.

"That broken whelk will be the nose," she said, taking from my hands a shell bearing zigzag-like streaks. "And how about those two sharks for eyes?"

We pushed them into our snowwoman and stepped back a foot. "Looks great, but I better get going before my father hires a search team," I said, noticing the sky getting darker. I walked over and picked up my straw bag.

"It wasn't my intention to get you in trouble," she said. "I do apologize."

"It's okay," I said. "It was nice meeting you."

"You, too. How long are you here for?"

"Six more days but I don't ever want to leave."

"Enjoy."

"I will."

"Goodbye, dear."

I waved and started meandering down the beach. A few seconds later, I heard her calling out to me.

"Oh, Lydia! Lydia! Wait, please!" "Yes?" I stopped and turned.

"I do think we met for a reason," she said, hurrying up to me. "I don't believe it was a coincidence. I hope I'm not wrong."

"Wrong about what?"

She took a deep breath. "Today was the first time in a long time that I poured myself a cup of coffee and went out to my lanai to sit and read. And then, I spotted you on the beach. At first I thought you were just reading, but then I noticed you writing in what looked like a journal." She reached into her bag and pulled out a very old-looking book. "Here," she said, handing me the book, but still clutching it herself. "This is what I went out to my porch to read today, but I've already read it so many times. It's a journal, and it's very old."

"You're giving it to me?"

"Heavens, no!" she said, nearly pulling it back. "I'm only lending it to you. The girl who wrote in it died long ago, but you reading it would be like giving flight to her words. I do believe you and she have some things in common. She loved Sanibel and, like you, didn't want to leave."

"Thank you," I said, the two of us still jointly holding onto it.

"There's one thing I ask of you," she continued.

"Sure, what?"

"That you not tell a soul about this. I don't think this girl wanted anyone and everyone rummaging through her priceless treasures, especially any man; so, please don't tell your father. I'm sure you wouldn't want your father reading your journal now, would you?"

"Of course not."

"Then, you understand. I think it's important that only the right kind of person read this. It's the kind of book that should be read by invite only. You're the first person I've chosen to share it with. Who knows? Maybe when you're done, we might pass it on to another. But in the meantime, can you promise to keep it a secret?"

"Oh, yes."

"Good. And remember, I do want it back. What you walk away with after reading it is yours forever, but the book itself belongs to me."

"Of course," I said.

She looked nervous. "Are you good at returning things? Give me an example of something you've borrowed, then returned properly."

"Library books," I declared. "Only one late fee in all my life, and I check out about fifty books a year."

"I thought you looked like an earthbound individual. Still, I need you to swear on your mama's grave you won't tell a soul and that you will return it to me before leaving the island."

"I swear."

"On what?"

"On my mother's grave."

"Thank you," she said. "When one returns a library book late, there is a fine to pay. Do you know what will happen if you don't keep our promise?"

"What?"

She thought a moment. "You will be cursed. Your ability and desire to write will erode and you will find yourself stranded forever in a place where ideas and creativity lie stagnant. Some people refer to that place as 'writer's block.' If you tell, you will wreck your destiny as a journalist. And I know you want to become someone important, famous maybe. What girl doesn't want the entire world listening to all the important things she has to say?"

"What if my father asks me what I'm reading? What should I say?"

"You're sharp." She reached into her bucket and pulled out another book.

"Here, take this. Its dimensions are a bit larger, so you can hide the journal inside it."

"*Catcher in the Rye?*" I asked, taking the book.

"Yes, and author J.D. Salinger autographed it for me personally. It's about a boy and nothing I'm too interested in reading. Are you familiar with it?"

"No."

"Figures," she said. "If anyone asks what it's about, tell them a generation of adolescents, overwhelmed with anxiety and frustration."

"Okay," I said. "I will."

She sighed. "I think that's it. Oh," she covered her mouth with her hand. "I almost forgot the most important thing. I live straight through that thin line of Australian pines." She turned and pointed. "See that yellow place with the green-shingle roof and shutters? The one on stilts?"

I nodded.

"There's a sign out front that reads, 'Bougainvillea.' If you don't see me on the beach, then please drop it by my mailbox before you leave the island. Now you better get back. It's getting dark. And keep that journal a secret!"

"I will, I will!" I said as I started walking briskly down the beach and a second later I thought I heard her say, "Go, you little feathery gold plume! Protect your destiny and don't breathe a word of this to anyone."

II

I HAD NEVER LOOKED into anyone else's journal before, and I could hardly wait to, hopefully discover it full of secret treasures. But dusk was quickly turning to dark, so I continued briskly down the shell-strewn beach. I didn't feel like facing Lloyd's wrath for getting back late.

As I rounded the large screened porch on the side of the cottage we had rented for the week, I spotted my father standing in the driveway. His right arm was bent stiffly near his face, and he was watching the hands on his wristwatch make their rounds. I stopped to decipher whether he looked worried or mad.

"Damn. Where is she? I don't have time for this," he muttered to his watch.

"Sorry, sir," I said, walking over and putting my arm on his and lowering it gently from his face.

"Where have you been, young lady?"

"I can explain," I said. "I met a very nice woman on the beach, and we were chatting. She said she got a nose job, and I felt too stupid asking her what that was. Do you know? What kind of work does she do? Smell things?"

"You're kidding, I hope."

I wasn't, but when he didn't look amused, I told him what he wanted to hear. "Of course. But I can still explain why I'm late."

"Never mind. I don't have time for any more stories. Save them for your journals," he scolded. "We're leaving the island."

"What? We can't possibly be leaving. We still have several more days left."

"Plans change. We're leaving. Haven't you noticed all our suitcases piled around me? I had to pack all of your stuff. Yours and mine."

I hadn't noticed them, but now I did, and mine were busting at the zipper lines. "Why?" I asked.

Lloyd took in a deep breath, and by the way he let it all out I knew something bad had happened. "It's my partner, Mr. Ashton. He's suffered a stroke and we've got to get back to Chicago immediately. I've arranged for a car to take us to the marina so we can catch a private charter out tonight. We'll be staying in Fort Myers, then flying out first thing in the morning."

"Is Mr. Ashton okay? Is he alive?"

"I don't know at this moment. But the bank can't run without him. They need me there right away."

"But can't we just stay until morning?" I looked to make sure the journal was concealed in my bag. It was.

"Sorry, dear. We're leaving immediately. If the driver ever gets here, that is."

"Why not one more night?" I pleaded.

He looked at me like he wanted to fire me as his daughter, or worse, hang me. And he was the type to do it. I knew he wanted to get back because a promotion was on his mind. "Lydia, a man is on his deathbed, and all you can think about is staying on the island? There are decisions to be made at the bank, and I don't want any of them made without me there," he said. "It's not fair for you to whine about your vacation at a time like this."

I wanted to tell him all about what the lady on the beach had given to me, and how I promised I would return it before leaving, but then I remembered that I swore on my mother's grave I wouldn't tell a soul about it. I didn't know what might happen to me for having sworn on someone's grave, and then not following through with my promise.

"Daddy, have you ever wanted to become famous?"

"Never, just wealthy and important and to play a man's part in the world."

I hadn't ever given it any consideration, either, but after hearing Marlena dangle it before me like she did, I now liked the thought of it. As I stood beside my father waiting for the driver to show, I no longer wanted to one day become the wife of someone important, but instead to be someone important myself. I felt selfish as a pirate for thinking the new way in which I was, but I'm sure pirates felt no guilt for wanting merry old lives for themselves. And all I really wanted was a life I liked. Marlena said I could do anything, and I believed her. She wasn't hired by my father to be nice to me.

"For Christ's sake, where is this guy?" Lloyd was starting to scare me. He was looking like he wanted the driver dead or alive.

I didn't want to add to his frustration, but I had to somehow think of a way I might return the journal to Marlena's mailbox before we left. "While we're waiting for him, sir, can I run back to the beach? I think one of the starfish in my pail is still moving. It's unethical to take a live shell."

"Lydia, you're making me question the progress I thought I've made in raising you. No! You cannot go to the beach—not at a time like this. Don't leave my side!"

When I heard a car round the bend of the road, I considered burying the journal in the dirt, anything so I wouldn't have to leave the island with a beach basket full of booty. But the men loaded the suitcases in the trunk so fast that I could hardly think. I only knew I never intended to loot Marlena like I was, and as I climbed into the backseat of the car, I felt more alone than I ever had before, even on the holidays when Lloyd worked and the nannies had gone home to their families and it was back before we had bought our first television.

As I watched the cottage shrink out the back window, I thought about what I was getting away with, both the journal and newfound belief that I had choices in life and I could be whatever I wanted to be.

"Daddy," I said as the car turned onto Periwinkle and headed east. "Did my mother ever want to be anything other than a homemaker?"

"No, darling. Your mother put in a good sixty to eighty hours per week working around the house. She was committed to that, and she didn't have any leisure time to sit around thinking about much else. Why do you ask?"

"I've been thinking," I said. "I'd like to be a journalist. Do you think I could be one day?"

He glanced back and looked at me like I was some feverish sailor losing her mind. Then he gave the driver one of those male camaraderie glances.

"I want a job outside of the house," I continued. "I want to write for a newspaper."

"Sir, if you don't mind my saying," the driver said. "There *are* female journalists, you know. It does exist."

"There may be a few, I suppose. I'm not familiar with any. I don't read the recipe and household cleaning sections," said Lloyd. "I do know there's a hell of a lot more women nurses. Nursing and teaching are suitable jobs for women who insist on working, Lydia. And secretaries are good. I appreciate all of mine. But if you're still set on working in five years, consider nursing or teaching. We'll discuss it then, dear. Could you go faster, please?"

A few minutes later the car pulled up to the marina. "I don't want to be a nurse or a teacher," I dared to say when my father opened the back door for me. "I want to be a journalist."

"It doesn't matter what you want, angel," he said. "No little girl of mine is going to work around a bunch of men someday."

"I'm not a little girl," I mumbled once he was ahead of me on the dock. "I'm fifteen."

The driver had already removed our luggage from the trunk and was handing it to the boat captain. I walked grudgingly toward the boat, listening as my father gave orders to the boat captain.

"Get us across this bay as fast as you can," he stated. "I've got innumerable phone calls to make tonight and we've already lost time waiting for that guy to pick us up."

My mind felt frazzled. I didn't want to leave the island with the journal. I wanted to read and return it to Marlena who had been so nice to lend it to me in the first place. As I staggered along, I feared the only fame I might own one day would be that of a notorious pirate captain who plundered a priceless, timeless treasure from a nice lady living on a barrier island in Florida. The driver must have thought I was trailing behind, moping for the way my father had talked to me.

"A couple of years back," he whispered to me, "some female war correspondent won a Pulitzer Prize for international reporting, you know."

"I didn't know that."

He raised an eyebrow at me. "Yeah, she reported from Korea, the first woman to win the award and shared it with five male war correspondents. You can do whatever you want."

"Thank you," I said, vigorously shaking his hand like a man.

He nodded and walked into the darkness and for a quick moment I thought about running after him and asking whether he'd do me a favor and return the journal to "Bougainvillea." But that was too risky. He was a man, and Marlena especially instructed that no man ought to ever lay eyes on the inside of this girl's journal. I could trust no one. And I had no choice but to step onto that boat with my treasure, hoping after all of this, that it would turn out to be filled with golden jewelry, silver coins, and bits of shining, priceless womanly wisdom.

III

AS THE BOAT PULLED away from the island, I told myself things would be different had I a mother. Maybe I wouldn't be telling lies or swearing on graves or embarrassing my father or turning to a life of piracy had I a mother to keep me in line.

And I would no longer look with envy and insecurity at girls who had mothers, if I had one of my own. I always wondered whether the girls with mothers knew more than I about the world or the handling or perceiving of situations. They looked so sure of themselves, as if they were wearing beautiful pearls of wisdom handed down to them from their mothers, who inherited the pearls from their mothers and so on throughout the generations of women in their ancestry. But a motherless girl like myself would have to figure the world out on her own, raiding others for scraps of knowledge and information.

As the boat entered the bay, I could feel the balmy air closing in around me like the walls of a jail, and I felt like I had already stood trial for piracy and was soon going to be made to walk the plank. That's when Lloyd tried talking to me.

"I'm sorry it was cut short, but did you like our little getaway, Lydia?"

"Yes, sir."

"Good because I was thinking we could start a tradition, you and I taking a leisure trip once a year. It doesn't have to be Sanibel. There's New York City, Martha's Vineyard, Lake Tahoe, San Francisco, Paris—You name it, darling, anywhere in the world and we'll go there."

"Sanibel," I muttered.

Returning there would be my only chance at returning to my life before pirating, for I could hand the journal back to Marlena and explain everything, setting my conscience free. I shifted uncomfortably in my seat.
"I don't want to go anywhere else," I stated. "I want to return to Sanibel."

"Did I ever tell you that you sound like your mother?"

I made a mental note to enter that new information about my mother
into my diary once we got to the hotel. "But my mother never returned to
Sanibel," I said.

"I know darling, but you will."

"Do you swear? Do you swear on my mother's grave that I'll return?"

"No. I don't like to swear on anyone's grave like that."

"Oh," I said. "So it's true."

"What?"

"A boy at school swore on his uncle's grave, and the next day his aunt
died. And the friend of a second cousin of my best friend's second-removed aunt once stepped on a crack and a couple hours later, my best
friend's second-removed aunt's second-cousin's mother fell down the stairs
and broke her back. I never met the woman with the broken back, but my
friend told me all about it. Is it true? Would I be cursed if I swear on
someone's grave, and don't stick to what I swore?"

"Never swear on anyone's grave," he said. "And never swear. It's not
proper."

I glanced back at the utopia that earlier had birds under a pink sky and
saw nothing but a lump in the darkness. I felt a burden within, one heavy
enough to sink the boat that was now speeding toward Fort Myers as I put
my hand over my mouth, ready to vomit over the side of the boat for having sworn I would return the journal before leaving the island.

"Mind if I borrow your flashlight?" I asked the captain as soon as my
queasiness subsided. "I've got some reading I'd like to do."

I pulled the girl's journal from my pail and as soon as I opened it I felt
my father's eyes aiming over my shoulder.

"J.D. Salinger," I told him before he asked. "I'm reading *Catcher in the*

Rye, a novel."

"Yes, I've heard of it. A couple of the young interns at the bank were reading it just last week. Isn't it a bit boyish for you, Lydia?"

I turned the flashlight off and closed the journal so he wouldn't give it a closer look. "No, sir," I replied. "I don't think so at all."

"I don't know that I want my daughter reading a novel about a school-boy at odds with society."

"Better a boy than a girl at odds with society, don't you think, Daddy?"

We both laughed, and I knew I was free to read. I opened the journal once more, feeling guilty for what I was about to do and wondering whether there were laws against this sort of thing, of reading another girl's diary. I had never been a law-breaking person and actually believed there should be more laws—against touching the wings of butterflies and feeding alligators and wild birds and taking live shells from the beach. Maybe there were laws for all of these things. I didn't know for sure. I only knew I felt like a criminal as I aimed the flashlight at the top of the page and let my eyes begin feasting off the handwritten words.

IV

SANIBEL ISLAND

1890

Ava

There is a beginning, middle and end to every woman's life. But once a woman arrives at what she thinks might be her end, all she must do is reach deep down into her innermost depths and there she will find a new beginning. A woman is as hardy as any perennial flower and deep as the sea.

I FEARED MY MOTHER had reached her end as the boat started across the wide bay on its trip over to the barrier island of Sanibel. The sun would soon be peeking out from the eastern horizon, and the island before us stood like a heaping black mound in the distance. The bay, having no natural light in these moments before sunrise, looked black as ink, and it made me want to dip my pen and start writing in my journal all that I was witnessing. But I knew this early in the morning my writing would only look like chicken scratch, and so my journal remained tightly in my hands. It was still too dark to write.

We were used to seeing dark rather than light. The winter in Kentucky had been wet, dark, and bitter, and my mother's eyes turned gray in the winter.

"You know what maddens me most about winter?" My mother, Abigail, asked, her eyes staring outward at the black silhouette of the shrimp-shaped island in the distance.

"No, what?"

"It couldn't care less about spring. Winter stomps right over spring. And poor little spring hardly gets noticed anymore. And do you know what I loathe most about fall?"

"What, Mama?"

"Fall is winter's predecessor," she said.

My father and I hadn't seen beauty in the changing seasons for some time. We only noticed Abigail's eyes turn colorless as the weather turned cold. Her face wilted downward, and her body crumbled to the ground when the sun disappeared in the fall. And come winter, her spirit retreated, surviving deep down in an underground, and all we could see was her crown, until spring, when her eyes, blue like the petals of an iris, opened widely again, turning us all into happily chirping birds.

I always paid close attention to my mother's eyes. They told me more than her lips ever did. And so I grew accustomed to watching everyone's eyes, for the eyes continue talking when the lips stop.

When her eyes suddenly looked awestruck, as if they were looking at the Lord Himself, I turned my attention ahead, for the rising sun had painted the sky over Sanibel with strokes of orange and pink and the clouds were now lit and floating before us like flames on candles. It was as if the old world I had known for all fourteen years of my life had passed away and a new world was appearing before me. There was now morning light and it was good.

Then creatures with wings of at least fifteen feet came out of the sky and were heading at us with outstretched necks.

"Flying beasts!" howled my grandmother Dahlia, seated on a bench at the front of the boat. "Woe, woe! They're going to kill us!" Dahlia's arms were stretched overhead in the form of a cross as if that alone might turn the things back to where they came from.

As they glided straight toward us, I could see they were mammoth birds with black and white wings. "They're only birds," I declared. "Nothing like we have in Kentucky, but they're birds."

I still jumped up from my seat, ready to take hold of a ribbon on Dahlia's sleeve so they wouldn't carry her off to where they might pick apart her elaborate dress and use its shreds for their nest and her soft, plump body for cushioning in that nest, but Dahlia dropped to the floor, and the birds soared by.

"Angels," I declared, shaking my head as they disappeared into the sky behind the boat. "They had the wings of angels, don't you think?"

"Pelicans," the boat captain corrected.

"Damn birds," Dahlia hissed. "That's what they were. Scared me to death. Now help me off this damn floor, someone."

"Mother!" scolded Abigail. "Watch how you speak in front of Ava."

I took my mother's wrath as a good sign. Whenever Abigail was feeling herself, she cared about the world, about her husband, and most of all about raising me to become a lady. But when she was down, she could care less that Dahlia liked the word "damn." And now her eyes watched me pull my grandmother up off the floor of the boat as if she knew she ought to be helping me. But I didn't want her help. I wanted her preserving all her strength for the adventure that lay ahead of us. Besides, I didn't mind pulling Grandmalia up by myself. I'd do anything for her. She had lived with us ever since I first learned to speak, and back then, I found it too difficult to say "Grandma Dahlia" and so I combined it into Grandmalia and everyone laughed and she liked it; so, it stuck and is what I call her to this very day.

I had to use most of my might to get her up and off the floor of the boat. Naked, Grandmalia probably weighed a ton, but her new dress and its bustles and nipped waist and yards of heavy fabric and lace added a good thirty pounds to her. It was the heaviest dress she ever wore, and my mother and I were wearing ones just like it. We had an independent seamstress make them for us for the day we arrived on the island. It was the day we had all been waiting for, and my mother wanted to make a good first impression.

The boat had reached halfway across the bay by the time I returned to my bench, sat down, and caught my breath. I had to write about the angelic birds. I had to write about everything, for there was nothing I loved more than to write. But the sun, now larger and higher, was bringing the water to life, and I couldn't reel my eyes in. They wanted to float forever in that water that God so carefully gathered into one place—the bay. It was green over there and blue over here! Turquoise surrounding the island! And in spots, the crests were glistening in silver as if Thomas Edison himself had turned on the switch to his electricity, setting light to the Gulf of Mexico. The water was a color I had never known water to be.

The pond behind our farm in Kentucky when we left had been a muddy color, and the lake on the way to town, a crap-like brown. The stream behind the school was rust-colored while the river that rolled past the cemetery, a clear gray. I thought the clear gray-like was nice-looking water.

But the San Carlos Bay surrounding us now sparkled like a sea of crystal, and it was clearer than any bath I had ever drawn for myself. I hadn't even drunk anything so clean, except maybe a sip of gin once, but just thirsting for the water around the boat made me feel tipsier than any sips of gin ever did. And this water was teeming with living creatures and they were doing what God had originally told them to do, "Be fruitful and increase in number and fill the water in the seas."

"They say Sanibel is a winterless paradise," Abigail muttered softly while squeezing my hand, "and that I will never have to hide from winter again."

"I think it might be true, Mama. I think it might truly be a paradise."

Lydia

When the boat touched the dock at Punta Rassa, I turned off the flashlight and closed the journal, still feeling a little shame for reading someone's diary, as if I was a vulture, one of those birds that pick away at a carcass and then fly off with a piece of it.

I was also disappointed. I didn't want to be leaving. I'd rather be her, a girl arriving at the island, than me, a girl leaving, and I'd much rather be on a boatload of women than one of men. Ava, her mother, and grandmother were much better company than my father who had already stepped off the boat without offering me any help.

I handed the flashlight to the captain and then glanced back across the bay toward the island that earlier was so green it looked as if chlorophyll had rained down upon it but which now I could no longer see. It had vanished into night. I thought about the boatload of women arriving to a place they had never seen and hoping it would meet their expectations.

"Yes," I whispered as I clutched Ava's journal to my chest. "I don't know about any paradise, but it is indeed utopia, same thing, I think. Your mother's eyes won't be disappointed."

I wished they could hear my reassuring whisper echoing across water and time, but I don't think they needed to. They already believed in a paradise before ever seeing it. Some people have such a way of doing that— of believing in things they cannot see.

My father was like that. He was a man of faith. He was faithful he'd be a millionaire within two years and CEO of the bank in five and that his investments would quadruple by the time he's fifty. No one could tell him otherwise. His faith was too strong, and we all feared his kind of faith.

"Lydia," I heard him call out. "I waited long enough to get off that island, and now I'm waiting for you. What are you doing daydreaming at a time like this?"

"Sorry, sir," I said, hopping off the boat to catch up with him. He was already climbing into yet another limousine, not bothering to give me a hand. I said nothing as I climbed into the backseat. I knew that when work was on his mind, my words bothered him like pestering mosquitoes. It's when work wasn't on his mind that I became his part-time job. He was training me to become a well-adjusted American woman, future wife of someone wealthy and important.

As the car headed down a dark road, I watched the bay out my right window. I thought about my own life and feared that it was ending before ever getting started. That doesn't mean I felt as if I were about to die, not this young, but that the kind of life I envisioned for myself was ending right there—going no further than a vision. It got me to thinking that maybe that girl Ava, the one who kept the journal, knew some secret truths about life. After all, she had both a mother and grandmother to pass such information on to her. And maybe it was true what she had written in her journal, that a girl is as hearty as a perennial flower and as deep as the sea and all she must do is reach into her innermost depths and there she will find a new beginning.

I didn't know what lay deep within me. I never went there before. I knew my outer layer—the clothes I wore, my hairstyles, the miniscule amount of makeup that I painted onto my face. And I knew my surface layer just under my skin—I knew boys gave me hives, and my father made me cry when he missed dinners and holidays. And sitting in a quiet church made me laugh with nervousness. I didn't go often, only when I slept over at a friend's house, but something about the quietness of it made my body shake from trying to hold in an uncontrollable burst of laughter. Maybe because I was playing a role that wasn't me, pretending I was a churchgoing girl and knew what to do when in reality my father and I never went. I knew my surface well. I was like any girl my age, wanting to fit in and be liked and hide anything about myself that might not be accepted.

If I were to dive deep within myself, I'm not sure I'd find much, I decided when I could no longer see the bay out my window. And when I noticed myself yawning uncontrollably, I scooted across the leathery backseat and rested my head on my father's shoulder.

V

THE NEXT MORNING I could hardly wait to read more of the journal. But our morning was rushed, and I sat too close to my father to read it on the plane. It wasn't until we landed at the airport in Chicago and I climbed into the backseat of the limo that I felt secure opening it up. Our usual driver was still on his vacation, like we were supposed to be on ours. My father and the temporary driver got along fine and once they engaged in conversation, I knew my reading would go unnoticed.

I had at least a half hour before my windows would come to life with the familiar sounds and sights of the windy city, so I opened the journal and began to read where I had left off the night before.

Ava

I stared straight ahead at the island looming before us, hoping it would meet our expectations up close. My mother had her hands clenched together as if she were praying, but her eyes were fantasizing instead.

She did her best to be a godly woman. When she turned sad in the winter, she believed it was Satan taking hold of her and she viewed our exodus out of Kentucky as spiritual. After all, it was a traveling minister in the general store talking about a "healing paradise" that prompted our journey in the first place. Abigail had overheard him describing Sanibel to a group of people, and that day she returned home so obsessed she could talk of nothing but her desire to find this island for months on end. My father and I agreed that finding it and moving there might be our only chance at salvaging her wilting spirit.

"Do you think we'll find any flowers on the island? I need flowers," Abigail said, her eyes blowing ahead with the spring breeze.

The boat captain's eyes skipped over to my mama. "Do you know what the name 'La Florida' means?" he asked.

"No sir, we don't," she answered.

"It means 'feast of flowers.' The Spanish conquistador Juan Ponce de Leon came up with it for a reason. You'll find lots of flowers on the island."

"Now isn't that something. I heard Sanibel was nothing but a remote island of fishermen, farmers, and smudge pots," Dahlia said from her seat at the front of the boat.

I whipped Dahlia with my eyes. I didn't want anything negative shooting from her mouth. I then looked back at Abigail. Her eyes told me she liked what the captain had said about there being lots of flowers.

"I believe the captain," Abigail whispered in my ear. "Men always know the world far better than a lady, and a proper lady knows when to be silent." She was reviewing a truth she already taught me the day Stewart announced we were moving to Florida.

"Are you sure you'll be able to find the state of Florida, Daddy?" I had asked that day. "You've never been out of the state of Kentucky."

He didn't answer, but my mama did. It was then that she first lectured to me that men know the world far better than any woman.

"We'll find you flowers, Mama," I said, giving her hand a solid squeeze.

And as the island grew larger before us, my heart pounded and my knees felt weak, for the sun was bringing out its brilliance and it looked as if the island had been dropped right out of Heaven. The sight of it all made me definitely know—not that I ever doubted—that there really is a Lord God Almighty. And before stepping foot onto the green fertile land flowing with coconut milk, I knew I had a decision to make. I could either collapse in grief on behalf of my father's absence, or I could find courage and become the leader amongst us three women.

I hadn't ever been the leader of any people before, just turkeys back on the farm, and that was challenging enough. They were far-roaming turkeys and so it was my job to lead the adventurous birds back to warmth and food. If it weren't for me building the temporary fences that I did, they'd have wandered straight through the cornfields and wouldn't have returned in time to be killed for the holidays.

My father, Stewart Witherton, liked holidays, and he liked winter. If asked, I don't think he wanted to leave behind our home and farm in Kentucky and move to Florida's little known West Coast. But his wife, when in her down days, had a beckoning way of luring him as if he were a spiny Florida lobster without any claws for fighting back. After Abigail had heard the traveling minister proclaim this island in Florida a healing paradise, he had no choice but to seek it out. I knew he was terrified that he might not ever find such an island. My father wasn't the type to believe in anything he couldn't see. When I had asked him if anyone in his line of ancestors had ever been to paradise, he looked at me blankly and said, "My great uncle Abraham. He's the only one to my knowledge. And he didn't bother to leave me a map."

"It's in the Bible, Daddy. The map to paradise is in the Bible."

"He didn't leave me any Bible, either."

I knew it scared Stewart that he might never make it to Heaven nor find Florida, let alone some remote island off its west coast. But he didn't have a choice. Abigail grabbed him by the head one cold night, pulling, twisting in an effort to dislodge him. I watched, horrified from the doorway as she took the broomstick and tickled him in the gut and then tapped him on the ass. The next morning he started to pack, and the morning after that we left on our pursuit of the Promised Land.

It pained me horribly to think of Stewart still out there, like a turkey let loose in the open range for the first time with no one to lead him back to safety. Getting pushed out of his homeland, and then wandering through Kentucky, Georgia, Tennessee, and Florida for forty days, he had suffered enough. And now it didn't feel right to me, arriving in the Promised Land without him, and I could only hope he was still alive.

It sounded like we were knocking at the gates of Heaven as the boat bumped into the lighthouse dock at the eastern most tip of the island. I felt like jumping up from the bench and shouting, "Holy, holy, holy!" at the multitudes of palm trees standing before us, royal and magnificent. Faith had me believing there was a Heaven in the spiritual, invisible sense, but now I also believed in Heaven on Earth, and I wanted to clap my hands at the sight of it.

As the captain tied the boat to the post, I tied my long black hair into a hanging knot and knew in my heart there was no going back. I only hoped that the island would accept me as a newly arriving songbird, but I knew at times I have a loud chirp for such a petite bird, a chirp that some think is slanted, opinionated, and way too unladylike coming from a mouth as prim-looking as mine. Until I open it and the space between my two front teeth shows. It's the space that everyone blames for my outspokenness, and although my parents don't really believe it, they use it, too. Whenever I say things that embarrass them, they're the first to tell people, "It's that space between her two front teeth. Things just slip out of it, and she can't help it. We don't know what to do about it."

And my eyes get me in trouble, too, for they're big and brown and strong as the color of coffee, and, like my mother's, they tell anything my tiny peach-colored lips forget to say.

I stood up and then glanced upward at the sky and spotted a flock of bright pink birds that were flying in long, strung-out diagonal lines. "Flamingoes?" I asked the captain.

"Nope. Easy to confuse them," he said. "Until you look up close at their bills. Roseate Spoonbills."

Lydia

We had just entered the city, I noticed as I looked up from Ava's journal. "Roseate Spoonbills," I remarked. "That's what those birds were."

My father was punching numbers into his calculator, so I knew he wasn't paying me any attention. "Roseate Spoonbills," I said again, this time looking into the mirror at the driver. "They were amazing."

The limo driver turned his rearview mirror so he could talk directly to me. "No, I don't think so, Ma'am," he matter-of-factly said. "Those were pigeons. I know for a fact. They just pooped all over my window."

"I know what pigeons look like," I said to his eyes in the mirror. "I've lived in Chicago all my life. I was talking about the bright pink birds that I saw when I . . . "

"Bright pink birds are called flamingoes," he said interrupting me. "And if you think you just saw flamingoes, then I must have made a wrong turn and we're at the zoo."

"I saw the pink birds running wild at . . ."

"Ma'am, they don't run wild in the city. I don't know what you claim you saw back there," he said, this time with a gleam in his eye for agitating me. "It might have been that old lady's hat. Damn, did that thing stick out in the crowd or what?"

I sighed heavily like the spring wind outside my window. Then I returned to my reading in hopes I might learn more of the birds I had seen on Sanibel.

Ava

"I didn't know such birds existed on Earth," I peeped to the boat captain.

"They're stunning."

"Just don't go hunting them down for their pink plumage," he said.

"Sir," I stated, "pink is my favorite color, but let me tell you, I wouldn't do such a thing."

"Ladies are doing anything for those pink hats. And over in St. Augustine, they're making fans out of their wings. It doesn't make any sense to me. Their feather color fades rapidly so the hats only have a limited lifespan. I guess the ladies don't care. They're the reason why the Roseate Spoonbills have been driven to the brink of extinction."

"Criminal," I said, shaking my head as the birds disappeared over trees. "There should be laws against that sort of thing, the poor birds, living in danger for their beauty. Women like that make me wish I were a man."

"Ava," my mother scolded me. "A lady knows when to add to the conversation with her gentle views, and she knows when to be silent."

I cast my eyes toward the east so no one would see them ornery; then, I reeled them back toward the captain who was lifting our belongings off the boat. My mother then handed him the name of the place where Stewart had arranged for us to stay.

"I'll see to it that your boxes are there and waiting for you, Ma'am," he told her.

"Thank you," chirped Abigail.

"I can do it myself," Dahlia with her nose in the air told the captain when he offered her a hand off the boat. "I don't need the help of a man. My son-in-law was supposed to be here with us but he's not worth a plugged nickel. Us women can manage fine on our own."

"Ava," my mother turned and called on me as a teacher does in the classroom when she wants a student to fill in the blanks.

"I know, Mama," I answered. "A lady never fails to be polite and accept help from a man."

"That's right," Abigail said as she hopped onto the dock. "I guess I'm not doing as poor of a job raising you as I had feared."

Lydia

Ava's words continued, but I stopped reading as the limousine pulled up alongside the curb outside the bank headquarters where my father's office was located.

"See to it she gets home safely and her bags are brought in," Lloyd ordered the driver.

"I don't need the help of a man," I blurted out. "I can carry my bags myself."

"Lydia," snapped Lloyd. "Apologize for what you've said."

"Sorry, sir."

He closed the door and disappeared into the skyscraper.

I didn't know why I said what I did. I didn't mean to be rude, but I had always felt passive and lazy as I watched our hired help do absolutely everything for me. I didn't think it was so bad of Ava's grandmother, Dahlia, wanting to step off the boat herself, without any help from a man.

The driver turned and looked at me and, once I smiled, we were off through the city in the direction of our estate. I continued to read.

Ava

"C'mon, Grandmalia. It's your turn," I said. "You can do it. Step off the boat. Onto the dock."

I noticed Abigail standing impatiently on the dock with her hands on her hips. We ladies had arrived to Punta Gorda by train, and we then took a steamer into Fort Myers. We did it all without any glitches. And it was a long trip. I wasn't going to allow Dahlia to accidentally slip and kill herself now nor waste any more time.

I put my arms out like a bed, ready to catch her, should she fall back. She had a big belly, so big we couldn't afford to have the seamstress make her a corset. It was that belly that made it so tough for her to see the ground where she was stepping, but she refused to blame anything on it. Instead, she blamed her large nose. No one disagreed about it resembling the beak of a hawk, and we tried telling her that hawks can still see past their beaks.

I could hear Abigail tapping her shoe on the dock, and it sounded like the tick tock of a clock. "C'mon, Mother. Step off the boat. We haven't all day. I'd like to find flowers."

Dahlia's eyes glided across her nose and landed on me. I shrugged my shoulder, hoping to nudge her round black eyes away from me.

"Oh stop with the rude look, Ava. Your mother and you were spared."

I rolled my eyes, knowing she was about to start talking about her nose again.

There were only a dozen stories Dahlia liked to tell and she repeatedly told them in a revolving manner like the revolving beacon of the lighthouse. And just as ships sixteen miles at sea can spot when the wick of the lantern is lit, I could recognize which story and which part of the story Dahlia was about to tell next by the tone of her voice.

"I got this nose from my grandmother, Myrtle, her name was. She was the fourth baby in her family."

"I know, Grandmalia. Time to get off the boat."

"Myrtle got it from her great-grandmother, also the fourth in the family.

You better be concerned for your fourth baby some day because this nose shows on all the fourths of the family, you know. At least it's not as big as that beak over there, is it?" Dahlia pointed to a white bird with a long, curved orange-red beak and matching legs, wading in the shallow water.

"That bird is beautiful—big beak and all," I said. "And so are you, Grandmalia."

"My nose is the reason I stopped having babies after Abby, my third," she mumbled, and I knew her story was ending.

Lydia

I closed the journal as the elaborate wrought-iron gates to our estate electronically opened. Then I ran my fingers alongside the contours of my nose. It was a small nose, like my father's, but unlike his mine had an upward tilt at the end that would send a downhill skier into back summersaults in the air. I had seen photographs of my mother and her mother, but neither had a tilt at the tip of their noses. I wondered the origins of my nose and whether the shape of it came from a great aunt on my mother's side or a not so great uncle on my father's side.

"Where did you get your nose?" I asked the driver as he opened the back door for me.

"I was born with it," he answered, wiping his nostrils with his fingers as if mention of his nose meant it had to be checked and cleaned. "Why? Do they sell noses at Marshall Fields? Do they have a nose department?"

He pulled out a handkerchief from his back pocket and blew. "Is that where you got your nose?"

I stopped and rubbed its contours once more. "I don't know," I said, wishing I had some matriarchs in the family to make such connections for me. Women do that. I've heard them. 'She's got her Aunt Nannie's sense of humor,' they'll say or 'You just laughed just like your grandmother,' or 'I know, she's got my strong will, all right,' or when a young girl throws a tantrum in public, 'You have your father's temper.'

When I saw the driver lift my luggage from the trunk, I put my arm over his and stopped him. "I can do it myself," I insisted, looking up at the stately steps leading into our mansion.

"Fine," he said. "Have a good day."

I should have let someone help me, I thought an hour later. After dragging my luggage inside and upstairs by myself, with the housekeepers watching, I landed on my bed like a bird, exhausted after migrating across hemispheres, and I was ravenous, but not for food. Instead, I opened Ava's journal, hungry for more tidbits about nature and the island. I wanted desperately to be there, not here inside my sterile bedroom, where I felt alone, pampered, and disconnected from the outdoor world.

Ava

"Mother," moaned Abigail. "Take my hand, please. And Ava," she said to me, "Get ready to catch your grandmother, should she fall back."

I still held my arms out like a bed behind her. But just as Dahlia did her little shuffle, and then worked up the proper momentum needed to step up and off the boat, she glanced back at me and started one of her stories.

"I remember when Abby was around your age, Ava, fourteen or fifteen," she said.

"Come on, Grandmalia, now is not the time for your story about the bugs. Step onto the dock."

She kicked off the floor of the boat with one leg, which would have been enough power to make it to the dock, but instead she arched around, flopping back down to where she started and said to me, "Some day I'll be dead, and you'll regret that impatience, young lady."

She reached out for Abigail's arms and once more looked ready to jump. "As I was trying to say, Abby used to gather a fistful of pink flowers for me every . . ."

Her foot missed and landed in the gap between the boat and the dock. "Damn," my mother screamed, then grabbed onto a ruffle on Dahlia's dress and pulled her safely onto the dock. And then she immediately followed up with, "I didn't mean that word I said just a moment ago, Ava. A lady ought to be even-tempered, for anything else is unsightly."

I smiled, glad that my mother was feeling well enough to care about my upbringing. "Hallelujah," I shouted jumping off the boat and putting my arm around my Grandmalia. "We're here!"

My mother also put an arm around Dahlia, and the three of us, connected by arms, took our first steps down the long T-shaped dock.

"You only liked the pink flowers, remember that, Abby? Pink was your favorite color back then," said Dahlia, continuing her same story from before.

My mother began to laugh, and I recognized the sound from years before when her laughing was the cockle-doodle-do of the rooster that started our days and the crackled pop of the fire that ended them. I didn't want it to end, so I chimed in, for the greater the number, the longer the laughter is sustained, and to my surprise Dahlia also joined in. I felt as if my old life and the order of things back home had passed away and a new life was about to begin.

"This is going to be a new start for us all," I declared as we took our first steps onto the white silken sand at Point Ybel, the easternmost tip of Sanibel. I wanted desperately to believe in something upon entering the Promised Land.

We stopped just before taking our first steps off the wood and onto the sand, probably to say our own personal thanks to the Lord for getting us here alive. We all have our theories as to why it took us so long to get to

Florida. If you ask Abigail in a good mood, she'd tell you my father lacked faith and courage and feared that an island this good might not exist. And if you ask her in a dark mood, she'd tell you her husband has the curiosity of a lobster and would stop the train just to watch a turtle cross the tracks. Enough excuses. We were here now and had no more time to waste.

"What are you ladies waiting for?" the boat captain asked us as he passed by. "Surely you must be eager to start your searching for seashells. They're the best in the entire Western Hemisphere and possibly the world, you know."

"Oh no, sir," I said. "We have more important things to do. We're here to claim land."

"Whatever suits you, Ma'am," he said and continued onward.

His claim about the seashells had to be true, for there were shells of every imaginable color and shape, and I hardly wanted to step, for fear of shattering any. I thought Abigail had bent down to pick one up, but instead she was licking her finger, dipping it into the sand, and then putting it into her mouth.

"My God, Mother!" I exclaimed. "What on earth are you doing?"

"It's white as sugar," she said, spitting the sand out of her mouth. "I just thought maybe . . ."

"No, Mama, it's only sand."

"Abby meant well, but those flowers were loaded with bugs," said Dahlia, continuing her story from before. I wanted to ring her neck for rambling irrelevantly at a time like this. "I'd keep 'em anyway, give 'em a good shake, then put 'em in a vase that stayed outside on the front porch."

My mother stood up and stepped over to me. "Do I do that, too?" She whispered in my ear. "Do I tell the same old stories over and over again?"

"No."

"Good, because I think she's losing her mind. I'm not losing mine, am I, Ava?"

"Of course not, Mama," I lied. I couldn't tell my own mother that I thought Dahlia was just getting old, but that she was losing her mind. Anyone who eats sand, even sand that's white as sugar, is surely losing her mind. I couldn't tell her that. I didn't want to accept it myself.

"That's good because if Dahlia goes mad, and if I lose my mind, then odds are surely against you, Ava," Abigail said into my ear. "It would only be a matter of time before you lost your mind, too."

"You're not losing your mind," I insisted.

Lydia

I rested the journal on my chest when the housekeepers came knocking for the third time at my door. "I'm fine," I said. "There's nothing wrong. I'm tired from our trip. And I've got reading to do before school tomorrow."

A second later, I could hear two of them mumbling in the hallway so I softly folded the corner of the page I was reading and tiptoed over to listen.

"Her mind isn't right today."

"She's acting crazy."

"What do you think it is?"

"I don't know. She's never behaved like this before."

I didn't bother defending myself. If they wanted to think I was crazy for a day, fine. Nothing I had ever done before warranted the diagnosis, but now, just because I wanted to be alone in my room and unsocial for a day, they're declaring me insane. I felt bad for Abigail. She didn't present as crazy. I didn't think it was nice of her daughter to treat her so. Ava should have been grateful she had a mother, and if she were to ask me, I'd tell her that Dahlia was the nutty one.

I returned to my bed and picked up where I left off.

Ava

We had just taken a couple steps when Dahlia started up again. "I told Abby," she said, "she was around your age, Ava—fourteen or fifteen—that flowers don't like being inside. That's how I kept the bugs out of the house, you know."

Dahlia stood close, spearing me with her eyes so I couldn't get away, yet there was nothing that my eyes craved more than the freedom to climb the royal palms and soar through the sky along with the birds. Her stop-everything-you're-doing-and-look-at-me stories had partially been to blame for it taking us so long to arrive here in the first place. I hadn't minded them on the train because at least we were still moving forward. It was every time we got off the train that her stories stopped us like boulders in our path.

If we were ever going to explore this island of seashells and to claim a piece of it for ourselves, then I had to rise forth as leader, shutting Dahlia up and keeping my mother's spirits up at the same time.

VI

LYDIA

COME MORNING, I FRANTICALLY searched around my bed for the journal. I looked everywhere, on the floor, the table beside my bed, the space between the wall and the bed and down near my toe area. At last I discovered it safely beneath my pillow, and I applauded myself for having slipped it there without thought. I couldn't afford to carelessly fall asleep reading it and risk my father or someone finding it.

Lloyd had come home from work way past midnight and was gone again when I left for school. Waiting outside for me was the same interim limousine driver from the day before, and he looked as glad to see me, as I was to see him, so I decided to stir things up a bit. I told him to drop me off at the nearest Chicago Transit Authority bus stop.

"Limousines bore me—they add to my feeling lonely, passive, sheltered and disconnected from the real world," I told him, expecting a debate. Instead, he drove directly to the nearest stop and let me out.

Fifteen minutes later, I found myself sitting on a metro bus, and it was going slow as a tortoise, which would never get me to school on time. In fact, if I didn't rise forth as a leader, like Ava felt she had to do, no one on the bus would ever get anywhere they wanted to go. So I made my way up the aisle and said to the driver, "Why are you taking Michigan Avenue?

Why not try one street over?"

"Because I'm the driver and you're the passenger," he said. "If you want to be the driver, then get a car."

"I don't need a car. I could walk faster than any car and especially this bus," I said, returning to my seat.

I loved Chicago. But today I didn't feel like being in any city. I wanted to be on my vacation, where instead of looking up at skyscrapers, I could see the towering lighthouse. Because we left earlier than we had planned, I never had the chance to see the lighthouse up close, and going to Sanibel and not seeing such a landmark was like going to Paris and skipping the Eiffel Tower.

I was in a Sanibel-sort-of-mood, and so I unzipped my school bag and pulled out Ava's journal. I opened and began reading like a girl diving into an ocean and drowning out the sounds and sites on the surface.

Ava

We passed the lighthouse, a towering throne before us with its slender, inner cylinder braced twenty feet off the ground by an iron column supported by a pyramid-shaped frame of latticed wrought iron. Its curtains up top were closed. The boat captain had told us that the keeper already made his daily trip to the top to extinguish the flame, trim the wick, polish the lens, wind the clockworks, and draw the curtains to guard against the damaging rays of the sun. The curtains wouldn't open, and the lamp wouldn't be lit again until this afternoon.

As we trekked toward the interior of the island, I was glad to discover it less densely wooded than I had feared it might be. We walked into late afternoon, following cart tracks to a narrow road blooming profusely with periwinkles. I felt as if my eyes had been sealed shut all my life and they were opened for the first time, witnessing miracles I had never known possible.

Dahlia had tears of delight streaming down her cheeks and dripping into her mouth, which was curved upward into a broad grin. "I hope my beloved Milton is in a place as Heavenly as this," she said, her voice cracking.

"I thought you said Granddaddy didn't believe in Heaven," I said.

"He didn't, but everyone in his family did, his grandparents, his parents, his brothers and sisters, cousins and uncles and maybe they all begged God in all his goodness to let him in anyway."

"Why didn't He embrace God if everyone in his family did?"

"We're talking about faith. It's not like a pair of trousers you can hand down in a family," she said. "You can still hand it down, but it doesn't mean the next person is going to wear it."

Abigail collapsed onto the flower-coated ground, weeping in hysteria. "Oh how sweet could this be?" she moaned, rolling from her back onto her stomach, looking as if she had swigged a bottle of spirits. I didn't dare say anything, but all I could think was, is that any way for a lady to behave?

"Look, each flower has five petals," she cried. "None of them have four. And they're perfect little pinwheel patterns. Oh, how my thoughts are spinning with jubilation." Then she stopped and looked at me. "The flowers aren't spinning, are they?"

"No, Mama, just your mind, I think." I was worried. I had watched melancholy wilt her to the ground in the dark winter months, but this was the opposite.

"Maybe it's her corset," I said to Dahlia. Everyone knew that corsets caused blood to flow to a woman's head, thus putting pressure on her nervous system, causing a personality change. But no one cared, and everyone wore the darn things anyway. Hers must have added a solid twenty pounds of pressure on her internal organs, which could be tolerable if she weren't rolling around in the ground.

"Mama," I said. "You ought to stop rolling on the ground like that. You could fracture a rib or collapse a lung or displace your liver."

But then I stopped scolding her because I'd rather see her gay like a pig in mud than down in the ground like a worm. In a way, her behavior was like a miracle. And she couldn't help herself. I don't think she wanted to be rollicking in the dirt with that new dress on but something—the Holy

Spirit maybe, the new corset probably, spring in the air for sure, or those flowers possibly—had taken hold of her.

I bent down and gave the flowers a closer look. They looked wild, ready to snap off and conquer the earth had they not been attached to their long, creeping, arching stems. There were multitudes of them. The vibrancy of their shiny dark-green leaves suddenly made me aware and grateful for my youth, beauty, and health. I felt alive and strong and ready to do great things. I knew Abigail was feeling the medicinal benefits, but I feared she had downed a dose bigger than she could handle.

I stood up to find two men with their sons around my age and younger standing nearby, their mouths hanging open as they gazed at my mother rolling around on the ground, stroking the petals with her fingertips, then tickling her own neck with their stems.

"I feel so fine. These flowers make me feel fine again," Abigail cried. "I haven't felt this fine in a long time. A woman should feel this fine every moment of her life, don't you think?" Her eyes blossomed in my direction, making my eyes bloom with tears, and when I turned toward Dahlia, I noticed her eyes opening widely. Together, the three of us women smiled at the men like a bouquet of wild flowers.

"I gave flowers to my wife once but they didn't make her feel that fine," said one of the men.

"Mine, either," said the other.

Lydia

I laid the journal on my lap and looked out the bus window. We were still on Michigan Avenue, and my eyes buzzed up and down like bees, desperate to land upon flowers in the city. I wouldn't feel content until they rested on something sweet and then, just as the bus closed its doors and started to go, I spotted something that might do the job.

"Stop!" I yelled, springing from my seat. "Stop the bus!"

"This isn't a stop," the driver said.

"Those flowers! See those flowers?" I shouted, pointing to a floral shop with every kind of flower imaginable and unimaginable blossoming out of buckets and overflowing out the doors of the shop and onto the sidewalk in carts. "I need those. I want those. I'll die if I don't get them right away!"

It was a childhood phrase that had always worked with my father, but the driver glared into his rearview mirror at me. I could tell by the way his eyes bounced back and forth between the street and me that he wanted to smack me like a spoiled little bug. And like a bug, I wanted off his bus.

"Sir," I said. "Stop this bus right now. I want to get off."

"I'll be stopping at the next street," he said. "You'll have to wait."

So I did, and when the bus stopped I flew out the door and back one block to the floral shop where I dove into bushels and buckets and up and down aisles inside and outside again searching for periwinkles. When I found nothing resembling what I recalled seeing on Sanibel or what Ava had described, with five petals and creeping stems, I settled for everything else.

I was a bee drunk on honey, and the owner of the shop liked me, I think.

"Is everything okay this morning?" she asked.

"Fine, I hope, but I'll tell you in a minute," I answered.

I pointed to the flowers I wanted, and in the midst of it all, I noticed her eyes rooting themselves into my purse, as if she didn't think I had the money to pay for all the flowers. I was glad she was looking at my purse and not my face, for my nose was twitching in an effort to stop from sneezing. It wasn't fair. The flowers that day didn't make Abigail sneeze. They made her feel fine.

Fresh cut daisies. Fragrant lilies. Ecuadorian red roses. Spring flowers. Blooming orchids. Blue iris. Belladonna delphinium. Yellow germinis. Festive orange Asiatic lilies. Yellow chrysanthemums. Yellow tulips.

"I feel fine. Just fine. Really fine," I muttered as I walked out of her shop carrying enough flowers in my arms to cover an entire island the size of Sanibel, or maybe Captiva, I thought as I took a seat between an old man and woman on a bench.

"Gesundheit," the man said.

"Thank you," I answered.

"You're a lucky girl," he said. "Looks like you've got a male admirer."

"Nope," I said in between sneezes. "Bought them for myself."

"God bless you," said the lady to my right. "If we don't treat ourselves, who will?"

"Excuse me," I said sneezing again and again and again, and then faking a sneeze or two.

I didn't feel like talking. I felt like sipping the intoxication right out of the flowers and nibbling away at their happy petals, waiting for the urge to fall to the ground and roll around like Abigail, or at least experience fineness in my own way, by singing, dancing, or maybe smiling.

I sat there stroking petals, waiting, but nothing happened. I sniffed a rose, then sneezed, then waited for a feeling of fineness to shower over me. Instead, I felt un-fine. I felt alone and isolated with thoughts that were strange and remote. The flowers on the island were free to grow wherever they wanted while the ones in my lap stood still and obedient as flowers in captivity do.

I longed to be free, to grow and extend out into the world, but I was surrounded by men who were dominant and hindering as Australian pines. If only someone asked my opinion, I'd say the male species is disastrous to the development of womankind and they ought to be removed promptly. But no one would ask and that's a good thing, for I didn't want to be called a freak of nature; me, the only girl in the world who thinks this way, probably.

If only I had a mother. Maybe she might understand or help me put my remote and isolated thoughts into perspective. A mother knows, I'm sure, how to travel that distance, risking mammoth waves and dangerous creatures in her path, but voyaging onward until she reaches the remote island of her daughter's innermost thoughts. Marlena reached me almost like that.

"I believe in you," she had told me that day on the island. "Anything is possible."

Hmm. Maybe the periwinkles on the island were magical, I thought, or maybe I'm not a typical woman who gets her contentment from a few flowers. I pondered what Marlena had said, and suddenly I felt fine, for I do believe there was magic in those words.

After sneezing three more times, I handed half of the flowers to the man on my left.

"Maybe your wife will like these," I said. "I hope she goes wild over them."

"So do I," he said.

"And here," I said, handing the other half to the woman on my right. "Don't wait around for some man to buy you flowers."

"Thank you. My husband has only brought home flowers twice in all our forty years of marriage. I think I'll start buying them for myself, like you did."

My hands were now free, so I reached into my bag and pulled out Ava's journal. I began to read where I left off.

Ava

"Flowers haven't ever made my wife act like that, either," said one of the men as he watched my mother roll onto her belly. "Maybe there's something different about the island flowers." He reached down and picked a handful of the periwinkles. "I think I'll bring some back to Florence."

"Worth a try," the second man replied.

I didn't want the men thinking they could linger around all day on the land we were interested in. We had found it first. I also didn't want any men knowing we had arrived to the island alone, without any men of our own. Such information might prove dangerous.

"Daddy should be here any second," I lied. "I know it's heavy for him to be carrying all his rifles alone."

"Ava, forgive me for saying this, but the only way your daddy might arrive is if he washes ashore like a dead fish," said Dahlia, destroying my plan of protecting us women from straying, stranger men.

"He's not dead," I snapped in my most non-ladylike tone. "My daddy wouldn't move us to Florida, then die, leaving us to claim land and fend for ourselves with all the wild animals out here." I glared at the men.

"Oh yeah? Remember the wild hog in Georgia? That thing was headed right for us," Dahlia said, her voice loud enough for our old neighbors
back in Kentucky to hear. She had one of those voices that reached a thousand miles out and pulled people in, and often she used it to convert innocent bystanders into her loyal sympathizers. "And your father, the only
man alive that would do such a thing stopped to swig gin before lifting the
double-barreled shotgun."

"No," said one of the men. "Tell us it isn't so!"

"So!" insisted Dahlia, her eyes consuming. "That's my son-in-law."

"I'd have taken two swigs," mumbled one of the men. "Where's he
now?"

Dahlia sighed. "We finally arrived in the Charlotte Harbor region, and
he had the guts to go fishing with some native."

"For Christ's sake," said one of the men.

"He spotted one of those silver fish," continued Dahlia.

"Tarpon?"

"Yeah, one of those."

"Did he secure it?"

"That man has never secured a thing in his life," Dahlia looked at me
and said, "You were on the boat that day, Ava. I'm not the only witness.
Tell the men what happened."

I did like to tell stories, and I know I inherited the liking and ability to
do so from my Grandmalia, although I never told the same story twice
like she did. I took a deep breath and stepped two feet forward. "My daddy's eyes glowed red, and he became entranced. After talking of nothing
but that fish for hours, Grandmalia pleaded for him to stop and..." I shook
my head and looked down at the ground, wanting to weep at the pandemonium I had witnessed on that boat. "He became physically violent with
her, wringing her neck over the side of the boat. I think he's possessed!"

The men laughed. I continued my story.

"The next day my mama wanted us ladies to stay back at the fishermens' hotel. But Grandmalia and I didn't want him drinking himself into
any trouble out there in the water, so we went out with him again. The

Floridian that owned the boat told us, 'shush,' then asked us if we heard it. Another fish as silver as the rim on Mama's tea set came to the surface to blow. And that's when it got bad."

The men raised their eyebrows, and their sons had huddled around my feet, so I continued my story. "In the flickering moment that its silvery side appeared before us on the crest of a wave, I gasped, for it was the most magnificent fish, and then, it vanished before our eyes, and I believed in magic, which I never believed in before."

"Tell us more," insisted a little boy sitting at my foot.

I sighed. "My daddy with his glowing eyes bossed the Floridian around in his own boat and made me wish I had stayed onshore like a typical lady. 'No, the other way,' my father had shouted at the boat captain. 'Cut off that school of mullet and drag the bait before them,' he had ordered. 'Go the other way again, then cast it among the mullet.' It had to have been two, maybe three or four yards long! 'Who's ready to hook it?' he had asked and it was then that he gazed at me for a moment with that tarpon-possessed look and said, 'Baby, how about we hook ourselves a Silver King today?'"

"Did he hook it?" asked a puny boy covered in freckles and dirt, knocking on my shoe.

I cast my eyes sadly upon him and patted his head. "No, he didn't. Not that day, nor the next, nor the next after that."

"It's not to say he didn't come close," added Dahlia. "He did fifty or sixty times, and we kept telling him that 'nearly' catching one was going to have to be good enough."

"But back at the hotel he nearly cried at the bulletin board that posted all of the names of men who caught Silver Kings," I added. "'Daddy,'" I told him. "'Us ladies are getting sick of staying at this fishermens' hotel. It's smelly, and Grandmalia claims the men are making lip-smacking sounds at her. You caught a 300-pound jewfish. Isn't that enough?'"

I turned to see my mother napping in the periwinkles. "The day he hooked the shark was the day my mama and Grandmalia decided to leave him behind and head to Sanibel on our own."

"Your daddy caught a shark?" asked a boy with no front teeth.

"Not really. The shark cut himself free the moment it closed its jaws on the bait," I said.

I lightly kicked the little boy off my toes, then tilted my head upward toward the afternoon clouds, and closed one eye. "Lord God Almighty," I said, and then paused. That is the way I prayed out loud, and that was my favorite prayer of all, for praying out loud and in front of anyone made me feel bashful.

"Lord God Almighty," repeated a male voice.

I gasped thinking it might be the Lord himself responding to my prayer, but when I opened my second eye I saw it was a boy around my age.

"Our Heavenly Father," his lips muttered, his head bowed and his eyes sealed. "Thank you for the fish in the sea and all that you have created. Forgive her daddy for abandoning his family and bring him back safely. And, please, help him secure a Silver King. In Your name, Amen."

I opened my other eye and cracked a smile at the boy. It was the first time in all my nearly fifteen years of living that I had ever smiled at any boy. He grinned back, and I saw he wasn't as ugly as all the other boys in the world. He was bony, puny, and smaller than me, but his eyes were a crystal green color and clear as a Florida freshwater spring. They were easy to look into and when I did, I think I measured depth.

Abigail lifted her head off the pillow of flowers, and I walked over and gave her my hand, pulling her up.

"That boy was a gentleman, finishing your prayer like that," she said to me. "A gentleman is tender towards the bashful. Remember that, Ava."

I felt my face turning red. "It's time we get going," I said. "Do you men think this land here is good for claiming?"

"Ava," whined my mother. "It's full of periwinkles. Of course it is."

"I'd probably give it a day or two," said the father of the boy who had prayed for my daddy, the boy with the deep eyes. "Wait for your daddy to show. He'd probably like to take a look at it himself."

"Thanks for your input," I said. "What land are you claiming?"

"We didn't come here to claim any land. We were cruising aboard a sloop when it went aground in San Carlos Bay. We're just passing time until the tide floats it off. We figured we'd explore the island before we head back to Punta Gorda."

"Oh," I said, disappointed. They had proven themselves to be gentlemen, and it would have been nice to know a kind boy around my age living on Sanibel.

"Location is everything," added the boy's father. "If I were here for that purpose, I'd probably claim a nice 160 acres extending along the Bay. I've met several who are taking up homesteads along the Gulf beach. I do think you have to prove you're head of the family before you claim."

"I'm temporarily the head," I said.

"You don't look twenty-one."

"I'm almost fifteen."

"Same age as my son, Jaden," he said, looking toward the kind boy. "If you were my daughter, I'd want you to hold off and give me a day or two to show up. I'm sure that's what your father would want."

I beamed a smile. "Then that is what we shall do," I said. "Thank you, sir."

VII

LYDIA

I CLOSED THE JOURNAL and returned it to my school bag. I wondered whether Lloyd might buy me a parcel of land on Sanibel. That way I could have a place to go to whenever I felt like getting away from the city. I'd have to ask him about it—if I ever saw him, that is.

I stood up and stretched my legs. I had been sitting there for some time, listening to some man preach the word of God, never noticing when the old lady and man on each side of me got up to leave. I felt small standing there with the towering buildings surrounding me, but when I glanced up, and saw that I had been sitting this entire time on a bench in front of the *Windy City Press* Tower, my spirits soared higher than the Sears Tower itself. For there are no coincidences, I told myself. One day I'll be sitting on this same bench, but it will be my lunch break, and I will be a journalist!

I felt so fine that I wanted to stay there in that exact spot and relish the coincidence of my getting off that bus and choosing a bench outside the tower of my dreams, but then, my eyes did what they wanted to do. They peeked at my watch and made me wish I believed in a God and in the message that one of our city's beloved homeless persons was preaching, for if I believed, then maybe God could make it so I wouldn't be late for school. Then again, if that handsome boy could pray for Ava's daddy to secure a tarpon, then I could at least try to pray for my own selfish needs. And whether I believed or not, maybe God, whether He existed or not, might hear me. And so I gave it a try, rattling off my first prayer, quick and simple as I took off sprinting through the city.

And when I saw that the crowds of people on Michigan Avenue spread apart creating a perfect pathway for me to run down, I nearly became a believer right then and there, but I didn't. Maybe it was because believing didn't run in my family.

When I arrived at school, panting like a panther, I told the principal, Mr. Smith, a big white lie about our flight getting in this morning and our limo breaking down and me running nearly a mile to get here. And when I noticed the secretary's questioning eyes, I pulled out from my pocket the single blue iris I had saved and handed it to her.

"The bell will be ringing shortly," she said. "Why don't you have a seat over there and you can make it to your next class. Actually, lunch is next."

"Fine," I said, my face blossoming into a smile. "I'll sit here and read until lunch."

I flipped open the journal to where I left off and began to read:

Ava

We left the periwinkles behind and treaded toward the east, asking directions as we went until we arrived at the house Stewart had arranged for us to stay at. Someone told him the woman of the house took in boarders, and after correspondence she and my father worked it out that we would stay there until we built a home of our own.

"I've been expecting you for over two months now," she said as she opened the door. "C'mon in. My name is Tootie. I'm glad you made it safely, but where's Stewart?"

"Sidetracked," I said quickly. "He'll be here any day, I'm sure."

"Fine." There was a no-nonsense air about her as she led us to the small, square room we were to share. "Your boxes arrived this morning. Make yourselves at home. I told Stewart in a letter it would be fifteen dollars a month per person," she continued, sizing each of us with her eyes, before they stopped suspiciously at Dahlia's big tummy. "That fifteen dollars was after he wrote and claimed that you ladies don't eat much."

"We do eat a lot," I said, annoyed. I didn't want to be made to feel awkward about all the food that was on my mind. "We eat like men. And we're famished right now from our arduous journey and exploration of the island."

"Of course you are," Tootie said with a smile. "Down this hall and in that room over there is where we eat. Looks like the other boarders are just now sitting down for supper. Why don't you go in and introduce yourselves, get acquainted. Several are just like you, new to the island and staying with me until they claim their land or build their homes."

I turned my nose toward the smell of food. "Let's go," I said. "I'm so hungry I could eat a raccoon about now."

My mother took hold of my arm. "Wait, young lady," she said. "I can't go in there looking like this."

"Like what?"

"A mess, all dirty, like I was playing in . . ."

"Dirt?" interrupted Dahlia. "You were, Abby."

"But we're meeting new people, and this is going to be a new start for us. It's important to make a good first impression. That's why we spent a fortune to have these new dresses made, so we might arrive on the island looking like classy Southern ladies for the first time in our lives. I just need to go wash parts of this dress before we go in there."

"Mama," I said, pulling her down the hall toward the room. "It's not important what we look like on the outside. It's all about our intellect and views on the inside. Besides, I don't care if there's dirt on my dress. It shows that I've got better things on my mind than striving to look like a prim and proper girl."

"I'm trying to raise a young lady," Abigail said to her mother. "Why is it so hard?"

Dahlia chuckled, then lowered her voice and didn't think I could hear as she said, "She reminds me of you, Abby, when you were her age. I prayed back then that one day you'd have one of your own to deal with. The good Lord does answer our prayers, doesn't He?"

When we entered the room, I noticed families eating at large wooden tables set up throughout and no one was wearing elaborate dresses like ours. They wore the kind of clothes that people wear when working the land and building homes.

Boys were looking my way. It was always they who watched me as if I were a rare and beautiful bird. I tiptoed to a table across the room, one without any boys my age. I didn't want them observing my every move, especially the way in which I was about to devour my food. I was ravenous and not about to pick away like a proper, dainty bird.

I chose a seat the farthest away from any boys, but still, they stared my way as if holding binoculars. I learned a lot from the way boys watched me. I learned I must be beautiful. Maybe it was my long, thick hair, with colors of auburn and chestnut, and streaks of black throughout. I got my hair from Grandmalia, although hers turned gray in her forties, I was told. I knew I should take advantage of my looks before they left, and I know most girls would find outer beauty a commodity, but I didn't want to be admired for my feathers or hunted down like those poor old Roseate Spoonbills. I wanted people to hear my whistle, to listen to what I had to say. I had a bold but honest whistle, the kind that hurts the ears of some and scares off others and only attracts a certain kind.

Dinner was good—grits and fried fish. I could tell Dahlia was tired by the way her head kept dropping to the table and Abigail looked calm and content after picking away at her food. All she ate were crumbs, but they settled her mind, and I was glad.

It was good talking to the other settlers. We learned of some who had been living on Sanibel under the pre-emption and homestead laws at least as early as 1884.

"I want to understand this," I said to a man sitting next to me. "We can acquire as much as one-hundred-and-sixty acres of free Sanibel land?"

"Providing," he said, "you are head of a family or over twenty-one, reside on the property or cultivate it for five years and pay proving up fees."

"And the Pre-emption Act of 1841?"

"It permits you to locate a claim of one-hundred-and-sixty acres and after six months of residency purchase it for as little as $1.25 an acre."

We talked with others, who, like us, had come for Sanibel's healthful climate. We were told there was a pastor on the island who, together with his family, moved here from Maine after he contracted tuberculosis. There was a childless widow, we were told, who saw life on an island as both an adventure and opportunity so she left her home in Cincinnati, Ohio, and came to Sanibel. Families had been arriving from Virginia, Kentucky, Maryland, and all over the country. Some members of their families, we were told, lived but a short time after coming to the island and were then buried on their land.

And we learned that Stewart wasn't the only man to become interested in tarpon. Tarpon stories from this area had been spreading worldwide, and wealthy sport fishermen, captains of industry, renowned politicians, and playboys were all arriving in Fort Myers for tarpon fishing and then falling in love with the area and staying.

I still couldn't imagine an obsession so strong that men were relocating their families across the country in pursuit of a silver fish. Maybe the fish, like the flowers, had a way of casting a mysterious spell on people because none of it sounded logical to me.

Lydia

When I heard footsteps crossing the room in my direction, I slid the journal under a textbook, looking up and returning myself to the administrative office at school, where I was still waiting for the bell to ring.

"Tell me, Lydia," Mr. Smith said. "Did your father do any fishing while in Florida? I've got a brother-in-law who went there back in the forties and came home talking of nothing but tarpon. The following year, he quit his job and moved his family there."

I laughed. "I wished that would happen to my father, but you could cast the strongest spell on him to quit his job and fish instead, and he'd still show up to work every day, maybe with a fishing pole, but he'd still work."

Just then, the bell rang, and I was off. "Mr. Smith," I called back. "What's for hot lunch today?"

"Turkey."

"Free-roaming?"

"I'm not sure I understand what you're asking, Lydia."

"Never mind. I'm so hungry I could eat a raccoon about now."

I could hear him laugh as I hurried out the door and down the hall.

But as I approached the lunchroom, there was nothing I desired more than knowing whether Ava's daddy returned to the family. There were times when I wondered whether my own father would ever return. He was always at that bank trying to secure, not a tarpon, but something just as silvery called money.

My friends screamed when they saw me, and we chatted over lunch, but then I excused myself and went alone to the bathroom. It was unusual, I know, for we usually flock together to powder our noses, but I wasn't in the mood for gossip or small talk or to hear about their latest purchases and adventures to the department stores. I found Ava's journey to the island so much more interesting, and as I walked into a private stall and locked the door behind me, I could hardly wait to read more. In my eyes, she was becoming the bold and courageous leader she had envisioned for herself. She was doing an excellent job taking charge in the absence of her father, and I wanted to study her words and learn her ways.

I took a seat on the throne and continued to read.

Ava

"Where's your husband?" I asked Tootie once she started stacking our dinner plates. "You're married, aren't you?"

"Ava," exclaimed my mother. "A lady doesn't blurt out such questions."

"It's all right," Tootie assured my mother nonchalantly. "I was her age once. I may have four wrinkles and eight gray hairs, but I remember being her age like it was yesterday." She carried the dishes over to a bench and returned. "It's good for a woman to remember the young girl she once was." She walked back to the bench with more plates and started scraping our scraps into the garbage. "I've got a husband. He's in Fort Myers, lingering around the saloons while I'm here doing all the work."

"Men," I said, hoping my mother wouldn't hear. "They sure can be lazy asses."

Tootie bent down and picked a fallen piece of bread up off the floor. "Ava, how old are you?" she asked me.

"Fourteen, going on twenty-one," answered Abigail for me. "Almost fifteen," I corrected.

"As you probably noticed," my mother told Tootie. "All kinds of bold and fearless words slip out of that girl's mouth. My Ava has a big space between her two front teeth, and I've never wanted her to feel self-conscious about it, so for years I never corrected anything she said. Now I'm in trouble."

"Outspokenness will serve her well," said Tootie. "Girls are trained to be perfect little ladies and then they enter the real world and don't know how to stand up for themselves or be rude to a rude person or strong in a bad situation. But what do I know? So what are you all planning to do with your land once you claim?"

"Grow watermelons," I answered. "They're the 'money crop.'"

"Oh, I don't know about that, Ava," my mama said. "I was thinking tomatoes."

"Muck. I hate tomatoes. Let's grow grapefruits—but only the pink ones." Dahlia shifted in her chair and pointed her forefinger at me, then shook it lightly as she always does just before adding her own opinion. Something about that finger gave confidence to what she was about to say and shushed us so we'd listen.

"Yellow grapefruits," she announced. "They're the easiest to grow."

I made a face, the kind of face one makes when they eat a yellow grapefruit. "Yuck," I whined. "The yellow are bitter."

"Some people like the bitter," she said.

"Yes, it's an acquired taste," added my mother.

I shook my head and shrugged my shoulders. "Well, unless they're a bitter person, I don't know why anyone in their right mind would ever like the taste of a bitter yellow fruit," I stated.

"I do," said Dahlia.

"Yeah," I said looking through her eyes and into the resentment she had toward her husband leaving her and my father disappointing her as a son-in-law. "I'd have guessed you to be the sort that likes the bitter fruit. I don't at all," I continued with a proud smile. "I only like the pink."

"People's tastes change," said Dahlia. "Just wait and see. One day you'll prefer the bitter as well. It's a natural progression. If we start growing the yellow now, they'll be mature and ripe for you when you reach that point in life."

"No way," I insisted. "I've still got years of pink in me."

"Stewart and I will be the ones to decide what we grow on our land," Abigail said, slapping me with her look that reminds me I'm still young and therefore I don't know as much about the world as an adult, yet I'm no longer a child and not yet a lady, but lingering between the two, like in that state called purgatory, only for a young girl no longer a child and not yet a woman, I call it a state of temporary frustration and I need as many prayers as possible to get me out of it.

When I folded my hands and tilted my chin down without any back talk, her eyes then softly patted Dahlia with that look that reminds her she's getting old and therefore must surrender her knowledge about the world, because the world has changed since her heydays, and now Dahlia is lingering between two states—wisdom, which I believe timelessly transcends a changing world, and senility, which grows roots around wisdom, eventually strangling it.

Grandmalia started fidgeting with a splinter of wood on the table, and I could see she was struggling not to talk back as well. She and I were alike in that we both liked having the last word on matters and speaking our minds without all the fake and sickly embellishments. I didn't think it was fair of my mama to shut her own mama up. I respected my Grandmalia for the portions of her wisdom unaffected by senility, and I wanted my own wisdom to start off where hers ended, and in order for that to happen, I needed the chance to hear some of her wisdom, which I never got to hear because my mother would shut her up.

I disagreed with which grapefruit color she wanted, but I didn't mind her expressing herself. I liked a good debate. I don't know why people were always so quick to end one before it ever started. And I was actually interested in what Dahlia was trying to say about the fruit and how a person's tastes change throughout life. But then my mama shut her up.

Is this what happens to us women? We spend our entire lives acquiring wisdom only for it to be covered up by a blanket of senility that others throw over us? The thought of it made my stomach curdle and it made the words that were rumbling deep within me start trekking upward through my system and toward my mouth as if I were going to puke. I knew what had to be done. I had to voice and express all my opinions and knowledge immediately before it was too late and before my own children would one day try to shut me up, like my mama did to Dahlia.

"We're growing the pink! Final word! I have spoken!" I blurted out so loud that heads from other tables turned my way.

"Ava," Mama said sharply. "You will quiet yourself."

"That's not fair," I said. "I'm smart, and I feel strongly about growing pink grapefruit on our land."

"Why, darling?" my mother said hoping the word 'darling' might soften me somewhat so I wouldn't cause more of a scene. "Is it because pink is your favorite color?"

I heard a couple of the boys snicker, and it infuriated me. "Of course not," I said, rolling my eyes toward them. "Sugar is expensive. You don't need any sugar with the pink."

"She thinks she's smart," a male voice in the crowd whispered loudly. He was the same man who before was scratching his chin and making a face, the kind that says, "You ladies, with all your irrelevant chitchat are not capable of productivity."

"She's got a good point," defended my mama when she saw the look on the man's face. "Sugar is expensive."

The man reared his ugly head once more, this time, more directly. "I think you ladies better sit tight until the man of the household returns," he said. "Let him make all the decisions."

I could contain myself no longer. I knew that a lady should never raise her voice or show a temper, that she is meek and humble and knows when to speak, but I stood up from the table, then slammed my hands down onto the wood, and looked directly into the man's eyes. "Sir, I beg to differ. Men know nothing in comparison to what women know, and it troubles me every time to think my fellow women were the ones who actually gave birth to men with attitudes as stringent as yours."

I looked away from him and over at my mother. Her eyes had darkened from blue to brown, and I felt sad and sorry for what I had said and for the anger it had caused her, not the man.

"Ava, apologize," scolded Abigail.

"No, Mama," I said. "I can't."

And I couldn't. As sorry as I felt for putting my mama through so much strife, I had to believe that the greater cause—of speaking up on behalf of all the women of the world who are shushed by men and told that they don't know anything—was more important than my momentary outburst of disrespect. And besides, verbal expression is a form of art. And all the eyes in the room were studying me as if they had just for the first time in their lives seen the art of rebellion. Some liked it, I think, but because art is all in the individual interpretation, my mama and a few others had a right not to like it.

"Ava," she snapped again. "You will apologize or you will go to the room now."

"Fine," I said, looking back at the man. "I don't give a damn what color grapefruits we grow."

All the eyes in the room were stuck on me like bugs stuck to damp skin. I knew now if I backed down further it would be one giant step backward for womankind, and so I remained standing and took this as an opportunity.

"Giving my opinion has nothing to do with lack of honor, or failing to be a lady," I said to the entire room. "Having an opinion and being able to express it is a natural right. We have left behind nearly everything we owned. We have said good-bye to everyone we ever knew. If we are going to survive on this island, we have to start from scratch! And that means leaving behind the archaic and ridiculous rules by which women live. For starters, we need to rid ourselves of the corsets that potentially harm our internal organs and change our personalities."

"Oh, Lord," my mother muttered, waving herself with a napkin. "She's onto the corsets again and how she wants to dress."

I continued. "Regarding all that ladylike stuff," I said, looking down upon some little girls, "toss it out to bay. We shouldn't have to hold our tongues pretending that men know more than us." I noticed the mothers of the little girls covering their daughters' ears, and a couple of them left the room, but I continued. "If anyone cared to ask me, they'd discover I know a lot of intelligent things."

"Someone shut her up," said a man's voice. But that didn't stop me.

"For instance," I went on. ". . . cattle, sugar, molasses, fish scales, shells, bird plumes—which I'd never consider profiting from—deer skins, hides of alligators, otters, bears, panthers and beavers are all principal exports. If a lady has to pretend to be ignorant, for the sake of a man's ego, then I no longer want to become a lady."

Suddenly my mother dropped her napkin to the floor, her eyes rolled back, and she slipped out of her seat and down onto the ground. Everyone jumped up from their seats and formed a circle around her and several started fanning her. I scooped her up in my lap and tapped her cheeks. "My God, is she all right?" I cried.

"She's fine," said a man. "She just fainted, that's all. Probably those crazy things you were saying."

"It's the heat," I said. We've had a long day, a long sixty days, and a long winter before that. It's been hard now for a long, long time. You have no idea."

The same man that ruffled my feathers from before picked her up and carried her down the hall and into our room. When he laid her on the bed, her eyes opened and looked around for me and then spoke her first words. "True gentlemen are merciful toward the absurd and never mistake personalities or sharp sayings for arguments, Ava. And true gentlemen make everyone feel at home, despite collision of feeling or suspicion."

The man gave me a smirk and walked out of the room. Dahlia and I removed her burdensome dress and corset, and then I rummaged through the boxes until I found her sleeping attire. I pulled it over her head and then rested her back down on the bed.

Dahlia collapsed beside her on the bed with her dress still on.

I kissed Abigail on the forehead. "I am sorry, Mama. I didn't mean to do this to you," I said, pulling a blanket up over both. She closed her eyes and fell asleep, and so I continued in a whisper. "But I can't help it. I think it's inherited, probably from Grandmalia." I was glad neither of them heard that. I wanted those to be my last words. I was too tired to debate any further.

I climbed into bed and pushed the blankets down to my toes. I was glad when Dahlia started humming. I loved her humming. It always made me believe the world was a good, safe place and that I could rest my eyes and fall into slumber with not a care in the world. She always hummed the same tune. Her mama had hummed it to her as a little girl, and she had then hummed it to my mama. Some day I'd hum it to my babies. Then again, I didn't want babies if having babies meant I needed a husband first. So, instead, I decided I'd hum it to my grandchildren, if that were possible without having to have children first.

But tonight, when her humming turned into snores, I was still alert, so I crossed the room to a dark wooden desk with a pineapple carving on it, lit a candle, and opened my journal. I had a lot on my mind, the move and all, and worried about my father and missing my friends back home. There I wrote until the wee hours when I heard a knock at our door.

"Are you awake in there?" It was Tootie's voice.

"Yeah."

She opened the door and peeked her head in. "I noticed light under your door. Don't go falling asleep without blowing it out."

"Oh no," I replied. "I'm sorry about tonight, about what my mother calls my wild and lawless temper and outspokenness and for causing a scene out there. It all just makes me so mad."

"What?"

"Men. They can drink and hang out at saloons while the women are living out their God-given roles as wives and mothers, keepers of the household and guardians of the moral purity of all who live therein, and we're the ones who are pagans if we don't feel like doing all that domestic stuff."

"Is that all you think women do?"

"It's what they're supposed to do, and if you ask me, they deserve to be married to angels, not men."

Tootie laughed loudly and then covered her mouth in response to a change in Dahlia's snore pattern. "What are you doing up so late?"

"Writing."

"Writing what?"

"About our journey here."

"You like books?"

"Love them, especially anything by Louisa May Alcott," I said. She was my favorite author, and at least one hundred cubic feet of tears per second spewed out of me for two weeks straight after she died. "I've read everything she's ever written. It's sad there will be no more books from her."

"I've got some of her books. I get them from a boat that comes by the island. Does your mama read?"

"Sometimes."

"Your grandmother?"

"Nope."

"You keep reading and writing, you hear? There's a school on the island I'm sure you'll attend in the fall. Reading and writing can change a girl's world, you know. There's power in creating a world for yourself."

I thought about what she had meant as she closed the door. I wanted a new world for myself. I wanted a world where my mama stayed happy dancing in flowers that blossomed year-round and where Dahlia could have her husband back and her senility gone and where boys would have to cook and clean and be nice and girls would be smart and in charge. I wanted a world where I no longer had to do chores from sunrise to sunset and where I had more time to read and write so I could know such a world or better yet, create one of my own. Reading and writing about an interesting and adventurous fictional world is far better than living in a plain and boring real world.

VIII

LYDIA

I ONLY CLOSED AVA'S journal when I became self-conscious that girls, entering the bathroom for a second powdering, might peek under the bathroom stall and recognize my same pair of shoes still there. And when the bell rang, I knew my behind belonged in study hall anyway, and not on the toilet reading.

It was the first time I ever enjoyed the quietness of study hall. I didn't want to write notes or toss spit wads or make faces at the gawking boys from two rows back. I wanted to sit there and think about the world I wanted to create for myself.

I wanted a bigger one—a world that stretched outside the walls of the mansion I lived in, a world I could discover for myself, not one I observed through the backseat windows of a limousine. I wanted a world where girls had choices, like up to a hundred bus stops and they got to decide when and where to get off. I wanted a world where I could set my eyes on the things I wanted, like I had the flowers this morning, and go after them with no one stopping me.

I thought about how I might get such a world. It wasn't something Lloyd could buy for me. And I didn't want to read about it in a novel or create a fictional one through creative writing. I wasn't creative. Besides, there was already a world out there, and I knew nothing about it. I'd rather get to know more of the one out there before searching for another, and I knew exactly how I'd go about doing that. I'd ask my nannies to order me a newspaper subscription in my name, to be slid under my bedroom door every morning. And I'd have them wake me an hour earlier so I could read it. I'd get to know the world one step at a time, like a baby osprey taking its first flight. I'd start simple and eager as a fledgling.

Learning about the world through current affairs all fit so nicely with my newfound plans of becoming a journalist. It was the most productive study hall I had ever sat through, I decided, and there was still more time; so, I opened the journal and continued reading about the world Ava lived in.

Ava

An hour later I was still sitting there at the desk listening to Dahlia snore while writing about the world when suddenly I heard a knock at the front door of the house and a man's voice, and the sound of something being dragged down the hallway toward our room. It startled me, causing a big blob of ink to form on my paper. I stared at our door, trembling in hopes it wouldn't open.

I looked around the room for a weapon, and when I spotted a broom, I held it high over my head and stood behind the door. I'd use it if I had to. I swear I would. I'd slam an intruder over the head the way Dahlia used to smack those turkeys back home. I liked the turkeys, and I agree with Ben Franklin who favored the turkey as our national symbol, and I didn't at all respect Dahlia for the way she treated the turkeys, but I'd do it for the sake of protecting us women. I'd do that and more. I'd do anything a man would do.

I held my breath as the door opened and a tall, thin figure sauntered in dragging something large. I nearly fell facedown to the wooden floor with pride at the sight of him. It was Stewart. I quietly set the broom down on the floor and covered my mouth, trying to keep all my jubilance from noisily parading out of me. He had secured a Silver King and had returned to us, his beloved family.

Tootie quickly tiptoed in behind him and set a bright lantern on the desk, lighting up the entire room. "Here, Stewart," she whispered, handing him a second lantern. "So you can get yourself settled in." She left.

"Daddy?" I whispered from behind the door. "Is that really you?"

His face was red as a lobster from the sun, and when he looked into my eyes I couldn't help but notice him tearing up. My daddy never cried before, and I didn't know what to make of his teardrops. They weren't clear like teardrops ought to be. I could only assume they were darkened from dirt, and I wondered whether they had left his ducts dirty like that or had picked up dirt on their trek down his dusty sunburned cheeks. As I got closer, I noticed his tears smelled like gin, but how could that be? God, my daddy would make a fortune if he produced gin droplets from his eyes.

"You did it," I said, choking back my own tears, for seeing Stewart, tenacious as a hemp plant, holding a silver fish of that magnitude over his head as if it were the ark of the Lord's covenant, made me believe that anything at all was possible. "What a merry thing!" I declared.

"I've never killed anything like this before, blossom," he finally said to me.

"It's a fish," muttered Dahlia, her head lifting from the pillow slightly.

"You've never killed a fish before?"

"Not one I loved," said Stewart, lowering it into a cradle position in his arms. "I've got more respect for it than I've ever had for any person."

"Looks like you love it more than your own family, your wife," stated Dahlia.

Lydia

I heard footsteps entering the study hall, and when I looked up to see the principal coming my way, I quickly slid my history textbook over Ava's journal and pretended to read about the Spanish Civil War. Mr. Smith stopped walking and placed a note from the office on my desk. It read:

Your father called. Just wanted to confirm you arrived safely
to school. Thought you might like to know.

Surely Lloyd must have found out that I refused to ride the limo this morning, that I was tardy for school, and that I lied to the secretary about our plane arriving this morning and the limo breaking down. But his note gave no indication of any concern. A part of me longed for a father who might stomp right over to school and address such issues with me, and I felt tears welling up in my eyes. I thought of Stewart loving that fish more than his family, and I only hoped my father didn't love his work more than me. But I thought he did.

I needed solace as I pulled the journal out from under the textbook and went on reading:

Ava

I watched Stewart, scraggly-looking, wobble across the room toward the end of Dahlia and Abigail's bed where they had the sheet pulled up to their eyes to escape the smell. "You weren't bit by anything, Daddy, a raccoon, dog?" I asked, watching him set the fish down on the bed, near their toes. "Because you're moving like you're rabid."

"Drunk, Ava. He's drunk," corrected Dahlia.

"In God's name, Stewart Witherton, get that stinking fish off our bed!"

Abigail opened her eyes and looked at him as if she wanted to grab him by his delicate antennae and drop him in a pot of boiling water, and I knew she too had smelled gin in his tears.

"But look at the size of it. One hundred and fifty pounds," he said, wiping the sweat from his face. "I've decided to preserve it, give it eternal life mounted on this board. You like it?"

"Yes," I said, thrilled to see him holding in his hands a fish that was more than a fish. To me it represented accomplishment. Stewart achieved what we all had feared he couldn't. He did it, and now he stood before us gleaming with pride. I grabbed a cloth and dabbed it at my father's hands that were covered with scabs.

"Ava, shut that door and get into bed," jabbed my mother. "Now that your father is back, we're homesteading in the morning, and we all need our sleep."

I climbed into bed, and Dahlia slipped out of her bed to join me in mine. Stewart then got into bed with Mama.

I lay in bed thinking of all the good that has happened. If Stewart could catch that fish, then maybe there were other things possible. Maybe things I could do with my life that I thought were impossible. I thought about the island. I had never known such beauty existed, but now I wondered whether there might be other forms of unknown beauty out there in the world. And maybe there was an oasis of hidden beauty deep within my own self, waiting to get discovered.

"Grandmalia," I whispered.

"Go to sleep," she said.

"I will, but there's something I want to tell you."

"Doesn't your tongue ever tire? What is it?"

"I want to be a writer one day, a famous writer."

"You got that desire from your granddaddy Milton. Did I ever tell you he wanted to be a poet?"

"Yep, you did. Was he any good?"

"Worst I've ever read," she said softly, then rolled over and turned her back to me and I knew she was about to talk about Milton leaving her. "Why did he, the love of my life, have to turn into a deranged, wandering writer?" she asked. "I'll tell you why," she answered. "I loved Milton more than he loved me. That's where I went wrong in life. Always marry a man that loves you more, you hear? Otherwise, they'll go off and leave you for something they love more."

"Don't worry about me. I'm never getting married," I said.

"You sound like your mother. She said that once. She also said she wanted to be a ballerina. Look at her now. She married your father, and that was the end of that. Eventually, your views will change. You'll realize a woman's place in the world."

I didn't like what she was saying to me. I tried telling myself that my desires and ambitions are gusty strong and that they're not going to be blown over by negative words.

"You just wait and see, Grandmalia. I'm going to write novels. I'll write novels that will make you proud."

"Then do it now, young lady, at your age, before the trivialities of domestic chores and insanity set in. I don't know if I ever told you this, but your granddaddy Milton may have been crazy. He'd have his lows and then his highs, and I'd give him hot salt baths to calm him down. Your mother is certainly reminding me of him. I just hope you don't have it in you. It's too early to tell."

As Dahlia began to hum, I began counting on all ten fingers how many years I had left before my own sanity, now blooming profusely, might whither away, and then I began counting how many years I had left before I'd have to get married, and I don't know which I feared more, the insanity or the domestic triviality. I did calculate that the triviality would set in first, then the insanity. And I wondered if the triviality is what causes the insanity. No, chores didn't make my mama sad. The dark winter months back north did. And I don't think sadness is the same as insanity, despite Grandmalia lumping it all together.

When her humming stopped and I could no longer see her beady eyes glowing red in the dark room, I knew she had fallen asleep. I wanted more than anything to fight back, to slay the dragon that tried mutilating my dreams. And she wasn't the only dragon. She was just one. The world was filled with cowardly dragons, people who chase after and tear down the dreams of others rather than chasing after and accomplishing their own.

"I beg to differ," I proclaimed softly to her snores. "I can do with my life whatever I want. And what is it that I want? For starters, a late-night walk on the beach and no one is going to stop me."

I stood up and tiptoed over to the door of our room.

Lydia

"You can do it," I muttered, wishing Ava could hear me. Instead, the boy next to me raised an eyebrow at me. "I wasn't referring to you," I snarled at him. "I was referring to all the girls in the world. They can do anything they want with their lives, even become presidents of companies or of America."

The bell rang, saving me from further conversation with the boy, and as the students burst forth from the study hall desks and out into the halls, I stood there a moment. "I believe in you, Ava, just as Marlena believes in me."

I felt bad that her grandmother didn't think she could ever achieve her dreams, and if only she could hear me cheering her on, she'd know there was one person out there, a dream buddy, who knows her intimate ambitions and supports them. Ava and I would be friends. We'd be walking toward our dreams together were we living at the same time. But still, I'd consider her my dream buddy. Dreams never die. Nor does the written word, and I could almost hear her voice. If she could become a fiction writer, then I could become a journalist, I thought to myself as I walked down the hall, quietly passed the teachers' conference room, and stopped near the main entrance of the school. I glanced out the windows, craving the outdoors, but I continued onward to my dreaded home economics. And like a robot so familiar with the programmed route, I didn't need to look where I was going, so I opened Ava's journal and read as I walked.

Ava

I knew I should be sleeping but I couldn't. I felt too inspired, so I walked down the hall, quietly passing a room of men sitting in the smoke of Cuban cigars. I stole my own whiff, then opened the front door and stepped outside. I walked to the beach, thinking the entire way about how badly I wanted to become a fiction writer.

And when I kicked off my slippers and set foot in the sand, I was aware that my mother and father would lock me up had they known their young lady was walking on the beach alone and at night. But by the time my toes touched the warm water, it also became clear to me what I didn't want for my life—a husband. Boys—all but the one who had prayed in the periwinkles for my daddy—were ugly, rude and dirty. Stewart was a good daddy, but the way my mama glared at him whenever he walked into the room taught me one thing: A man doesn't make a woman happy. Quite the contraire! I wanted happiness. I wanted a world where girls grow up to be happy ladies. And besides, having a husband would mean having babies and I didn't want to risk dying during childbirth like so many women had been doing.

When I looked up at the stars, I missed my friends back in Kentucky. I could only hope they too might reach these revelations. There was no way for me to share my new worldly views with them. Before moving to Florida, we shared books and lunches, and the basic, primitive belief that boys were nasty and that we'd rather swallow a raw shrimp than kiss the lips of any boy. We never took it any further than that. By no means had we ever said we'd never marry. And we never shared our ambitions. I had no idea what my friends back home dreamed of doing one day or whether they'd given it any thought.

But as I stood alone, ankle-high in the water with the moon beaming down, it was time for me to act on behalf of them and all the girls of the world, and I had to imagine that herds of them would be standing here with me, if they could.

Lydia

"Here," I answered without looking up from the journal when the civics teacher called my name on the attendance roster. "I am most definitely present with you, Ava," I muttered under my breath.

Only physically was my body sinking lower into the wooden desk at school, for my mind was standing beside Ava, ankle-high in the water way past dark with the moon beaming down on me. And I couldn't stop reading, not now.

Ava

I stood there with my toes sinking into the sand. I was just one girl in a large world, but I stood there for us all, for all the girls who believe what I do. Yes, I stood there as president of the unladylike club, and I could almost hear others from around the world and throughout the past and future ages cheering me on. I bent down and scooped up seashells in my hand. I didn't know what they looked like, for it was too dark.

"I will not behave according to rules set forth by men," I murmured as I dropped one shell. "I will never do what a lady is supposed to do but what I want to do," I whispered as I threw another out to sea. "I will pursue my own dreams," I said louder as I tossed one further than the last. I felt bold and courageous as I threw the entire handful of shells in my hand and then waited to hear them make their splashes. "I declare I will never marry a man!" I shouted at the top of my lungs with arms raised and head hung back and eyes wide open toward the moon. None of what I did was for the rudimentary purpose of childish rebellion, nor dramatic art, however one might interpret it, but for the advancement of womankind.

Lydia

I sat with the journal wedged between the pages of my home economics book. My mouth hung open. I had never in all my life heard such things coming from the lips of a girl. I didn't know such girls existed in the world, at least not where I lived.

"And Mary Beth," I heard Mrs. Fields say, glancing three seats behind me.

"What do you envision for yourself?"

"To be a happy homemaker, Mrs. Fields," Mary Beth answered in her perky voice. "Although I'm horrible at ironing business shirts. My mother wants me to learn, but I've burnt three of my father's necklines."

"It's okay to admit that," Mrs. Fields said with a warm smile. "We're going to spend an entire week on laundry. And there's still plenty of time to master it before you get married."

"How about you, Judy? What are your aspirations?"

Judy sat two seats behind me, and that meant Mrs. Fields was working her way up my row. I could feel my breathing becoming shallow, as if

I were standing on a humidity-ridden beach. When I closed my eyes, my thoughts soared across the sea and I never knew how large the sea was, and then I saw stars scattered throughout my mind like options I never knew I had and they were infinite. But when I opened my eyes, I was still in class, and the reality of the world in which I lived.

"Maintaining a perfect home and keeping my husband happy," Judy two rows back answered in her soft, dainty voice. "But after that, I may want to become a nurse," she added.

"Don't forget the children, Judy," said Mrs. Fields. "It takes a lot of time to create the ideal home life. We're up to Suzie."

"Marriage," she answered from the desk behind me.

I closed my eyes again and joined Ava on the beach. I, like her, may be just one girl in the world, but one plus one equals two girls and two girls can make a difference. I wanted more than anything to join her un-ladylike club, to be one of its official members. So, quickly, I opened my eyes and the journal at the same time and found the part where she bent down to pick up seashells.

There were no seashells on my wooden flip-top desk, but there were erasers. I had an entire collection of pencil erasers, and I scooped them up into my hands.

"Marriage," said Mrs. Fields "is the highest achievement. We're up to you, Lydia Isleworth. Lydia?"

"I will not behave according to rules set forth by men," I read softly, dropping one eraser to the floor. "I will never do what a lady is supposed to do, but rather, what I want to do," I murmured as I threw another out into the aisle. "I will set and pursue my own dreams," I said louder as I tossed one toward the front of the room. I felt bold and courageous as I threw the entire handful of erasers in my hand and then waited to hear them smack against the chalkboard. "I declare I will never marry a man!" I shouted at the top of my lungs with my arms raised overhead and my head hung back and my eyes wide open toward the moon, or maybe it was the fluorescent light above me.

VIII

"LYDIA!" I HEARD MRS. Fields yell. "In God's name! In the name of patriotism."

It was then that I realized what I had done. Girls were flapping about their seats like fish jumping up from the water and their eyes were bulging with fear. I heard one with her head out the door yelling, "Help us, someone help us. Lydia's going insane."

"Girl! Get a hold of yourself!" Mrs. Fields took hold of my shoulders, and as she glanced around at the panic-stricken girls, I had just enough time to break free from her grip and tuck the journal into the waist of my skirt.

"Order! Order!" Mr. Smith demanded as he tapped my desk with a ruler. That's when the pandemonium settled and the girls returned to their seats.

"What were you thinking?" he asked me.

I hadn't meant to shout out the words of Ava, but they came rattling out of my mouth like venom I couldn't contain. When I didn't answer, Mr. Smith took hold of the sleeve of my blouse and pulled me out of my desk and toward the door. I could hear girls snickering and Mrs. Fields saying to them, "Girls who express masculine characteristics and behaviors as Lydia just did will not achieve any form of satisfaction in their adult lives, most especially personal fulfillment as wives and mothers."

Still in the grip of the principal, I managed to cast Mrs. Fields a look before leaving the door. And as our eyes were hooked, I blurted out in a voice that wasn't at all mine, and one that sounded the way I imagined Ava's to sound, "I beg to differ, Mrs. Fields."

I sat in the principal's office all afternoon as Mrs. Cross, his secretary, repeatedly rang for Lloyd at work. She still had the blue iris sitting on her desk, I noticed.

"It's an important day at the bank," I said to her. "I don't think my father will have time for this."

"Oh, I think he'll find time once we inform him of what happened today in civics class," she said, putting down the receiver and looking at me. "Do you really mean what you said? Because anyone who does not embrace marriage and parenthood risks being perceived as perverted, immoral, unpatriotic, and pathological."

Then, she shifted in her seat, her voice softening. "I've known you since you first started school here, Lydia. You're not any of those, are you? Do you know what all those words mean?"

"Just because a girl has her own plans for life doesn't mean she's a deviant," I said. "And besides, why would any girl want to get married? Why would she want to enter into a contract where she must serve and obey a man? If you ask me, it's a form of master and servant."

Mrs. Cross didn't answer. She stood up and walked out of the room and left me alone. A few minutes later I heard Mr. Smith and my father talking in the hallway outside the door. Mr. Smith had one of those voices that carry. It had always amused me that successfully whispering hadn't been a prerequisite for him getting a job as principal. I heard every word he spoke to my father in the hall and I'm sure the nearby classrooms did as well.

"I'm mostly concerned about deviance," Mr. Smith announced. "The disturbed, hostile, and rebellious child is a danger to herself and to the community and a poor risk as a future citizen."

"Now, wait just a minute," said Lloyd. "I do believe that the great task of parents is to see that their child's individuality develops naturally without harm to himself or society. I am aware that Lydia is going through a phase in which she wants to express her individuality and she's testing authority and boundaries in an effort to feel secure. I will discipline her accordingly. But I know my daughter. And she is not disturbed, hostile, or rebellious.

She's a respectful, charming young lady."

"I had always thought that, too, but there's apparently another side to her. She wasn't so charming when she used a Southern accent and told Mrs. Fields that she 'begs to differ.' "

"A Southern accent?"

"That's right, sir."

"I don't get it," said Lloyd. "I'm horribly confused. I'm distraught, I'm beside myself."

"I don't want to overstep my boundary, but I'm wondering about your home life."

"Our home life? That girl has everything she needs and more."

"But she doesn't have a mother," said Mr. Smith.

"No, but she has nannies and helpers and . . ."

"Do they do everything for her? Do they let her do anything domestic?

Does she wash dishes or help with laundry?"

"There's no need. I pay for it to be done."

"That's my point. A girl, from the time she is little, finds it exciting and challenging to be like her mother," Mr. Smith said. "In caring for her dolls, she takes that attitude and tone of voice of her mother. She absorbs her mother's point of view toward men and boys. Observing a mother is a major way for a daughter to accept the distinction between a man's role and a girl's."

There was a pause. "Maybe I should have remarried. I should have found a mother for Lydia years ago," said Lloyd. "But I became so entrenched at work. I don't have time to . . ."

"Have her help with dishes. You've got too many nannies, maybe. They're doing everything domestic for her, and in that, you risk the possibility of raising a social misfit."

"She's never washed a dish in her life."

"That's concerning. She must learn to appreciate the distinctions between men and women and to think and act as members of her own sex are expected to think and act in marriage. There are books and articles I can give you. They'll help put it into perspective."

I could hardly listen any more, and when tears of shame began pouring down my cheeks, I opened the door and ran into my father's arms. "I'm so sorry," I cried. "I didn't mean to make you leave work and come here like this. I'm sorry."

"Lydia," said Lloyd. "I love you and I'm going to correct your unhappiness."

"You're going to work less and stay home with me more?"

He looked up at Mr. Smith, who shook his head sadly and walked away.

"You're my number one most important asset, Lydia. I'm taking the rest of the day off, and you and I are going home. And we're going to spend all evening together."

"Can we stop for ice cream?"

"No," he said. "Maybe," he added, analyzing my unhappy face. "Okay."

The ride to the soda parlor was taking so long in traffic that I felt as if I were aging by an entire year. That's how limousine rides made me feel, like the world was passing by through those windows and I was passively watching it go.

I unrolled my window. At least I could then feel the breeze outside. But there were so many cars honking that it sounded like wild animals outside my window.

The ride wouldn't have been so bad if Lloyd and I spent the time talking, but instead, he chose to read. It looked at first as if he had opened the newspaper, but I caught a glimpse of what he was really reading, an article Mr. Smith must have given him called, "Raise Your Girl to be a Wife."

So I opened Ava's journal, eager for words of advice from the president of the unladylike club. I may have felt a year older, sitting in the limo listening to the car horns bemoaning the tempers of the drivers, but Ava truly was a year older.

I was stunned to discover it had been an entire year since our president's previous entry.

IX

SANIBEL ISLAND

1891

Ava

According to my mother, a girl is like an island in that she is constantly changing with time. And elements such as sunlight, wind and tides are constantly at work, altering her. When I asked her how a girl becomes a woman, she said it's a process consisting of waves, gentle ripples, crashing surf and shifting sands. It's the coming together of small things over time that creates a woman.

I KNEW THE SEASONS on Sanibel had fully revolved, and it was spring once more when I awoke to the sound of alligators bellowing in the swamp outside my window. I first heard their sound last spring when we first arrived, and it was a sound I'd never forget.

"Why are they making all that noise? What are those gators doing out there?" I pulled the pillow off my face and called out from my bed to Dahlia and Abigail, who were up before dawn doing laundry.

"Alligator noises are none of a young lady's business," my mother replied from the other room. "Ava, get out of bed. There's work to be done."

"They're mating, aren't they?" I asked, kicking the blanket down off my body and past my toes. "Why do they mate?"

Dahlia poked her head in my room. "It's how they make baby gators," she murmured.

"I knew that, Grandmalia, but how exactly do they do it?"

"I think you better get your mind off that and think about something else." "How can I think of anything else when all I hear are those gators mating out in the swamp? What else should I think about?"

"How about Little Ben?"

"Benjamin Harrison? The president? Why on earth would a girl want to think about anything or anyone political? I'm not interested in any of that. I do want to know more about mating."

"It's not for me to tell you."

"Why? Why won't anyone ever tell me anything I want to know? Oh come on, Grandmalia, tell me how babies get made."

I didn't know my daddy had been standing outside the door, listening, but he made his presence known by clearing his voice loudly, and when I saw his shadow on the wall outside my door it looked like the spooky branches of a swamp tree. He staggered into my room like a creature and said in an eerie tone, "You hear all those roaring bellows and splashing head slaps out there?"

"Yes," I said, reminding myself why I never ask my daddy any life questions in the first place.

"It's the fellows courting the females with nose-taps, nudges, and shoves. That's all there is to it, dear," he said with moody eyes.

"That's disgusting," I said.

"It sure is and it's exactly why I'm warning you to stay clear of boys. They're disgusting. That's all you need to know, coconut."

"Yes, sir," I replied, disappointed in our stagnant conversation.

"You think maybe you've got too much time on your hands, Ava?"

"Hardly any."

"Okay, because I could always add to your chores."

"More chores?" I asked. "Unless you want to create an eighth day of the week, Daddy, my seven days are already full with nothing but chores. Look at me," I said, wiping the tears from my face. "I'm fretful, frazzled, and fraught with tension as it is, and I'm starting school in the fall. If I take on more work, I'll die."

"No additional chores, then. But you better pull yourself together and get out of bed. I've got to get going myself."

"Where are you going this morning?" I asked him.

"To the bay to catch us something good. I'll be back soon."

"Bye."

"Bye, blossom."

I once again sat up in bed and touched my feet to the wooden floor but collapsed back down again. I didn't know what was wrong with me, other than I dreaded Mondays. I couldn't tell my mother how I loathed doing laundry on Mondays, because a lady ought to joyfully fulfill her womanly role as keeper of the house and I didn't want to be chastised, but it saddened me to think we spent at least forty-four hours a week making meals and cleaning up after them and another seven hours each week cleaning and doing laundry. It's great for those who enjoy that sort of thing, but I didn't enjoy it. I was different, and it was burdening to me to be so different, but I couldn't help it.

"Don't let that sun rise before you, dear," Abigail said as she walked into my room with a vase of flowers. She had been walking with a bounce ever since we arrived on the island and more so once Stewart had started bringing flowers home to her on a daily basis.

No sooner had she set the vase on my bureau then Dahlia came following after with a broom. "When Abigail was a little girl, around your age, Ava, fifteen, sixteen, she'd pick me flowers," Dahlia said slamming the broom down on escaping bugs. "But I told her the flowers had to stay out on the porch." She tossed the broom aside and started stomping the bugs with her feet instead. I frowned.

"Don't make that face or it'll freeze like that. You look like a dented coconut," she said as she stopped her bug smashing and sat down at the end of my bed and began rubbing my toes. "You should be up by now.

What's going on this morning?"

"I'm not sure," I said, pulling my knees to my chest. "My body aches. I feel no cheerfulness left in me. I hope it's not tuberculosis."

"Lord," my mother said as she pulled the sheets from around us and off the bed. "Could it be, Mother?"

"No," Dahlia insisted. "She's been working too hard. For over a year now that child has been beset by long days of labor. She's exhausted, mentally and physically. No wonder her bones are aching."

"She just turned fifteen," added Abigail. "She's still growing into a young lady. They're growing pains. That's what she's feeling. Haven't you noticed? She's growing like a sea oat, and those legs of hers are tall and long like a wood stork."

"Should you send for a doctor?" I asked.

"No. You don't need any doctor," said Dahlia, turning to look at my mother. "I'll tell you what she needs. She needs time off to be a girl before she turns into a lady."

"Should we have her stay in bed today?"

Dahlia stood up and walked over to the window and looked out. "If that's what she wants to do. I think she should do whatever she wants today."

"I think I agree with you for once, Mother," said Abigail. "I don't know why I didn't think of it myself. I'll bet any day now she'll become a young woman, and that alone deserves a break, doesn't it?"

X

I GOT DRESSED IN my black puffed sleeve wool bathing costume and walked out the door of the small, palmetto-thatched house we erected with the help of our neighbors just one year ago. I felt like I was walking away from Monday itself. To me, president of the unladylike club, all the never-ending housework over the last year had become absolute drudgery.

I passed our garden, where the tomatoes would grow, and walked past clumps of palmetto trees and then through rows of citrus trees. Our crops had proven successful, and we had been sending them to the mainland aboard steamships. It was the first time I had ever walked away from it all long enough to feel any pride.

Beginning the morning after Stewart returned to us with the tarpon he had caught, we marched around the island of wild, untouched beauty six days in search of our land, and when we found it I had wanted to shout and blow trumpets, but there had never been any time for that. We laid claim to a 160-acre tract not far from the Gulf of Mexico and started work immediately.

When Dahlia told me to do whatever I wanted today, the only thing I could think of was walking out to the beach to hop over waves, as slight as they were on this side of the state. There, maybe, I could get a different look at the sunrise. I no longer liked sunrises and dreaded them representing the start of chores. But this morning, I wanted the sunrise to mean something other than time to start laundry on Mondays, ironing and mending on Tuesdays, baking on Wednesdays, and deep household cleaning on Fridays. And now I wanted to remember why I ever thought the sunrise was beautiful in the first place, which I did, a long time ago.

While rounding Sanibel's eastern end, I noticed plovers, least terns, and black skimmers nesting directly in the sand, which they do in the spring, and an ibis was flaunting its iridescent pink bill and legs. I stopped walking and listened carefully, for I thought I heard the Spirit of God hovering over me, subtle as the first signs of spring in Florida. I'm sure the Spirit of God was with me year-round, not only in the spring, but I've been too busy to stop and listen for it.

I felt blessed with a sense of worth and dignity as I glanced up at the horizon. The sun had already woken and was making its way up, faithfully and dutifully, as always, never skipping out a day here or there, and I wondered how that sun did it. Even on rainy days, there it went, hiding behind clouds but still getting up to make the world more beautiful.

If I could spend my days writing, I'd rise up faithfully each morning as well. I envied the sun for doing its one significant task, for lighting up the world and making it more beautiful. I wanted to write of a beautiful world.

I sat down a moment in the sand and yanked off my lace-up bathing slippers, then my long black stockings and, finally, the fancy cap I had over my hair. I felt free and naughty, for the sun was now touching parts of me that I knew it shouldn't be touching. As I glanced out at the bay, which looked like a bucket of blue-green paint, I spotted my daddy sailing about. I hoped he was too far out to see that my ankles and feet were naked and exposed. I stood up and continued to walk, watching the bay for his boat, but then I looked down, which was a good thing, or I'd have stumbled over some boy as if he were a piece of driftwood.

"What are you doing?" I asked the boy. He was down on his knees in the sand, kneeling over a half-dead pelican.

He glanced up. "Fidgeting with the bird," he answered. "It's injured. A fishing line."

"Need my help?"

"No," he said, struggling to hold it down.

"Sure looks like you do."

"Maybe I'd want your help if you weren't a girl," he said.

"That type."

"What?" he asked. "What type?"

I wasn't going to waste time telling him he's the typical boy who doesn't think a girl is of help except with household chores." Look, my daddy's out in the bay. I can signal for him to come help, but by then your bird might die a slow torturous death. Or, I can help right here and now. What's it going to be?"

"Get down and restrain him. Hold his wings against his body."

I tossed my wired sun hat on the ground. I hadn't ever helped a bird before, or any boy, especially one I did not know, a stranger boy, but it's not to say I have never done the work of a man. If I weren't wearing a clumsy dress and bloomers trimmed with ribbons and bows, he'd see the wonderfully un-ladylike muscles on my arms, shoulders, and back that prove I've done more physical labor than most boys, maybe more than this one, although he had an impressively solid build himself, I might add objectively.

I yanked a cloth out from under his shoe and then wrapped it around the bird's body. The boy without flinching pushed the hook's barb through the skin. He then cut off the barb and slowly backed out the hook.

"He didn't swallow it. Thank God," he said, standing up with the bird in his arms. And then his eyes met mine for the first time and I knew him. He recognized me too for neither of us blinked until the bird started fussing.

"I've seen you before," I said. "But I can't place it."

"My name is Jaden. I know exactly where I've seen you," he said, rubbing the head of the pelican in his arms. "It's going to be okay, fuzzy head," he told the bird. "I'll take you home with me and feed you pureed fish."

"Where?" I asked. "Where do you know me from?"

Jaden smirked and casually started walking.

"Tell me!" I demanded, following suit. "Where do you know me from?"

He kept walking, grinning. "You like periwinkles as much as your mama?"

I tried not to blush. It was him, from a year ago, the boy who had prayed for my father as my mother rolled around lustfully in the dirt. I should have known it was him, not by his square jaw or his sandy blonde hair (sandy as in Midwestern sand, and not at all white as Sanibel sand), but by his eyes, for they were a clear green, almost as if I could see into them and know where I was stepping. His body looked stronger, thicker, and not at all puny like it had been a year ago. He was taller than me by about a foot and more handsome than any of the other boys in the world.

"You look different than you did a year ago," I said.

"So do you."

"How?" I asked.

His eyes were exploring me up and down, as if searching for a treasure, and I wondered whether this was the reason my daddy had warned me to stay away from boys. No girl should allow any boy to reach into her chest and grab her jewels, not without a fight. And there should be laws that protect women from this sort of thing and from the way boys are allowed to look at them.

"How have I changed since the last time you saw me?" I asked again.

"I might get myself in trouble answering a question like that," he said, looking at me now as if he wanted to hunt me for my plumage. "What about those flowers? You like them as much as your mother?"

"I hate flowers," I said, offended that he'd bring my mother and the periwinkles up and rub it in my face after I just helped him with the bird. "I hate them all—roses, hibiscus, dandelions—and I especially hate periwinkles."

"But you're a girl." He stopped walking and looked cockily at me. "Girls like flowers."

"They do," I replied. "But I'm not an ordinary girl."

It wasn't that I disliked flowers. I didn't mind them. But I was my own person and didn't want to be lumped into one big category of what I was supposed to like just because I was a girl. I also wanted to forget about my mama's behavior that day we first arrived.

"If flowers aren't your thing, what is? What do you like?" he asked.

I looked up at the sky over the bay. The rising sun had lent some pink to it, the same color as the cover of my journal, which my mama had given to me shortly before we left Kentucky. She gave it to me on a day where she had been feeling well and told me that if ever a time returns when she's not feeling good and where I didn't have anyone to talk to, I could write my thoughts in the journal. She hand-made it for me herself using the fabric from an old dress of mine to make its beautiful cover. "You still like the color pink, I hope," she had said when she presented it to me.

"It's my favorite color, Mama," I had said to her.

"Oh good," she answered, taking me in her arms. "You're still my little girl. You'll always be my little girl."

I did like pink, but I would like any color journal and anything she made for me. The first time I wrote in it, I felt like I was stepping into a world of vast lands, both unexplored and undeveloped, and along with it came responsibility to fill it up with beauty, and to leave only meaningful footprints behind, for starting my new journal was like being a pioneer arriving in a place of natural, primitive potential where I could cultivate whatever I wanted and I could hardly wait to plow through its pages.

"I like to write," I said, holding my neck tall and proud like a great blue heron.

"What do you write?"

I looked up at the sky. It was such a beautiful pink that even a boy would have to admit pink was beautiful. "Stuff," I said. "I write about stuff."

"Good stuff?"

I didn't know what was good and what was bad. I'd have to read what I wrote to determine that and it had been nearly a year since I last wrote. I stopped writing after our first night at Tootie's boarding house. After that, Abigail was feeling fine. She was there for me to chat with as we waited for weeks for our lumber to arrive on a sloop from Punta Gorda. Then we built our house and worked our land and my journal is still under my bed as it was last spring, unless Dahlia found it and swept it up on a deep-cleaning Thursday.

"I write good stuff," I told Jaden. "Novel material. Unpublished, but one day it will be good enough for all the women of the world to read. Sorry, but no men will ever be allowed to lay their eyes on anything I've written. It's a rule and should be a law!"

"So it's girl stuff," he said, making a face.

I was offended. "No," I corrected. "Good stuff, not girl stuff. In fact, I take back what I said about all the women of the world liking it. In truth, I don't think everyone will. I know my own mama won't. But I'm sure there'll be at least one girl out there, somewhere, one day, who will hopefully read what I've written and maybe like parts of it."

"You sound different, smart."

"Thank you. I am, but I haven't been to school in a year. I can't wait to start up at the schoolhouse in the fall."

"I'll see you there."

Just then the pelican started fidgeting in his arms. I bent down to pick up the cloth that had fallen and wrapped it once more around the bird the best I could. "Did I tell you my name was Ava?"

"I'll be seeing you, Ava." He turned and walked away.

"Wait," I called after him. "That day I met you, I didn't know you were moving here. I thought your boat went aground and you were just here for the day."

"Yeah, but we liked what we saw and homesteaded 160 acres overlooking the Gulf." He looked as if he was about to turn and walk away once more, but then he said, "Are you as good as a boy at keeping secrets?"

"I sure am. Why do you ask?"

He stepped up close. "There's an old shack on our property. Us boys call it 'Fighting Conch,' " he said in a low voice. "We've never invited a girl there before, but since you're a writer and you're smart, I was thinking, why don't you come by one of these nights. We're usually there around one o'clock in the morning. Don't bring anyone."

"How dare you! Why would a lady like me show up at some fighting shack alone in the middle of the night? I should report you to my daddy."

"First of all, we don't fight there. We have fun. And secondly, you don't present like a lady, and thirdly, you're a writer. I'm sure you're always in search of good writing material," he said, his eyes now a deeper green like the depths of the bay. "But you don't have to accept the invitation."

"I could never," I said. "My daddy is as protective as a sea oat."

"He doesn't have to know about it. I told you, it's a secret. You've got to wait for a full moon, then follow the beach west until you spot a piece of driftwood big as a bench, then head up and there you'll find us and the shack. We're only there on full moons so don't try coming on any crescent moon or quarter moon nights."

I shook my head in disbelief and gave him the look I reserve for pagans.

"Forget it. I'll see you at the schoolhouse in the fall."

"See you then, Ava."

He walked the beach where the bay lets into the Gulf and I walked a pine-laden trail inward. "Dear Lord," I muttered, wanting to say a prayer for him. Despite him being a typical boy trying to get a girl in trouble, he had prayed for my daddy that day, and I always liked to return prayers for people. "Please bring that boy's pelican back to flyable health." And then I looked back at the sun peeking through the branches and whispered, "Thank you," to God for letting the sun mean something different today and for making me care less that it was Monday.

But as I headed back to our home, I knew that come Tuesday, the sun would mean ironing and mending, and Wednesday, Thursday and Friday more of the same, and if I wanted to become a true lady, I would have to rise to the occasion and find joy in it all.

But I didn't want to be a lady, a joyless one anyway. And I didn't want to spend my youth growing old doing never-ending chores that, except for gardening, kept me inside all the time.

So instead of heading back home, I rerouted myself to Tooties and when no one answered her door, I walked in and helped myself to a book in her library. *Flower Fables*, by Louisa May Alcott—her first book and probably the only one I had never read before, but always wanted to. I did like flowers. I had lied about hating them.

I found myself a shady place to sit under a tall tree and opened the book and began to read out loud, but softly.

The summer moon shone brightly down upon the sleeping earth, while far away from mortal eyes danced the Fairy folk.

I read until the sun reached me through the branches of the tree, disrupting my canopy of shade, and then I closed the book and walked home. All the while, I wondered about joy. While in a good mood, Grandmalia once said that joy is an abundant and limitless natural resource within every woman, and whenever it feels scarce, all she must do is tap into it. Grandmalia always said neat things when in a good mood.

But after today, I questioned whether that was truth or just one woman's perspective, for if anyone asked my opinion, I'd have to say joy is found outdoors only. It's out there wading along with the birds as they show off their breeding colors and the ibis flaunting its iridescent pink bill and legs and the red-eyed vireos and all the other migrating birds that were singing with joy. I wished I was one of them, but I was happy to discover how generous they were, sharing some of their joy with me.

And so I had a little jar of it stored up inside me as I walked into the front door of the house, and because I didn't want to spill it out into the hot soapy laundry water, I tiptoed quietly into my room, not wanting anyone to hear me, especially anyone that was doing chores and might need my help.

There in my room, I pulled out my journal and began to write all about my day outside. I poured my joy into my writing as a way of preserving it forever. I was glad the birds had shared some with me, and I longed to go back out and search for more, gathering it up so that I had more pleasant things to write about. And I wondered where I might find more. Could there actually be joy in a boy? Maybe one night I'd have to find out.

XI

LYDIA

CHOCOLATE BRINGS JOY, I felt like telling Ava as I walked into the soda fountain with my father. A boy, no matter how clear and green his eyes might be, does not! I thought she, president of the unladylike club, knew better, but I was wrong.

And it made me furious to think I had followed in spirit someone as wishy-washy as her to the beach earlier today, declaring I would never marry a man nor get involved with any boy. And now, after making a fool out of myself, she made it sound like she was changing her views. But I wouldn't know for sure until I read some more.

And so I was left wondering whether she deserted the greater cause, but also, where in fact does one find joy? It was something I hadn't ever thought about before. If I asked Lloyd, next to me, where we might find joy, he'd most certainly say money, for he didn't at all look to be getting any pleasure from his soda, and his bank reports were open on the counter beside him. As I sipped through my straw, slurping like a boy when I reached the bottom of my ice-cream soda, I knew joy could only come from chocolate. I could think of nowhere else to find any.

I hated drinking my soda so fast. I hated watching my father slowly sip his while I sat there with an empty glass. And I hated reading about Ava and that boy, especially now that none of the boys at school would be interested in me. I was mad. It was she in the first place who inspired me to act like a wild, raging deviant of nature, and now I didn't ever want to return to school, where everyone would be talking about me as if I were some rabid creature. I could never go back there with my head held high again.

I suddenly questioned everything about Ava, even whether she felt under the weather at all that morning in bed, or did she feign it as a way of getting out of Monday chores? Hmmm, she really stumped everyone with her lie about feeling poor, and it got me to thinking, if that lie got her out of chores, than maybe it might get me out of school, which I used to like, but now, after my outburst, I didn't feel like returning to on Tuesday.

"Get me home, Father," I moaned, holding my hand over my mouth. "I'm sick."

Lloyd set his bank documents down and looked at me. "What is it? Too much chocolate?"

"Of course not," I said. "Chocolate doesn't make a person sick." And then, being a horrible actor, I slinked off my stool and dropped onto the floor. To make up for that poor acting, I then pulled my knees up to my chest and started rocking. "I'm sick," I moaned again. "It has nothing to do with chocolate."

"Should I call for an ambulance?" he asked, scooping me into his arms and examining me with alarming eyes. "What's going on, baby? Are you okay?"

"No ambulance," I said. "Just take me home." And then I recalled the words Ava spoke that morning in bed as she dreaded her day of chores. "I'm fretful, my body aches and I feel fraught with tension," I said. "I hope it's not . . . It must be . . ."

"What?" he asked desperately. "It must be what?"

"Polio," I answered. "It must be Polio."

My father carried me to my bed and then gave orders to all the housekeepers and nannies and chefs that were on duty. Within minutes, I had cold cloths on my forehead, tea by my side, someone massaging my toes, and a burst of cool air coming through an opened window in my room.

I enjoyed all the fuss, but what I really wanted was to be alone, so I could read more of Ava's journal. I quickly closed my eyes and pretended to snore, louder than I ever snored before and when everyone left the room, I pulled her journal out from my school bag and began to read:

SANIBEL ISLAND
A couple of nights later

Ava

There is nothing wrong with being out after dark, I told myself as I briskly walked in the direction of the shack that Jaden had told me about. Birds migrate by night, and moths fly, and besides there was nothing dark about tonight.

Thanks to the moon, the ground in front of me was well-lit, and I wondered if this were the reason God created and placed the moon up there in the first place, so girls like me could effortlessly sneak out in the midst of night, or maybe so their fathers might catch them. I didn't want my daddy catching me, and I prayed that God put the moon up there for the first reason and not the second.

As I stood outside the dilapidated shack on Jaden's property at around one o'clock in the morning, I could hear boisterous shouting and laughing from inside, and I wondered whether my parents might be right. Maybe there were places that a lady ought not go.

The mosquitoes and sand flies were attacking my neck and hands, and I was smacking them with a vengeance. "You're here as a writer, Ava, not as a lady," I uttered under my breath as I crawled over to the window and peeked up just enough to catch a glimpse inside.

There was a group of boys standing in a large circle, shouting like fools, and I remembered a girl's number one right—to change her mind. I turned and crept away from the window, wanting to return safely to my own bed, but then, I felt something slithering around my ankle and it could only be a snake. I hated them more than boys.

As it twisted tightly up my leg, I charged through the door of the shack screaming my head off. I raced in circles like a lunatic until a couple of boys tackled me to the ground. There I stayed as two held my arms.

"Red and yellow could kill a fellow," said a laid-back voice that sounded like Jaden's. "Red and black, venom lack."

"What's he saying?" I cried to the boy holding my arm.

"That if the snake's stripes were in the order of red, yellow, then black, it could kill you."

I looked up, first at the snake. I saw red, black, yellow, but I was trembling and couldn't tell the order. I then looked at the boy that was carefully untwisting it from my leg. It was Jaden.

"Help me, Lord!" I moaned, tossing my head back onto the hard floor.

"Relax," he said in a voice that could tame a rabid raccoon. "This snake is red, black, then yellow. You're fine, but it's a good thing I'm a gentleman and got it before it slithered any higher than your knee."

I would have normally hit a boy for a comment like that, but he had saved my life; so, instead, I let my eyes follow him as he carried the reptile outside. The boys holding onto my arms lifted me up off the floor. "Jaden didn't think you'd ever show up," said one.

"I did, and now I'm curious about what you boys do with your spare time. I've had it up to here with household chores. They give me no time whatsoever to pursue what I really want to do and that's to write." My ankles were wobbly, and my legs were shaking but I didn't want them to know.

"Here," a boy said, handing me a large gold goblet. "Everyone that shows up at the shack must drink from this cup."

"What is it?" I asked, taking it.

"The sacred Casine, or 'Black Drink.' It was drunk three hundred years ago by the French explorer, Rene de Laudonnier, and one hundred years later by the shipwrecked sailor, Jonathan Dickinson," he said. "Swig, then hand it off. It sets all of our bets in stone; so, whoever doesn't carry out their bet, is cursed."

"What bets?"

"Jaden will explain that. Take your sip so we can pass it on."

I touched my lips to the drink. "Gin!" I declared. "It's only gin."

"You have any friends you could bring along next time?" another boy asked me.

"No," I said blankly. "I don't. I'm too busy for friends. I told you all I have time for are chores."

I stared at them, wondering whether I should tell them how different I am from most girls, that I'm stronger, and more brave, except when it comes to snakes, and that I know the world better than any men, having led my family here all the way from Kentucky.

"Hey, doll face," Jaden said as he walked up beside me and touched my cheek softly. "I had a talk with that snake out there. I told him it's not nice crawling up a girl's leg like that, but I thanked him for not biting you."

I blushed, for I was stuck on "doll face." I had never been called "doll face" before. I didn't know whether I liked it. I had never seen an ugly doll, so I guess he meant it as a compliment, but I wasn't used to such verbal niceness from a boy. Usually I just got their silent stares and gawks.

"If you hadn't pulled it off my leg," I said to Jaden, "I would have run myself right into a swamp. Snakes are my only weakness. I'm sorry you all had to see me like that tonight."

"No need to thank me," Jaden said. "I did what any boy would do and that's going after a snake that is going up a lady's leg."

"You make me want to slap you," I said. And then I felt my opinion of him softening. "But you're my hero for the night, one night only, so I'll thank you, instead."

The boys were forming a circle again, and Jaden took my hand and pulled me over to the corner to a bucket filled with crabs. "Pick one," he said. "Hurry up. They're waiting on us."

"Crabs," I said, slowly reaching down into the bucket. "Crabs pinch, don't they?"

"Sometimes," he said. "But I could pry it off your lips like I did that snake off your leg," he added with a cocky smile. "Or you can just point to one, and I'll pick it up for you."

"That one."

"Good choice. What do you want to name it? According to our rules, it's got to be a name from Florida's history."

I hadn't been to school in over a year, so my mind was rough, but a name came to me, and when I saw that the boys were impatiently eyeing us from the circle, I announced, "Queen Isabella."

Jaden picked up a brush, dipped it in ink, and wrote, "Queen Isabella" on its hard shell. He then placed it under the bowl in the center of the circle. He waved me over, so I went and joined him on the circle.

"I stand here as a reminder that we boys will repeat the heroic acts of men who came before us while vowing never to repeat the atrocities of the ill-hearted," a boy in the center announced, then took a sip from the gold goblet. "Everyone that drank the drink, know that your bets are etched in stone and you will face the consequences if you don't carry them out."

"How much money did you bring?" Jaden asked.

"None. Why?"

"You've got to place a bet. Everyone who races must place a bet."

"I've never bet before."

He took hold of my hand and pulled me close and said, "It's okay. I'll set the bet for you."

Just then the boy who gave the speech said, "So in the name of exploration and adventure they're off!" He bent down and pulled the bowl off the ground and out came the crabs, climbing over each other and racing outwards toward the circle line.

Jaden got down on his hands and knees and pulled me down beside him. "If my crab, Juan Ortiz, is the champion," he said into my ear. "I kiss you . . . on the lips."

My mouth dropped, and I wanted to slap him, but he must have read my mind.

"If yours wins," he continued, "you punch me as hard as you like and wherever on my body that you like."

"Look at them hauling shell!" A boy next to me also dropped to the ground hollering at his crab. "Go Juan Ponce de Leon! It's not like this is your first voyage!"

"Is your crab any good?" I asked Jaden.

"Juan Ortiz? My God—champion six rounds in a row, a real motivated racing crab that I've been training personally now for six weeks."

"You didn't just pick him from the bucket like I did mine?"

"Juan Ortiz," shouted Jaden. "Come on, hero! This is why I've been working you so hard. This is it!"

As I stood there cheering my crab on, I could think of nothing worse than kissing a boy and nothing better than punching one. I hadn't ever kissed any before, and my hands and feet felt tingly at the thought of it, as if I had just been attacked by some jellyfish. At least Jaden wasn't ugly. And I had to believe he was a gentleman, not in the way his eyes grabbed and pulled me close, nor in the way his mouth spoke of kissing me, but in the way he was doctor to that injured pelican and personal trainer to a crustacean and a hero that saved me from the snake.

He was special; so, maybe it might not be so bad if I had to kiss him before night's end. Then again I'd also probably enjoy giving him a good punch. Either way, I'd turn out a winner, I decided. But I preferred a punch.

The crabs were nearing the outer circle. "Go, Queen Isabella!" I shouted louder than I had ever shouted anything before, and I'm sure my shout made it all the way to Spain and spanned the centuries after that.

XII

LYDIA

I DIDN'T WANT TO stop reading, but when I heard my father talking to the doctor in the hallway, I knew I had just seconds left to skim ahead and find out whether she kissed or punched that boy. But as I turned the page, I found nothing but blankness through to the end of the journal. It wasn't fair that Ava would so abruptly end her writing, and if I didn't feel sick before, I did now.

I wanted to read more, to find out what happened that night at the shack and with the rest of her life. I wanted her to tell me what to do next, but that was all she wrote. I was disappointed as I slid the journal under my pillow. It wasn't like I could walk to the local library and check out the sequel.

When the doctor approached my bed, I knew there was only one thing to do. I had to look as sick as possible, for tomorrow was Tuesday, and that meant 4H after school; and then would come Wednesday, glee club; and Thursday, honor society meeting; and Friday, piano lessons; and then back to Monday again. I couldn't stand to think of how the boys and girls had gossiped about me after my outburst, and I didn't ever want to show my face at school again.

"I've got a headache, I'm fatigued, and I've got pain in my extremities,"

I said to both my father and the doctor.

"Lydia," Doctor Conroy said. "Those are textbook symptoms for polio. But I don't think that it's polio. Let me check your pulse and listen to your heart."

"Hmmm, I'm perplexed," he said to my father moments later. "Everything looks fine. Why don't we let her rest, and you and I can talk more," he continued, signaling for my father to follow him out the door.

I hopped out of bed and listened as they walked down the hall and into Lloyd's study. When they closed the door, I quickly tiptoed outside the door and stopped. It was my health they were talking about, so I had a right to hear.

"I'm concerned about her," Lloyd said. "I told you on the phone what her school said to me, that unhappy girls are a potential threat to national security. They're as bad as sissy boys, according to the principal. I'm just trying to figure out why she's so unhappy. I've given her everything."

"How was your trip to Florida?"

"We had to leave early and that upset her. That may be why she's acting out."

"You think she's doing all of this as a means of getting your attention?"

"I don't know, but she's got it. I took the entire afternoon off work for her."

"One afternoon isn't enough," said the doctor, clearing his voice. "Lloyd, I've known you for years. I was at your wedding. I saw how you loved her, but has it occurred to you that maybe you did get remarried— that you're married to your work? I don't want to be too direct. My God, it's impressive how far you've gone at that bank, but you're also raising a daughter by yourself."

"Not by myself," he replied. "I've got so many nannies I don't know them all by name. I thought that was a good thing, but the school is telling me different. They're suggesting that Lydia is too pampered, that she has to start doing domestic stuff on her own. They're afraid she might not understand her female role in life."

"They may have a point," said Dr. Conroy. "What if you were to take Lydia away from the pampered life for awhile, take time off, a leave of absence so the two of you can get away from it all?"

"Maybe, but it'll have to wait. This is probably the most detrimental time in my career. With my partner in the hospital, I've got to stick around. A man can't up and leave when there's about to be a changing of the guards. I'll consider taking time off once things settle."

"If you don't," said Dr. Conroy, "it's going to be you in the hospital next."

"I won't let that happen. I'll give myself a break before I reach that point. I'll take another vacation, a longer one."

When I could hear them no more, I climbed back into my bed and let the underground river of tears break through. I didn't know how I'd ever survive returning to school tomorrow. There were only a couple of weeks left, and I'd be done with tenth grade, but next year would come eleventh, and the year after that, twelfth. Everyone would be talking about me as if I were a headline in today's news:

GIRL TURNS REBEL IN A SINGLE DAY

I felt as if my life had once again reached its end, even more so than the day I was forced into piracy, leaving the island with Marlena's historical treasure. But then I remembered what Ava had said and my tears stopped abruptly. I reached deep down into my innermost being, past the surface debris, and into the dark private depths, and there I pulled out a branch of an idea.

The newspaper.

DESPITE ODDS GIRL PURSUES DREAM OF BECOMING A JOURNALIST

I was starting young. I still had a couple of weeks, plus two years left of high school. And I would do whatever was necessary. I would subscribe today and become entrenched in current affairs. And the issues at school and in my own little world involving me would become miniscule in comparison to those I was reading about in the real world.

AVA WITHERTON, FORMER PRESIDENT OF THE
UNLADYLIKE CLUB, RESIGNS AFTER KISSING A BOY.
NEW AMBITIOUS PRESIDENT STEPS UP TO FILL HER SHOES.

It was a personal story, and it affected me deeply. There were so many details left unsaid. I could only assume that Ava allegedly kissed the boy, later
married him, and then went on to Monday being laundry day. I didn't want
to smear her name any further, for I liked Ava, and I had dirty laundry of
my own. I was still a thief—a troubled one. Parts of the treasure I had sto-
len were missing. I examined its pages once more and discovered jagged-
ness near its spine, as if pages had been torn out. Foul play, maybe.

But *Who*? *What*? *When*? *Where*? And *why*?

XIII

SANIBEL ISLAND
1955
THREE YEARS LATER

Lydia

LIKE GUSTS OF WIND, those five questions blew through my mind for the next two years. And they had been the driving force that pushed me to the *Windy City Press* that very summer, where I landed a job as errand girl. When school started again in the fall, I switched to after-school hours, and I remained working there until graduation.

At first, Lloyd didn't like my working at all. He tried getting me to quit, but I gave him a silent treatment so strong it felt as if an Iron Curtain had descended between us, and he eased up a bit. I reassured him I was doing mostly secretarial-like things, as well as making coffee. But really, I was twig-by-twig building my nest, where one day I would sit comfortably as a successful journalist, and just as an osprey never hides its nest, I would no longer have to hide my success.

I mastered the percolator with only a few burns on my arms, and coffee fast became my specialty. I allowed no journalist's coffee to reach below the half-full point. And I learned who liked it black, with cream, with cream and sugar, or just sugar. I never had to interrupt their interviews or discussions to ask who wanted more. I could see who did.

It was in these moments of pouring that I learned I had a natural sense of determining the newsworthiness of things. "McDonalds," I heard one journalist say to another as I was pouring his coffee one afternoon. "They want me to look into it as a possible story."

"And why would some hamburger stand in California be newsworthy to Chicagoans?" asked the journalist next to him.

"Ordinary people are lining up for fifteen-cent burgers, five-cent coffee, and twenty-cent milkshakes, and they're being served within fifteen seconds."

"And that deserves a headline?"

"Not to me, it doesn't. It's a fluff story."

"I disagree," I said, unable to keep my mouth shut any longer. "We're talking more than burgers, here. These guys are doing what Henry Ford had done for cars. To me, that's news."

Then that journalist took a sip of his coffee—for he was on a fifteen-second sipping pattern—and he looked at me and said, "Lydia, the biggest challenge to my job is deciphering what's newsworthy and what's not."

"Mass production of hamburgers sounds like news to me," I said.

"You may have a good point," he said. "Thanks for the coffee."

I poured so many cups of coffee over the course of two years that the paper got thicker and deadlines were hardly missed and journalists were talking and thinking faster than ever. I also started drinking it, and ideas flooded my mind. I even wondered whether I should desert my pursuit of journalism and open a drive-through coffee shop instead. If people were lining up to buy hamburgers, then maybe they'd line up for coffee. But it was only a coffee high that gave me that thought, and when it died down, I knew I had a better shot at becoming a journalist then opening a place where people actually drive by a window to buy coffee.

Besides, I liked working at the paper. All kinds of exciting and newsworthy things were happening in the world: the school desegregation ruling, *Brown v. Board of Education*; cigarettes cause cancer; the first nuclear-powered submarine launches in Connecticut; the first mass vaccination of children against polio begins in Pittsburgh; the first successful kidney transplant; a Memphis, Tennessee, radio station is the first to air an Elvis Presley record; Boeing unveils its jet aircraft, the "707"; and the Red Scare has families building bomb shelters.

The more I became absorbed with what was happening out there, in the world outside my front doors, the more I wanted to go out and cover that world myself. And I still believed wholeheartedly that anything was possible. Marlena's words had landed on me like seeds on fertile soil, but it was up to me to nurture them from dreams into accomplishments.

I also looked up to other women who were paving the way and I enjoyed reading articles by Virginia Marmaduke. She was one of the first women to cover hard news in the "windy city," and to break away from the fashion, entertainment and society pages.

And I knew of a female working as a journalist over at the *Chicago Defender*, the African-American newspaper. Payne, her name was. She began her career while working as a hostess at an Army Special Services club in Japan. She let a visiting reporter from the *Chicago Defender* read her journal, and in it were detailed accounts of her own experiences and those of African-American soldiers. The reporter then took the journal back to Chicago, and soon her observations were being used by that paper. I thought, "If she could do that, then I can do what I plan to do."

But then my father suffered a minor heart attack several months before my high school graduation, and I had to quit my job at the paper. I told myself it was only temporary, until he got well again. He didn't need any stress coming from me. He had enough from the bank. While he was in the hospital recovering, they worked a plan out with him. As he had explained it to me, he was now like a consultant, a financial consultant. He could do his work from anywhere, and Doctor Conroy strongly suggested he take time off.

After several months of seeing Lloyd do nothing but lie around watching *The Millionaire*, *The Ed Sullivan Show*, *The Jack Benny Show*, and his favorite, the *The $64,000 Question*, I reminded him of his promise from two years ago, to take a break and spend time with me.

"Sit down," Lloyd insisted as the ferry pulled away from the dock at Punta Rassa. I had been pacing back and forth, like a prisoner ready to be set free, and I was nervous about returning the treasure to Marlena. But I had kept it all this time safely buried deep within my pajama drawer, and I only hoped she would see that I had taken very good care of it. I sat down beside my father and pulled out the day's newspaper. It was already late morning, and back home I usually had the entire thing skimmed by sunrise.

"Lydia," he said. "You're seventeen. You shouldn't be reading all those nerve-wracking stories. They're not good for you."

"Pop, the Reds don't scare me," I said. "I like staying in orbit."

"In what?"

"Informed," I said. "I have to stay informed with current events if I am to become a journalist."

He rolled his eyes. "Whatever, darling," he said as he bent down and reached into the bag he had been toting around since the airport. "I did buy you a gift. I think it might come in handy now that it's just going to be you and me for a few months. Why don't you put that paper down and peek inside?"

I set the paper on the floor of the boat and set my foot over it so it wouldn't blow away in the spring breeze. I couldn't stand the thought of missing a day of news. I took the bag from my father and reached inside and pulled out a heavy book... *A Betty Crocker Cookbook*, I said. "Thank you, Father." I could feel the smile on my face turning into a frown.

I didn't want to disappoint him, not now. Although the cardiologist assured us there had been no damage to his heart and all looked fine, I didn't want to add any additional pressure. I hid my disappointment so it wouldn't burden him any. It pained me that he wasn't proud of anything I had been working for over at the newspaper. To him, the criterion of success for a daughter was still whether or not she got and kept a man of good reputation and background. There were many occasions in which he would bring home a young executive from the bank for dinner and I knew he was trying to fix me up. But once I started talking about my job at the paper, the two would raise their eyebrows and often their glasses and quickly lose interest in what I had to say.

"So, what are you going to cook me for dinner tonight, dear?" Lloyd asked as the ferry headed across the bay.

I quickly flipped through the pages of the cookbook without really looking at the recipes and said, "You know I've never cooked before. Do you think it was a mistake not bringing along a chef or housekeeper?" I closed the book and dropped it in the bag.

"I regret not giving you a more female orientation toward life earlier on," he said. "But it's time you learn now."

I bit my lip, for he had rattled my cage. It suddenly dawned on me that maybe his taking me on a getaway was more than just that. It was a ploy to domesticate a girl that didn't want to be domesticated. I didn't want to cook elaborate meals. I didn't like eating them. I could get by on coffee—a good strong cup of percolated coffee—and a bagel. My stomach felt queasy. My father giving me the cookbook made me feel like a victim of a smear campaign, the kind I read about in the papers all the time. And I wanted a confession from him, but I knew he would only profess his innocence.

When the ferry dropped us off, we checked into the cottage we had rented on Sanibel's east end. Lloyd and I differed on what we were to do first. He thought I should go grocery shopping and he would go fishing, alone, and then return for a home-cooked dinner. I wanted to go for a walk on the beach, alone, so I could secretly find Marlena's cottage and after enduring endless days and nights with a guilty conscious, return the journal to her.

"If you could just wait a couple of hours," I told my father. "I'll be back and I'll go fishing with you." I didn't want him going alone. I was nervous about his health and didn't want him doing much of anything without me.

"Fishing is for men, dear. Maybe I can catch something good and bring it home for you to cook," he said, flipping to the index of my new *Betty Crocker Cookbook*. He was looking up fish recipes for me.

"That's it," I said. "I'm going fishing with you. I'll go to the beach when we get back."

XIV

"DUNGAREES?" LLOYD ASKED WHEN he saw me.

"What's wrong with dungarees?" I asked as I tied a scarf around my head, babushka style. "We're going fishing."

His eyes looked at me as if I were a project at work that went bad. "You'd rather I slip into a party dress and white gloves?" I laughed and shook my head.

"Party dress, no," he said. "But a blouse and jumper might have been more appropriate."

"There's so many injustices in the world, Daddy."

"What do you mean?"

"Girdles and petticoats namely," I said as we strolled along a pathway through dense trees. "There's a reason why men are considered more athletic and physical than women. It's because, historically, women's bodies have been squelched inside corsets and girdles, and if you ask me, it was a victory for women when the corsets were tossed, but it's time we toss the girdles as well and the skirts and catch up physically with you men."

"Lydia," he said. "Promise me you'll never share your views on that with anyone but me, you hear?"

I rolled my eyes, and when I noticed Lloyd breathing heavily, I stopped talking of things that upset him and slowed our walking pace as well. Doctor Conroy said that walking was a good activity at this point in his recovery, but walking and talking about my views toward life probably wasn't.

"Do you hear that music?" I asked as we reached a sandy road. "Where's that coming from?"

We stopped and listened. I liked it, and so I walked further until I saw a boy around my age sitting under a tree playing an instrument. He was wearing a Hawaiian shirt, and like the fronds of a palm, his hair stuck out in all directions and hung down shading his eyes.

We stood there still and silent like two audience members at the symphony, front-row seats. I squeezed my father's hand to let him know how amazing I found the music. When the boy blew into his instrument, his cheeks puffed out as if he might float off into the air and pop, but when he cast his eyes toward me, the music stopped, and he stared as if he hadn't ever seen a girl before. I stared right back at him, into his eyes, brown like a puppy dog's. I typically never rested my eyes on a boy for more than a two-second count, and unless he were a journalist and I had something important to say, I usually had no desire for talking with boys. But this one played his music so passionately that I stared for about three and a half seconds before looking away and probably another four seconds or longer after that. Still, he was all boy, dirt on his face and all, I noticed.

"Excuse me," Lloyd said, interrupting the way the boy and I were looking at one another. "We're looking for the Sanibel Fishing Pier."

"You're just about there," he answered, reeling his eyes off me. "I'm about to head over there myself. Just give me a second, and I'll go with you."

He put the tip of his finger over his lips like he might blow me a kiss but instead closed those lips and blew hard. I watched for his cheeks to blow out like they had before, but they didn't this time. He put the instrument back up to his mouth and did it all again, this time on the mouthpiece. When he finished, he tucked his instrument into a carrying case and looked up at us again. "I'll bet you're looking for Max Crowe."

"We are," said Lloyd.

"Max is my dad. He's out there waiting for you." We started walking, and the boy looked at me and asked, "You're going to watch the big boys fish?"

I was offended. "What do you mean by that? Do I look like I'm on my way to a soda fountain?"

"She says she wants to fish," Lloyd said on my behalf.

The boy smiled. "We sure could use something pretty to attract the fish our way."

He epitomized the definition of a huckster, and I wanted to slap him. I wanted to tell him "D.D.T.", which means drop dead twice. I wasn't used to any boy telling me I was pretty. I know the men my father took home for dinners were attracted to me. I could tell by the way they said "hello" and shook my hand and watched me before dinner was served. But then, once I opened my mouth, they did everything but cover their ears with their hands, trying to make me believe that a girl that talks of ambition is noisy and boisterous and belongs in a rookery full of nesting birds.

"A girl who fishes is a fine thing," the boy added, interrupting my per-colating thoughts.

"I appreciate that," I said.

Just then a tan-skinned man carrying fishing poles and a bucket greet-ed us on the pier.

"Hi, I'm Max. You must be Lloyd."

"Pleased to meet you. And this is my daughter Lydia."

"Pleasure, Lydia. Looks like you've already met my son, Josh. We send him off a couple hundred yards to practice his music. We don't let him play here on the pier. He'd scare the fish away and probably attract the kind we don't want," said Max. "Son, give me a hand with the bait now."

Josh walked over to the white bucket, and I followed. "So, what are we using for bait?" I asked.

He tilted the white bucket for me to look inside. It wasn't what I ex-pected, and I tried not to have a cow, but when one of the translucent, monstrous creatures spilled out onto my sandal, I jumped and screamed, "Lord God Almighty!" It was the second prayer I had ever said, one sto-len from Ava, and I didn't know where to go from there, but I think I felt a bit of peace and was able to regain my composure for having uttered those three words.

"So tell me," I said, switching to my journalistic tone. "What exactly are those things?"

"Shrimp," Josh matter-of-factly said as if he hung out with them on a daily basis. "Shrimp are the most universal bait. What did you think they were?"

"I have no idea—Cooties, maybe," I said, and we both laughed. But all of a sudden, I felt my stomach curdle, so I sauntered to the edge of the dock, where I bent over and gagged, then dry heaved a moment before standing straight again to look if Josh had seen.

"You going to be okay?" he asked.

"Fine," I insisted as if it never happened. "I'm just used to seeing shrimp wrapped in fried coconut and coated in lime sauce, not at all naked like those shrimp."

We walked over to our fathers, and I was handed a pole. I looked around at all the men that were fishing and I felt good about what I was wearing. I'd look like a fool hooking bait in a jumper and blouse and vomiting over the pier. I intended to do whatever it was that men who go fishing do, and if I was going to catch the biggest and best fish, then I had to be wearing dungarees to do so.

I could hardly wait to begin. I had so many questions. "*Why* do you use shrimp?" I asked Max.

"Most fish are line-shy so from the dock we use the smallest hook, lightest sinker and thinnest line possible," he explained. "Shrimp are easy to keep alive. They're cheap and all, but sharks will bite on shrimp."

"*What* types of fish might we catch in this water?"

"You sound like a journalist," Josh noticed.

I could hardly speak I was so flattered. It was the best thing anyone had ever said to me, and I could feel a smile appearing on my face. "That's exactly what I plan to be," I said. "I've been working at the *Windy City Press* now for two years every day after school. I've applied to college, and I'm waiting to hear if I get accepted. If so, I'll start in the fall."

"Good for you," he said.

Lloyd cleared his voice as one does before speaking into a microphone.

"I've been trying to tell Lydia," he said, "that nurses are in demand. She's got steady hands. Look at her with that fishing pole. I think she'd make a great nurse."

"But it sounds to me, sir, as if she wants to be a journalist," Josh replied.

I tried giving Josh the look that says, "don't go there," but instead my eye did its own thing and winked at him, and my mouth, with a mind of its own, gave him a smile.

"So tell me, boy," said Lloyd. "You look like you're about my daughter's age. What do you plan to do with your future?"

I felt tremors inside my gut, telling me something was about to erupt. My father had a reputation at the bank. When someone impressed him business-wise, he would carry that person straight to the top, but if they made an error or said anything he perceived as stupid, look out! He'd become like a volcano, his words hot as lava.

"I just graduated from high school, sir," he answered. "I'm spending the summer fishing with my dad. Then I'm thinking of chartering."

"I wish you the best of luck, son."

It was my chance to rescue Josh from the volcano. "So as I was asking before, Max, *what* types of fish might we catch in these waters?"

"Pompano, cobia, redfish, grouper, snapper, shark, sea trout, hogfish, amberjack, barracuda, whiting, flounder . . ."

I was beginning to relax and understand why it was that men fish, when all of a sudden I felt commotion at the end of my line. "I've got something," I announced with loud pride and confidence. I looked at the men on the pier to be sure they had heard me, and I said it again. "I think I've caught my fish for the day."

"Start reeling," instructed Max.

"*How?*" I asked, bobbing my wrist up and down as if playing with a yoyo.

"I've never reeled before." But then I felt Josh's strong hands over mine, and I knew he was standing behind me making sure I was reeling just fine. I may not have been reeling fine, but I was feeling fine.

"Lydia, why don't you hand the pole over now?" Lloyd suggested. "I think you've done enough."

"It's my fish," I said. "I'm reeling it in—with a bit of help."

Everyone's eyes were floating on the water in anticipation of what I may have caught, and I was ready to win all records set by man for having so easily secured the largest, most desired fish out there, perhaps a tarpon, but when my fish surfaced, I nearly peed my pants. The most hideous-looking sea monster, worse than the see-through shrimp, was dangling from my line.

"Lord, help us all," I screamed. "What on earth is that thing?"

"Puffer," said Max.

I tried loosening my grip so I might drop the entire pole into the water, so we might never have to deal with that monster again, but Josh tightened his hands over mine and steadily forced my hands to do what they didn't at all want to be doing. Together our hands lifted the creature up and over the rail so it landed smack onto the pier where all of us were standing.

"Get it away from me," I cried, jumping up and down and spinning in circles.

"It's just a harmless puffer."

The thing was yellow with brown stripes and coated with pointy, sharp spikes, and within seconds it inflated itself like a balloon.

"It's going to explode!" I shouted, jumping two giant steps backward and landing on Josh's feet. "Get out of its way!"

"Relax," Josh said touching my arm. "Relax."

"I can't. The thing is blowing itself up."

"Pull yourself together," he said. "You've got to for all our sake. We've been trying to tell you, it's just a harmless puffer."

"A what?"

"A blowfish," said Max as he unhooked it with a pair of pliers, and then tossed it back. We watched it deflate and swim away.

"So it wasn't anything that might win me a tournament?"

"No," said Josh. "But that performance might win you an Academy-Award nomination."

I looked around at the other men on the pier and noticed a couple of smirks. I tossed my hands up in the air. "Haven't you ever caught a blow-fish before?" I asked.

When they started laughing, Max jumped in. "She's from Chicago."

That's when the men nodded, waved, and continued their own business of fishing.

"Shall we call it a day?" I asked when I saw Max reaching in the bucket for more bait.

"We're just getting started," he said.

"I know, but my father needs to rest, and I've got things I need to do."

"What could possibly be more important than fishing?" Josh asked.

"I could think of a million things," I said.

"I'm sorry to hear that," he said. "Life's too short to have so much to do."

"That's easy for a male to say," I replied. "But it's a different world for us women. You men like to eat, right? Who do you think has to make your dinners? And guess who has to go shopping first and then do all the housework? I'm glad you have time to fish. I don't. My father is going to get hungry soon."

I said too much and didn't mean to take all my frustration with men out on him. He actually ranked better than any of the boys I had known from school and the ones my father tried setting me up with all the time. But now, I had opened my big mouth the way I've done too many times before, and I waited for him, turned off and terrified, to turn his back to me and pick up conversation with the men.

"Your father seems like a pretty intelligent individual," Josh said, nearly knocking me off the pier with surprise. "I'm sure he'd survive just fine if you weren't around to cook and clean for him."

I thought about it a moment, then said. "He is smart. But I've never seen him pour his own cup of coffee. I don't think he's capable."

"Women like you give men no credit, so you do everything for us. You think we're stupid when it comes to the basics."

"Not at all," I stated. "I believe men don't think women are capable of success outside of the home. You men want us in the kitchen baking cookies all day and then waiting on you hand and foot when you walk through that door."

He raised his eyebrow and laughed. "This could get ugly," he said, shaking his head. "First, I'm as man as man gets, but don't stereotype me. You don't know me. Second, yeah, I love home-baked cookies and a woman mixing up something good in the kitchen. But, third, if baking cookies ain't your thing, don't spend your life crabbing about baking. Do whatever turns you on in life. That's what a guy like me finds attractive in a woman."

I was speechless for the first time, and my mouth hung open as wide as an open-mouthed bass. I felt stupid for not knowing what to say as Josh shrugged his shoulders, smiled at me, then turned to go join our fathers who were off the pier by now.

"Josh," I called after him.

He stopped and turned.

"We're going to be here for the next few months. Would you like to go fishing again some time? I don't mean catch a blowfish again, but maybe something prettier."

He smiled. "Yeah, I think so, and it's not so bad catching a blowfish. We'll be in touch."

"*Where? How? When?*" I said, stopping myself with a mental kick in the behind.

"Let's not complicate things," he said, and then smiled. "I know I'm on the pier every morning around sunrise. That's all I need to worry about."

"Thanks," I said as if getting the only answer I needed. "Bye."

"Bye."

XV

WHEN WE GOT BACK to the cottage, my father was hungry, so I walked into the kitchen and leaned on the counter with my head in my hands. I took a deep breath to prepare myself and then I opened the cabinets, only to discover there were hardly any utensils.

"Great," I moaned. "I'll bet the pre-Columbian Indian housewife was better supplied than this. How am I supposed to make anything in this kitchen? There's not even any food to work with."

"You can go to the store and buy whatever it is you need," my father said.

I was glad he didn't expect me to make my own knives out of bone or shark teeth. But grocery shopping and preparing a meal sounded just as challenging in the mind of a girl who hardly ever had to make her own sandwich.

"Coffee," I said. "We need coffee, or at least I do. I don't think it's good for you right now."

"Buy yourself some. Buy whatever you need. This is all good practice for when you get married one day."

"One day maybe a zillion years from now," I said. "But Josh was a nice boy, don't you think?"

"Of course he was," said Lloyd. "Boys without any ambition are always nice."

It wasn't a fair and balanced statement, and it upset me at first, but then

I told myself to forget about Josh. I wasn't the sort of girl who needed any boy in my life, ever! There were more important things to think about.

"It's not fair that I've waited so long to return here only to grocery shop and cook," I said. "If I don't set foot on that beach within ten minutes, I will die," I told my father.

"Fine," he said. "I can take care of myself. But you are grocery shopping first thing tomorrow morning, you hear?"

"Yes, sir."

The map to Bougainvillea was imprinted in my mind. Over the last couple of years, I had imagined myself walking through that fine line of Australian pines a million times, and I had rehearsed everything I would say.

As I stopped short of the steps that led up to the yellow cottage on stilts, I could hardly wait to clear my slate and return to feeling the way I did before my act of piracy. I had lived every day with this secret weighing on my mind, and when a girl keeps a bad secret like this all to herself she builds four prison walls around herself, walls invisible to everyone but her.

Marlena's forgiveness would set me free at last, I thought. There is nothing I wanted more than forgiveness.

Knock. Knock. Knock. I took a deep breath. *Knock. Knock. Knock.* I let it all out.

I knocked harder. Freedom. I could taste it. I knocked faster. Freedom. I could smell it. I knocked louder. Freedom. I could see it.

And it was staring me in the face. Marlena stood in the doorway, as beautiful as I remembered, wearing a sexy pink Capri outfit and her dark hair now in a poodle cut. I said nothing as I reached into my straw bag and pulled out the journal, then handed it to her.

"I need your forgiveness," I said, my lips quivering. "I can explain."

The door opened wider, and I walked in with a spring breeze and joined the classical music playing softly. She walked quickly, and I kept up. Then, she stopped and took a sip of her coffee, allowing me to study her profile. I remembered her nose, still perfect as if a sculptor had shaped it from clay. She turned and stared down her porcelain nose at me with a look in her eyes that made me feel like a bitter-tasting bug she just spit out.

"Thief," I thought I heard her say. But her lips didn't move so it had to be my own conscience reminding me I was still behind bars.

"I need to explain what happened," I said, breaking the silence.

"One moment, dear. Let me have a look at the journal."

I stood awkwardly before her as she set her mug on the coffee table and slowly began perusing the pages of the journal as if inspecting its condition. My mind started recalling the impact those pages had on the last couple of years of my life.

Marlena glanced up at me. "And what have you learned from all of this?" she asked.

"That a girl is as hardy as any perennial flower," I answered, recalling what Ava's grandmother had said.

Marlena continued her inspection of the book, and I felt myself tearing up just thinking about the day I learned Ava's writing ended. I not only lost my unladylike president, but a friend and in an odd way, a mother and a grandmother that came along with her. I liked Abigail. I liked Dahlia. Of course they belonged to Ava, not me, but in reading about them, I felt as if I had a family of my own. I liked hearing what a mother and a grandmother had to say about things regardless of whether we shared the same blood.

"You're crying," Marlena said, when she closed the journal and set it on the coffee table. "Sit down, dear."

I did as I was told, wiping my tears with the sleeve of my blouse.

"Don't worry. I'm not going to charge you any late fee," she said, handing me a handkerchief. "Now what's with the tears?"

I sniffled and sobbed and sniffled more before gaining my composure. I felt like a fool, for I hadn't ever cried like this in front of my father, or anyone come to think of it. "I need your forgiveness," I replied.

"I forgive you. Now why are you really crying?"

"She changed my life," I said.

"Who? Who changed your life?"

"Ava," I said. "She inspired me to think things I never would have thought before. And I did things, crazy things, as a result of what I read. I joined her unladylike club and lost my own friends and any chance at dating any boys at school and then I felt so driven to pursue my dream of becoming a journalist that I rebelled against my father and got a job at the paper and now, just today, I met a boy I can't get off my mind and I'm not sure what to do. It makes me wonder what Ava would have done—what she did with Jaden. I know it's just a journal, but I feel like I know her, like she's a friend of mine, and she just left me hanging."

Marlena stood up and walked over to the window and stared out at the banyan tree. "My dear," she said. "Ava wanted more than anything in life to become a novelist. By enjoying and valuing her writing as you have done, you are helping to complete her dream. She'd be honored that a girl some seventy years later was appreciating her writing."

"Then, why did it end so abruptly? I couldn't believe it. I was dying to know if she ever met up with him again."

"She did," Marlena said, turning to look at me. "Why? Are you thinking of meeting up with your boy again?"

"I don't know. My father wouldn't want me to. He wants me marrying some young and rising bank executive and living properly ever after in the suburbs," I said. "How do you know she met up with Jaden again?"

"I've got the torn-out pages. Ava tore them out so her parents wouldn't ever find them. But after hearing the impact she has already had on your life, I'm not so sure it's wise of me to let you read further. Did you say the boy you met lives here on the island?"

"Yes, he does."

"And how long are you here for?"

"The summer."

She shook her head. "I don't think I should let you read them, dear."

"Please," I begged.

"Excuse me, but you're how old?"

"Seventeen. How old are you?" I asked.

She pushed her neck back like the pelicans do and it made her look as if I frightened her. "How old do I look?" she asked.

"I don't know."

"Do I look the same age as Debbie Reynolds did in 'Singing in the Rain'?"

"You look young but not that young," I said.

"I never got an audition for that. I thought it was my nose back then, but I know now it was my age. For the record, in case you're wondering, I'm a solid eighteen years older than Debbie. What about Katharine Hepburn? Do I look her age?"

"I saw the *African Queen*. My father doesn't know I went to see it, but I did. You look younger."

"I'm liking you more and more," she said. "Vivien Leigh?"

"Who?"

"Tell me you've seen *A Streetcar Named Desire*."

"I haven't."

"I'm her age, just a year older. Didn't get that audition either. Makes me question why I ever surgically altered my nose in the first place. I've got this perfect nose, and I'm still not getting any good roles. I'm forty so now I'm wondering if it's my age. And you know there's no surgical intervention for age. Oh well, I can't feel all that bad. I have done my share of acting."

"You're a movie star!" I exclaimed.

"Not quite a star. I'm transitioning over from a successful career as a theatrical actress. I've appeared in more stock and Broadway productions than I can count, but Hollywood is where I've always wanted to go. I've been trying to break in now for five years, but now I'm competing with all these younger women. I wished I'd started with screen earlier, that's all."

"You're more beautiful than any of them. You'll get in," I said.

"You're saying that because you want to read more of Ava's journal."

"No I'm not, but, yes, I do want to read more. Do you think I'll be able to?"

"There's a different set of rules this time around," she sighed. "The pages don't leave my house. You'll have to come here to read them and only a little at a time."

"Thank you!" I said, wanting to shake her hand, hug her, and tell her the real reason I was crying. I was so relieved she had forgiven me, and was now sharing the rest of the journal with me, but really, I was starving to know whether she still stood behind the words she spoke to me that day on the beach. I wanted to know if she still believed in me. But I'd take the forgiveness. That would have to be enough for today.

"When can I start reading?" I asked.

"Why not start now? Follow me."

The cottage was charmingly small, with wooden floors and windows that ran the entire length of the great room, and because the walls were painted lime green, it looked as if the sea grape leaves outside had come in. I followed her down a short hall and into a yellow room with a high, pointed ceiling and wooden fans hanging in parts where the ceiling was lower and flat. There were windows in that room too, and a banyan tree beyond one window made it look like we were standing in a tree house.

"Have a seat," she said pointing to a mahogany desk with elaborate pineapple carvings. "You'll find the torn-out pages in the drawer on the right."

I took a seat and pulled out a bundle of pages that were tied together with a thin rope. I glanced at the door and noticed Marlena had already left. After carefully untying the rope, I recognized Ava's handwriting immediately.

XVI

SANIBEL ISLAND

Ava

There are three treasures inside every woman: a heart, a mind, and a soul. Each is priceless and worth far more than gold, silver, or diamonds. However, keeping these treasures locked up and hidden from the world will do her no good and bring her no pleasure.

I GOT TO KNOW the new yellow-crowned night herons and the little blue herons and the baby ducks, before summer's end, and I also got to know Jaden. I wanted to be fair to my heart, to at least give it an opportunity to do what I had heard hearts do best—love.

I snuck over to the shack three more times before the hotly humid summer had ended. I only went on clear, bright nights using the moon to guide me, and I rubbed my face, neck, and hands with a mosquito salve. It was a secret recipe Jaden had created and when I no longer felt the bites, I believed I could survive anything with that boy. I could walk through a swamp by his side and still feel safe.

But I never gave him any indication that I needed a boy to feel safe, and I proved I was good and strong myself. That first night at Fighting Conch, my little Queen Isabella did surprisingly well, proving I was better than that roomful of boys at coaching crustaceans. Then I took twelve sips of the "Black Drink" and still walked a straight line across the broken piece of dock the boys had balancing on two chairs—another competition of theirs.

I saw the way the other boys watched me and I knew they had never seen a girl do things so well before. I felt pride in myself and walked in a confident way, one that says, "I'm president—president of the unladylike club."

One night, after the boys had deserted Fighting Conch, Jaden, his best pal Riley, and I stopped by the beach. After Riley threw a coconut into the Gulf, I laughed out loud and said, "I can throw further than that."

"You think you can do anything us boys can do, don't you?" Riley asked as he jogged to the water to look for his coconut.

I'd rather show my skills than tell all about them; so, I stretched my arm behind my head and threw my coconut with the same force as a shooting star. A second later there was a splash, a loud one, too loud to have come from the coconut and when the moon poked out from a passing cloud, we spotted Riley down in the water.

"God almighty!" I cried as Jaden handed me his coconut and ran to lift his friend's head out of the water. He pulled Riley's body up onto the sand. "Did it hit his head?" I asked.

"His nose. It's a nasty one."

As the cloud passed and the moon beamed fully down on us, I covered my mouth with my hands. I had never made a person bleed before. He lay in Jaden's arms, his eyes slowly opening, only to spin for a moment and then they scanned the beach from left to right before stopping on me like the eyes of a male panther on a kitten it's planning to eat.

"Forgive me, man," Jaden quickly said, interrupting the way Riley was looking at me. "I can't believe I did that."

"I thought she did it!"

"No way. Ava can't throw that hard."

"The Hell I can!" I snapped, but when Jaden jerked his head toward me I added, "But I didn't, not this time."

"That's funny, because I swear I saw her raise her arm just before . . ."

"She did, but so did I. She's still holding her coconut. Hold it up, Ava. Show Riley you've still got yours."

I held up the coconut Jaden had given me to hold after I had thrown mine toward the water and hit Riley with it.

"If my nose weren't bleeding so bad," Riley told Jaden as he stood up, "I'd throw you a hard punch. Instead, give me your shirt. I've got to stop the bleeding."

It was at that moment that I knew for sure Jaden loved me. A boy who lies to protect a girl almost always does it because he loves her. And as I watched him take the shirt off his back and hand it to his friend so that he could wipe the blood from his nose, I tried not to stare at his chest, which was strong as any conquistador. Instead, I tried focusing on how Jaden's kindness made me feel. His fibbing to his best friend made me feel as important as that wounded pelican, the snake around my leg, and his crab getting personally trained. No one has ever made me feel that way before.

When Riley's nose stopped bleeding, we parted from him, and Jaden and I walked back to my parents' property. It was then that I decided to surprise him with a second kiss. And this time, I'd kiss him like a hero ought to be kissed, not like the first kiss I had given him the night of the crab races. I was nervous that night and didn't know what to do but had since gone over it a zillion times in my mind, rehearsing what one might say. I wasn't nervous any more, and I felt embarrassed thinking back to that first night we kissed.

"You're shaking like a live starfish grabbed from the water," he had said sometime after his crab came in first and mine second.

"I am?"

"Yes. Are you afraid to kiss me?"

"No," I lied. "But do you hear all those frogs quonking?"

"Yeah. Male frogs. They're calling for mates."

"How romantic," I laughed. "But you're only kidding. How would you know what they're doing?"

"I've watched them before. It's true," he said, softly taking hold of my chin and looking into my eyes, conquering my heart the way no boy had ever done. "And you know what else is true?"

"What?"

"I'm going to marry you one day."

"How can you say that?"

"I've watched you tonight, and I just know certain things."

"You're just saying that so I'll hurry up and kiss you. I'm not so naïve."

"I do want a kiss, but I mean what I've said. Just wait and see. One day, you and I will be married. I promise."

And then he kissed me, at first like a boy who wants to marry, but then like a conquistador going for gold, and all the time I heard the chorus of croaking frogs growing louder all around us. His kiss changed me on the insides and the flattering idea of him wanting to be with me forever made me want to do everything better—throw harder, run faster, shout louder, talk more interestingly, look more beautiful, and kiss better the next time—just so I could further impress him. His kiss sent me on a mini crusade in search of how I might attain for myself more beauty, intelligence, personality, and wit.

His kiss made me overzealous in the weeks following, and it almost got me in trouble at home.

"Ava," Dahlia snapped at me one Monday morning. "You just swept that floor, scooped up the dirt, then dumped it back down again. What's wrong with you, girl?"

I stopped rehearsing my kiss with Jaden in my mind and began focusing instead on the look of bewilderment in Dahlia's eyes. And I didn't at all mean to dishonor her, but when I saw what I had done with the dirt, I started to laugh and couldn't stop. There was a lot of it, and normally I never minded a bit of dirt on the floor. Dirt made me feel like I was outdoors, and I loved the outdoors, but this was too much, I had to admit.

I had tears rolling down my cheeks because moments before I felt like I was standing in a room full of gold and silver, not dirt. That's how thinking of Jaden made me feel. I bent over, trying to stop myself from laughing any louder, but then my mama entered the room and that stopped me abruptly.

"Is there a boy, Ava?" she asked.

"Ick," I groaned. "You're talking to me, Mama. You know I've never tolerated boys."

"You're acting as if some boy is making your mind wander off."

My daddy had a way of showing up and shaking my jar of joy any time the word "boy" came up in our household. "Boys are dirty as the dirt on that floor, blossom. I've told you that," he said and then walked out the front door. It made me mad that my daddy spoke willfully and then left without further conversation. They knew full well I loved a good debate. In fact, I craved it but could never get it, at least not to my contentment.

As my mama watched me from the doorway, I tried one more time going after the same old dirt on the floor, and I know I did so in a way that reflected my views on dirt, that dirt would never truly be gone, for it was probably two-thousand-year-old dirt and the same dirt the Calusa Indians walked across. I could see from her face that my mama disagreed with my belief that dirt never goes away. It just finds a new place new to hide.

"Okay, there is a boy," I finally said when I knew she wasn't going to leave the doorway. "A nice boy. In fact, he's the one who prayed for Daddy that day in the periwinkles."

Abigail drew a blank look, and although she had said that day that a boy who prays is a good thing, I knew she no longer remembered her periwinkle ways so I decided to skip over that and get to our second encounter.

"He was helping a hurt bird that day you and Dahlia gave me the morning to myself."

"See, Mother, why I don't believe it's wise to set a young girl free for a day?" Abigail said, raising her I told-you-so brow at Dahlia.

"You can't stop natural progression," said Dahlia. "You can delay beach erosion, but sooner or later it's going to happen just as a girl is eventually going to fall for a boy."

Neither of them thought to ask me how many times I have snuck out of the house in the middle of the night to go see him; so, I decided not to offer that information. They weren't ready for me to fall in love. And I think it was because they still needed me. I was their only child, and they liked having me at home. And whenever Abigail started wilting, I was the only one she'd open up to slightly. She wouldn't survive without me, I don't think. And neither would Dahlia, nor my father, nor Jaden come to think of it. Jaden made me want to live forever, not that I didn't want to live forever before falling in love with him, but now my life here on Earth was appreciated by another person, and that felt good.

"A boy that is nice to animals," Abigail said, taking the broom from my hand, "is usually decent to women. But you should still stay away as your daddy warned. Now go start the laundry."

Lydia

I closed the journal and thought about the ingredients that, according to Abigail, make up a good man—one that prays, and is kind to animals—and I realized something was missing in this recipe, a very important spice: A man who supports a girl's ambitions. Josh was made up of all these things and he was like a cookie I had never tasted before. My father had me believing men rule the world and women clean it, but when Josh talked positively about my plans of becoming a journalist, I learned for the first time that there were men out there that truly do respect the individual minds and ambitions of a woman. And I wondered if maybe I was ready to let my heart try what hearts were meant to do.

"Done reading?" Marlena asked, poking her head in the room.

"No," I said, jumping in my seat. "There's more."

"The sun is about to set."

"It is? Then I've got to go," I said, neatly setting the pages I had read atop the stack. "Can I come back and read more?"

"Of course, you can," she said. "But my agent has set up a few more auditions for me. I'll be in California for about two weeks. Why don't you come back after that?"

"I'd love to," I said, disappointed to wait so long, but I had made her wait a couple of years. Besides, I was thrilled that Marlena might become famous and I could say I knew her when. "I hope you get a role opposite Marlon Brando. He's gorgeous, don't you think?"

She laughed and waved me out her door.

My father was resting on a hammock under a palm tree when I returned to the cottage, and he had confessed that he walked to the store for a bag of basics, which would get us through the night. I felt concerned that he would do such a thing and risk his recovery, and I felt bad for having not taken care of him like I should have.

We ate the snacks he bought and played cards out on the lanai until way past midnight, and I could hardly keep my eyes open. I thought my yawns were going to kill me, but I didn't want to say anything or let on as to how tired I was. I didn't want our game to end. Time together like this would never happen back home, not when he had to be at the office by five in the morning.

XVII

I SPENT THE ENTIRE next day doing what women do on a regular basis. I skimmed through the pages of the *Betty Crocker Cookbook*, selecting recipes I would make for the week. Then I created a list, four pages long, of all the ingredients I would need for those, seven times three, twenty-one recipes, plus seven desserts equals twenty-eight. Doing all of this was like exercising parts of my brain I never knew I had. I found it excruciating.

With my list in hand, I went to the island's general store and shopped for over three hours, going up and down every aisle about eight times each until I could find what I was looking for. It was helpful to learn that the fruits and veggies were stocked together in one section and the meats in another. I had no idea there was organization to a store. Next time, I decided, it would be simpler since I knew where everything was.

I hated to do it, but I called for a driver to pick me up and take me home. I then had him set all the bags outside. I wanted to carry them in myself, which I soon regretted, because it then took me another hour to do so and put it all away. I then collapsed on the sofa next to my father who had been reading a novel all day. He went ape when I handed him my grocery receipt. I had spent over one hundred dollars.

"What do you mean, watch my budget, father? I didn't know we had one."

"Yes, you should always look at the prices of things and try to pick the least expensive cheese, that is, without compromising quality. You didn't do that?"

"I was too busy finding things. If I sat there comparing prices, I'd still be there now. Grocery shopping is more time-consuming than I ever imagined."

"I hope you bought food that will go far," he said.

"I've got enough for twenty-one meals, plus seven deserts, so roughly, one week's worth of food," I said.

"Damn, I better find you a wealthy husband." He looked at his watch. "It's nearly time for dinner. What are you going to make? I'm starving."

I spent the rest of the evening doing things I never thought I'd do. I chopped and minced and peeled and cried. I boiled and soaked and drained and shriveled up a few times mentally. I stirred, blended, mixed, and tossed my hands in the air with frustration. I dropped, spilled, and cracked eggs onto the floor, and even slid myself, landing beside a pile of breadcrumbs. I grieved over the fourth egg yolk dead on the floor.

Dinner was ready by ten o'clock. But first, I had to set the table. If I had children, or a husband, I thought, I could make them do that for me. A man that sets the dinner table is—Abigail might disagree—another ingredient that goes into the making of a good man, I thought.

"Did you buy any Scotch?" I heard my father call from the other room. "I'm ready for a glass with ice."

"No, father. I'm only seventeen. I can't buy liquor."

"Damn," I heard him say. "I'll get it myself in the morning."

We ate. I don't remember a thing about the meal. And that's a shame. I went to all that work and don't remember the meal. I did offer Lloyd seconds, which he refused. And I was glad, for there was nothing I wanted more than to dive into bed. "Good night, Father," I said, pushing my chair away from the table. "I'm turning in."

"Lydia," he said with a frightened look in his eyes. "The dishes. The mess."

I was so fatigued I forgot we didn't pack our housekeepers and assistants in our suitcases. That meant there was only me to clear the table, wash the dishes, dry them too, put them away, and clean the stove and oven, cabinets and floor. By the time I finished all of that, my father was sleeping. I climbed into bed, but still my mind went on working, worrying about the kitchen corners I might have missed cleaning, places the ants might find. I tried falling asleep, but my mind had chased my body around in that kitchen all night, and now it didn't know how to turn itself off.

I had a new respect for my fellow women, for the wives and the mothers and the daughters who help their mothers and for anyone who had ever gone through the agony of preparing a single meal. I wanted to look up each person that has ever made me a dinner, whether in our home or in a restaurant, and thank them personally for their behind-the-scene efforts.

I also wanted to sleep, but Mr. Sandman never came. Maybe he figured there was already enough sand on Sanibel. I felt mentally lopsided, and so I remembered the words of Ava and allowed myself to think of Josh. It was as if thinking of him inflated my heart, and I felt as if I were riding the peaks of the waves.

I felt so ready to live and way too excited to sleep, and so I climbed out of bed and headed for the kitchen. There I pulled out the *Betty Crocker Cookbook* once more and flipped to the dessert section. I then took out sugar, brown sugar, flour, baking soda, butter, one egg instead of two—since I dropped so many on the floor while making tonight's meatloaf—and a bag of chocolate chips.

As I watched the sun rising through my kitchen window, I also watched the cookies rising through the oven window. And I wondered, as I sat on the tile floor, which would rise first. It turned out that the good old sun defeated my cookies in many ways. The sun was beautiful, my cookies ugly. The sun continued rising, my cookies fell. The sun was only getting warmer, my cookies cold, by the time I scraped them off the pan and dropped them into a bag.

"Oh well," I mumbled as I headed for my room to get ready. "At least my cookies are comforting as the sun. I'm sure Josh will appreciate them."

I quickly got dressed, not in my dungarees this time, but in a nice yellow dress with short white gloves. I then applied eyeliner to my top eyelid only and peeked into the room at my father. He was still sleeping and would be for hours. I would have just enough time to sneak over to the pier and find Josh and return home before he awoke. Ever since his heart attack, he had been sleeping way past ten o'clock. I never believed that was possible.

XVIII

JOSH, POLITE AS HE was, ate three, and the other men standing by us on the Sanibel Fishing Pier each took one, but a few minutes later I spotted large crumbs, chunks, and then whole cookies floating by in the water below the pier.

"Are they that bad?" I asked Josh.

"We'll know in a couple of days if a bunch of dead fish wash ashore."

I punched him on his shoulder and laughed as I spotted one fisherman whipping his cookie across the water as if trying to skip a stone. It didn't skip, but rather fell apart in mid-air. "Baking is not one of my strengths. It should be, I know. I am a woman, but I guess I find it rather . . ."

"Where are your shoes?" Josh asked looking down at my naked toes. "What if you step on a hook out here?"

"It's a risk I'll take," I said, smiling. "There's nothing better than the feeling of toes touching the ground. I want to feel grounded, connected, and in touch with the Earth, you know what I mean?"

"You are unique."

"Thank you. That's the second nicest thing you could say to me."

"What's the first?"

I looked down at my toes and thought about whether or not I wanted to tell him. I didn't want to live my life confined within a limo or the walls of a house. I didn't want a mansion to become my world. It's why journalism continued to interest me. The stories brought me out there, into that world full of different kinds of people with different backgrounds and perspectives and quotes so unlike what I had been raised with inside the sheltered walls of the limo and mansion. I curled my toes along the splintery edge of the pier.

"The first nicest thing you said to me," I told Josh. "was that you thought it was great that I wanted to be a journalist."

"You've got to be kidding me," he said. "It meant that much to you?"

"Yeah," I laughed. "I've never heard any guy say anything supportive like that before. My father and the men he introduces me to, the ones we have dinner with occasionally, certainly don't think my career aspirations are a good thing."

"Sorry to hear that."

"Yeah, me too. It's screwed up, don't you think?"

"Yeah, but if you don't mind my asking, what is it that you're after? Because I'm guessing it's not the money. I may be wrong."

"You're right about that. I don't care about money."

"Then you've probably never gone without, right? Because anyone who has ever gone without money does care."

I thought good and hard about what he said, and maybe, to an extent, there was accuracy in it. My father was just turning into a man and entering the workforce when the Great Depression hit, and he witnessed firsthand how the loss of fortunes, big or small, devastated everyone he knew and didn't know. It was nearly impossible for him at that time to land any job at any bank because thousands of banks were failing and closing back then. He watched his own father lose his job and with it the house when he could no longer pay the mortgage.

"I guess you're right," I said. "I've never gone without money. Maybe that's why I'm not at all concerned with making it. But my father, he's gone without, and maybe that's why he works so hard at his career. He's gone without a job and a house before, but you should see now the way he stores up his money and works all the time. I don't know. For me, it's not at all about money. It's all about having choices in life and maybe one day women won't think about this because they won't have ever gone without choices. Everyone should be able to have choices in life, don't you think?"

"Absolutely," he said. "Isn't that what freedom is?"

I nodded. "Do you believe women should be free to work in whatever field they choose?"

"Why not?"

"You're the only one who thinks so. You, and my friend, Ava." I stopped there. I didn't want to tell him that Ava was just some girl whose diary I had been snooping through. And I also stopped talking too deeply about my career aspirations, for the more I talked with Josh, the more I liked him and the less I wanted to spook him away like I did all the other men, although he didn't appear to be the type to be spooked away by a woman like me.

After that first morning of not catching a single fish, I stopped thinking about career aspirations and started having fun, pure and simple fun that continued for the next fourteen mornings in a row. Every morning on that pier was fun with Josh, despite my not catching any fish. Josh said it was because they tasted my cookies and were scared about what my bait might taste like, but I didn't care. To me, fishing was no longer a competition with the men. Somewhere into our second week together, fishing became all about standing alongside Josh, talking or not talking. I liked both, for even when we were quiet, I felt like I was getting to know him by the way he moved, patiently and relaxed, never in a hurry, nor angry even when I dropped a pole in the water.

My father didn't know about my early mornings out. But if Ava could sneak out at night to meet up with Jaden, I told myself, then I could sneak out at sunrise to meet up with Josh. A woman does what she must to see her man, and with all the cooking and domestic responsibilities I was attempting for my father, there was no time for me to get together with Josh during the day. Besides, I had a gut feeling that my father wouldn't like the idea of me spending so much time with him.

"Why are you looking at me like that?" I asked Josh one morning as I stepped onto the pier carrying our two cups of coffee.

"Like what?" He had an unusually large smile on his face, like that of a dolphin, and I didn't know why for sure, but I suspected it was because he had fallen in love with me as I had with him.

"That grin," I said. "You're grinning more than you usually do."

I handed him his coffee and turned down the pole he handed me. I didn't feel like fishing. I just felt like standing there beside him, and there were other things I wanted to do with my hands this early morning and holding a fishing pole would only get in the way. I had been up all night thinking about Ava kissing her guy, and it bothered me that a girl living nearly seventy years before me was getting more action than me, a modern-fifties chick. Maybe it was because she and Jaden were getting together in the darkness of night while Josh and I had that morning sun and the other fishermen all around us. But, still, it was early summer and even the dolphins had just gotten done with their spring courting and copulating. It wasn't fair, and I decided to do something about my craving to kiss him.

"Josh," I started. "The world is so large."

"Sure is," he said.

"Sometimes I want to experience everything it has to offer. Do you ever feel that way?"

"What do you mean?"

"Kiss me, Josh."

He turned and looked at me, and still holding his fishing pole in one hand, he softly touched my chin with his other hand and pulled me close. I closed my eyes, and as we kissed I swear I saw multitudes of dolphins bursting forth from the water and lightning bolting across the sky and a thousand hawks circling above in an aerial performance before moving on.

But that was all impossible. I had only spotted two dolphins that morning when my eyes were open, and it couldn't have been lightning, for that usually comes in the late afternoon, and the hawks, well, they aren't scheduled to arrive in these skies until fall. But I swear I saw all of this when my eyes were closed and my lips were kissing Josh. I guess anything is possible when you love someone.

"I like your world," I told Josh after our kiss. "It's a nice world you live in."

"The best," he answered, and I wondered if that might be true.

That kiss and the ones following filled me with joy, and I wanted to tell Ava that now I knew exactly what she was talking about. It was as if there was a summer breeze fueling my footsteps each morning after my time on the pier with him and whatever it was, it made my burned casseroles smell like apple pies and my eyes brighten as if Thomas Edison himself had been conducting experiments on them. And maybe it was my newfound sense of joy that made me serve my father dinner with pleasure and then dance the jitterbug with him.

"Looks like you're starting to enjoy being a woman," Lloyd said over dinner.

"I sure am, sir," I said. "Would you like more tea?" I didn't wait for his answer but sprung up from my chair and got him more.

"Is there a boy, Lydia?" he asked when I returned with the kettle and started to pour.

I made a face, one that if frozen, would be the world's most shocked and insulted-looking ice sculpture. "A boy? Why do you ask?"

"I'm observant. And when I suspect things, I'm usually never wrong."

I wanted to be strong, like Ava had been when she confessed to her mother that there was indeed a boy. "There is," I said. "And you met him."

"The one at the pier? The one who wants to spend his life fishing?"

"Yes. Josh. It's a great way to spend one's life, don't you think?"

Lloyd cleared his voice. "A boy who wants to spend his entire life fishing is not the right man for my daughter."

"We all have choices. Not every man wants to live his life inside the walls of a bank, like you. Everyone is different, you know." And just as I said it I over-poured the tea, and it flowed out of his cup and onto the floor.

"Watch how you talk to me," he snapped as I headed for a towel in the kitchen. "I think it's best you stay away from him."

Impossible, I thought. Can a river otter stay away from water and an archeologist keep from an Indian mound and pelicans not go near Florida and the waves stop reaching the shore and a person spot a rare Junonia shell on the beach and pick up an olive shell instead? Can lovebugs separate?

"Impossible," I said when I returned with the towel and began wiping the table. A girl can't stay away from the boy she loves.

"You will do as I say."

"I won't. Why should I? My mother never cared about her parents' wishes."

And the second I said it I regretted it, for I had never spoken back to my father so badly, and I saw a look on his face I had never seen before, one that told me he didn't know what else to say and was actually frightened of me. If only in the silent moments that followed I had a name to pull out, someone to blame for my outspokenness, an aunt, a great, great grandmother maybe but I knew of no one with a history of sharp nasty tongue.

I only knew of my mother, and she married my father against her parents' wishes. She was Irish, and he was not, and there were consequences long after my mother's death. Her family never let us in, and I hardly know of them today. I knew all about their history, and I knew my father was trying to make it so that history might not repeat itself. He wanted so badly for me to marry a man he approved of. But he didn't have the power to change history. I was the one who had that. It was my choice who I loved and who I would one day, if ever, end up with.

Neither Lloyd nor I spoke the rest of that night, and in the next morning's silence I awoke to the sound of my beating heart. There may have been an alligator or two bellowing outside my window like Ava had heard, but I wouldn't know. My heartbeat was louder than any alligators. I quickly and quietly got dressed, percolated some coffee, and started tiptoeing toward the front door so I wouldn't wake Lloyd.

"I guess you don't need this." His voice startled me as did the music on the radio. He was in the armchair in his robe, smoking a cigar and waving an envelope in the air.

"You shouldn't be smoking that cigar," I told him. "What would the doctor say?"

"I'm celebrating," he said.

"There's healthier ways to celebrate. But what's going on? Another pay raise at the bank?"

"No, but give me another seven or eight months and the answer to that will be 'yes.' This time, it's about you," he said taking the cup of coffee meant for Josh, and then handing me the envelope. "Read it for yourself."

I set the other on the coffee table and opened the envelope. "North-western University," I announced a second later. "I've been accepted."

I tried keeping a straight face as I quickly folded it and stuffed it back into the envelope, but I couldn't keep my emotions inside. "It's a dream come true," I said, and then ran into Lloyd's arms like a child. "I've done it," I said. "I'm going to the college of my choice and I can hardly wait!"

He was laughing and got up from his chair and started to dance. "Your mother and I once danced to this song," he said. "She loved it. It's a good one, isn't it?" I smiled as he spun me around and then dipped me. I pulled him close and hugged him, fearful that celebrating might be a shock to his typically intense nature and dangerous for a recovering man like himself.

"College is expensive, dear," he said into my ear. "I'll pay quarterly. I'll support you fully. Just don't do anything to disappoint me. You are my only child. Don't get mixed up with the wrong man. I don't think you could afford the cost of that school on your own, let alone on a fisherman's salary."

I stiffened. Lloyd was living up to his reputation. I had seen him threaten associates like this throughout the years, but this was the first time I was personally on that side of it.

I didn't want to dance anymore, so I broke free from his dip and stood there breathing in the smell of his cigar, feeling queasy. This was no longer about choosing between family and boy. He had added a twist, and it was more like the dreams a girl has for her life versus boy. History was repeating itself, but in a different way.

I didn't know what to do. My dreams had been with me longer, yet my feelings for Josh had become more intense. I needed a friend, someone I could turn to for insight with this matter. I thought of Ava and wondered what she might do and what she did do with regard to Jaden. Did she stay away from him forever like her parents advised? And I thought of Marlena. Two weeks had gone by. Maybe she was back from Hollywood. I was eager to hear if she landed a big role and more anxious to hear from Ava.

Then I remembered Ava saying she feared there was only a small win-

dow in a woman's life in which her wisdom is taken seriously. And it bothered her that her young voice wasn't heard and that soon senility might set
in; so, there was only that brief period of her life during which anyone
would listen to anything she had to say.

Well, I couldn't let that happen to my friend. To me, she was chock full
of wisdom she collected, gathered, and inherited, and I was ready to hear
anything that might help with regard to my own situation. And I trusted
her words now more than ever. After all, it was she who suggested in a
round-about way that joy can be found in a boy, and thanks to her I found
it and my jar of joy was filled to the rim. But now, this dilemma had me
stumped.

XIX

BREAKING A HABIT IS never an easy thing to do, and it was difficult for me not to meet up with Josh on the pier at sunrise the next morning. Instead, I skimmed through the pages of a local wildlife book, then made breakfast for my father, swept and mopped the kitchen floor, washed windows, did laundry, and, finally, walked to Bougainvillea.

Marlena opened the door and gave me an enormous hug. "I just got home last night," she said, pulling me inside. "And I bought an amazing assortment of pastries. Sit down while I make some coffee, and I'll be right back."

"Need some help?"

"Not at all. Make yourself at home." She disappeared into the kitchen and returned moments later with a tray full of a breakfast goodies fit for a celebrity.

"How was your trip?" I asked, taking a golden pastry with raisins.

"Hollywood is marvelous, but there's no place like Sanibel."

"Did you meet Marilyn Monroe?"

"No, but tell me the truth—I'm not thinner than her, am I?" She stood up, licking icing off her fingers and spun slowly around in a circle.

"You're about the same size, maybe a bit bigger in the rear."

"What about Elizabeth Taylor?"

"I don't know," I said.

She plopped back down in her chair and reached for another cinnamon roll. "I don't want to look thin. Thin is not sexy. My agent has been tell-ing me to gain weight, and so I have and I've had fun doing it." She picked the raisins off and tossed them aside, making a face. "But maybe I need a bit more sensuality added to my hips."

"You don't look thin," I said and meant it.

"Thank you," she said. "I'm expecting big things to come from this lat-est trip. But we've talked enough about me. I don't ever want to become one of those egocentrics. What's your tale, nightingale? Tell me your story." She crossed her legs Indian-style and made herself comfortable.

"It's sad," I said setting my coffee down. "I don't know what to do."

"A male?"

"How'd you know?"

"Every role I've ever auditioned for involves a man and a woman, and there's always a problem between the two. So what's your problem?"

"I like him, but my father doesn't."

"Parents. They always want the best for their daughters. Maybe your father is right."

"Not mine. To Lloyd, the right boy would be rich, rude, and powerful."

"I see. And this boy is none of that?"

"He's the opposite. He's laid-back, simple."

"Oh," she moaned. "This is the good old classic story, isn't it?"

"What do you mean?"

"Well, you're certainly not the first woman on earth to be put into this sort of plot. In fact, there's one gal in particular that comes to mind."

"Who?"

"Ava."

It was the first time I had cracked a smile all morning. "I already feel like we're friends, like I know her. I do relate."

"Then you might want to go read more of her journal."

"Does she meet up again with Jaden despite her parent's wishes?"

"That's not for me to tell. I'll let her tell you all about it. Go ahead. You'll find it in the drawer."

I walked down the hall into the yellow room. There I looked out the window and spotted an owl perched on the tiniest branch of the banyan tree. We stared eye-to-eye, but then once I tried opening the window, it flew off. I sat down at the desk and pulled out the next set of pages. I was eager to read. To me, Ava was a girl with the world's largest collection of wisdom that she sought and chased after, gathered and caught, as well as inherited, and I wondered if maybe somewhere in her writing she might instruct me as to how I might go about finding some for myself. And wherever wisdom sits, whether perched on the branch of some special tree, or in the mind of some older woman I might meet, I needed a bit of it right now, at this very age, and not when I'm ninety.

"I can't wait that long," I muttered and then started to read. "I need wisdom now."

1892

Ava

If any of you lacks wisdom, he should ask God, who gives generously to all without finding fault, and it will be given to him.
—James 1:5

Orange-crowned warblers and orioles were frequenting the island, and it was fall. I was walking through the mudflats to get to school, appreciating the migrating songbirds, when all of a sudden what I thought was a wild creature came running up behind me, sending me splashing down with fright. It was Jaden.

"Look what you made me do," I said. "This isn't what a lady is supposed to look like on her first day of school."

"I didn't think you were a lady," he said with a smile. And when I wiped my dirty, glaring face with the sleeve of my blouse, he gave me a hand and pulled me up. "Let me rephrase that. You're too fun to be a lady." I took that as a compliment, but when he tried brushing dirt off my behind, I turned and slapped him across the face.

"Don't you dare!" I scolded. "I may be more fun than any other lady, but I still share the ladylike morals."

"Fine," he said. "But there was a grunt worm on your behind."

"No!" I laughed.

"Yes. You want me to find it?"

"Forget it. Why were you running so fast? We're not late for school, are we?" I asked.

"No, but I spotted tracks way back there and knew they were yours. I wanted to catch up with you."

"Footprints? There's no way. You couldn't possibly have recognized them as being mine."

"I did. You've got squiggly tracks, like those of a beetle."

"I do?" I asked, looking behind me.

"Yeah. It tells me you're not dull. You don't walk a straight line."

"What about your tracks?" I asked, looking back at the soft ground behind him.

"I don't know. You tell me. What do they look like to you?"

"Full-foot prints," I said.

"That's right, like those of a tortoise. It means I place both heel and toe into the ground. I'm not in a hurry. I want to enjoy my walk to school, the slower the better. I couldn't care less if I'm late. People are in such a hurry to learn what a textbook has to teach that they miss what nature is trying to teach them. There's wisdom in nature, you know?"

I laughed. "I want to believe you, but you looked like you were in a hurry to me, the way you charged toward me like that."

"I was only hurrying in hopes I might catch you. But I'm not hurrying any more now that I've found you." He was blushing, which I hadn't seen him do before. After that, we made plans to wait for one another under a certain tree every morning and walk together the rest of the way. And neither of us ever missed a single day of school that year, or starting the next.

"Do you like school?" I asked him one early-October morning.

"Only my walks there with you."

"What are you going to do when you're done with school?"

"Fish."

"I'm serious. What are your plans?"

"I told you, fishing."

"What else?"

He moved his hands as if he were reeling in a catch. "Fish, then fish some more," he said.

"You've got to do something other than fishing all day. I'm sure one of these years my daddy is going to need help with his land. He wishes he had a son."

Jaden smiled. "I can't wait for the day when I can tell your daddy I love you," he said, pulling me off the trail and behind the trunk of a banyan tree.

"Don't you dare tell him, not yet," I cried. "They know I've crossed paths and walked to school with you a few times. But they think we walk with a group."

"Then we'll wait. By spring, we'll tell them. They'll be ready to hear it come spring, I'm sure."

I didn't want to tell Jaden that my parents might never be ready to hear it, or at least not until I'm in my thirties. I was still their only child, and I don't think they'd ever fully accept my leaving them to go live with a man, albeit a husband one day.

"Doll face, you're too beautiful to look so worried," Jaden whispered in my ear, then kissed my neck. I took his hands in mine and led him back to the path so we could continue our walk to school.

"Maybe when you're eighteen," he said, "your daddy will understand. I'll wait as long as I have to."

Lydia

I held the page I had been reading close to my chest. "That's it," I whispered.

"Time. All I need is enough time. It's okay to slow things down."

But it already hurt me thinking of him there at the pier this morning with no one to hand him coffee and stand by his side, or plant a quick kiss on his cheek. But I'd have to stay away a little longer yet, at least about a week so my father might no longer suspect. And then I'd meet up with him again but not in the morning sunlight anymore. We'd have to come up with another time and place to meet. None of it was fair. My father didn't even know Josh, but he knew well what he wanted his daughter marrying. He didn't care whether it was a man I truly loved. He only wanted me marrying someone just like him, who loved money and work more than anything. And maybe I'd have settled with that, but now thanks to meeting Josh and to Abigail for sharing with me the traits that make a good man, I wanted differently for myself. That's not to say any man would ever override my goals.

I continued to read in hopes Ava might further lead me in the right direction.

Ava

It didn't matter that there were close to one hundred people living year-round on Sanibel. When Jaden and I walked to school together, I felt like we were the only two on the island—just us, and the wildlife, that is.

He taught me so much about nature that at times I felt it easier living in harmony with it than with people. There were so many mornings when I walked out my front door feeling bad for my mama or mad that no one could possibly understand the love I had for Jaden, but all of a sudden, once I reached our path and spotted him, I changed, like one of those frogs that change their colorings to match their surroundings. And I felt at peace. I felt invigorated beside him and walked with a hop in my step, occasionally glancing back at my tracks to make sure I was still human.

With Jaden by my side, I felt wilder and freer than any girl could ever hope to feel, soaring like one of those bald eagles in the sky. I felt eternally alive and beautiful as if I had discovered the Fountain of Youth and would continue loving him forever, simple and pure.

Together we trekked our way through autumns with the eagles court-ing above us in mid-air, then into winters when passing cold fronts cast millions of seashells onto the ground below us. And always in the spring, like two shorebirds we walked wing to wing. I wanted to cry with the first drops of rain, for it meant summer was coming and school was ending. It was already hard enough each day after school when my tracks continued eastward toward my house and his turned and headed south.

Lydia

There was more to read, but I wasn't ready. I tied the pages together and placed them back in the drawer as I had found them.

I sat there a moment, thinking about what I should do, but my mind was as indecisive as Florida's summer sky. Come fall, I'd be leaving the island to start school. If I were to continue seeing Josh, he and I would be one of those long-distance love affairs, nothing like Ava and Jaden, living year-to-year on the same island.

"Ours would be trickier," I said as I stood up.

"What would be trickier, dear?" Marlena asked me. I didn't know she had been standing in the doorway.

"I wish I could stay and talk, Marlena, but I've got to get going. I've got to figure everything out."

"What do you think you're going to do?"

"I don't know. For starters, I'm going to read everything I can about the wildlife on this island. Ava and Jaden have inspired me like that. Then I'll try and figure out what to do about Josh."

"Can you come back tomorrow?"

"I'll try," I said. "It'll be soon."

XX

AS THE REMAINDER OF the week and the following week sauntered by, I felt like one of those fanatical birdwatchers, for everywhere I went, my eyes were looking for Josh. And I thought I had spotted those eyes of his a few times, at the general store, the library, the beach, and the wildlife refuge. But they belonged to other creatures, ones I didn't feel like watching.

I knew where to find him, perched on that pier every morning at sunrise. But I was still a coward when it came to Lloyd threatening to pull my finances. So I spent my mornings walking ankle-high in the water, searching for shells. I think it turned into an addiction, for I did it for hours and found it quite hard to stop, and, then, well into the night, I'd glue those shells to mirrors, heart-shaped boxes, picture frames, anything I could think of, and I considered talking to someone about the long hours I was putting toward this activity, but I figured no harm done, other than feeling tired the next morning.

I went to Bougainvillea often, carrying with me my morning bucket filled to the rim with shells. The bucket and the shells gave me more of a lift than a strong cup of coffee, but I still drank the coffee Marlena made for me whenever I arrived. She was the only person who made coffee nearly as good as I, and I greatly respected her for it, but I knew her secret. Double the amount of beans until it is dark as mud, and so after a few sips it has one believing she might conquer the world.

We drank coffee, talked, and laughed a lot. I stayed away from the yellow room with the wooden desk. I needed a break from Ava's journal, and Marlena agreed. She saw the impact it was having on my life. I needed to make my own choices on loving Josh and didn't want Ava's romance with Jaden to influence my heart in any way.

"Have you heard anything from your agent?" I asked her one morning.

"No, and patience is not a virtue of mine."

"Mine, either. It's been eleven days since I last met Josh for a sunrise on the pier. You'd think he'd at least come find out what happened to me, don't you?"

"One would think," she said. "Maybe he doesn't know where you're staying."

"No. He knows."

"Then maybe he's busy."

"No. He's not."

"Then you may not like what I'm about to say, but there's one thing I know from my own personal experience and that's when a man stops actively going after a woman, it means only one thing: The fish doesn't like the bait any more."

Those words pierced me, and I didn't want to believe them to be true, so instead I asked Marlena about her own love life. She said she chose her dreams of becoming an actress over her love life, having dated numerous men throughout the years but always ending things before there was ever talk of marriage. I liked talking with Marlena. She told me good stuff, and I told her things I wouldn't have told anyone else, and in doing so, I no longer felt as remote as I once did.

When I wasn't laughing over at her place or compulsively gluing shells together, I was spending time with Lloyd. We had been enjoying a good amount of father/daughter time together in the evenings while our mornings and afternoons were our own. He went golfing or fishing, not on the pier, but out in a boat with a guide. And come evening, we'd catch a sunset together and then go out to a restaurant, which meant I was making dinner less and less. Somewhere between Tuesday's Sloppy Joes and

Wednesday's baked hamburgers, Lloyd decided he needed a break from my cooking. And so did I!

"I've been thinking," he said over dinner at a restaurant. "Remember Leo Fairbanks?"

"Yes, that young guy you mentored at the bank some time ago? The one who said he gets along better with numbers than people?"

"That's the one. You remember him, don't you? I spoke to him the other day when I called the bank. He's rising quickly."

"Doesn't surprise me, Daddy. Everyone you mentor rises quickly."

"I guess, but he especially made a good impression on me, and when a young man does that, I enjoy investing my time in him for the betterment of the bank. I was thinking of inviting him out here for a visit. He's not that much older than you."

I put my fork down. It made a loud noise and people at the next table turned. "What are you trying to say?"

"You wouldn't have to cook for him. I wouldn't want you to. The three of us could go out for dinner every night. We've got three more months here. It might be nice to have company and for you to spend time with the right kind of man."

I handed my plate full of food to the waiter and pushed the napkin off my lap and onto the floor. I was disgusted. He had put thought into it. He just didn't get it after all this time that I didn't want to marry a man for his money, his title, his education, nor the house he could buy me in the suburbs. And up until I met Josh, I didn't think I wanted a man at all.

"Ever since we went fishing on the pier our first day here," I said, "I haven't been able to get Josh out of my mind. It's time for me to step up and be honest with you, myself, and Josh."

"Dear, you better get him out of your mind because I don't think Josh is interested in you anymore— At least he wasn't when I spoke to him last."

My mouth fell open. "*What?*"

"Josh and I had a nice discussion."

"*Where?*"

"The pier."

"*When?*"

"About two weeks ago."

"*Why?*"

"I'd have to give an entire presentation, slides and all, to get you to fully understand my perspective on why I went to talk to him," said Lloyd. "But I'll try to sum it up. You're my only daughter. You're all I've got. I've put all my hopes into you."

I pushed my chair away from the table and stood up. I wanted to leave. Then I sat back down again. I wanted to throw a tantrum. I wanted to pick up a plate of food and throw it across the room like a child, but also like a woman I wanted to calmly discuss and persuade my father over to my point of view. I looked at him as he continued chewing his steak as if nothing had happened and I wanted to hate him. But I loved him.

"Daddy," I said. "I'm a woman. You can't tell a woman whom to love."

"True, but you're also my daughter."

"You shouldn't have interfered in something that wasn't your business like that."

"If you marry a man who can't provide for you, it'll become my business. Believe me. When you come crying home for money and I start writing him checks, it'll be my business all right."

"Money!" I shouted and the ladies at the table next to us gawked. "Is that everything to you? I'll bet my mother got sick of hearing you talk about money all the time, too, didn't she?" I shouldn't have said it, but I did.

"Your mother was too busy doing her duties to get mad and opinionated like you all the time. She was a good woman and a good wife and would have been a great mother. She knew her place and she loved it. It's where she wanted to be."

"Really? If it's where she wanted to be, then why'd she . . . ?" I stopped there. I couldn't go on. And I knew it had nothing to do with it. There was no connection whatsoever and I was trying to make one that wasn't there. I felt bad.

I picked my napkin up and tossed it like a parachute across the table and then I left. I hurried outside and down the sandy street like a journalist who had just gathered most of the information she needed but still had one more important source to talk with. Josh. I had to find him. I didn't know exactly what Lloyd had said to him, only that it probably wasn't true and it definitely wasn't nice. I went to the pier, but he wasn't there. They told me he might be at the marina. But the people at the marina said he left to get a beer at the bar. I gathered all kinds of information at the bar, most of which I didn't want or need, but then someone told me he left for his place over an hour ago. That source was very valuable and gave me directions as well.

And there, I knocked and knocked aggressively on his door, proud that I was no longer acting like a proper lady. And when the door opened and I saw Josh, as well as a beautiful woman behind him, I felt stupid for being anything but.

XXI

"LYDIA," HE SAID, WHEN he opened the door. There was a bottle of wine in his hand. "Haven't seen you in a while. Thought I might never see you again."

I looked past him at the woman sipping from her glass. "I hope I'm not interrupting," I said.

The woman turned and smiled at me. I noticed her brown eyes. They were dark against her blonde hair, and she and Josh made such a couple. They were a perfect, matching pair.

There are advantages and disadvantages to having a journalistic mind. It's great when you're trying to find out clues as to where someone might be. But it's bad when you assume every situation is potentially a major story when maybe it's no story at all. But it's great when you're so observant of details that you quickly put things together.

"Your sister?" I asked.

"You could tell?"

"You two look like twins. Are you twins?" I said, walking over to the table and holding my hand out.

"No. We're a couple of years apart."

"You had me fooled in more ways then you can imagine," I said, grinning.

"Hi, I'm Lydia. So nice to meet you."

"You too," she said. "Would you like to join us? I'm sure Josh wouldn't mind."

"Oh no," I said. "Thank you, but I've got to get going."

The table was set for two and the platter of roast beef was steaming and there was a plate of freshly steamed vegetables and a bowl of mashed potatoes.

"How long are you here for?" I asked her.

"I've been here a week already. I fly out in the morning."

"She lives in California," said Josh. "Northern."

"It's nice she cooks like this for you, Josh," I noted. "What a sister!"

"I didn't cook it," she said. "Josh did."

I swore a wave slapped me across the face and stole my breath. "Did you say . . ." I was choking on my own words. "Josh, you cook?"

And all this just when I was about to surrender, to take up cooking again, and reconsider my plans of going to college and pursuing things that typical girls don't pursue, I was hit with the news that Josh cooked this Norman Rockwell-looking dinner. I've never heard of a guy cooking before. He must be the only one in the world capable. But it reinforced something for me. If a guy could cook, then a woman can do whatever it is a man does outside of the home.

"Do you cook often?" I asked him.

"Every night. I've done it since I was a kid. I love it."

Wow, I thought. A male who cooks is a good thing, another trait added to our list of good-man qualities. I'm sure Abigail would have agreed.

"How's your father?" he asked seriously.

"You tell me," I said. "Sounds like you two had a talk. I don't know what he said, but . . ."

"He said that if you and I spend any more time together, he'd take away your finances for college."

I felt like I was drowning as I gasped for air. "Is that what he told you? Is that why you haven't come looking for me?"

"I'm not getting in the way of your plans. I know how important they are to you."

It was then that I broke every etiquette rule in the book "What are you doing tomorrow night at around ten o'clock?"

"Are you asking me out?" He looked at his sister and smiled. "Do women do that?" She shrugged her shoulders. "Ten o'clock is a late start for a date, isn't it?"

"Yes, but my father falls asleep at nine-thirty."

"I'm asleep too at nine-thirty," he said rolling his eyes. "I do get up to fish at sunrise, you know."

"Do you want to or not?"

"I do," he said. "But I'm not crazy about being your little nighttime secret. Maybe for a short while, I can play along sneaking out at night to meet up with you, but sooner or later you're going to have to tell your father. Is that something you're willing to do?"

"Of course," I said. "Just give me a little time."

"I can do that. Now which window is yours? What side does it face?"

"The west."

"Leave your bedroom light on, and I'll come knocking tomorrow night at ten o'clock. It's a date."

"I look forward to it."

"So do I. I'll see you then."

XXII

I WAS IN A carnival-of-a-mood when I started knocking on Marlena's door. It was July and one of those mornings where the sun coats the clouds with pink, blue and streaks of purple, turning them into puffs of tasty-looking cotton candy. My knocking turned into a song, and I actually enjoyed standing out there thinking about the times Josh and I had been enjoying.

As I crawled out my window each night, I entered a whole other world, a simple one I never knew existed. We'd walk beneath the moonlight to the dock behind his house, our hands interlocked like the roots of a mangrove, and from there we'd leave on his boat. Some nights we fished and other nights we sat quietly in each other's arms until the gentle laps of water would rock us to sleep. He always had me back through that window by sunrise, although a couple of times we came close to getting caught with the sun at our heels, and those were the mornings he introduced me to the herons, ibis, and other characters nesting along the coast.

When staying out all night started making us both tired out during the days, we changed our routine and started meeting up in the early evenings, just after I finished dinner with my father. We spent the month of June bike riding through the refuge and swimming in the Gulf. I shuffled my feet, paranoid at times that my father might be lurking nearby, and if he found out what I had been up to, he might sting. It would be a nasty sting. I couldn't imagine not going to school in the fall just as I could hardly think about leaving Josh. Running off with him was like leaving all my worries behind and entering a sanctuary where there was nothing but peace and beauty.

When my knocking song on Marlena's door ended, I pounded a few times more with all my force, as if I were playing to win the stuffed-animal prize at the carnival. It hurt my knuckles, but the door opened and there appeared a sad, sick creature peering out. Her poodle cut, glamorous two weeks ago, now looked a wild mess and in need of grooming. Her eyes were red and puffy.

"Is this a bad time?" I asked, wondering whether I should have given up my knocking and moved on ten minutes ago.

"It's fine," she said.

"Are you okay?"

"Fine. Why?" She looked at me as if she was a blue crab and I had trapped her.

"I don't know. You look tired today."

"I'm fine," she said in a monotone. It sounded nothing like her typical dramatic tone, the one of an actor.

"Is now a good time for me to read more pages? I can come back."

"It's fine. You know where I keep them."

"Thank you," I said, walking toward the yellow room. Her home smelled like the interior of a seashell might if the mollusk inside dies without draining out. "It's dark in here," I said, turning to look at her. She was still standing in the doorway. "Were you sleeping? Did I wake you?"

"No. I've been up. Make yourself comfortable."

"Thank you," I said, looking around the yellow room for a lamp. The shades were down and the house was dark and Marlena looked like she was sickened and dying. I opened the window, hoping the life outside might fly in. I then pulled out the pages from the top right drawer and stared at them, but I was too concerned about Marlena to start reading.

"Marlena," I called out. She didn't answer. I stood up and glanced down the hall. "Marlena?" Again there was no answer. I quietly crept back into the great room and there she was, sitting on the couch with a martini in hand, her eyes open but looking full of debris like the gulf does after a windy storm. I tried looking deeper, but I couldn't get past the sur-face layer. I wanted to scrape the soot away and see the color once more but I didn't know how.

It spooked me, so I tiptoed back into the yellow room and sat down, hoping that Ava might provide some insight into all of this.

I began to read:

SANIBEL ISLAND
1894

Ava

There are those times when a woman fears that she is on the brink of extinction or that the dreams and wants she had for her life are endangered. It is then that she must declare herself a refuge and take whatever measures to preserve her nat-ural elements.

Whoever says there are no seasons in Florida? There are, they're just subtler, and there are moods to go along with those seasons. When the shorebirds returned, I felt like cheering and clapping my hands at this year's opening sight of spring, but instead I hopped out of bed and went for a walk.

How could I not go out and greet the return of the migratory birds? But as I stepped outside to welcome them back, I wondered where Abigail had gone. Back in Kentucky spring was the season that sent my mama blooming again after her long winter doldrums. Here on the island, she remained full of color all winter along, but in recent days she started pull-ing a disappearing act. Sometimes I found her still in bed, like yesterday, and other days sitting on the wooden floor of the kitchen. And when she finally did stand up or speak, let's just say she wasn't trying to please or en-tertain any audience. I was as worried as a ringleader when he suspects his top lady of deserting the act.

But the others on the island were performing fine, I noticed as I walked toward the shore. Talented herons were perching themselves on thin branches like circus performers while brown pelicans were doing acrobatics, starting thirty feet in the air and then diving headlong into the ocean in search of fish. Their fuzzy newborn chicks appeared magically out of thin air, flaunting around without any feathers. And those shorebirds, how they dazzled us all, dressed in their fresh molted plumage and adding festivity to the mudflats.

Despite its beauty, this spring morning didn't smell right and it smelled as bad as a heronry. When I didn't see Abigail swirling the spoons, kneading the bread, or twirling the mop in the kitchen this morning, I feared the worst—she was sinking like a grunt worm into the ground. As I sat down with my back against a tree, I feared my faith was sinking too. All of us were believers that Abigail had been reborn that first month we arrived here and that the climate had healed her fits of sorrow. Faith had us believing she would live happily ever after on Sanibel, but since early May when she no longer joyfully buzzed around her chores, I began to privately question my faith.

I closed my eyes and buried my head in my hands and mourned for Abigail and the joy dancing in her eyes and for the part of her that so rigorously tried churning me into a lady and cared for the details of our home. It was as if my mama had a costume change and the new her couldn't perform a single act, not even crack a smile. It was like curtains were closed across her eyes and I couldn't see in.

And as I watched Abigail in her new dark, drab costume, I tried tapering down my own brightness. If anyone asked what my favorite color was, I'd no longer say pink. I had moved on from that. I was no longer a child. My mama doesn't know this, but it was this missing Abigail that taught me most how to be a woman. Not a lady, but a woman. I sprouted forth from my girlhood that spring when I watched the Abigail who loved me disappearing into the ground.

If there were questions I could have asked her, I would have. If there were cheerful quotes or versus that might have made her smile, I'd have recited them. If there were dances I could have danced to keep her from slipping further, I'd have danced them. If there was a magic word I might say to make her reappear, I'd have said it. I would have stood center stage and done just about anything to make her laugh and clap and jump up and down with joy.

There had been many acts. It wasn't like all of a sudden she'd just disappear on me. And on this fine spring morning, she was at the part where she still answered my questions. But she was entering that stage where her answers weren't making sense. Next would come the silence. As in a circus, the silence makes me nervous.

Lydia

My eyes slipped off the journal like toes from a trapeze. I put my elbows on the desk and let my head fall into my hands, and there I cried. I cried not for Abigail, but for my own mother. I was just a baby when she pulled the disappearing act. There was nothing I could have done to help, and it made me sad. I needed her then like I do now. I didn't want to think about it; sometime, maybe, but not now.

Now I thought of Marlena. She wasn't herself today, and there was an uncanny similarity to the way Ava had described Abigail's appearance. I wiped my eyes and nervously stood up and went to find her sitting in the same position she was in before I started reading.

"Did you see the *I Love Lucy* episode where Lucy impersonates some Hollywood notables to impress her nearsighted girlfriend visiting from New York?" I asked as I sat down on the armchair across from her.

"No."

"It was the funniest thing. Lucy impersonates Gary Cooper, Clark Gable, Marlon Brando, and Jimmy Durante, and then Harpo Marx just as the real Harpo arrives at the apartment with Ricky. It was the funniest thing in the world!"

Marlena didn't crack a smile, and I stopped my humor there. "You look tired today," I said. "Why don't you go rest in your room? You might be more comfortable in there."

"I'm fine," she answered.

"Are you sure? Are you sick?"

"Not really, no."

"Then what's wrong? Why are you sad?"

She turned and looked at me for the first time. "Are you writing a book?" she asked.

"No."

"Then stop with all the questions, please!"

"I'm sorry. Maybe I should come back another time." I started to stand up.

"Remember the day we first met and we made that snowwoman?"

"Yes," I said, sitting back down again.

"Did I ever tell you it was destroyed by some boy a few days later?"

"Are you serious?"

"Trampled it to nothing," she said. "Do you know what that means?"

"No," I answered. "What?"

"It means that sometimes the dreams we have for our lives make it no further than a dream."

"What are you trying to say, Marlena? I'm not following you."

"I didn't get the part. Any part. My agent says I'm not suitable for the screen. It got me to thinking. I had a great reputation for the stage so I could go back to that."

"Why don't you?"

She stared me in the eyes, and suddenly I felt as if I was on stage with a strong overhead light beaming into my eyes. I wanted to look away, but I didn't dare. "The dreams we set for ourselves are like fingerprints," she said rubbing her fingers together. "They make us unique, and they're with us for life, whether they're trampled on or not, they're still embedded in us. I'm not ready to give up on mine, not yet."

"That's motivating," I said. "Then don't give up. Keep trying."

"I have every intention of doing so, but there are things that keep getting in the way, things I can't seem to control."

"Like what?"

"Things," she said. "At first I thought it was my nose, and then my weight, and then my age. But now I see there is something else going on, something I don't know how to change."

"What?"

"You couldn't possibly understand," she said. "And I don't mean that rudely. It's just that unless you go through it yourself..."

"Go through what?"

"Never mind. I don't feel like talking. It's not you. It's me."

"Is there anything I can do to help?"

"I don't know," she said. "Why don't you finish your reading?"

"All right," I said, standing up. "But please call me if there's anything I can do to help."

As I returned to the yellow room and stared out the window at the green sea grape leaves, I wondered whether it was her not getting any roles that got her down. If so, then it was situational, and her getting a role would lift her up again. Abigail's spirits, on the other hand, lowered for no apparent reason. At first it was triggered by winter, but then she started sinking in the spring as well. My mother, from what I gathered, fell into a state shortly after my birth. I don't know the details surrounding it all; I only know it was bad, and from the moment I first overheard someone talking about it years later, I privately declared I would never have a baby of my own, for fear it might happen to me. Depression. Is it all the same? I don't believe so. There are different classes of it just as there are different seashells on the shore, and each must be identified, and while some can be left alone, others must be spotted and treated and cared for properly.

I sat down at the desk and continued to read:

Ava

A couple of weeks after spring's opening act, I was sitting with my family at the breakfast table eating smoked mullet, biscuits, and sea grape jelly, and smiling at my father, who went to great lengths to lure my mother out of bed. It was the morning I picked to announce my love for Jaden, and I had prayed the night before that the news might miraculously bring a smile to my mama's face.

I had also prayed heartily for Dahlia, who was lying on her tummy in the bed I dragged out of our bedroom, down the hallway, and into the kitchen myself so she could join us for breakfast and hear my declaration of love. A stingray had stung her on the behind the evening before, and I stayed up all night, soaking her in a nearly boiling bath after the attack. I then pulled pieces of the stingray's spine out of her wound and applied a cloth to stop Grandmalia from bleeding to death.

"I don't know if anyone else heard it, but I heard moaning last night," Abigail muttered.

"Maybe another woman was giving birth over at the lighthouse," said Stewart. "Apparently this is the season. The midwives can hardly keep up."

"Impossible," I said. "There's no way we could hear the screams of a woman all the way over at the lighthouse."

"Oh yeah?" Abigail said, looking up from her plate at me. "Until you give birth one day, you'll never have any idea how loud it makes a woman scream, Ava."

"Then I better start moving forward with securing a husband so I can endure all of that kind of torture while I'm still young and strong, don't you all think?" I asked, hoping to break into my news shortly thereafter.

"You're too young for boys," Stewart said.

"I'm eighteen."

"Yes, but your mother needs you still. Look at her."

"I see, but what's that have to do with my . . . ?"

"Ava!"

"Sorry, sir, but I could still be here for Mama and love a man, don't you think?"

I looked over at Dahlia, who was swigging from the medicinal whisky. "That depends, Ava," she said. "If you get married, you're going to have babies and you might be aware that a woman loses an ounce of sanity with each child she has. That's why I stopped after the third, you know."

"Thank you for that explanation," Stewart said. "Now I understand you better."

She flicked her fingers at him. "Is that any way to talk to a woman full of venom?"

I pushed my chair away from the table, having lost my appetite, and I walked over to Dahlia's bed and kneeled down to take a look at her wound. It hurt her horribly, I'm sure, but I was hurting, too. One would think it a good thing for a woman of eighteen to be in love, but not my parents. I think they were afraid that I might leave them, and then my mother would have no one to open up to anymore. As I dipped a clean cloth into water and gently scrubbed Grandmalia's wound, I thought of Jaden who would soon be standing there by our tree, waiting for me. Today was the last day of school, and I could hardly stand to think that the walks we took together to and from school each day had reached their end.

No one in my family knew that he was the reason I loved the sunrise and getting up in the morning and running out that door to start my day. I knew I had to tell them. I promised him I would in the spring. But spring's opening act had come and gone, and still I hadn't made any announcement. I hadn't told the world that Ava Witherton loves a man and wants to get married and have his babies. I hadn't told anyone and I didn't know whether I could keep Jaden patiently waiting a minute longer.

"If anyone heard any moans last night," I said, looking up, "they weren't from any woman giving birth over at the lighthouse. They were all from Grandmalia as I pulled pieces of stingray out of her behind. It was bad."

"How's it looking now?" Stewart asked.

"Slightly blue and swollen, but there's no more pus. I just don't want her dying from any allergic reaction," I said. "I wish you'd let someone other than me, a doctor or my father, take a look at it," I said to Dahlia.

"Don't go there," she snapped. "I already told you that no one but dear Milton's eyes have ever seen that area of my body."

Maybe she truly had lost three ounces of sanity for having three children because it made no sense at all that she'd let nobody but me see the wound on her ass, yet she got it from something as risqué as skinny-dipping in the first place. Stewart and I must have been thinking the same thing at the same time.

"With all due respect," he started at her. "I don't think it's wise for a woman of your age . . ." He stopped and cleared his voice. "I mean any woman to be skinny-dipping in that water, or any water. It's dangerous."

"A gal knows she is in the winter of her life when family members nearly half her age start telling her what she should and shouldn't be doing," she said, sipping more of her medicine. "Besides," she continued. "I'm not alone out there when I skinny-dip. I know my Milton is watching down from Heaven, keeping a close eye on me."

I laughed as did Stewart and even Abigail, I think.

"Those years before we were wed," continued Dahlia, "back when I was around your age, Ava, we used to skinny-dip together all the time, I might add."

Stewart cleared his throat. "I'm sure you did," he said, "but we're trying to raise a lady, and you're talking about an activity that ladies don't do."

"Leave me alone." She flagged her hand through the air. "I can say whatever I want. I'm in the winter of my life." She rolled slightly over on her side and continued. "I may not be the definition of a lady, but I don't care. I've lived life, and I don't want to forget the girl I was when I lived it to the fullest. We took all our clothes off and jumped into that pond outside the shed one spring night."

Stewart slammed the jar of jelly down on the table. "Too many details," he said, glancing over at me. I was kneeling beside her bed like a girl at a campfire, eager to hear more of the story and feeling a bit envious that my own grandmother, as old as she was, had more juicy details to share than I did at age eighteen. "We get the idea," Stewart said to her. "All I'll say to you is that if you go back out into that water, just stay on your feet and shuffle so the stingrays know you're coming. End of story."

Dahlia turned her head toward me and grumbled, "Why is it that everyone thinks they've surpassed me in knowledge?"

I stood up and took the bottle of whiskey from her hands. "I don't know," I said. "Everyone knows more than me, too. I guess you and I are both in those phases of life where no one thinks we know anything." I walked over to the hooks on the wall and took my school bag. I couldn't wait to open that door and run out, to meet up with Jaden, the boy I once knew and the man I still knew I would one day marry.

"Everyone on the island is having babies, it seems," muttered Abigail as I opened the front door. I turned to look at her, and she was gazing into space, holding the same piece of bread she had clutched the first moment she sat down. "I always wanted more than just one child," she said, then focused her eyes on me. "Don't ever leave my side, Ava. It would kill me."

The news I had all morning on the tip of my tongue now worked its way down my throat and into my gut where it secretly churned about, making me nauseated. I thought about Jaden, who was probably already there at the tree waiting for me and waiting to hear how my family reacted to the news that I loved him, madly loved him. I would have to tell him that this morning wasn't right. My mama couldn't handle the news. I walked over to her and planted a kiss on her cheek.

"You didn't follow me out there last night, did you, Ava?" she asked me.

"Follow you where?" I asked.

"To the beach, because if you plan to follow me, you've got to be quiet or you'll frighten them."

"Here we go again," Stewart uttered under his breath. "Who? Frighten who?" I asked her.

"The mother turtles."

"The turtles again. If you're really sneaking out at night to watch those giant-headed turtles on the beach, why don't you bring some home so we could cook up some soup at least?" asked Stewart.

"Why do you like to watch them, Mama?" I asked.

No one truly believed that my mother wandered out alone at night to watch any turtles, but we played along with her anyway. And if she did indeed sneak out, Stewart wouldn't know. He was the type to sleep through a hurricane.

Abigail stood up and ghost-like sauntered to the window and looked out at the darkness that would soon turn to light. "The full moon was shining last night," she said in a monotone. "And my friends arrived from the sea, dragging themselves along the beach in search of a good place to dig their nests."

"Did they find one? Did they dig their nests?" I asked.

"Yes. Then the mother turtles went back out to sea." She turned and walked over to where I was now sitting and combed her hands through my long hair. "They followed a glistening pathway that the moon created atop the water."

"It sounds beautiful," I said.

"It was. I'm thinking maybe I might head out to sea myself," she said, then kissed the top of my head and walked toward her bedroom. "Who knows? Maybe I will."

I followed her, but the door closed in my face. I felt queasier than when I tweezed the stingers out of Grandmalia's butt. What did my mother mean? Why would she want to head out to sea? I didn't want her going anywhere. I wanted her here, in the nest with me, but her mind had already swiftly propelled itself out there, to that portion of the sea where the sea turtles swim. I'd just have to wait for her to return again. It is a mystery to me how she does return, how she finds her way back to us after being gone so long, but she does. And I'd just have to wait and watch.

"Ava," Dahlia called out to me as I stood with my ear up to my mother's door. "None of what she says makes any sense."

"But why would a mother turtle abandon her eggs?" I asked.

"Why should you care if they do?" Stewart asked, looking at me as he always does when I try turning simple things into in-depth connections. "Never mind your mother. She's talking nonsense again," he said. "Now get yourself off to school or you'll be late."

I looked at Grandmalia. "Are you going to be okay today without me?"

"I'm fine," she said. "Especially now that my fever is gone. Listen to your father and get your behind out that door, young lady."

I did as I was told, and when I opened the door and stepped outside, I entered the world I loved, the one full of beauty and anticipation, and I ran as fast as a panther to meet up with Jaden by our tree.

Lydia

I was about to put the pages away and quietly leave when Marlena stepped into the room.

"Lydia" she said.

"Yes?"

"How did the reading go today?"

"Fine," I said. "But did Abigail ever go out to sea?"

"Don't take her literally," she said.

I didn't know how else to take that one, so I stood up and gave her a hug and then reached into my purse and pulled out a tissue.

"What is going on?" I asked her. "Is this really about your not getting any of the parts?"

"I'm not sure," she said through sniffles. "I get like this from time to time. It takes a few days, other times a few weeks before something happens to me."

"What? What happens?"

"I feel fine again. I function. I audition. I go out with friends. And then it hits me again, and I don't feel like doing anything."

"Is there anything I can do to help?"

"No. But do me a favor. Take some of Ava's pages with you. That way you can read them over at your place. I've got some cookies a neighbor brought over. You want those, too?"

"Are you sure?"

"Yeah. I'm just not in the mood for any cookies or company. Like I said, it's not you."

I felt disappointed as I gathered up a stack of pages. I liked coming to her place to read, but I also liked seeing her. But if space is what she wanted, I'd give her some, and then I'd return, and hopefully she'd be okay again. I tucked the pages into my bag.

"I'll read and return them soon."

"I know you will."

"Bye," I said, not sure whether leaving her like this was the right thing to do. "Would you like me to bring you flowers tomorrow?"

"No. I'll get outside and get some for myself. I need a task to get me going. Don't worry about me."

"Would you like to go to the beach with me?"

"Lydia," she said. "You better get going. This is my problem. I can't rely on someone else to restore my happiness. It's not that kind of sadness I'm dealing with. I'm not lonely, so you keeping me company isn't going to fix it."

"All right," I said. "I'll be going, then." And as I walked out her front door, I turned and said, "Did you know there's a patch of periwinkles at the bottom of your steps?"

I thought I saw her smile. Or maybe she just nodded. I waved and was on my way.

XXIII

JOSH AND I HADN'T snuck out at night for some time, but I told him there was something important that I wanted to do and it could only be done in darkness. There was a lot on my mind as I lay in bed waiting once more to hear his gentle tapping on my window. I had told him all about my relationship with Marlena and how she was letting me read an old journal belonging to a girl who once lived on the island. I told him I felt like the girl and I were friends. And I shared with him how Marlena filled a gap I felt in my life from not having a mother. I decided not, however, to tell him about the way Marlena looked and how she talked today. It troubled me, and I didn't know what to make of it.

"Hey, baby," he whispered as I opened the window. "You ready?"

"I am, but no fishing, boating, or sitting on my bed whispering, not tonight."

"You name it," he said. "What are you in the mood for?"

"There's a full moon, and there's something I'm itching to do," I said pulling the sheet off my bed and draping it over my shoulders.

"Sure, anything." He took my hand and helped me crawl through the window.

"Take me to the beach so I can see if it's true, if those mother turtles really dig their nests and then return to the sea."

"They do," he said. "It's a fact."

"I need to see it with my own two eyes."

On our way to the beach, Josh asked me why the sudden interest in watching turtles, but there are those things a girl doesn't feel like telling a boy. He asked me again as we quietly lay on our stomachs, watching and waiting for turtles, but there are also things a girl doesn't want anyone in the world to know.

And things nobody knows that she knows. I don't know what sort of depression propelled my own mother to take her life shortly after I was born. Weren't there any other options or steps she might have taken? I've never come to terms with how she could have done that, or why, and I don't think I ever will. It's not natural. Even parent pelicans stick around because their featherless newborn chicks need to rely on their body heat for warmth. No one tells them to, they just do, naturally. So why would a mother leave her babies motherless inside their eggs?

I have never asked anyone and never has anyone talked to me about it. I found out accidentally one day when I overheard Lloyd and Doctor Conroy talking about it. I can't imagine any mother laying eggs or giving birth and then disappearing. It makes no sense to me.

Josh and I hadn't been there long before a silent mother sea turtle emerged from the water and made her way across the sand. Soon she used her curved flippers to toss sand to the right and to the left. And when the holes were deep enough, she laid her eggs. She covered her nest with sand and, sure enough, she headed toward the shore. The moon was bright, and it formed a glistening pathway on the surface of the water, just as Abigail had mentioned. The mother turtle followed it out to sea.

"What's out there, Josh?"

"Water," he answered matter-of-factly.

"No, I mean after death. What is there after we die?"

"Heaven," he said.

"I don't know that I believe in any Heaven," I said. "Nor any God."

"Look at you," he said. "You're beautiful. You're a work of art. You don't think you just happened, do you?"

"I don't know what I believe. My father once told me people evolved from fish. He was busy analyzing a report when he told me, so I don't take it all that seriously. Do you believe anything about what he said?"

"No, I don't. I believe God created the Heavens and the Earth and . . ."

"Oh, shush," I said as I jumped up from the sheet and pulled him by his hands. "Don't get so serious on me. C'mon, let's go for a swim." I ran to the shoreline stopping just as the warm water touched my toes. I laughed thinking of poor Dahlia sick in bed, but then, stingrays or no stingrays, I decided I wasn't going to let some old lady living a century before me have more fun then me, so I slowly started unbuttoning my blouse.

"What are you doing?" Josh asked.

"I'm not going to wait until I'm an old fart to go skinny-dipping," I said as I pulled my blouse off my shoulders and tossed it to the sand. "Aren't you going to join me? It's not right for a lady to skinny-dip all alone."

I only had time for a quick peek as he unzipped his jeans and pulled them down, and then kicked them off his feet and into the air a bit too far, only to land down in the water. I laughed, and so did he, then I got back to my own arduous task of gracefully struggling to remove my easy stretch, cool lacey hug girdle without looking like a fool. It took so long to get the dang thing off that it ruined my spontaneous mood, and I started to have second thoughts, mostly concerning the recent tourist boom on the island.

"What's taking so long?" Josh called out. He was standing waist-high in the water and facing the moon.

"What if a tourist spots me?"

"They're not interested in you," he said, turning his head to see my rounded foam rubber contour shell bra drop to the ground. "Anything short of beaches, sunsets, shells, manatees, alligators, shorebirds, or dolphins would only disappoint them," he continued as I quickly tiptoed toward the water like a shorebird that might fly away at any moment. And when I stepped up beside him, waist-high in the water wearing nothing but the transparent light of the moon beaming across me, he smiled and said, "But if I were a tourist, I'd be interested in you, very much so."

I no longer cared about any tourist or local resident or even my father finding us there in the water. When Josh took hold of my hand and kissed me I felt as if we were the only two people on the island and I felt as much inner peace and calmness as one might expect from spending time at a wild- life refuge, exploring and observing, with lots of respect and restrictions, of course.

"We can't be a secret anymore," Josh finally said. "You've got to tell your father about us."

"What would I tell him?"

"That we've been seeing each other a lot and that I love you."

"You do?"

"Of course I do."

I looked up at the moon and for a woman in that moon, hoping she might tell me what to say, but there wasn't any woman up there and I never ever believed there to be any man in the moon and so I simply said, "I love you, too, but what about my father not paying for my tuition come fall?" And I said both together in one sentence.

"Isn't what we have together more important than any of that?" Josh asked.

"Any of what?"

"That—that which you're chasing after and hoping to find out there in the world."

"My education and career? Is that what you mean?"

"I guess," he said.

"It's time we get going." I started walking quickly toward the shore. "We've been out here too long, and I'm started to feel creepy."

"Look," he continued when we reached the shore and started putting our clothes back on. "I didn't mean to upset you, Lydia. I support you doing whatever it is you need to do in life, but I know what all of that means. It means you're going to leave here in a few weeks and we're going to have to say 'good-bye.' I just want to make sure that leaving is what you really want. What is it that you want, Lydia?"

I beat him in getting dressed, shoes and all, and just as he asked me again what I wanted, I spotted a lump on the sand. I walked over to it, only to recognize it as my girdle. "To never wear this wretched thing again," I said, picking it off the beach and bunching it into my arms. "That's what I want."

He didn't find it as funny as I did. "Seriously now," he said. "What is it that you want?"

I took a tight hold of his hand and said, "I want to get back now. C'mon, let's go." And as we walked back to my place, I thought about what I wanted and I wondered whether it all fell into that category of things a girl shouldn't or should tell the boy she loves. Freedom. I wanted the freedom to make my own choices. To marry or not. To work or not. To both marry and work or not. To marry who I want and not who I should. To have one, two, three, or four babies or to have no babies whatsoever. It's a woman's right to have the opportunity to make such choices in life, isn't it? Something inside told me that 'yes,' of course it is, but along with such freedom of choice comes responsibility to later accept the choices a woman makes for her life. When she makes her own choices, there's no one down the road she can blame.

"Freedom," I said as I opened my window. "I want the freedom to make my own choices, Josh." I climbed through and into my bed and rolled to my side so I could still safely talk to Josh as we had done so many nights before.

He didn't balance himself halfway in and out the window like usual, and his whisper was different, too. "I respect how you feel," he said. "When you make your choice regarding me, let me know. Until then, maybe I'll see you around." He started to close the window.

"Wait," I said, jumping up and putting my hands on the window to stop it. "What do you mean?"

"You know exactly what I mean. You're the one with choices to make." He was talking louder than usual.

"Shhh," I insisted. "My father will hear you."

"Good," he said. "I'm sick of sneaking around. I don't like being your little secret anymore; so, until you feel sure of yourself, there's not much I can do but continue as I do and as I did before we met."

Both my hands and his were on the window, and he was ready to close it while I was keeping it open. When it closed, I grabbed my pillow off my bed and whipped it at the window. He left.

As much as I wanted them, I also hated having choices because there was nothing easy about them. I laid back down again and let my mind drift down a potential road where I saw myself watching the sunrise every morning with Josh, and it was good, but then, I wondered what might happen if we ever chose to have a baby. I couldn't stand to think about what happened to my mother, the depression and all after she gave birth to me, and I wondered whether I had any choice with regard to that or not.

I thought of Ava. Her mother also had a form of depression. I wondered whether that might stop her from moving forward with Jaden. When I couldn't turn the thoughts off in my mind, I turned on the light and reached under my bed for Ava's journal pages. I began to read.

XXIV

AVA

I STOPPED RUNNING TO say a quick prayer to God, that he might heal Dahlia's wound, and just as soon as I said, "Amen," I took off running once more, this time, smooth and relaxed as an osprey flies in the direction of our tree. But when I arrived, Jaden wasn't there, so I hovered around a moment, unsure whether I should continue on to school without him or wait. I had been coming to this tree now year after year, and it was comfortable as a nest, I thought as I leaned against the tree and let my mind wander.

My thoughts soared off to a world in which I wanted to live, one where Jaden and I would anchor our boat out in the bay before sunrise each day. His line would already be cast by the time the sun peeked over the horizon, and my mind would be conjuring what it wanted to write. With the first beams of light, I would enter my thoughts on paper, and he would reel in his fish. And soon babies, then children would join us in the boat, and probably, I thought with a chuckle, replace my writing. It didn't matter. We'd live, "Happily ever after," I declared out loud.

"Whom?" A nearby voice asked.

It startled me, and I jumped away from the tree with a quick scream, ready to attack an intruder, but then I spotted his shadow and knew it was only Jaden.

"You scared me to death," I said, kicking him in his shin. "I thought you were an owl. What were you doing?"

"Waiting for you," he said. "I waited so long that when I heard you coming, I thought I'd hide behind the tree and make you wait for me. Then I heard you say, 'happily ever after.' Whom were you talking about?"

"Us," I said with a smile.

He laughed. "Does that mean you've told your family that you love me?"

I couldn't answer him, so I turned my head and let my eyes travel far off across the Gulf of Mexico. Other than her strangeness that day in the periwinkles, Jaden knew nothing about my mama's bouts of sadness. I couldn't possibly tell him how she sank into the ground all the time and that according to the stories, my granddaddy Milton experienced the same. What would it say about me and who I might become? According to Dahlia, I was at risk. She says these sorts of conditions are often passed down through families, and I feared she might be right. I hadn't fully sunk, but there were days here and there where like a sand dollar I want-ed to partially bury myself beneath the sand, and it confused me because I wasn't shy by nature. But this wasn't the sort of thing I could tell the man I loved. I didn't want it interfering with the way he loved me.

He gently took hold of my face and turned it toward him. As I looked him in the eyes, I could think of nothing worse in life than losing my zest and joy and freedom to love him the way I wanted to love him.

"You look off to sea," he said. "Did you tell your family about us?"

"No, but I'm closer than you think," I said. "Do you know anything about mother turtles?"

He smirked and walked off. "You've got to be kidding me," he said. "What are you trying to do? You think you can just keep me hanging and then just switch the topic over to turtles when you know there's only one thing on my mind and it's us? Why the hell would I care about mother turtles at a time like this?"

"Because I do," I said, following after him. "There's a reason for it. I was wondering if you knew why they come to shore to lay their eggs and then return to sea. Isn't that abandonment?"

He stopped walking and I bumped right into him, annoying him more than ever. "Of course not," he said, looking at me as if I were stupid. "It's the opposite. It's not safe for them on land. They follow the light of the moon as it shines down on the water and they go out to sea to survive. They're doing what they must to survive."

"Oh," I answered just as the sun reached through the branches of a tree and touched me on my cheek. "That makes sense."

I know he was hurt that I hadn't yet told my family about us, but I could hardly keep from smiling as I took his hand in mine and we walked the rest of the way to school. I felt peace just thinking about the glistening pathway atop the water, for it had represented survival, not abandonment. Jaden didn't know it, but as we walked, I silently vowed that if ever I felt down to where I could hardly get out of bed, I would force myself to think of the glistening pathway that the moon by night, and perhaps more so the sun by day, creates atop the water, and it would prompt me to get up and take my own glistening steps to survival, whatever those steps might be. I'd have to determine when and if the time should ever come.

Just before I stepped foot into school, I glanced back out at the sky with its spring thunderstorm brewing and gave a silent thanks to the Creator for giving us an intricate and infinite world, one that if we look closely enough only leads to a respect for life and healing, not destruction. And there's wisdom in it, too.

Lydia

I stopped reading. It pained me to think what my mother had done. Taking one's own life is so unnatural, a thing to do it defies the laws of nature and she abandoned me in the act. I set the journal down, held my left hand up and closed my eyes. "I am with you once more, Ava," I declared out loud. "If ever the time comes, I, too, will take whatever glistening steps are necessary for the sake of my survival."

When I opened my eyes, I noticed the most colorful-headed bird sitting on a branch of the banyan tree outside the window, and I thought about God. I wondered if maybe Ava's belief were true, that a supreme being was indeed the creator of Heaven and Earth. Just in case, I closed my eyes once more and muttered, "Dear God, thank you for such beauty." I opened my eyes, not sure whether He heard me, but it felt nice having someone to thank.

I continued my reading:

Ava

When the doors of the school house opened, and I stepped out, I felt like losing my temper at the rain, not that I had anything against the rain, but I had to get mad at something, for I had sat all through school feeling angry with my family for not wanting me to fall in love.

"We can wait over there, under the canopy of that tree," Jaden said, taking my books and shoving them under his shirt so they wouldn't get wet.

"To hell with the rain," I said, the first to step outside. "It can do to me whatever it likes." I started walking with an attitude as if I wanted to prove that rain could do me no harm. I knew Jaden was following close behind. He was a nature boy, and nature boys love getting wet and dirty and all that good stuff. But then once lightning struck probably five feet away from us, I stopped my tough-woman act and let myself run straight into his arms. We stood there a moment, unsure whether we should out-run the future strikes or lie down and pretend we were just two innocent sticks tossed to the ground. I never saw such fear in Jaden's eyes before, but I wasn't sure whether it was fear of lightning or fear of what might happen between the two of us.

"Ava," he declared, once we decided to take a few steps. "The time has come. You've got to tell your daddy that you love me and I love you and we've loved each other for a long, long time now."

I looked up and let the rain slap me across the face. "I can't," I said. "You just don't know. You wouldn't understand."

"Understand what?"

"Everything," I shouted and took off running through the mudflats.

Jaden would never understand. A man can't feel what a woman feels when she's worried about her mama. I could hear him running behind me and knew he was probably creating tracks that resembled a squirrel bounding over the ground, leaving marks that were wide apart with the foot flared. Wide apart always meant running. My hind feet were also paired and placed ahead of the marks left by my front feet. Tracks such as the ones we were leaving might make someone wonder who was chasing whom, and with what result?

I probably could have outrun any other boy in the world, but not Jaden. He followed me through the mudflats, and when he caught up with me, he grabbed onto my waist, and we both went smacking down into the shallow marshy water. I looked as bad as I looked the very first time we ever walked to school together, after he startled me and I fell.

"This is what I'm going to do," he said, pulling me off the ground.

For a moment, he searched my eyes, and I wondered whether we were both thinking the same thing. I wondered whether he wanted to risk everything and kiss me in broad daylight.

"I'm going to give you space," he said instead.

"What kind of space?"

"Just space. I'm not going to show up outside your bedroom window, knocking in the middle of the night."

"You're not?"

"Nope," he said. "I'm not that nutty. And, believe me, I was thinking of it. I was planning to take you out to that beach, to let you observe for yourself those turtles, but not now."

"When am I going to see you again?"

"You're not, at least not until you're ready to tell your parents everything and to marry me."

"Wait a minute. What did you just say?"

"You heard me. I'm not going to repeat it."

I laughed like I did the first night at the shack when he told me he'd one day marry me. But then he reached deep into his pocket and started fishing around for something.

"My God," I said, expecting to see a diamond, my first diamond.

"It's not what you think," he said, pulling out a shell with brown squares all over it. "It's a Junonia shell."

"It's beautiful," I said, taking it from his hand. "It's better than any diamond. Where'd you find it?"

"A trip to Captiva the other day. I thought you'd love it. Keep it as a reminder and a promise that I plan to marry you and that I'm waiting around. It's all up to you right now. I don't know what else to do."

"It's not up to me," I said, softly. "I don't know what to do. It's impossible to know."

"What is? What's impossible?"

I thought of all the things I hated in the world, of our walks to school ending, of ironing and washing, of being too busy to read a fine novel or to write one myself, of winters back in Kentucky and how I hated them so and now of spring and my mother's gloom. Then I thought of the two things I loved: Jaden and writing. Both felt impossible to me now, with my mother's latest relapse and my taking on extra household chores in her place. I felt a chill, the kind that only comes in the winter. But this was spring, and it was Florida. "Impossible," I stated.

"Nothing is impossible," Jaden said.

"Oh yeah?" I said, searching in my mind for something that was indeed impossible, something he couldn't argue with. "Snow on Sanibel. It's impossible."

He shook his head. "You've got it wrong, Ava. Anything is possible. I'm sure of it."

I laughed. "Damn," I said. "Why are you always so optimistic?"

We walked arm-in-arm until the point where our paths usually went separate ways, but that day we continued hand-in-hand along my path, and then we kissed beneath the rain, and I was glad he couldn't see the tears rolling down my cheeks at the same time. When the rain stopped, but my tears continued, I turned and walked toward my house, and headed back in the direction of his. I knew I wouldn't see him for quite some time again.

Lydia

So that was that. I closed the journal, turned out the light, and got back into bed. If Ava could take time off from the boy she loved, then so could I—not that I wanted to be the sort to wear red or jump off a cliff just because my best friend was wearing red or jumping off a cliff, but in this case, I didn't know what else to do. Taking time away from Josh suddenly made sense to me. And how difficult would that be?

XXV

LYDIA

SOME THINGS IN LIFE are difficult, I realized as I faithfully studied the shore, hoping to spot a Junonia. It was late summer, and soon I'd be leaving without that one rare and special shell.

I had been spending much of my time searching for shells, and I especially liked doing it an hour before or after low tide when everything was more exposed. The tides and the rain told me as much as any clock or calendar ever could, and they constantly reminded me that summer was progressing by the way the rain that once hit early was now coming later in the day. The seashells at low tide, the ninety-degree temps thanks to a sea breeze, and even the later afternoon thunderstorms that cooled things off and forced me to nap, were all simple. It was finding a Junonia that was difficult.

My aching back from stooping, my devoted yet unfulfilled desire to spot a Junonia, and my decision to go without seeing Josh were not simple. They were difficult, and I floated aimlessly around like a spineless, brainless, heartless, bloodless blob, a jellyfish ready to sting anything or anyone that came too close.

By late July Lloyd had fully regained his health. I had noticed him talking money more than golf and knew he was returning to his old self again. And I was glad for him when his one true love, the bank, called and welcomed him back. It had been simple for him to leave the island and return to work a couple of weeks earlier than we had planned, and it was simple for me to stay there on my own and finish up my summer on Sanibel before starting college.

I left the beach, losing faith that I would ever spot a Junonia and doubting whether they existed on the beaches of Sanibel at all. Maybe it was all a hoax and they were occasionally planted out there by some tourism promoter. I was disappointed and wondered if this was how devoted people feel when they want a miracle so badly and don't get one.

When I got back to the cottage, I checked on my latest shells soaking in a solution of half bleach and half water. The bleach in no way altered their color, and I was glad. Then I reviewed my latest arts-and-crafts project—shells turned into twenty-five Santa Claus ducks lined up along my windowsill. They were dry, and that was good. I didn't know whom I was going to give them to when the season finally rolled around, but I'd worry about that when the time came. I was ready to move onto something new, like a seashell mirror, maybe.

Later that day, after the thunderstorm and my nap, I decided to go to the local seashell shop to buy a Junonia. And I felt like I was buying myself a miracle as I handed the girl the money and she handed me the shell—that simple.

"I know I get obsessive about things," I muttered to myself as I walked out of the shop carrying a bag filled to the rim with every other type of seashell. It had been my fault that I couldn't see over the tips of the lightning whelks and I bumped into someone, but I didn't care. I was more worried about my shells crashing to the ground. I fell to my knees and started gathering them up.

"Lydia refuses to tell father about the boy she loves," a male voice said from above me.

I don't think that's what he really said, but my mind sometimes heard things in the form of headlines only. "Josh?" I stood up, leaving a few of my purchased seashells in the gravel so someone else might experience what they consider a miracle to be. "Sorry for bumping into you. What did you just say?"

"How are you and your father doing?"

"Good. He's back in Chicago."

"So you're here alone?"

"Yes, just for another few days," I glanced down at the driveway and spotted my most precious of all purchased shells, the one with the brown squares all over it, still lying beside someone's tire. "I wanted so darn bad to find a Junonia on the beach before I left," I said, bending down to pick it up.

"I bought one today. I guess I've given up."

"Don't ever give up," he said. "Why would you give up?"

"On to new things, I guess. I'm headed back to the city and to school and finding a Junonia in the city is definitely impossible."

"Good point, but you'll be back one day, won't you?"

"I hope. You think you'll always be here?"

"Where else would I be other than here?"

I smiled, but he looked grim. "I'll look you up when I return," I said, formally.

He smirked, then took a couple of steps away as if he were about to wave and be off, but then he drew close, looked up to the sky, then back into my eyes. "Humor me for a moment," he said. "There's something I need to know."

"Sure, what is it?"

He took his hat off and ran his hands through his hair. "Do I mean anything to you?"

"Of course you do," I said, wanting to tell him he meant almost everything, but I couldn't. My education and career plans back home meant something, too, and I was so close to starting my journey toward accomplishing them. "You are the rarest boy I've ever met."

"I'm not a damn seashell," he said, rolling his eyes and laughing.

"I know you're not," I said, laughing as well and mentally kicking myself for letting my Junonia obsession slip out via my choice of words. "But here, take this. I don't want it anymore." I picked the Junonia off the pile of store-bought shells and handed it to him. I no longer wanted it. It wasn't like I had found it the authentic way. "Keep it as a reminder and a promise that I will return and I will come looking for you."

"How will you recognize me? I'll probably be an old man by then."

"No. I'll come back before then. I've got to. I want to be young and beautiful when I find my own Junonia on the beach and get my picture in the paper."

"Your picture in the paper for finding a shell? That's ridiculous."

"Josh," I said. "If there's one thing I'm confident in about myself, it's deciphering what is and what is not newsworthy. Believe me, the Gulf of Mexico handing over such a priceless and prized possession is definitely newsworthy. I'm telling you now that I will return and I will find what I'm looking for." I stepped close and kissed him on his lips.

"What if I'm married and have six kids by then?" he asked when the kiss ended.

"You won't be," I said. "You can't get married without me here."

"Okay," he said, tossing the shell up into the air, then catching it. "But you're gambling with time and a guy's heart. I just want you to know you're taking chances, Lydia." He put the shell into the pocket of his jeans. He looked at his watch. "Unfortunately, I've got to get going now."

"I understand," I said, then kissed him again. "You want to come over tonight?"

He smiled and didn't answer. It was the sort of smile that made me think he wasn't going to come over. He was better than that. And I felt uneasy about the space I had placed between us and the space to come.

He got into his truck. and I watched as he backed out of the parking space and turned onto Periwinkle Way. He waved. and so did I. And I wondered if he ever shed a tear. I did as I stood there another five minutes, wondering whether I was making the right choices in life. How could I know for sure? Doesn't it take years of hindsight to know whether the choices a woman makes are for better or worse? Why does it have to be so hard, all these choices in life? Why can't anything be simple? And why can't I be a typical woman who just fell in love with a man from the suburbs and got married?

"Because you're not a typical woman," I said to myself as I started to walk toward Marlena's. "And because you fell in love with a different guy. It's just the way it is."

XXVI

MARLENA HUGGED ME IN the doorway. "I'm sorry for how I've been," she said. "Please come in. It's nothing you've done or said. I just haven't felt myself."

"Don't worry," I said. "I'm glad you're okay."

"Yes, so am I. How much longer are you here for?"

"A few days."

"I'm sorry to hear that. I'm going to miss you."

"I know. I'm going to miss you, too."

"Your eyes don't look right. Have you been crying?" she asked. "Is it your father?"

"No. Josh and I said goodbye today. It was my decision to say goodbye for now."

"For now? What does 'for now' mean?"

It suddenly sounded so ludicrous to me. "For now means college, then maybe graduate school, then my career and . . ."

"Sounds more like forever to me."

"No," I insisted. "It's just for now." I then reached into my bag and pulled out the pages I had read last. "Here, I brought these back."

She reached out and took them from me. "Let me see just where you're at with your reading," she said, her eyes scanning the last page. "Ah, yes, I was wondering if you got that far." She looked up at me. "Why don't you go into the room and start the next pages while I make us a lunch."

"Sounds good," I said as I walked into the yellow room, glad to have the old Marlena back. And I think she was glad to see me return. It was like old times again, and I could hear her humming the tune "Jingle Bells" softly from the kitchen as I pulled out a stack of pages. I thought it odd that she'd be humming a holiday tune now, in summertime, but I was more curious to find out how Ava was faring during her time off from Jaden. I began to read:

SANIBEL ISLAND
1894

Ava

There ought to be a refuge inside every woman whereher joy can flutter and her wisdom breed and her dreams nest and her mi akes land softly and the words her mother or grandmother or others have spoken flap about like butterflies and all these things can mingle and thrive harmoniously as long as they like, or they can enter the world by way of her lips.

"Jingle shell, jingle shell, jingle shell, rock," I sang out loud as I sat down at my desk and shook a handful of seashells. It was a late December evening, and it was unusually cold. But there was so much to be joyful about. A strong northwestern had cast millions of seashells upon the beach, and my mother and I spent the day together stooped over in search of treasures. We came home with a ton of pearly translucent shells and discovered that a handful of them would "jingle" when we shook them.

I placed the shells in my drawer and pulled out my journal. I opened it to a blank page. It had been way too long since I last wrote, and I had some catching up to do. I dipped my pen in the ink, ready to leave tracks all over the smooth white pages of my journal as to where I had been and where I was going.

After my last day of school, I had worked hard through summer, and come fall I felt as drab as the warblers looked, doing my own chores and those belonging to my mother. And since Dahlia was getting older and doing less, I took on her work as well. They both needed me as much as mollusks need the water to survive. I tried to be there for them, physically extending myself around their every need, but my mind was its own, and I let it drift toward Jaden. I hardly saw him but in passing, and I missed our walks to school together, but the schoolhouse blew down in an eerie autumn wind, so even if we were still of age to be students those walks would have ended.

Just then there was a knock at my door. It was my mother. "How'd I know you'd be sitting here without stockings on your feet?" she said with a scolding smile. "Here, I brought you your favorite drink."

"Warm milk, honey, and butter?"

"And cinnamon." She set the teacup down on my desk, and I took a sip.

She stood there for a moment, running her fingers through my long hair, and I wondered whether she were trying to read what all I had written; so, I closed my journal and shifted in my chair to face her. "The tea is good, but it tastes different tonight."

"Yes," she said, rolling her eyes. "You can thank your Grandmalia for that. She added an ounce of brandy. Thought it might take the chill out of the air."

"It's working. My toes are warming up," I said, taking another couple of sips.

"Good." She reached down and kissed me on the cheek. "I'll let you get back to your writing."

"Thanks, Mama. I love you."

"I love you, too, darling. I love you so much."

In early December hundreds of white pelicans had arrived, and my mama started rising before the sun like she used to. We could hear her tinkering with the pots or filling the water, and it was as if someone waved a magic wand and turned her back into the other Abigail once again. I was so ready for the happy Abigail to reappear that I jumped up from bed one morning clapping my hands and skipping around the house. But how long until she disappeared again? None of us knew. The Bible says we can ask

for anything at all, and so I prayed that the happy Abigail might stay forever. I tried not to think about the part of scripture that says if it's God's
will. I only wanted to think about my will, and it was plain and simple—
that Jaden still loved me after all these months apart.

After several more sips of hot tea, I noticed it was harder to write and
easier to think about Jaden. I was preparing to tell my parents any day now
that I loved him and could hardly wait for the moment when I could go running over to his house with the news that we no longer had to be a secret and
that we could start back up again loving each other where we left off the last
day of school. The time was right. Mama was feeling good again, and things
were going well for my parents. They had a fine winter crop of tomatoes; so
fine that earlier in the day a man offered my father a hefty sum for it all.
Stewart was only playing poker when he told the man to come back in a day
or two. The crop was beautiful, and we all agreed we could get a bit more
out of the man if we strung him along for a day or two.

I stood up from my desk and tippy-toed over to my bed and pulled the
Junonia Jaden gave me out from under my pillow. "Tomorrow, the last Friday of December is the day," I whispered. "I will tell my parents everything and get back together with Jaden in the morning." I climbed into
bed and tucked the blanket around my body, and a few minutes later I
heard Dahlia entering the room and crossing the floor toward her bed. I
was so tired from the day and from the brandy that I never said
"good-night."

I slept deeply, like a bear hibernating through winter, but when I awoke
the next morning, way before sunrise, something didn't feel right. The ef-
fects of the brandy had long worn off, and the coldness in the room felt
more like Kentucky cold than Florida cold and it made me feel delicate as
a dainty bird.

"Grandmalia," I whispered across our room. "I'm cold. Aren't you?"
there was no answer, just the wind blowing outside our window. "You're
not snoring," I continued. "So I know you're awake. Talk to me,
Grandmalia."

When there was still no answer, I feared she might be dead, and because I didn't feel like facing that right now, I pulled the blanket up over

my head, but then my toes stuck out so I sat up to cover them and lay back down again, only to feel my toes exposed once more. I refused to believe that Grandmalia might be dead; so, I tried once more to strike up a conversation.

"I'll bet granddaddy Milton would love this weather," I said, knowing she never passed up an opportunity to talk about Milton. "He loved the cold, didn't he? Didn't he used to say if life dumps snow on you, build a snowman? Tell me something new I don't know about Milton."

When she didn't respond by starting her same old story about the snowman Milton built in the sand one year, I sat up and glanced over at her bed, ready to face the sad truth. But there was no lump under her covers, and I knew by the flatness of her bed that she was alive but missing, which in this chilling weather could turn out to be just as bad. It was too early to start chores, so where could she be?, I wondered, as I placed my feet on the wooden floor. She long ago gave up skinny-dipping for spending early mornings wading along with the large flocks of shorebirds, gulls, and terns that arrived with the start of winter. That's probably where she was this morning, I thought, wondering why the cold air didn't stop her.

Just then the door in our bedroom, the one that leads outdoors, flung open, slamming against the wall, and a gust of bitter air howled in and whipped me across the face. I froze with fear, as a dark figure wearing a cape appeared in the doorway. "Get out of here," I yelled, "whoever you are. I've got a rifle and I'll use it."

"Milton used to say that too," said the body in the doorway. "But he had the worst aim. Everyone knew it, even the bandits. I always feared we'd get robbed because of it." The floorboards creaked as Dahlia, wrapped in a blanket, not a cape, crossed the room, and then sat down on the side of my bed.

"I was worried about you," I said, putting my arm around her shivering body and laying my head on her shoulder. "You shouldn't be out in this cold weather all by yourself so early in the morning."

"I know. It's blowing great guns."

"Then why did you go out? What were you doing out there?"

"Would you believe me if I told you it's snowing out there?" she asked.

"No," I said. "It's impossible. It can't snow in Florida."

"I swear I'm not fibbing."

"You swear on granddaddy Milton's grave?"

"I can't swear on his grave. We don't know where it is. If I were to bet you on it, I'd say Egypt or California. Did I ever tell you . . . ?"

"Yes, you did," I said, draping the blanket from my bed over my shoulders. "C'mon, show me that snow." I took hold of the damp, stiff sleeve of her nightgown, and we scurried to the door, tugged it open, and stepped into a subtropical winter wonderland kingdom where anything was indeed possible.

It looked as if billions of white egrets were shedding their feathers, but, no, it was snow, pretty and white as the island sand. Heaping mounds were forming atop the green fronds of the palms while single flakes were landing on my nose. Crystal icicles were hanging from wooden posts nearby, and I thought for sure the sun had overslept today or taken its first day off in the history of the world, but then the ground around my feet lit with orange and one hundred shades of pink, and I knew that the good old sun was reporting for duty.

I felt like collecting the snowflakes in a jar before they melted or running into the house to enter everything I was seeing into my journal so it would never be forgotten. But I didn't want to miss anything as it was happening. I would write about it later, once my fingers weren't so stiff.

"Grandmalia," I said, looking deep into her eyes. "What's the one thing you want most?"

She must have been in an inspired mode of thinking like me, because her answer came without any hesitation. "That Milton and my love for him won't ever be forgotten."

I rubbed her hands vigorously and said with a smile, "That's it? That's all you want?" I shook my head as she nodded. "I can help you with that. That's easy," I said.

"How?" she asked.

"I'll put your love for Milton into writing. I'll write all about the two of you in my journal. Then, I'll turn it into a novel one day so the whole world will read of it. Novels last forever, Grandmalia. That's why I want to be a novelist. So I can create something that lasts forever. Do you believe I can do it? Do you believe that anything is possible?"

"With God," she said. "Don't forget God. Anything is possible with God."

I took hold of her other hand as well, and we circled around like two little girls playing "ring around the rosy." I was full of purpose in my life and happier than I had ever felt before. I already knew I wanted to write a novel, but now I saw it as a way of keeping Grandmalia and the man she loved alive and remembered forever. I'd pass it on to my own daughter who would then hand it to hers, then hers, and hers straight down the line until, by golly, some futuristic great-, great-, great- and so on granddaughter of mine, living in the new millennium, if the world still exists then, if our Savior doesn't return by then, will know all about Grandmalia and her love for Milton and me and my love for Jaden. And because anything is possible with fiction, I could even create between Abigail and Stewart a love that would make the lovebirds envious.

And thinking of birds, in my book I would make Grandmalia's nose smaller and more feminine. There's no need for the world to think of her with a beak. And Abigail would be such a happy character that circus clowns would travel from all over to train with her for a week.

"Anything is possible with God," I said as we stopped circling and bumped into each other out of dizziness. "As it is with fiction."

We tried walking, but we slipped, and since I was the leader I made sure to fall first and then catch Gandmalia in my lap. I posed there on the ground like a frozen statue, holding her as both of us tilted our heads back and welcomed more snow, like flakes of chilled coconut into our mouths.

"Dreadful," a man's voice rang out. "Do you two have any idea what this weather means to us?"

I felt numb and couldn't answer. Maybe I didn't want to. The world around me was glowing pink from the rising sun, and there was no room for anything negative in a moment as fleeting as this, where I believed anything at all was possible and close at hand. But then a dark shadow showed up on the ground in front of me.

"Our crops have been killed to the ground. Our crops, everyone's crops— dead, frozen," said the shadow. It was Stewart, and he was looking ornery as a stone crab.

"People are saying this is the coldest morning in the history of Florida," my mother said walking up beside him. "We've lost it all. So much for that man and his offer—the tomatoes are ruined. The oranges, too, and not just the oranges," she continued. "But the trees. They're also dead."

I no longer felt ripe with inspiration, nor numb, but rather bruised, dented, and destroyed as I jumped up from the ground and pulled my grandmother up as well. "What does this all mean?" I stepped up eye-level to my father. "What's going to happen now?"

He shook his head and kicked an icicle beside his foot. "You're talking to a man who just lost one hundred and sixty acres of fertile land. I haven't any answers, blossom."

"You've got to have answers," I insisted. "I mean, what are we going to do?"

"First thing that comes to mind is leave."

"No. What do you mean by that? You mean leave the island? Us?"

He shrugged his shoulders and then meandered over to the icicle hanging from the post. He gave it a nudge and it swung back and forth before crashing to the ground.

"We've got to look on the bright side," I said. "We still own land on Sanibel."

"It's worthless now," he said, stomping his shoe over the ice.

"Land is never worthless," I cried as my father walked into the house. "We can start over."

"Everything," Abigail said through violet lips. "Everything we grew together. Our tomatoes, peppers, eggplant, and watermelon—destroyed! It's not just us. I was over talking to the neighbors on both sides, and it's the same for them, for everyone."

"The damn freeze," stuttered Dahlia. "The damn freeze has killed us all."

"How can you say that?" I said sharply. "You just said anything was possible with God."

"Yes," she said, "be it His will."

I was mad now, madder than ever. I couldn't possibly believe that it was God's will for us to be defeated and not start over and not see the slightest good in it all, that we were still alive and our land was still here, frozen and our crops destroyed, but the land still intact. My mama stared trance-like at me, then put her arm around Dahlia, and as I watched them walk into the house together, I felt like hollering after them. "Where's your wisdom?" I mumbled under my breath. "The two of you, as old as you are, ought to have lots of it stored up deep within, ready to be pulled out in such moments as this."

I feared my mother heard my words because just as she arrived at the door of the house, she turned and said back to me, "You better come in now. We can't stay on this island any longer. We'll be making arrangements to leave."

"Leave Sanibel? Where? Where will we go?"

"I don't know, yet," she said, and then disappeared into the house.

I wanted to cry, but my ducts were frozen shut so nothing could drip forth. Instead, the tears swelled up inside my head and flooded my thoughts. I didn't know which way to turn, and I reached down into my own jar of wisdom and rummaged around for ideas, anything I might grasp to keep from slipping under.

Go in that house. Go for a walk. Find Jaden. Find Jaden. Go in that house. Pour yourself some brandy. Find Jaden. Go for a walk. Brandy. Jaden. Find Jaden. Find Jaden. Find Jaden—it was the one idea that kept surfacing above all the others so I took hold of it, knowing it was the wisest and strongest branch of an idea.

I had to find Jaden.

Lydia

My hands were shaking as I returned the pages to the drawer and jumped up from the desk. "Marlena," I cried as I ran through the halls. "Marlena!"

"Lydia, what is it?"

"It's Josh," I said. "I have to find him."

"Wait, darling," she said, following after me to the front door.

"I can't wait. I have to find him."

"Lydia Isleworth, you will wait right here for just one moment, and if you don't, I won't let you read any more of Ava's journal."

I stopped at the bottom of her steps and sat down in the dirt, then watched her go back into the house. Yes, I'd sit in dirt just to read more of that journal. It was better than sitting on ice. A moment later Marlena returned.

"Here, take these with you," she said, handing me more pages. "I think it's important that you read what happens next."

"Does she leave the island or stay behind with Jaden? That's all I really need to know."

"Why don't you read it for yourself. I suggest you find a nice quiet spot, like the lighthouse, maybe." She raised her hands up in the air. "Look at me," she said. "I should stop meddling. Read them wherever you like. Now go, young lady. Go find that boy of yours!"

XXVII

UNLIKE AVA'S WINTRY DAY, mine was a hazy lazy humid one, and I wondered under which conditions was it easiest to run fast. But it wasn't a race, I decided, as I took off running toward the marina as fast and erratically as a hawk flies, creating my own breeze as I went. Ava and I were on missions of our own, but very much alike, both en route to tell those boys that we loved them and we were no longer leaving the island. We were staying because of them.

As I spotted the marina and Max hosing down a boat from a distance, I circled the area while wiping sweat from my forehead and thinking about all that I would be giving up but also gaining by telling Josh about my decision to stay. And my love for him gave me a lift and nearly made me crash-dive as a hawk does, right to the spot where Max was standing.

"Is Josh around?" I blurted out as if hunting for prey.

"Hi, Lydia, good to see you," said Max, turning off the water. "He left a little while ago."

"To *where*?"

"Key West with a few of his buddies."

"*What*?"

"Guys' trip."

"*How* long ago did he leave?"

"A couple of hours ago."

"You're kidding me."

"No, they've been wanting to go for some time now."

"*When* will he be back?" I asked.

He gave me the same look the ranger had at the start of summer when I asked when I might see the hundreds of hawks up in the sky. It was the kind of look that told me you're not going to see that amazing sight until September.

"In about a week," Max replied.

"That puts us into September, doesn't it?"

"I think it does. I haven't looked at any calendar in quite some time, but . . ."

"I'll be starting school by then."

"I wish you the best, young lady. You're smart. I'm sure you'll do great."

I stared Max in the eyes, wondering whether I should tell him what I came here to tell his son, that I love him and would have stayed for him. But then I thought about the guys' weekend in Key West and that maybe Josh wasn't missing me as much as I thought. Besides, it had only been a summer. Suddenly I questioned how I could love someone after only a summer, and I wondered whether it was love or obsession.

"I better get going," I said. "I've got a million things to do before I start school. Just tell Josh I stopped by to say, 'good-bye.'"

"I sure will. and I wish you the best with all your plans."

"Thank you, Max," I said and turned and walked off slowly. Despite my wanting to get away, I couldn't run. It was no longer early morning and not yet late afternoon, but rather that in-between time of day that made me walk slowly. Besides, there was no need to hurry. I wouldn't be around in September to see Josh return nor the hundreds of sharp-shinned hawks passing through Florida's skies.

There was only one thing left to do. I walked to the lighthouse. There, I sat down under a tree for shade and pulled out the journal pages. I could only hope that Ava got to Jaden faster than I did to Josh, or, better yet, maybe she caught her prey in midair and was now enjoying a pleasant feast.

I began to read:

Ava

Ice was everywhere. But it didn't slow me down. As I ran toward Jaden's house, with the tawny-colored blanket from my bed wrapped around me like the soft furry skin of a buck, I paid little attention to on-lookers and near-collisions on the slippery trail. And when I saw his father standing out front, I wasn't at all shy. I walked right up to him and asked if his son was around.

"You just missed him," he said. "He was up all night. And like all of us, not in the best of spirits this morning. I tried telling him to get some sleep, but I think he needed to do some thinking."

"Darn," I said. "Tell him I stopped by."

"I sure will. How'd your family fare?"

"Not good. They're leaving the island, giving up after this."

He looked just like Jaden, but for his age, and even then he didn't look that old, not the bad kind of old. He was a good old, and it made me smile knowing that Jaden, too, would be looking good twenty years down the line. And he looked at me with sensitive eyes, and I knew then where Jaden had gotten his eyes from.

"I'm sorry to hear your family is leaving the island," he said. "You know where Jaden likes to go when he needs to think?"

"No."

"The lighthouse. I'll bet you anything that's where he is right now."

"Thanks," I said. "I better get going."

"Keep that blanket around you. Keep yourself warm, young lady."

"I will."

I started for Sanibel's east end, quickly picking up a trail of tracks etched in the shallow snow that I knew instinctively were his. They were only about eighteen inches apart, so I knew Jaden had walked his way to the lighthouse, whereas mine would probably measure some three to four feet, for I was trotting as fast as a buck.

My lips were numb, and I could hardly talk when I walked up to Jaden, who was sitting on a bench of driftwood. He was staring out at the bay, and he looked moody and bothered, unlike that fine spring morning when I first found him doctoring the pelican to life and the bay was sparkling and swarming with life.

I sat down beside him and opened the furry blanket I had clutched around my neck and waved it in the air so it would land softly over the two of us. "How are you?" I asked.

"Been better. And you?"

I was glad to know the heart can't freeze, for hearing his words warmed my body and made me tingle down to my toes. "Horrible," I said, feeling a pout spread across my face as wide as the sky. The sky was slate-colored and it was pouting too, I noticed. "I'm horrible today. This is not my day."

"We lost everything, too," he said.

"At least your family is staying. I talked with your father. My family is leaving the island. We're moving elsewhere because of this."

He cleared his voice, and I waited for him to say something, anything. He didn't, and I wondered whether he was thinking what I was, that our dream of one day being together was now freezing into a nightmare.

"I'm not sure yet where my parents are planning to go next," I added. I just know we're leaving."

I listened and swore I heard hoarse-sounding chirps of birds about to die, probably the white pelicans that just days before were forming straight lines in the water, then beating their wings and scooping fish up in their bills. "The birds didn't know this weather was coming, did they, Jaden? Don't you think they would have flown off if they sensed it coming? Are birds special like that?"

He turned for the first time and looked me in the eyes. "No one knew this was going to happen, not even the birds. But you know what a bird does when its nest is destroyed? It rebuilds. That's what it does, without giving it any thought. It rebuilds."

"I wish my parents would do that."

"That's their choice. But you and I are of the age now where we have our own choices to make. Me? I'm starting over in the same spot on the same land, no thought given to it at all."

"You're so strong," I said. "You're stronger than most people I've known. You're more like a bird." I laughed and he almost did. "And you're wise as nature. I think nature is wise, don't you?"

"You know I've always believed that. I think nature is worthy of our respect."

When I felt his breath on my face, I knew I had to get on with what I had come to tell him, and I knew before I even spoke that my words would screech forth like the chirps of the dying birds. "I've come to say good-bye."

His eyes were judging me as if I were the dumbest girl in the world, but in them I still saw everything I ever wanted, one thing at a time leaping forth like dolphins from the water but then disappearing back under again.

"Stop staring at me like that," I said. "Say something."

"What's there to say?" He smirked. "You already know."

I shook my head. "Know what?"

He smiled as he gazed out at the bay. Then he laughed. "Don't play dumb with me, Ava. You know you don't ever have to leave this island or say good-bye to me again. You know I'd love to marry you. In fact, we could marry tomorrow around dusk at the base of this lighthouse."

"You make it sound so simple. You make everything so simple, don't you?"

"Why not? I love you, and you love me. It is simple, and I know of someone who can marry us without any fuss." He was still grinning when he took hold of my chin and held it tightly. "But you realize it's up to you right now, don't you?"

"Sort of." If he hadn't been holding my chin so tightly I could have told him it was also up to my parents.

"You do see that you have choices, Ava, right? Because a lot of people don't see they've got any choices until it's too late, and they wish they had done whatever it was they didn't do. I want to make sure you know all of this so one day you don't look back and think to yourself that you should have married him and could have been loved genuinely and would have lived happily thereafter."

I moved his hands off my chin, not liking the grip he had on me. "Impossible," I said jumping up from the piece of wood we were sitting on. "Everything you talk of is impossible, and you don't understand, you couldn't possibly."

He raised an eyebrow at me. "Everything? Now aren't you exaggerating just a bit, Ava?"

I thought for a moment about all the impossibilities in the world. A manatee can't survive in cold water. A starfish can't move as fast as a shark. An osprey might look the part but can never turn into a bald eagle. My mother can't always be smiling, and Dahlia can't tell a story just once. They were all impossible, so I didn't think I was exaggerating at all.

"C'mon, Ava, is it that impossible for a girl to start acting like a woman and to start making some choices of her own?"

I bent down, desperate for the kind of snow we had in Kentucky, the kind in which I could make a strong snowball, one I could throw at his nose, but instead all this Florida snow allowed me to make was a cold, sandy mixture that fell apart in the air. I think Jaden felt sorry for me at that point because he closed his eyes and said, "Marry me, Ava."

All at once my thoughts thawed and came tumbling through my lips like an avalanche. "I'm thinking of my mama, Jaden. If she leaves and I stay . . ." I stopped.

I didn't know how to explain to him that Abigail's sad times no longer followed a seasonal pattern and that she had been down in early November, then back up again in December, and now, like this weather, there was no predicting what might happen next. She needed me by her side to care for her, bathe her, and feed her when she was down.

"Look," Jaden said, taking hold of my hands in his and resting them on his chest. "I'm not going to talk you into anything. I shouldn't have to talk any girl into marrying me. But if you want us to marry, then let's do it. We can keep it simple. We don't need much. Look around us. Everything we love is right here. We don't even need time to plan. Why should we? We know we love each other, so why make it all harder than it has to be? Meet me here at the lighthouse tomorrow around dusk. I'll have the minister here. If you're not there, I'll accept that you've chosen to leave the island for good with your parents."

"If I'm not there," I said, "I'll leave you a letter."

"A letter?" he said, releasing my hands while laughing and frowning at the same time. He turned and walked toward the lighthouse. "Like a piece of paper is going to sit around waiting for me to find it? Surely it'll blow away, Ava. It's been kind of windy, you know."

"I'll bury it," I said, hurrying after him.

"Oh, that's a great idea," he said sarcastically. "So I spend the rest of my life digging around in search of a buried rejection letter?"

"It won't be a rejection letter," I said. "And you won't have to search. I'll place the Junonia you gave me atop the mound where I bury it. Look for the Junonia."

"Sounds like you're plotting your escape."

"That's ridiculous," I said. "I'm just making provisions."

He had it all wrong, I thought as I stepped up to him and touched my hands to his red, icy cheeks. I pressed my lips to his, and with my kiss I told him I could live happily ever after with him. And soon he loosened the blanket I had wrapped around me and tucked into the neckline of my nightgown, and he spread it over top of us, and there we stood in a warm, private world that I never wanted to leave. But then he reached down and slid his hands over my thighs and up toward my hips and over my waist— all of which I didn't mind—and up toward my breasts. It took me a moment to come to my senses and wonder why he'd dare such a thing if we were to be married tomorrow. I also thought why he'd dare such a thing if we were to part forever tomorrow. Regardless of what the outcome would be, he ought not to have done such a thing at a moment like this, I realized minutes later, and so I yanked the blanket off the two of us and slapped him across the face.

"How dare you assume a lady wants to do such things?" I asked.

"Ava Witherton, you're not a lady."

"Not a lady?" I could feel my mouth drop open and the cold mist shooting out like fire from a dragon. "Then what am I to you?"

"A woman."

"Oh," I thought, as I bent down and picked the blanket up off the ground.

No one had ever called me a woman before. I took it as a compliment. He had a point. A lady wouldn't like what he was doing, but a woman probably would, I assumed. I didn't know the definition of a woman. Mama had only taught me the ways of a lady, and despite my rebelling against those, I always considered myself a girl, but not a typical girl, more of a boyish-type girl. Now, at eighteen years old, I felt for the first time in my life a woman. But I was a stupid woman, for there is nothing I wanted more than for Jaden to touch me there again.

"Did you like what you touched?" I asked sweetly.

He raised an eyebrow at me. "I'll tell you after we're married," he said. "That is, if you decide to show."

"I love you," I said, then turned and let a gust of wind push me in the direction of my home. I looked back once, and he was watching me, so I blew him a quick kiss. I didn't turn again. My tear ducts had thawed, and I didn't want any man seeing me cry.

I wanted to be a woman, a strong woman.

XXVIII

LYDIA

"THEN BE THAT STRONG woman, Ava," I said under my breath as I tucked the journal into my bag and stood up. "This is your chance to exercise your right to make a choice for yourself. It's what strong women do."

I walked slowly around the base of the lighthouse, keeping an eye out for an ancient Junonia shell and wondering at the same time if vows were ever exchanged on the ground where I was standing.

I had to find out, I decided, as I left the area and headed toward Marlena's. I had to know whether Ava showed up at dusk or dropped off a shell and left on a boat forever. I had to know all these things because maybe I still had choices of my own to make. I was flying out soon and had lots of things planned for myself, but reservations and plans can be cancelled. Just as a woman has the right to make her own choices, she also has the right to change her mind.

"Let me guess," Marlena said as she opened the door. "You're here for the wedding, aren't you?"

"So there was one!" I exclaimed.

"I didn't say that. I just asked if you were here for it."

I walked past her into the great room and laughed. "Of course I am. I'd probably be maid-of-honor, don't you think?"

"Yes," she said. "In all honesty, I do think you and she would have been close friends. I think she could have used a friend like you. She really didn't have a lot of girls she could relate to."

"Well, I'm here, and I'm relating to her, all right. Mind if I get reading? I'm already nearly sixty years late for the wedding."

"Take your seat," Marlena said, ushering me down the hall and into the yellow room where, outside the windows, the birds were performing music fit for a wedding. She sat down as well, and we chatted a minute.

"I'm dying to know," she said. "What's happening with you and Josh?"

"Nothing," I said. "For now, absolutely nothing."

"You look uneasy about that."

"I am."

She stood up and patted me on the knee. "I'll be in the kitchen making you a nice warm drink, one my own mother, grandmother, and even great-grandmother once enjoyed. It's one of those family comfort recipes that I think you'll like." She left the room and I could hear her walking down the hall.

I could hardly wait to hear Ava's footsteps walking down the aisle, ready to join Jaden so their tracks would become one. I picked up the pages and began to read.

Ava

There should have been blue-winged teal, red-breasted mergansers and white pelicans there to give us their blessings, but there weren't any. Probably the cold got in their way, but that's okay, I told myself. "I'm not going to let something like that ruin my day."

"It's a beautiful day," my mother said to me, sensing my nerves. "Wouldn't you know it? Of all days, today is turning out to be one of the most beautiful days I have ever seen."

"I know it is," I said. "Now take your seat, Mama." I looked at the lighthouse, tall and regal as any cathedral steeple might be. "It's time everyone takes a seat. You too, Grandmalia." I took hold of her hand and steadied her down, and then I looked around for both my father and Jaden, but neither were anywhere to be seen. I wondered whether my father would show at all, but I knew Jaden would. We all make our choices in life, and we all have to live with the lives we've created, I thought as I stood nervously watching to see whether my father would choose to say good-bye to me or not.

He had made a big choice yesterday, one he had announced to me as I walked in the front door after returning from my chilly morning with Jaden.

"Key West," Stewart had said, his feet up on the table and his hair a wild mess as always after he's run his fingers through it during a decision-making process. "We're going to Key West to manufacture cigars."

"What did you say, Daddy?"

"Financially, it makes best sense for us to move to Key West, coconut. I hear that wages paid to the cigar makers alone amount to three hundred thousand dollars in a single year. You know what that means?"

I shook my head.

"Sit down, and I'll tell you," he started. "It means I'd buy you every-thing you ever wanted. Hey, Abby," he called out, turning toward the kitchen. "Abby, our little Ava has grown into a beautiful young lady. She'd look good in a few new dresses, fashionable ones, don't you think?"

My mother stormed out of the kitchen and slammed a teacup down on the table in front of me. "Here, Ava, this is for you." Then she bent down and pointed her finger at my father. "I am not moving my daughter to a place where cigar manufacturing is the chief commercial enterprise."

I sipped the tea, wondering whether brandy had become a permanent ingredient in our family's favorite comfort recipe. Warm milk, honey, but-ter . . . I took another sip . . . yep, I think I tasted hints of brandy like I had the night before. Heading into the third generation, the family comfort recipe had indeed evolved to now include brandy, I decided. It was histo-ry in the making. And the brandy, I think, replaced the cinnamon. I couldn't detect any cinnamon. "How far is Key West from here?" I asked, not believing that any of my father's talk would ever turn into action.

"This discussion is between your father and me," Abigail said, not looking at me. Instead she cast a smoldering look back at Stewart; so, I sipped more of the comfort drink and watched my mother and father communicate with their eyes. It annoyed me when they did that because they thought I didn't know the eyeball language and that it was only for married couples, of which club I was not a member.

When my mother walked away, my father pulled his feet off the table and scooted closer toward me and then whispered, "Key West isn't too far from here. It'll take a week by sailboat to get there."

"I heard that, Stewart Witherton," Abigail said, returning with her own cup, some of it pouring over the rim as she walked. "Key West is out of the question." She sipped, and I wondered whether her cup, with its amount of brandy, would have any lasting impact on our family recipe. She shook her hand to dry the spillage. "Did you forget we don't speak Spanish?" She gulped and slurped from her cup and I could tell she was desperate for comfort. "I'll tell you exactly what you're going to do," she said, setting her empty cup on the table. "Stop dreaming and take us home to Kentucky where they at least speak our own language."

"What about the winters there?" Stewart asked.

"Never mind the winters. I'll be fine."

Dahlia came out of the bedroom and sat down beside me. "I've got an idea," she said. "What about Hollywood? I heard men on the dock the other day talking about it as a place people are moving to."

Stewart shifted in his chair and gave her a face. "Did all that cold weather out there freeze parts of your brain because you're scaring me now?" he said.

"Be nice," Abigail warned. "My mother's idea isn't all that ludicrous. I've heard people talking about Hollywood, too, but it's for wealthy mid-westerners, which we certainly are not. They're buying up residential lots there to build homes, so they can winter in California."

"Then if Key West doesn't pan out, we'll head for California," Stewart said.

"No, no, we won't," said Abigail. "We're going home to Kentucky. The discussion ends here."

"Wait a minute," I said, standing up. "How could it end here when I haven't even had a chance to say anything?" Standing made me feel taller then when I sat, and more powerful, and if I didn't want to be a writer, I'd probably want to be a speech giver, for I liked giving speeches when I had something good to say. "We'd be fools to leave this area," I began. "This is a good place to live. People are pouring in from all over the world."

"For what? Fishing over at Punta Rassa?" Stewart asked. "Those tourists aren't helping our farming any."

"I'll answer questions when I'm done. Please don't interrupt," I said. "It doesn't matter why people are moving here, just that once they get a taste of it, they're smitten and want to move their families here." I stopped for a moment, sipped some tea and prepared to tell them that I had fallen in love here as well, and his name was Jaden, and if they tried forcing me to leave, I'd be getting married tomorrow at dusk. "I myself am madly in love with this area," I continued. "I couldn't possibly imagine living anywhere but here, and I'm also in love with . . ."

"Save your words for a situation in which they might actually be helpful," my mother broke in. "Our decision is made. You, your grandmother, and I are headed back to Kentucky where we can at least reunite with some family members, and, Stewart, you're headed off to Key West, only long enough to make a fortune and bring it all home. That's it, that's all there is to discuss," she said, waving her hands through the air at me as if I were a bug she was trying to shoo away.

"Kentucky?" Dumbfounded, I dared to ask, "But why? I don't get it."

"It's home," said Abigail. "There's something normal about returning home. Now get into your room and get started with your packing. We'll leave not tomorrow, but the morning after that, early."

I ran into my room, not to cry, nor get packing, nor collapse onto my bed, but to open my journal and get writing, for I had to chronicle everything that happened. Doing so might put it all into perspective and help me make my decision. I could marry Jaden near the lighthouse tomorrow at dusk, then say farewell to my parents the next morning, or I could not show up at the lighthouse and leave with my family the next morning. It was that simple, I told myself. But If I chose to marry, I would most certainly invite my family. It would be up to them whether to show or not.

When I finished writing, I started to pack. Regardless of what my decision would be, I'd have to pack. Packing would be simple. I was glad not to be rich or to have acquired and collected a bunch of material stuff without meaning that would only weigh me down. All my belongings would easily fit into three large bags.

Everyone had taken seats but me. I was still standing, my knees wobbling, and the lighthouse was standing too. "Ava, the ferry is ready to leave. What are you waiting for? Sit down," Grandmalia said to me.

I smiled at her through my tears. I couldn't possibly tell her that my private hopes that Jaden might still show were getting slighter by the moment. As I stared over at the lighthouse in the distance, I thought of him arriving there the evening before only to find the Junonia I had left him in the dirt. It pained me horribly to think of him digging into the mound and finding my journal, filled with pages of my love for him and descriptions of my mother's situation. Surely, he would see how torn I had been, and that despite my decision to stay with my mother I loved him more than anything else. And maybe he would recognize that I made the wrong choice in not showing up to marry him and he would take off in search of me before it was too late, before this ferry pulled away.

"Ava, sit your buttocks down now," Grandmalia insisted again. "What is your problem, girl?"

And just as I sat down I saw the other man in my life, my daddy, running along the dock, giving the "just one minute" signal to the boat captain. He hopped aboard and kissed Dahlia on the cheek and then walked over to me.

"Good-bye, coconut," he said. "I'm just going long enough to make a fortune, and I'll be home."

I jumped up from my seat and threw my arms around his neck like the tangling roots of a banyan tree. "I wish I could come with you, instead," I whispered in his ear. "I'll bet I could roll cigars like any man."

"I'm sure you can, but your mother needs you more," he said. "I've promised your grandmother I'd send her cigars, and I'll send a couple to you as well. Just don't tell your mother." He winked over at Dahlia, and when the captain cleared his voice, he quickly said, "I'll send you the finest, and I'll send money, too." Then he walked over to my mother and got down on his knees, and I couldn't wait to hear what he had to say to her, but to my surprise, he didn't have a chance to say anything because she reached out and grabbed him and pulled him close.

As I watched them embrace, I thought about the man that I loved and how I might never be able to put my arms around him again. It wasn't fair to think that soon I'd be gone from the island like a living seashell yanked off the beach. It was as wrong as picking a sea oat and bothering a resting or a nesting bird and littering on the beach and there should be laws against these sorts of things, and of taking a girl away from the one place she wants to be, the place she belongs. Life was so brittle, I thought. It could be going along so beautifully and all of a sudden a branch breaks and everything you were sitting on collapses to the ground.

A moment later my father struggled out of her grip, stood up, and stepped onto the dock.

"Daddy," I called out without emotion. "After being with all those Cubans and Spanish-speaking Negroes, what if we don't understand you anymore when you come home?"

"That's not how it works," he reassured me from the edge of the dock. "Learning a new language doesn't mean you forget your old one, baby. Don't worry about a thing."

"I love you, Daddy."

"I love you, too! I love you all," he said, waving, and then as he started to tear up, I saw him rub his eyes, then turn, and venture down the path. I could hardly think. My mind was dizzy with anger and love for him. I had turned down the man I loved so I wouldn't abandon my parents, and now my daddy was selfishly off to Key West for a wild adventure of his own. As the boat pulled slowly away from the dock, I considered changing my mind. The boat was only a couple of inches from the dock, an easy hop. Find Jaden. Find Jaden. Find Jaden, my heart pounded out to me. The boat was about a foot from the dock, but I could jump. Jaden and I used to compete to see who could jump the farthest. And as the boat continued a few feet from the dock, I knew Jaden would be proud to see me jump this far. "It's still not too late," I said, trying to motivate myself. "You might think it is, but you can still change your mind."

"Ava," my mother said. "You shouldn't be standing so close to the edge. Sit down, young lady."

I didn't listen. I couldn't. I was still watching to see if Jaden might come running down the path, at least to wave good-bye, or maybe swim out to meet me halfway in the water. The boat was several feet from the dock now, but I was a good swimmer, slow like a manatee, but steady. I could swim far, and distance, not speed, is what I would be facing now more than anything. Then again, the water was cold. Manatees hate cold water. So do I. The cold could kill me. And if my mama jumped in after me, it could kill her. I didn't want that.

Lydia

"Don't be a fool, Ava! Jump!" I said when I reached the end of her writing. "Jump, or you'll regret it."

I stood up and walked into the great room. Marlena was sitting on the sofa and there was a tray with teacups on the coffee table. I sat down and stared into the cups. "Looks like milk," I said, unsure that it was anything I wanted to try. "What is it?"

"I told you, an old family recipe."

I picked up a cup and tasted slowly. Warm milk. Honey. Butter . . . "Brandy too?" I asked. I didn't need any answer. The brandy was quite strong. I took another taste, trying to piece it all together. "Did you say this was *your* family recipe?"

She was smiling and nodding and raising her own teacup to her lips, and then she slurped and gulped in the most unladylike manner.

"Has anyone ever told you," I said, as I watched a little spill over the rim of her cup, "that you sip your drink exactly the way your grandmother Abigail once did?" Marlena laughed and put the cup down. "Have I got it right? Abigail was your grandmother?"

"Yes, and Ava my mother. I never got to meet my grandmother, yet I do believe some ways of doing things are carried on through the generations, simple things most people probably don't know about, but I do, thanks to Ava's journal. I guess I do slurp and gulp like my grandmother once did." She laughed some more. "And I did have my great-Grandmalia's nose. Sometimes it makes me sad that I erased that part of her from my face, but, my God, Lydia, you should have seen my nose before."

"Wait a minute," I said. "Then you can tell me whether Ava makes it work with Jaden. You know the ending of this story. You *are* the ending."

"No. I like to think of myself as the continuation."

"Who's your father? Is it Jaden?"

"There's more to the story," she said. "It gets complicated."

"Tell me," I insisted. "Did she jump from the boat and swim back? Did she marry him after all? Marlena, you can't keep me waiting any longer. I've got to know."

"When are you leaving, dear?"

"Tomorrow. I'm definitely leaving the island tomorrow. But I'm not sure yet where I'm leaving to. Chicago or Key West."

"I don't think you stand a chance at getting a job rolling cigars, dear."

I rolled my eyes. "That's not why I'd go to Key West," I said with a laugh.

"Josh is there. I figure I could take a speedboat and get there right away." I stopped and gave thought to what I was saying and thinking. "Am I crazy?" I asked. "I think maybe I am. Or maybe I'm confused. I've never loved a guy before. Can you tell me whether Ava jumped from that boat and how it all turned out?"

"Ava's choices were Ava's choices, and Lydia's choices will be Lydia's," she said. "I don't think Ava wrote about her life with the intention of telling anybody what to do. That's not why women share their stories."

"Can you at least tell me if she wrote more?"

"Of course she did. Ava's life doesn't end there. You're looking at her daughter, you know. Why don't you make up your mind, and then stop by in the morning, and I'll give you the next set of pages."

I felt like throwing my arms around her, for Marlena was more precious to me than ever. She was Ava's daughter! "I'm glad there's more to read."

"Ava loved to write. It's hard to keep a girl from doing what she loves to do. Now drink up. It's comforting, isn't it? And there's more, although I'm thinking of deleting brandy and returning it to the original recipe with the cinnamon. What do you think?"

"Keep the brandy," I said with a grin.

XXIX

LYDIA

MARLENA WAS OUT FRONT gardening when I stopped by the next morning. She put her hose down, walked over to the steps, and picked up a bag filled with cookies and biscotti and the next set of pages.

Neither of us said "hello" to one another, and I imagined it was because no one likes to say a simple hello when they're about to say a big farewell. Besides, there was something weighing heavily on my mind.

"Why me?" I asked when she handed the goodies and pages to me. "Why did you tell me all that stuff on the beach that day? The day we made the snowwoman?"

"I said a lot of things that day. What exactly are you referring to?"

"The part about you believing in me."

"Oh," she said. "You remember my words well."

"Of course. You were the only one who had ever said anything like that to me."

"I said it because when I was a little girl, someone spoke similar words to me. And to this day, whenever I feel as if my dreams are starting to drown, I grab onto the words that woman spoke to me. She was just a stranger, but her words were powerful. When I saw you on the beach that day, you were around the age I was when that woman approached me. I've always been grateful for the way she came up to me and told me I'd be significant one day, and I wanted to pass that on. When I saw you sitting there all alone writing, I couldn't resist."

"Thank you," I said.

"You're welcome, but enough with the sentimental stuff. Did I mention I got a call from my agent and she's hooked me up with an independent film company over in London?"

"Marlena, that's wonderful!"

"Yes, I'll be playing supporting actress, and they start filming in three months."

"In England?"

"Sure. Why not?"

I threw my arms around her, and she spun around like we had both been smoking something bad, or good maybe. "Congratulations," I shouted. "I knew you'd do it."

"I guess so. I wondered at times."

Then, when we stopped spinning like tops and released our grips, but for our hands, I grew serious. "Do you still believe in me?" I asked. "Do you think I can do all that I want to do?"

"Of course I do, darling," she said. "But that no longer matters. What matters is that you believe in yourself. A magical transformation occurs when someone tells you they believe in you. All of a sudden, you start believing in yourself. And soon, you start expecting and no longer need others believing in you because belief in yourself becomes enough."

She pulled me close to her and we hugged as I had watched mothers and daughters hug throughout the years. "Write me," I said, wiping the tears from my eyes. "Tell me all about the filming. I want to go see it when it comes out."

"If they show it in this country," she said with a laugh. "But, yes, we'll keep in touch. Send those pages back to me when you're done, and I'll send you more."

"There's still more after this?"

"Yes, but you're not ready for those just yet. Soon you'll be entering the summer of your life, dear. I'll give them to you then."

An hour later I took my seat on the ferry, and as it pulled away from Sanibel Island, I pulled out the journal and began to read what Ava had decided to do.

Ava

"Ava," my mother's voice was bouncing up and down like a buoy. "Take your seat. We're not going to ask you again."

I looked at Abigail's pale face, then back at the green island. The boat was far offshore now, too far for me to safely swim back, but I wondered whether I should do it anyway, jump overboard and risk whatever came my way. The further the boat drew from shore, the stronger my love for Jaden grew, and could hardly stand the thought of living without him.

"Ava," Abigail cried. "I'm feeling faint. I need you, darling."

I glanced down at the water, to see if it had suddenly turned into a chop, but it hadn't. It was smooth as a sheet of glass and there was nothing to explain why I felt the boat rocking or why I stumbled across the deck, stopping midway with my legs wobbling and my heart tumbling about inside me. I tried taking hold of my heart, securing it down, but it palpitated about like a flapping fish and slipped through my hands and into the air, landing smack down in the water.

I obediently took my seat next to Abigail, and my Grandmalia sat next to me. I could hear her faintly uttering a prayer of appreciation to the Lord God Almighty, specifically praising Him in detail for the good times she had on the island, for skinny-dipping and not dying from the infection due to that stingray sting on her ass and for sea grape jelly and coconut milk and much more. I could hardly listen and didn't want to join her in prayer. I didn't want to thank God for anything.

As Sanibel grew smaller, I noticed Abigail's eyes also shrinking and looking beady, like those of a hermit crab forced to abandon its home.

Then I saw a gold object glistening like a treasure in the water behind the boat. It bobbed up and down for a moment, a beautiful piece of gold. And when it disappeared beneath the surface of the water, I knew it was my heart.

I was leaving it behind. It was a solid heart and would surely sink. But first it would struggle as long as it could to remain just under the surface of the water, in that layer where the sun still penetrates, and soon it would travel down to the dimmer twilight zone, passing by strange and bizarre fish, and from there, maybe around midnight, it might turn a deeper red or even black as it entered the deep ocean layer where no light goes.

I don't know how long it might take for my heart to reach the pitch-black bottom layer, where the water is nearly freezing and its pressure immense. And it probably wouldn't stop there. My heart would continue downward to the forbidding trench at the very bottom, and I could only hope that there it might dwell comfortably beside a starfish or a friendly tubeworm.

Despite such depths, my heart was strong and would go on beating in that deep dark underworld. But I have no idea what happens to a woman when her heart sinks to that portion of the sea.

"Mama, did you know that periwinkles are adaptable flowers?" I asked when the boat was about halfway across the bay. She didn't answer. "They like the full sun, but they also do well in shade. I think you'll do fine in the shade, too."

"Read to me, Ava," she said. "I like when you read to me."

I took out a book I had once borrowed from Tootie's library but never returned, and I opened it randomly. It was *Flower Fables* by Louisa May Alcott, and I had kept it knowing that one day my mama might need to hear about flowers. As the boat made its way toward Punta Rassa, I began reading the words in front of me:

> *"But while I eat, tell me, dear Violet, why are you all so sad? I have scarce seen a happy face since my return from Rose Land; dear friend, what means it?"*

I didn't mean to take and never return the book to Tootie, but instinctively I must have known the day would come when my mama would need it like a dose of medicine.

Abigail lay down and rested her head in my lap, and I continued to read:

> *"I will tell you," replied little Violet, the tears gathering in her soft eyes. "Our good Queen is ever striving to keep the dear flowers from the power of the cruel Frost-King; many ways she tried, but all have failed. She has sent messengers to his court with costly gifts; but all have returned sick for want of sunlight, weary and sad; we have watched over them, heedless of sun or shower, but still his dark spirits do their work, and we are left to weep over our blighted blossoms."*

I stopped reading just long enough to wipe a tear from Abigail's face. I looked over at Dahlia, who finally stopped telling everyone on the boat about Milton's agitated side and how nothing but a hot salty bath used to calm him down. When our eyes met, she signaled me over to her with a jerk of her head.

"What?" I asked.

"I'm worried about Abby," she whispered in my ear. "I think she has reached her wits' end. If you know anything about ends, it's close to the grand finale of all ends, dear."

I stood up and slowly walked back to my mother and opened the Alcott book and continued to read. She needed another dose of medicine.

XXX

CHICAGO
1959

Lydia

UNLIKE AVA, I STILL owned my heart when I returned to Chicago. I was too stubborn a woman to leave a vital organ behind. And I was a strong woman and strong women drag their hearts along, no matter how heavy. Mine, stuffed and bursting at the seams with feelings for Josh, weighed a ton.

When the doors of Northwestern opened in the fall, I gave my heart permission to continue loving him as long as it didn't disturb the studies my mind had to do. Occasionally, I'd set my books down and hold my hand over my left chest and feel for its beat. My heart was still there within its private chambers, and it was more than beating. It was spinning, dipping, and double-stepping within. Maybe it was rehearsing for when I might see him again. That's what a woman's heart does when she loves a man—it dances all the time.

I dated here and there, nothing serious, and I wondered whether Josh was doing the same. I feared it would only be a matter of time before he found a new girl or no longer remembered me but there was nothing I could do about it, so I tried the best I could to keep my mind busy learning the fundamentals to reporting—accuracy, fairness, and balance. I was achieving a perfect grade-point average at Northwestern University's Medill School of Journalism, where, once, *Chicago Tribune* editor Joseph Medill had said, students learn to "write boldly and tell the truth fearlessly."

My second year of college, I could stand it no longer, so I sent Josh a letter and waited months for him to return one to me. And when he did, I found his words a breath of warm, comforting fresh air, so I wrote back immediately, and in a few weeks I received another. Our letters continued, and each got longer and more detailed. And by my third year of college, we were exchanging letters once a month, and in my fourth year, twice a month. I told him all about my classes and professors, and he told me about the seasons on Sanibel and the fish and the novels he was reading. He enjoyed Hemingway most. I had no time for pleasure reading, but it sounded nice to be on a boat with a coffee in one hand and a novel in the other and nothing but Florida's dramatic sky above.

His was a world away, and yet it felt so close. His letters made me feel like I was sitting there beside him, going through those seasons on Sanibel, with the love bugs in the spring and the afternoon thunderstorms of summer and the migrating songbirds lining the trees in the fall and the passing cold fronts of winter. We never mentioned in any of our letters whether or not we were seeing anyone else, which I wasn't, except for dinners or movies here and there with guys that came and went. We also never wrote about the feelings we had for each other. Mine were growing stronger with each letter of his that I read.

I wanted many times to tell my father how deeply I had fallen and through letters was still falling for that boy on the island, but that would rob me of the financial support I needed to attend such a prestigious, private university. So, instead, I privately savored his letters, much the same way I once reread over and over all the things written about my mother in my journal. Reading Josh's letters brought me comfort much like reading about my mother once did. But then, in my fourth year of college, something happened. Our letters dwindled down to two the entire year, and I was too busy to realize it until looking back. I don't know how time fooled me like that, but the year flew by, and I hardly had time to wash my hair daily, let alone write any letters. And I was so focused on my goals and graduation, both fast approaching. That is not to say my interest in Josh faded, but that things that were geographically in my face took on precedence that last year of college. I knew in my mind that was normal. It was the way it ought to be.

And Lloyd was proud, I think, the day I graduated with a bachelor's degree in journalism, and he set me up in an apartment downtown with new furniture. He no longer questioned why his only daughter had no fiancé, marriage proposals, or boyfriend.

I landed a job at the *Windy City Press*, thanks to the good coffee I made while working there in high school. The journalist who wrote about the opening of McDonald's that day remembered me and pulled strings, and I got hired to write obituaries. Actually, I was offered a job working on the women's news section, writing about shoes and clothes, but I'd rather die than write about that kind of stuff, and when I said just that to the hiring editor, I was sent down to obituaries.

I wrote to Josh, giving him my new address and telling him about my new job, but I didn't hear back. Naturally, he moved on as well, I assumed. Marlena and I wrote several letters back and forth through the years, and she filled me in on all the juicy details of the English films she was starring in and the producers and directors she had dated and the roles that were getting bigger and better. She was flying from London to Florida to Hollywood, where she was still auditioning for major motion pictures, but not getting those roles. She was most upset for not getting a part in some movie about pillow talking. I wrote her back and told her a movie about pillow talking would never make it and that she was better off without a movie like that on her portfolio.

I had just finished hanging up the last of my brand-new career wardrobe when there was a knock at the door. A package from Sanibel, for me! I sat down on my new sofa that faced the window that overlooked Chicago and I tore open the package. The letter inside read:

Dear Lydia,

Congratulations on your new job. Remember a first job is only a step-
pingstone to something else, but how fortunate you are to be writing
obituaries, which are like sacred summaries. A person's life and what
they did with it while here on earth are sacred, indeed. It will be the
most inspiring job, I'm sure.

I've enclosed the next set of pages that Ava wrote. I think you're ready
for them. You're at a critical point in your life, dear. You have many
choices yet to make. Hope you enjoy your visit with Ava. I know you
mean as much to her as she does to you. She always wanted one special
reader, someone to appreciate what she wrote.

Sincerely,
Marlena

I didn't know for sure what Marlena was referring to. At twenty-one years
old, I felt I had already made the major choices of my life. I chose not to
get married and not to move to the suburbs. In the back of my mind, I
knew that one day I might choose to reconnect with Josh, but for now, I
liked exactly where I was. I was working for a newspaper, another choice
of mine. Maybe it was Ava who regretted the choices she had made.

I felt mine were good ones and they weren't strange, as Lloyd and the
rest of the country had me believing. I was glad to have chosen print journalism since it already had a long history of women working in it, whereas television news was a new frontier with a new group of groundbreaking
women. I appreciated women who paved the way.

I tucked Ava's latest journal entries into my briefcase and walked out my
door. I took the elevator to the lobby, then walked to Michigan Avenue and
sat down on a shady bench. I pulled out her journal, eager to know how my
poor old friend had fared after leaving the island a heartless woman. How
could any woman survive without a heart? I had to read quickly for it was
my first day of work and there was no way I was going to be late.

KENTUCKY
1899

Ava

There is a reason why so many women look back on their lives and regret the things they've done or haven't done. It's because they didn't notice the options and choices arriving on the shore until it was too late and those options and choices floated back out to sea. Rarely do the important options in life smack us in the face like a cold wave. Often those are the ones that come and go quietly with the tide and blending with our lives so that we didn't pay them any attention.

I arrived in Kentucky a heartless woman, and, off and on throughout the next year, I wondered whether I was losing my mind. There are certain circumstances, when put together all at the same time, that make any woman lose her mind, even those who haven't any history of mindlessness in their families.

While Stewart was off in Key West rolling cigars, Abigail's days of rolling happily on the ground with the flowers were gone for good. She was overtaken once more by the spell of sadness, and I cried out each night with prayerful pleas that a prince might come along to kiss and wake her from the spell.

My mama looked like a dead person as she'd lie in the bed in the middle of the afternoon, her eyes open, but not looking, and her lips pressed together softly, but not saying anything. With the tips of my fingers, I'd touch her lips and try shaping them into the beautiful smile that my daddy once fell in love with.

Our first year back in Kentucky, I tried many things. And so did the doctors. We all did. Even Abigail herself did. But when a flower is picked from the ground where it wants to be, its days are numbered, and she lost all desire and eventually her ability to take in and keep down food or water.

"You need this," I tried insisting as I held her head back and poured water into her mouth. "You've got to drink it, Mama."

And the first day she let it dribble down her chin; I tossed the water onto the floor, not caring that I broke the glass. "Mama," I cried. "Remember that glistening pathway? The one made by the moon on top of the water? The one you said those mother turtles followed?"

She stared through me.

"I need you to walk that glistening pathway or at least take a couple of steps. Please, you've got to do whatever you can to pull yourself out of this and survive."

But when she stayed in the crumpled-up position, her condition had gone too far and she was too weak to go for any walk or to take any strengthening measures of her own. I knew then she had already taken her final glistening walk, and it was years ago when she uprooted our family and moved us to Florida, despite our extended kin thinking she was nuts for moving us to a place far away and one that we had never been to before. Now that we were back, I think she made the decision not to go for any more glistening walks.

"I don't know what to do," I said one day when I was buying wheat in town. "I've got a plant that's dying."

"Water it," said the woman after handing me my change.

"I've given it water. Three to four times a day or more."

"Too much water. Try sunshine."

I shook my head. "That once helped, but not any more."

"Have you tried talking to it?"

"It doesn't talk back."

"Of course it doesn't. Plants don't talk, but they still hear."

So that day I returned home with the wheat and sat down on the end of my mama's bed and began to talk. I thought I noticed her eyes opening wider, and they were the color of mine as I told her all about the boy I loved on the island and how we'd meet up in the moonlight, like two owls wanting to love without any interference from daylight or people. I told her all about our walks to school and the tracks we left behind in the mudflats and how he was a boy who prayed and who cared for animals and believed in my dreams. I continued to tell her how my heart had leaped over the side of the boat the day we left and I watched it sink.

She liked my story, I think, for it was the first time in weeks that she sat up in bed and placed her feet on the ground, as if she were about to stand on her own. And then I told her why I thought the Lord put the moon up in the sky. It was so that even in the dark of night there would be some light and somewhere it would be glistening down on earth. And there would be no excuse. The glistening pathway would always be there, and it's up to us to go out and walk it. I waited for my mama's reaction, for her to conjure up in her mind a simple step she might take, but just as I thought she was about to stand, she fell onto the floor instead.

I cupped her in my arms and caressed her pale soft skin.

"No, Mama. Don't leave me. Please don't go," I cried.

"Ava," she uttered. "Your soul."

"What did you say, Mama? What about my soul?"

"Listen to it."

"But what does it sound like?"

She took a slow breath in and said, "The sea," then let it out like the tide.

"What if I can't hear it?"

"I see it," she said, her voice trailing off.

"My soul, Mama? You see my soul?"

"No. I see Heaven. I think."

"What does it look like? You've got to tell me."

She closed her eyes and never got to tell me. I could only imagine.

Hours later the men tried taking her from me, and I cried and screamed and kicked. And soon I stopped kicking, but I screamed in my sleep for weeks, and when that ended, I cried night after night for months on end.

At first, Dahlia would hear my cries, and she'd sit beside my bed, holding my hand. "Those damn winters," she'd say. "They killed her, you know." We both needed something to blame, and winter was the easiest. The season lasted long, like our sorrow, and I could kick the snow and let the ice knock me down to my face giving me a reason to lie there cold and crying and feeling sorry for myself.

But when spring came and we both still felt upset over my mama's death, we knew winter wasn't truly to blame. There had been something else. It was as if Abigail's mind went through seasons of sickness.

I had hoped that with the arrival of spring I might pick myself up again and get on with my life, doing all that I wanted to do. But I wasn't ready when the flowers started blooming.

XXXI

LYDIA

RAIN WAS A GOOD THING. If it hadn't started to rain, I'd have gone on reading. Instead, I glanced at my watch, threw Ava's journal into my brief-case, and took off, sprinting faster than any Chicago bus or earthly man or Florida panther. And when I collapsed into my chair at work, I was heav-ily panting and didn't catch my breath until I finished writing my first obituary. It read like this:

> *Abigail Blake Witherton, 51, of Kentucky, died Sunday, June 24, 1896 in the arms of her daughter, Ava. The damn winters killed her.*
>
> *She was born and raised in Kentucky where she worked on the turkey farms. She and her husband, Stewart J. Witherton, later moved their family to Sanibel Island, where they lived amidst the flowers and worked the land before returning to Kentucky. The flowers of Sanibel brought her pleasure, as did the white sugar sands. Abigail's soul is now soaring, not in an earthly paradise, but across the everlasting kingdom of God where the periwinkles bloom year-round into eternity.*
>
> *She was the daughter of Milton and Dahlia Blake.*

I didn't turn the above obituary in, but it served as a good warm-up activity, I thought, as I folded it tightly and stuffed it deep inside the seashell I had placed on my desk for good luck. I would keep Abigail's obituary there inside the seashell on my desk to remind me of the significance of my job.

I was glad to have a job, my own job and my own desk with a seashell on it and a telephone just for my use. Things were going well now, and I was close to doing what I wanted with my life.

I wrote and turned in several obituaries, and when lunchtime came around, I decided to spend it with Ava. I didn't yet know anyone else, and I felt like being with her, so I opened her journal and continued to read.

Ava

Abigail was survived by a mother: Dahlia, who day-by-day was losing more of her mind; a husband: Stewart, who, after a short stint rolling cigars in Key West, regained a portion of his mind and returned to his family and turkey farm; a brother: Henry, who, after losing his own wife just two months prior, was walking around grief-stricken and despondent; three nieces: Violet, Lilly and Rose, ages 12, 14, and 16, and who, after losing their mother, and now facing a distant father, were like raging wildflowers, nasty but with good reason, closing their petals on anyone who came too close; and finally, Abigail was survived by a daughter: Ava, a girl who once was full of dreams. But now, in the wake of losing her own mother and her aunt, her dreams were pushed aside, for she has been given three nasty flowers to care for.

Those three girls were craftier than any wild beasts roaming the earth. And they hated me. They were out to get me for the simple fact that I wasn't their mother and they wanted their mother. I think I understood, for at twenty years old, I wanted mine, too. But no one gave me any pity, for I was now an adult, and since there were no men calling for me, the care and responsibility of those three girls fell into my lap.

At first, I naturally tried churning them into ladies, for that's what a mother does, and I remember my own mama passionately trying to turn me into a lady, but the girls didn't like it at all. If I tried being sweet to them, they accused me of handling them like babies. If I told them I didn't like their behavior, they thought I was being judgmental. If I tried giving them my opinion on things, they swore I was ruling their lives and telling them what to do. If I tried asking them questions out of interest regarding boys or anything at all, they thought I was being nosy and invading their privacy. If I tried telling them anything about myself when I was their age, they looked at me, bored, as if I was comparing my life to theirs or lecturing and preaching in some way. In reality, I was only trying to relate. And it felt like yesterday when I was their age. Years are only big to young girls. To older girls years are nothing.

They made me feel like twenty going on one hundred. And those girls made me feel like a bossy, judgmental, opinionated old spinster, which I wasn't. I was the opposite of it all, but that is how those girls wanted to view me, and I could say nothing pleasing to them and nothing that wouldn't offend them. I didn't want those girls changing who I was or how I felt about myself, but they were starting to do it to me. They were starting to make me self-conscious of everything I said and asked and how I communicated, and I had never been one to worry about my own words before. Those girls were changing me, and they were changing the way I would have been there for them had they not been sensitive to me in the first place.

"I think you ladies could use fresh air. Your faces are pale," I said one afternoon. "How about we go outdoors and let the sun shine down upon us. I'll bet you didn't know that being outdoors is my favorite thing."

"And why would we listen to anything you said?" Rose had the sharpest tongue.

And Violet's words were like digesting a poisonous flower petal. "Men don't like you and women say you're heartless; so, I agree with Rose. Why should we emulate you in any way?"

"I'm not wanting you to emulate me. Be your own selves. Each of you has your own uniqueness. Identifying and feeling comfortable with your-selves is what a true lady is all about."

I walked outside and insisted that the three of them follow me. We walked alongside the house, and I knew that my father and their father were far out working in the field and wouldn't be able to see us. I took hold of the handlebars of my bicycle that had been leaning against the house, and I hopped onto it and rode a short distance from the girls, then circled slowly around and returned. They and everyone had been whispering about the way I purchased the bicycle from a mail-order catalog and rode off on it every day.

When Stewart had returned from Key West, he had made only a little money off his cigar rolling, but he gave a lump of that money to me. I was free to do whatever I wanted with it; so, I bought a bicycle. No woman in our family had ever owned one before, and I viewed it as a means of per-sonal freedom. I could ride off for hours on my own and travel farther and faster than by foot. I liked the independence that it brought me. And I often wondered what Jaden would think if he saw the tracks my bicycle was leaving behind.

"Here," I said to Rose. "Your turn. Give it a try."

"Bicycles were not made for women," she said.

"Maybe not," I admitted. "But women are adapting. I'm not the only woman in the world riding a bicycle, you know. They are becoming popular."

"My father says it's not healthy for delicate, fragile ladies to trust them-selves on such a contraption," little Violet mumbled. "And it takes up too much concentration."

"And that it's not safe. What if your dress gets caught in it?" added Lilly.

"Then you fall down," I said. "And then you get back up again. It's okay for women to do that, to fall down from time to time."

I noticed a look in Rose's eyes. It was the look a girl gets when she wants desperately to try a new thing but she is afraid she might fail and disappoint or embarrass herself in front of a laughing world or, worse, be judged by that same world. But then her hands reached out, and she took hold of the handlebars and slowly, as I held the bike steady, she climbed on.

"Now take it slow," I said. "I'll hold on. I won't let go."

Together, with me briskly walking beside her, we went a good fifteen yards, and I was just about ready to shout a loud "hooray," when she shouted louder, "Let go! I don't need your help."

"Dear," I insisted. "I think you do. This takes practice."

"Stop treating me like a little girl," she said. "I don't want your help!"

And so I let go, regrettably and two seconds later a heavy wind caught her skirt and wound it around her pedal, and her upper body dashed over the front end of the bike, sending her down into a puddle of muddy water, and a second later the bike landed on top of her.

I rushed down onto my hands and knees beside her in the puddle, pushing my bicycle to the side and then wiping the blood on her chin and nose with the sleeve of my own dress. "Rose," I cried. "Are you okay?"

Her sisters were there too, and they were holding her hands and rubbing her cheeks. She was crying, and her face was full of mud, and when she opened her eyes and looked at me, I feared she was a demon-possessed pig ready to yank my soul out from me.

"Look what you've done!" she shouted. "My mama always told us you were unladylike, even as a little girl, and now I believe her. She was right."

"Leave us alone," cried Lilly, as she pulled her sister up from the mud, and together the three girls hobbled into the house.

I pulled my bike up and tried straightening the dented handlebars the best I could. The girls didn't talk to me the rest of the evening, and their father scorned me for urging his daughter to try such a thing.

"Bicycle riding is a bad idea for women," he said. "Don't you ever let her try that again, do you understand?"

"Yes, sir," I said.

And that night, I felt guilt-stricken for having ruined her dress, so I stayed up all night long, turning sturdy, heavy, upholstered curtains into dresses for all three girls. I put a catalog I had gotten in the mail in front of me and tried to create the stylish hourglass silhouette by stitching stockings to the buttock, hip, bosom, and sleeve areas to exaggerate the desired wasp-waisted effect. And as I worked, visions of the girls and me dressed like ladies danced in my head.

"We don't like those dresses that you made for us. They look like curtains," they said the next morning.

"Yes, they were curtains yesterday," I said, sleep-deprived. "But today, they're dresses. It's my way of making amends for what happened to Rose's dress yesterday."

"They look like what a man would make if a man ever tried to sew." Rose's words always pricked me like thorns.

"That's a generalized statement, and it's not fair to men," I said. "There are male fashion designers, you know."

"We're not going to wear ugly dresses that you've made out of curtains. Our mama could turn curtains into ball gowns. She was good at sewing, but these? They look like tarp we'd use to cover the turkeys during a freeze. Why'd you put stockings inside them?"

"To give you ladies the appearance, the illusion of hourglass silhouettes. The boys will go wild over you. That's what you want, isn't it?"

At first, they looked disgusted, but then they started laughing, and soon we were all laughing, and I felt proud, for maybe they no longer viewed me as old and judgmental, and hopefully we were bonding. Two months went by before Rose started wearing the dress, and I suspected there might be a boy she was after.

And then one day my bicycle was missing for at least four hours, and so was she. I was horribly worried for her safety and ran through the town, searching for bike tracks and looking near every mud puddle out of fear she had fallen and drowned. I wanted desperately to tell my father and her father, but that would be disastrous. I would wind up being the tattletale, the one who allegedly thrives on getting Rose into trouble, rather than the one who was concerned with teaching her never to disappear like that again. Yes, everything I did was viewed as bad with regard to those girls, and it wasn't fair that I was given the job of looking after them, yet I was given no authority or respect in terms of guiding, instructing, or disciplining them. It was too much to bear, and it was ruining the life I had envisioned for myself and the person I wanted to be.

I said nothing to Rose when she returned four hours later with my bicycle. I smiled at her, dumb as a happy rock. That's what they wanted me to be, a happy rock they could hop over, stand on, and blame when they tripped and fell down.

"Why don't the four of us go for a walk? There's a full moon out and everything looks beautiful under a full moon," I suggested one evening after dinner. The men had drunk beer and were already asleep for the night, and Dahlia too was asleep and snoring, and there was nothing I craved more than good nighttime air. "What are you all staring at me for?"

I asked. "Let's go for a walk."

They were giving me the same look I remember their mother, my aunt, once giving me when I was little and I started to cry as she cut into the Thanksgiving turkey one year. "I don't want any turkey. I can't possibly eat old Rickety Tickety Turkey," I cried. "I liked him. He was the wisest of turkeys and good at giving speeches. He started them all with riddles. It's why no one ever slept during his speeches."

"You're weird," my Aunt Agatha said. "Abigail, you better watch Ava. She's got a weird imagination. It's ruining our feast today, but what's it capable of next?"

"She views the world differently, that's all," my mama had said to her sister. "She's a creative child. There's nothing wrong with that."

My mother was right. She understood me like that. And if she were around today, she'd know I had no interest in judging the girls or doing anything to make them hate me. She'd know my mind preferred other things, like standing out under the moon and thinking up stories I might write.

So as the girls and I stood alongside the dirty pond out back, I tried talking to them on a deeper level. "What dreams do you girls have for your lives?"

As I waited for them to answer, I noticed that even in a mud puddle one might catch a glimpse of the moon glistening across the water. "That my mama will come back," Violet said a moment later.

I put my arm around her. "That's a good wish," I said. "And you will get her back in heaven one day, but you need another dream, one you can focus on in the meantime, sweetie."

I held my breath, fearful that tagging "sweetie" on to the end might be seen as belittling, rather than the term of endearment that I meant.

"Do you have a dream?" Lilly asked me.

"I do," I said, although I hadn't thought of my dream in some time.

"What is it?"

"To write," I said. "I write all the time in my journal, but one day I'd like to write novels."

There were giggles and wiggles and whispers.

"Proper ladies don't whisper," I said, and then remembered I had given up trying to teach the girls anything. "What are you all whispering about?" I asked.

"I can't see you ever writing anything significant," declared Rose. She reminded me of the turkey that tried gobbling up all the other turkeys. It wasn't that he was hungry, just empty, and eating took his mind off his emptiness. "Your journal was lying open on the floor in your dirty room one day, just waiting to be read, so I took a look, but there wasn't anything good in it, so I closed it and slid it back under your bed where you keep it. Unless you go off to writing school, I can't see it happening."

It was the last time I tried reaching the girls on a deeper level like that, which was a shame, for I had in me the desire to make a difference, to coach them, not into becoming ladies, but into pursuing what they wanted in life, but they were going to fight me until the end. If I had been running for my second term as president of the unladylike club, they'd urge the men of our household not to vote for me, that's for sure.

So from that day on, I started focusing on their most primary needs, cooking and cleaning and waiting on them, as well as Dahlia, Stewart, and my Uncle George. I waited on everyone hand and foot, and I felt as if I were aging rapidly.

One morning I went for a ride on my bicycle, looking toward every seed-bearing plant and every tree that has fruit with seed in it, anything that might tell me what season it was. I was gone so long I grew hungry and laughed at myself, a woman with better things to do than say farewell to the spring of her life. When I reached the house, there was nothing I wanted more than to sit down and rest, but I couldn't. There were too many chores to do.

And those never-ending chores allowed my mind no time for living on a deeper, more creative level, for they meant waking up two hours before sunrise every morning to get the girls fed and dressed and out the door to school. And once I had the quiet house to myself, I worked non-stop just to get their clothes cleaned for the next day and dinner on their plates at night. It all made me miss doing chores side-by-side with my mama.

As months went by, I noticed myself longing for solitary confinement, for then I'd have quiet time with nothing to do and I could fill that silence and time with writing. I guess life is bad when you start fantasizing about spending time in a prison cell.

My cravings for a getaway spooked me, so out of my own guilty conscious I started making the girls get down on their knees every night to pray for one solid hour. It was an activity no one could critique me for enforcing. But at first, the girls tried.

"Why do you make us do this every night?" asked Lilly.

"You've each got three treasures—a heart, a mind, and a soul," I said.

"You've got to appreciate them. Don't keep them locked up inside collecting dust. And your soul, it's probably worth more than all the treasures put together. And your body is the chest that carries those treasures, so you want to keep that fit and looking good as well. And besides, without a body, you can't ride a bicycle."

"We don't like riding bicycles, and you can't make us pray."

"Then, I feel sorry for you girls, having to spend eternities with the souls you neglected to care for while you had the chance."

I suppose good and bad traits get carried down from one generation to the next and all the rudeness got wadded up and those three girls were the by-product of that wadded up rudeness. That had to be the case, I told myself when they pushed me over the edge.

"Your mother was insane. Are you?"

"Am I what?"

"Insane like her?"

"I hope," I said. "Because I'd rather be insane like her than evil like you three. You think you got your evilness from your mother?"

"Our daddy says you might turn crazy one day."

"Oh yeah? I think your daddy ought to instead be grateful he has me to care for you girls."

"He says it won't be for long. His cousin Mary is coming from Alabama, soon. She's going to take over, I think."

"Is that so?" I asked. "Then let us all pray for poor Mary."

I dropped to my knees beside them and truly prayed. I believed the girls were evil and needed all the prayers they could get. I don't believe evil is handed down throughout the generations. It's a choice, and those girls needed my prayers.

I had been going through the motions of prayer alongside them but hadn't actually prayed in some time. I felt bad for it, like something very important was missing from my life, and I felt ashamed, for my mama had done her best to instill in me the significance of constant, daily prayer. I felt distant from it and from all I once loved and who I was and where I was headed. I knew I couldn't blame anyone but myself for distancing myself from God, for a relationship with Him isn't inherited. It's a personal choice.

But tonight was different. The girls and I needed all the prayers we could get, even if they were only coming from me. "Lord God Almighty," I prayed silently. "I'm thinking of committing a crime. Can you forgive me in advance?"

Lydia

My lunch break ended, and so did Ava's writing. I put the journal back into my briefcase, frustrated that once again I was left hanging. Did she commit the crime? And what was it? I wanted to know.

Poor Ava. I spun my chair toward the typewriter and started typing her an obituary.

Ava Witherton, 21, of Kentucky and Sanibel, slowly and gradually died, the date is uncertain, while getting caught up in a life of tedious drudgery.

She was a strong woman, surviving without a heart. And when she was living, truly living, she believed that anything was possible.

I stopped typing there. Ava hadn't died. She was the sort of person that walks outdoors in the burgundy air of night to listen for possibilities as if she were listening for owls. And although possibilities are sometimes invisible, she'd call out to them, and they'd come. They'd line up on a perch, and she'd walk right over and observe them.

Ava was a faithful believer that all things were possible. Maybe she stopped writing in the journal and started writing a novel instead. And since I was now a journalist and tired of waiting for Marlena to send or not send me new pages, I decided to gather my own information. After work, I ran over to the public library and looked up novels by Ava Witherton. None. Poor Ava.

And because I wasn't an investigative journalist, but rather an obituary writer, my searching ended there. I would have to wait for Marlena, in her uncanny way, to send me more pages when she felt I was ready.

In the meantime, I could only assume that Ava went on to do one of two things: either she committed that crime, and hopefully nothing too serious, or she went about life not really living and eventually died amidst the drudgery.

Those were the only choices I saw Ava as having. But she was the girl who once believed that anything was possible. Maybe she would come up with more options.

XXXII

1960

Lydia

Buddy Holly, George Reeves, Lou Costello, William Bishop, Max Baer, Walter Williams, and Clark Gable were some of the famous obituaries to come across my desk over the next year, but none of them touched me more deeply than the one I had to write for my own father.

> *Lloyd Isleworth, 54, of Chicago, Illinois, died April 14th, 1960 in the arms of his daughter. He was best known for his contributions at Metropolitan Bank.*

My father was taking his last breaths when I arrived at the hospital. I missed his last words, which he spoke to the nurse just five minutes earlier but I got there in time to wrap my arms around him and tell him all that I had to say.

Now that I had uninterrupted time alone with him in the hospital room, there was so much he needed to hear. I told him I loved him and that we had some things in common. He knew and loved my mother. I never knew my mother but loved her anyway. And as I rubbed my fingers over his cheekbones, which were high and prominent like mine, I thanked him, not for the things he bought me, but for the traits he gave me. Along with his cheekbones and high forehead, I had his stubbornness and determination, and those two traits of his, good or bad, would live on in this world through me, his daughter. And I told him I felt a responsibility in some way to keep parts of him remembered forever, and the only way I could think to do that would be as I once did with my mother, to write about him and, secondly, to remember the good things he taught me. I would store his lessons in my very own jar of wisdom and pull them out whenever they were needed.

As I lay next to him in the hospital bed, I knew my personal time with him was running out. He no longer had to be at the bank in ten minutes, but he still had to go and I had to let him go. But, first, I had to tell him not to be upset with me for living my life like an unconventional woman. I liked the fact that he could no longer argue with me, but it didn't make it any easier telling him what I had to tell him, for tears were pouring out of my eyes, and I was sobbing as I said my last words to him, and I tried my best to say it in a rationalized manner that I knew he'd like.

"My ambition, Daddy," I cried. "I got that from you. I, too, am ambitious, maybe not to your extent, but a much smaller percentage of your ambition lives on in me. I do want to figure out how to proportion it all, so that maybe I could find a way to spend 50 percent of my time pursuing ambitions and the other 50 percent loving or spending time with people I love. I'm not sure. I need to play around with those numbers and figure it all out. Maybe from where you are you'll have a different perspective on it all, and you can help me with this."

I gained my composure and left the hospital room, but his death sent me crashing into a solemn mood for weeks, and despite having written hundreds, thousands of obituaries, his made me aware of my own mortality for the first time. And the reading of the will a couple of weeks later made me feel more alone than I had ever felt in the world.

I received nothing. All of Lloyd's assets, stocks, bonds, paper money, and the estate went to people from the bank he had worked with for years, including two of his long-term secretaries. He also gave a lump of money

to three nurses who had helped after his heart attack and sums of grati-
tude went to teachers from his past, from grades kindergarten through
high school. All I got was a letter.

My dearest Lydia,

*The will is not my way of punishing you, but rather, my way of respect-
ing you. I worked hard to give you all you might want in life but all you
wanted was to do it yourself.*

*My paying for your college education was all you needed, for you're the
type of woman who goes out and makes her own money in life. Now is
your chance, dear, and I wish you the very best of luck.*

Sincerely,
Your father

"Bastard," I mumbled to myself over the next several weeks. My father
said nothing in his letter about continuing payments for the apartment he
had set me up in. Rent was now my responsibility. I wasn't making enough
money at the paper to stay any longer in Chicago's Gold Coast District;
so, I placed ads in the paper and sold the nice furniture he had bought me
and moved into something more affordable on the other side of town. I
bought a double and triple-lock for the door and a pocketknife to keep
under my bed. It was a cheap bed, one that served as a sofa by day. I never
wrote to Josh. I never gave him my new address. It had been months since
he last sent me a letter. I could have sent him another, but I didn't. Life
had me busy, and I knew better than to turn my thoughts back to the romantic fantasy of some ghost.

The apartment was the size of a shoebox, but I could afford it fine. The
only closet, converted into a sink and stove, left me no place good to hang
my professional wardrobe; so, I hung it across the shower pole. When that
broke, I laid it all neatly across the floor at the foot of my sofa bed. I used
the kitchen table as a desk and told myself the place would be fine tempo-

rarily until I could afford something nicer. I would be saving a lot of money by living in such an apartment.

It was noisy at night. There was music, children crying, a man and woman fighting. When I couldn't sleep, one night, I gave in and reread the bundle of letters Josh had sent me. Those letters started me thinking of him again, and I didn't know why I always did that, why I let my thoughts linger back to some guy I only knew for a summer and then wrote to for nearly three years after that. Maybe there was something wrong with me. A normal woman would have moved on by now.

I gave serious thought as to why I held onto Josh so tightly. In a way, I had done the same thing with my mother, whom I never knew, yet thought of daily as a young girl. Maybe I had trained myself to hold onto the fantasy of someone because that is all I ever had. I again told myself it was time to let go of a guy so far removed from my real everyday life and place. Josh and I were over for good, I convinced myself. We as a couple were officially declared extinct.

I felt a world away from him and lonely, and when I walked into work several months later with dark circles under my eyes and my clothes hanging on me, I considered writing an obituary for myself. Once I started budgeting for the sake of survival, I stopped buying the things I liked to eat and instead bought what I could afford. I had lost a lot of weight and gained a new appreciation of the value of the dollar.

I started drinking three cups of coffee every morning and eating nothing but an apple for lunch, then rice and beans for dinner. Maybe I was grieving. I don't know, for sure, but getting out of bed in the morning felt like too much of a task and it only made me want to fall back down again and rest.

I no longer walked to work as I once loved to do, but now clambered up the steps of the bus and sat with my eyes closed until it reached my stop. "Bastard," I still mumbled every time I thought about my father leaving me nothing, but then I suddenly stopped. For a word like that wasn't mine. It was his. I had heard him say it a million times, every time he disliked someone at work. I swore I would never say it again. I wanted to be nothing like him in that regard. I wanted to be better. I felt a new inner energy the last week of July. At work it had me hurrying through the halls toward the elevator. It also made me smack into someone, sending all the papers in his hands crashing to the floor in a big mess.

"Sorry," I said, dropping to the floor to gather them up.

He kneeled down as well and started to help. He looked to be in his late twenties, and he was handsome in a classic, stately looking way with wavy brown hair and matching brown eyes, and he was in a hurry by the way he shuffled through the papers, not caring that the edges were getting all ruffled.

"I should have been at the convention ten minutes ago," he muttered, hardly looking at me.

"The Republican convention?"

"Yeah. My intern was supposed to have made all these copies for me, but he never showed, so I had to borrow two interns from the human interest department, and they were slow as turtles."

"There's a ton of copies here," I said.

"Thirteen hundred," he said, shuffling a handful of the papers into a neat pile. "One for each of the thirteen hundred GOP delegates. Darn intern! So much for his resume."

"I guess you pay the price for having power at your fingertips," I said with a grin. "But I wouldn't know. I don't have any interns."

We both stood up. He was over six feet tall and had to look down on me. He was handsome and intense-looking. "I've never seen you before. I'd remember if I did. What do you cover?" he asked.

"Obituaries."

He studied my eyes. "Aren't you too pretty to be covering those?"

"Watch it," I said, offended. I handed the papers back to him.

"I didn't mean that," he said. "I mean, you are pretty . . . but I shouldn't have said that here at work." He paused and said boldly, "Now if I bumped into you out on the street, I could say it and not get in trouble, right?"

I laughed. "I guess."

"I didn't introduce myself. I'm Ethan Blake."

I had seen and heard his name several times. He was fast gaining a reputation as a young and rising political journalist, and his byline was everywhere. "I'm Lydia Isleworth. Nice to meet you."

"I'm sorry for crashing into you like I did. I was in a hurry, still am."

"My fault," I said. "Hope you're not too late."

He started to turn and walk away, but then walked back. "I always wondered, do you people write obituaries at night or by day?"

"Day mostly. There's laws that don't let women work that late, you know."

"Then you're done for today?"

"Unless someone important dies before I catch the bus, yes I am."

"How would you like to attend the convention with me?"

Thoughts of my lonely little apartment rummaged through my mind and GOP delegates nominating Nixon sounded better than me collapsing onto my sofa bed as I did every night. "I'd love to," I answered. "Although I'm not used to all the excitement of a convention. The department where I work is a bit quieter, you know."

He laughed and handed me a pile of the papers. "You mind holding this half?"

"Not at all."

The convention turned out to be a lively and patriotic experience for me and, without any reference to political parties, it as a whole reminded me that freedom and self-government are for everyone, not just for some, and they are worth fighting for, if need be. The message was simple, I thought.

That night, after the interviews were over and the energy died down, Ethan and I parted outside the front doors of the convention hall. He insisted on driving me home, but I knew he had deadlines to make, and, besides, I didn't want him knowing where I was living. It was my problem, and I'd work my way out of it soon enough.

The next morning, Ethan was like a burst of living energy when he showed up in the obituary department.

"I was wondering what time you break for lunch," he said. "Maybe we might try someplace quiet being that last night we were surrounded by thirteen hundred GOP delegates."

"Yes, quiet does sound nice," I answered. "I just have to finish this last obituary. Did you get everything in last night?"

"Of course. That speech by Barry Goldwater removing himself from the race, where he called on the conservatives to take back the party, was the highlight of the convention. I got a great interview with him outside after we said good-bye."

Over lunch, Ethan and I discussed the other side of things, of Senator Kennedy's theme of getting the country moving again, and how he assailed the missile gap with the Russians and denounced the Eisenhower administration for allowing a Communist regime to come to power in Cuba. And we talked about how Nixon criticized Kennedy for his lack of experience.

We went for lunch again the next day and the next and the next after that, and soon we started going for dinner after work, long and quiet at a nice restaurant or quick as a midnight snack, depending on the hours we worked and the deadlines we had to meet. And once, we went to see Marlena as supporting actress in an independent film that made it to the States! It was playing at a little art theater on the south side of the city, and I could hardly contain myself, for when she showed up on the big screen, playing the part of a nasty school teacher at a private girl's boarding house, I jumped up from my seat, whistled, and screamed, and Ethan had to pull me back down again. I went back and saw that movie five more times by myself. I was so proud of her!

Ethan and I could analyze the news for hours, turning headlines into major discussions. We differed on what constitutes newsworthiness, or which story should have made the front page and why, or which story appeared slanted, or why one story was given abundant coverage while another got a blurb. Events I hadn't paid attention to were escalating in Vietnam, and Ethan insisted it was newsworthy and would only become more so.

But I was mostly interested in things happening locally, in the windy city, until one September evening another wind from far away caught my attention.

"Hurricane Donna is headed for the Caribbean," I said to Ethan over dinner. "I hope it doesn't hit Florida."

"Too soon to tell," he said. "There's uncertainty at this point."

"Donna is moving into the Gulf to the west of Sanibel," I said the next day over lunch. "With winds over a hundred miles per hour."

"I didn't hear any mention of Sand-ball," he said. "What exactly is Sandball?"

"Sanibel. It's a barrier island in Southwest Florida. Maybe they didn't actually mention Sanibel. Maybe I just thought I heard it. I know it's still too soon to tell where the thing is headed."

I didn't want to say more about Sanibel, for the weather forecasts were already stirring up thoughts of Josh in my mind, and I didn't know what to do about it. Ethan and I had become romantically involved just a few weeks prior; so, the thoughts and concerns I was having for Josh were only confusing me. I didn't feel like going back there in my mind, to some guy I hadn't seen or spoken to or written in ages. But still, my feelings for Josh felt stronger than those I had for my current man, the one who was a realistic part of my everyday life. I scared myself but couldn't help it.

"Many lives were lost as Donna skirted to the north of Puerto Rico with one hundred-and-thirty-five mile-per-hour winds," I read from the paper to Ethan over dinner.

"It doesn't look good," he said.

"Its course suddenly changed to almost a true west heading," I told him over coffee Wednesday morning, September 7.

"You still don't know for sure that it's going to hit your little Sanibel Island."

I wandered in and out of the weather department all morning, and, later in the day, Donna had begun to move more to the northwest, and the Hurricane Center issued a hurricane watch for southwest Florida.

Shortly after, the watch had been upgraded to a hurricane warning, and I pictured both Marlena and poor Josh boarding up their windows and securing anything that might blow away. I knew from a letter that Marlena had returned to Sanibel after finishing work on her first film, and I worried about her.

It was mid-afternoon on Thursday, September 8, when my phone at work rang.

"Hi Lydia," said a female voice.

"Marlena! I saw your movie! You're going to win an Oscar for that. I just know it. You were amazing!"

"Thank you, but did you know there's a hurricane headed for us?"

"Yes, I've been tracking it. Are you okay? What's happening there?"

"I'm using the pay phone at the ferry landing, and there's a line behind me like you wouldn't believe. And there's also a line to get off this island. I'm the thirteenth car."

"Good. You're leaving. That's wise. You'd be crazy not to. Where are you going?"

"I've got an actress friend, aspiring, who lives in Chicago. She's trying to break into television. I haven't seen her for some time. I could visit with her, and maybe you and I could meet up for dinner if you're not too busy? I don't want to interfere with your job."

"I'd love to. When are you flying out?"

"I'm not. I'm driving, but I drive fast and straight through. It might take me awhile to get out of town with all the evacuees, but once I'm out, I plan to cruise. Long car rides relax me."

"You've got both of my numbers?"

"Yes, you gave them to me in your last letter."

"I'll give you one more number, just in case. I might be at that number over the weekend."

"Got it," she said. "I'll see you soon." And then, just as we were about to hang up, she added, "Guess whom I bumped into here at the ferry landing a few minutes ago?"

"Who?"

"That guy you used to like. I didn't know it was him until we got to talking, and I mentioned I was leaving for Chicago, and he said he knew someone who lived there, someone pursuing a journalism career and what a small island. We put two and two together."

"Josh! Did he tell you we wrote letters for three years and they just stopped?"

"No. He was with his father and . . ."

"Did you say he was in line for the ferry?"

My stomach swirled, and rudimentary questions thrashed about my mind like debris flying around in a hurricane. *Who* did she say he was with? I know I interrupted. *What* was he doing with his life? *Why* was he on the dock? *When* was he evacuating? *Where* was he going? And *how* was he getting there? I'm sure they only spoke small talk, but still, I had other questions, like *what* did he look like and it's not one of the "w" journalistic questions, but *did* he ask about me?

"No, he wasn't in line for the ferry. They're hunkering down, weathering out the hurricane. He said weather doesn't upset him at all. Hey, I've got to go, Lydia. There's a line of people behind me waiting to use this phone."

"Wait," I cried into the phone.

"Can't. I just watched nine cars in front of me board. I'm not losing my spot in line. I'll call you once I'm in Chicago. Bye."

She hung up.

The next morning, Friday morning, the Miami Hurricane Center had positioned Donna's center at 175 miles south of Miami, heading northwest, and it was reported that the storm was releasing energy equivalent to a hydrogen bomb exploding in the atmosphere every eight minutes—and it had been strengthening.

"Its forward movement is becoming erratic so its true direction is difficult to predict," I said as I stopped by Ethan's desk.

And that night I too was becoming erratic, for I no longer knew whether I wanted to move forward with Ethan. How could I when my thoughts were with Josh? It wasn't right. It was criminal to lead one guy on when I still loved another. I hoped it was love. It had to be. Obsession or infatuation is over a movie star, I convinced myself, someone you've never known or truly loved. I knew Josh, and what I was feeling now was simply a love that wouldn't go away.

"Let's stay in and have dinner at my place tonight," he said after lunch. Did you pack your things for the night?"

"Of course," I said, preferring to spend the next two days in his cozy arms as opposed to my lonely rundown shoebox of an apartment.

But when I slipped into his arms that night, I could only imagine Josh and his father in the darkened midst of the deafening, howling winds, with objects striking their house, fearing for their lives.

As dawn approached, Donna's eye passed through the central Florida Keys. I tuned Ethan's radio to the weather and insisted we stay in bed, listening to any changes in its course. It was both of our days off, and neither of us could remember the last time we stayed in bed without rushing off. For me, I think it had been way back when I faked having polio, and for him it was mononucleosis in college.

At eight-thirty, the Weather Bureau's Miami radar had shown the eye approaching Everglades City, and the hurricane's forward speed at 20 miles per hour.

I got out of bed and showered, and at around noon, about the time they had predicted Donna's eye to arrive near Sanibel, Ethan's phone rang. It was Marlena. She had arrived to Chicago early and wanted to meet for lunch instead of dinner.

XXXIII

ETHAN KNEW AND MET every politician in Chicago, but he had never met a movie star before; so, I invited him to walk over with me to the John Hancock Building on Michigan Avenue, where I was to meet up with Marlena. On the way over, he tried telling me she wasn't technically a movie star until she starred in a leading role or won some awards. He was probably right, but still, she was the only person I ever knew to play any role in any movie, and I was proud.

"There she is!" I exclaimed when I saw her, looking more glamorous at age forty-nine than she had ever looked before. "Isn't she amazing? She's more beautiful in person, don't you think?"

Ethan nodded. "I guess."

I dropped his hand and threw my arms around her.

"Lydia, my darling, you cut your hair," she announced.

"You like it?"

"Professional. There's no hint of little girl left in you."

We held hands long after our hug ended, and I wiped a tear from my eye as she consoled me about my father. For a blink of a moment I felt like pouring it all out about his will and where I was living and how I had barely been staying afloat financially, eating like a pig whenever someone brought donuts or bagels in to work and lying awake at night amidst the noise of my apartment, but I refrained from all of that and accepted her words of sympathy regarding my father instead. I didn't in any way want her to assume I was hinting for money now that she was rising to fame. And, besides, Ethan was standing close, and I wouldn't want him hearing. I wouldn't ever want any man feeling sorry for me. I was a strong woman and could manage fine on my own.

"There's someone who is dying to meet you," I whispered to Marlena, then turned to signal Ethan closer. "Ethan," I said when he stepped up to us. "I'd like to introduce you to Marlena DiPluma."

"Nice to meet you," he said shaking her hand. "You were wonderful in your movie. Congratulations."

"Oh please," she said. "I swore that if I ever made it big, I'd never become one of those types that have to be the center of attention. Maybe that's why I don't like talking about my performances. But thank you."

Ethan glanced at me, and I nodded back, and we both knew it was best that he didn't ask for her autograph. That had been my plan. I thought it might boost her ego, but I don't think she wanted that.

"I heard you two spent your first night together at the Republican Convention. Are you Republican?" she asked Ethan.

"Off the record," he answered. "Yes, I am."

Marlena looked as if she were about to pull a shotgun out of her purse as her character had done in the movie. "I'm a Democrat," she said, and then broke into laughter. "But that doesn't matter. I'm not the one dating you, am I?"

I kissed him on the cheek and told him we girls had better get going. We didn't have much time together, just a lunch. Marlena and I walked up Michigan Avenue until we reached the Lincoln Park area and then walked into a good Irish pub.

"The eye of the hurricane is probably over Sanibel," she said, glancing at her watch. "That means it's peaceful there now."

We both knew that in about an hour onshore winds could bring the highest tides and likely do the most wind-related damage. There was nothing we could do but wait and hear the news after it happened. We tried talking of other things. She had recently found six gray hairs, and it bothered her, as did talk of a causeway going up that would link Sanibel to the mainland.

"It's only talk," I reassured her. "It probably won't happen."

"I think I've heard you say that before."

"What?"

"That it won't happen. If I remember correctly, it was when I told you I didn't get the role I wanted in that movie, and you told me, 'Don't worry, Marlena. That movie probably won't even happen.'"

I rolled my eyes, knowing exactly what she was referring to. "So did you go see 'Pillow Talk'?" I asked.

"Who hasn't seen a movie that got nominated for a half-dozen Oscars?"

"What do I know?"

We laughed, and Marlena took a swig of her beer. "You think I could have done as well as Doris Day? Be honest."

"Better," I said. "I know she got nominated for her first Academy Award, but she overacted in my opinion. You could have done much better."

"You think? You think Rock Hudson and I would have looked good together?"

"Great together."

"Damn," she said as the waitress set our fish platters down. "We probably would have."

I took a few bites of my sandwich and then dared to ask what I had wanted to know the moment I gave Marlena the hello hug.

"That guy I used to like, you bumped into him on the dock?"

"Lydia," she said with a gleam in her eye. "He's hotter than Rock Hudson! And he was pleasant, too."

"Anything else?" I had been starving for news of him, anything at all, but like an egret perched on the Sanibel Fishing Pier, I wanted my tidbits without looking too eager.

"Nope. I told you everything there was."

"What do you think of Ethan? He's an ambitious man," I said. "His coverage is excellent. I could learn a thing or two from him."

"If there's anything to learn from a man," she said, "I suppose."

"You're not one of those man-haters, are you, Marlena?"

"Of course not," she said, batting her false eyelashes at me. "But I think men are for loving, not learning from. Do you love him?"

I took a deep breath. "I'm still gathering information," I said coyly. "Not to change the subject, but did you talk with Josh for awhile?" I feared she might hear my stomach growling for more. "I hope he is doing well."

"I only paid him attention because he's darn good-looking, the best-looking thing I've laid eyes on. All man."

I was glad when the waiter brought another beer so I had something to down before my curiosities poured out further. But I could see in her eyes that she had more scraps to toss my way.

"He was holding hands at first with a blonde," she said, glancing at me as she drank.

"What else?" I insisted, wondering if that was why he stopped writing. He could have had the courtesy of telling me. Then, again, our letters weren't the mushy sort. Neither of us described any relationship or feelings we had for each other or whether or not we were seeing anyone else. We only wrote about our lives, our philosophies, and our day-to-day thoughts. Pretty much we wrote about things that turn friends into really good friends, and I feel like I grew to love him on a deeper level through those letters, a level that couples don't get to unless they've been separated by time and distance and keep on writing through it all. I wrote gooey stuff once in a letter, but then I held it over a candle flame and burned it to ashes!

"Nothing else to report," Marlena declared.

But there had to be. She wasn't looking at me straight on, but still from the sides of her eyes. I always knew sources had more to say when they looked at me like that. "It's not nice to tease a bird," I said. "What else?"

"I did ask him what he was doing, and he said he's chartering by day and something about practicing his music at night."

"Good for him," I said. "Sounds like the life he had wanted for himself."

"Write him, Lydia. Why don't you write him?"

"Why would I write him a letter? He's got a girlfriend."

She gave me a suspicious look. "Yeah, but it looked more like that girl was hanging onto him. She was holding his hand, if you know what I mean. The way in which couples hold hands tells you everything. And it looked to me as if she liked him more than he liked her. Does that make sense?"

It did. I knew that to be the case with Ethan and me, only he had stronger feelings for me than I did for him.

"You think I should write a letter to Josh?"

"Absolutely. Your eyes tell me you're still interested, and I think his eyes said the same."

"Maybe, but it's impossible," I said, then stopping what I was about to say to correct myself when she rolled her eyes. "I mean, nothing is impossible, but right now, it would never work out between us. We can't go on writing letters forever without ever seeing each other. I think that's why our letters ended in the first place. He probably got bored or fed up with just writing. Besides, I only knew him a summer, you know. And now I care for Ethan and we're in a relationship, a real one. So did Josh say or do anything else?"

"Yes, as I was getting into my car, about ready to close the door, he nonchalantly walked over and told me to tell you he found a Junonia shell on the beach. Is that supposed to mean anything to you?"

"Yeah, he's rubbing it in my face that I couldn't find one," I said. "Or it's another one of life's reminders that anything is possible. I think I'll write him."

Marlena smiled as she reached into her bag and pulled out another set of pages. I should have known Ava was up to something I might relate to in my own life.

"Tell me this," I said, taking them from her. "Did she do it? Did she commit a crime like she was talking about?"

"Oh, did she ever!"

But that was all Marlena would tell me, for it was up to me to find a quiet spot to spend with my friend Ava so she could tell me all about it in her own words.

Marlena and I finished lunch and then walked back to Michigan Avenue where we shopped without buying and stopped for coffee twice before continuing on to the art museum. She wanted to look at beautiful art as a way of forgetting about the hurricane for an hour.

After that we parted. She left to meet up with her friend, the aspiring actor. And tomorrow morning, the two of them would drive back to Florida together. It sounded like a chaotic, poorly thought out plan to drive this far for just one night, but there was no convincing her otherwise. Her mind was elsewhere. It was on Sanibel, along with everything precious that she owned, and from what she claimed, bits of her soul lingered there. She had to get back, to assess the damage and to simply be there. And then she'd be flying off to London the following week to start filming on a new movie.

It was early evening when we parted, and I walked to the corner of Michigan Avenue and Chicago Avenue and sat down on a bench near the Chicago Water Tower. It was one of my favorite places to sit in the city, and I found it as relaxing as one finds sitting near a lighthouse. It, like many lighthouses, had survived through disasters.

I opened Ava's journal and started to read, wondering whether it was going to be a journal entry from prison.

NEW YORK CITY
1905

Ava

As surely as God created the sun and the moon and put the stars up in the sky and the granules of sand on the beaches, so do I believe we have natural resources placed within us as abundant as the sea. But if we don't believe and we don't tap into those resources, they'll lie dormant within. And our lives will never change.

I was twenty-two years old, and it was the summer of 1898—two years after my mother's death and one year after inheriting the responsibility for those three despised girls—when I committed my crime. It wasn't the sort of crime that sends anyone to Hell, I don't think. I didn't strangle anyone—nothing like that. But the crime I committed was a premeditated one. I had given it thought, knowing it would rescue me from my life in Kentucky, from the never-ending daily chores and tedious doldrums of life on the turkey farm and from having to look at the hurt, angry faces of those nasty flowers every morning and from turning myself into a heartless spinster.

What did I do? I married a wealthy man. There's nothing wrong with marrying a wealthy man, but I married as a heartless woman, meaning I didn't love him. And marrying a man, when your heart is elsewhere, is a criminal thing to do not only to the man, but also to yourself.

Leonardo DiPluma was an advertising executive from New York. I met him when he was traveling through the Midwest conducting demographic surveys for a mail-order catalog. He came through Kentucky to interview farmwomen on their likes and dislikes at about that time when I had been pondering how I might escape my life. I had been receiving the catalog in the mail for years, and when he walked up to me in town one day with a clipboard in hand and introduced himself, I told him I liked what I had been seeing in the advertisements.

"I know some ladies are put off by your catalog. Maybe because they can't afford anything, but I hope you keep sending it. I love getting your catalog in the mail."

"Tell me, what is it that you like so much?" he asked, removing the pencil from behind his ear and writing something down.

"The pictures remind me there's a whole other world out there, so unlike my own."

"Can you be more specific?"

"Yes," I answered. "I especially like the ads that depict women outside of the home in nondomestic settings."

"Advertising is leaning more in that direction," he said. "A few men I interviewed earlier criticized it, saying it's the advertisements that are pushing women out into the world. I disagree. I believe the women are doing that on their own and the advertisements simply reflect it."

"Yes, I agree with you," I said, amazed at how interesting this man was.

"You're an intelligent demographic," he said, flipping to a new page on his clipboard.

"I am? Why thank you," I said. "But what's a demo . . . demographic?"

"We break people into categories, age, gender, income levels . . . things like that."

"Well, I'm flattered to be one of your demographics and to be on your mailing list," I said. "It's about the only mail I get. I especially like the postcard with the handwriting. Are you the one who personally writes that to me?"

He laughed. "No. There's no way. We send out eight thousand of those postcards. It just looks like someone personally took the time to handwrite it." He smiled and added something to his notes.

"Now tell me," he said. "How often do you purchase from our catalog?"

I was embarrassed. I wanted to lie. I didn't want to tell him that I never had any funds to place an order, but it didn't mean I didn't like all the watches, jewelry, shoes, garments, wagons, stoves, furniture, china, musical instruments, baby carriages and glassware. Those items reminded me of all there was in the world and of potential. "Please, don't be offended when I tell you this, but I've only ordered one item. Everything looks lovely and it's all displayed so nicely, but . . ."

"What was that one item you bought?" he asked.

"A bicycle."

He looked up from his clipboard and raised an eyebrow at me. "Really?"

"Yes, I love it. It was like a burst of freedom the day it arrived. I take off on it whenever I'm upset or frustrated or bored. I'm gone for hours, and no one knows or cares, I don't know which."

"I see." His hair was dark and slick and his eyes blue, the color of deep water, and it was the first time I noticed them. I had been preoccupied with his clothes. He wore a brightly colored shirt with a hard, white tubular collar worn under a sporty sack-suit jacket, and he looked like he just stepped foot off the pages of his catalog. He was around thirty years old and good enough looking to be a model.

"With regard to clothes," he continued. "If you were to purchase any clothes from our catalog in the near future, what would they be?"

"Sport clothing," I said without hesitation. "A bicycling costume. I saw one where the wearer can buckle the skirt around her legs for complete coverage of the ankles. The same skirt could then be unbuckled for a more ladylike traditional look when not on the bicycle."

His questions made me feel important, and when the sun that was above us when the survey started was now leaning to the side of us, I noticed Leonardo no longer looked to his clipboard for the next questions. I think he was making them up because he didn't want our conversation to end.

"Ah, let me remember what else I'm supposed to ask," he said when I started pacing back and forth impatiently. It wasn't that I was bored, but nature was calling. "Do you plan to stay in Kentucky or are you interested in ever moving to New York?" he asked.

"I love Kentucky," I said. "But I'd move just about anywhere. There's nothing keeping me here."

"Are you engaged?"

"Is that really a question on your survey?"

"It does apply," he said. "It's the awkward part of gathering demographic information."

"Oh," I said. "No, I don't have time for men. I'm too busy chasing after the turkeys and these three wretched girls I care for and . . ."

"You don't sound so happy."

"Is there a demographic category for unhappy women?"

"No," he laughed.

"Then I don't have to answer that one."

"No, you don't," he said. "But are you available tomorrow, same time, same place? I've got another survey I'd love to conduct on you. You're a great demographic."

I laughed. I was not only flattered, but I was interested. Ours was the first stimulating conversation I had since . . . since I was in Jaden's arms and we had been talking about my being a woman and the choices I had since becoming one.

"I've taken too much of your time. Thank you."

"Your welcome," I replied, snapping out of my Jaden daydream and re-membering where I was now and who I had become—a woman dressed in a curtain standing in the middle of town answering a list of questions about my life, which suddenly didn't sound anything like the life I could have chosen for myself had I stayed on that island and married the man I loved.

The next day we met again, but this time I brought a blanket and a pic-nic basket and suggested we sit under a tree instead of standing for two hours.

"I don't want to damage your reputation by doing this," Leonardo said as he took the basket from me and watched as I flipped the blanket up into the air and let it land flat on the ground. "This is a professional survey, you know. I am here on business."

"To hell with everyone," I said as I took the basket from his hands and sat down. "I'm tired of living in fear that I might offend someone. I wasn't put on this planet to properly please others and pretend I like doing so."

He stood there staring down at me. "I'm thinking you fall into a dif-ferent demographic category now that I'm getting to know you a bit bet-ter," he said. "You're not the typical woman."

I rolled my eyes and opened the basket. "Yes, I do live in a lonely cate-gory all of my own, don't I?"

He sat down beside me and took the bread I handed him. "I wouldn't say that. I see women like you in New York all the time, and I'm thinking there might be more of you out here in the country, as well, but they're not being honest in their survey answers. They're in hiding, and they're afraid to come out of the haystack, maybe. I appreciate your honesty."

"Why?"

"My job is to interview all kinds of women and then create a publica-tion that appeals mostly to the masses but also to ladies living on both sides of the spectrum. Because of you I'm thinking of going out on a limb in future publications. I'd like to start gearing my material more toward the women out there who actually want to be doing more in life, meaning sporting costumes and so forth."

He asked me a bunch of silly questions and then took a break to eat bread and cheese. And then I pulled out a secret stash of brandy I carried with me from time to time, and I sipped just enough to tingle my toes.

Soon, I took charge and started asking him the questions. He was thirty-one. He came from a wealthy but small family. He was the only son and inherited his parents' wealth. His father had been a banker in New York and died a couple of years ago. His mother died five years before that. He knew people in New York, and it had been simple for him to get a job at the catalog. They paid him well, and because I was now trying to figure out what sort of demographic he was, I asked him to be more specific with regard to his financial status. I liked his answer, and I liked him. Had my heart not sunk to the bottom of the sea, I probably could have fallen in love with a man like him.

"Do you have time for one more survey tomorrow?" he asked when we stood up a few hours later.

"I do," I said. "I do," I said again after the next day's survey. "I do," I said the day after that. "I do," I said a week later and again two weeks later.

"Do you?" I started to ask ten surveys later, when I learned he wasn't as interested in my information as he was in my long, dark hair, heart-shaped face and brown oval eyes. It was the first time anyone put shapes to my features, telling me I had a heart-shaped face and oval eyes. "Do you want to marry me?"

"I've never heard of a woman asking that before," he replied. And then he said, "Yes, I do."

I didn't love him, but I liked him. I especially liked the way he complimented my features, making me feel like I was an exquisite and detailed object straight off the pages of his catalog. I was also flattered that beneath my old faded dresses I still possessed beauty, for I hadn't felt any since leaving Sanibel Island nearly two years ago.

And when he placed a ring on my finger, a ring I had only gawked at in the catalog for years, I cried, for I never thought my hands or fingers could ever look feminine, not after all the work they had done.

Dahlia gave me her blessing, as did Stewart. And the girls were giddy as river otters the day I married Leonardo out back, behind the pond with the sun glistening down upon the brown, muddy water. Their Aunt Mary, the one they adored, had arrived from Alabama, and she was as excited to take over as their caretaker as they were to see me go.

I left Kentucky and moved to New York with Leonardo, him having no idea he married a heartless woman. He was a good man and attractive, too, and I felt bad marrying him when my heart was elsewhere, but I couldn't see I had any other choice. I carried the burden of my crime within me for years, trying never to make it difficult on Leo, the innocent victim of my heartless love. But every night I faced the consequences of the crime I had committed.

I quietly cried myself to sleep thinking of Jaden and how I loved him. At first, it was horrific trying to love a man when my heart was settled on the bottom of the sea, longing to be rediscovered by the man it belonged to. I thought about what dear old Grandmalia once told me: a woman would be wise to marry a man that loves her more. That way, he'll stay devoted. I now disagreed with her and had to catch my mind from fluttering off to a time and place where I loved someone who loved me equally. That sort of balanced love is out there, but it's rare.

Soon, I became like any other woman who simply thinks back fondly to the boy she once loved and wonders how his life turned out. Had he any hardships? True joy? A woman to love him? And, most importantly, had he ever in the course of time thought of me in any way?

Leo loved me aggressively, and his words of affection read from his mouth boldly and confidently as if they were coming from one of the advertising campaigns he was working on. I never had to question his love for me. If ever I was ten minutes late after shopping or having tea with the ladies, he came in search of me. His kind of assertive love made me think Jaden never loved me as intensely. If he did, he would have come searching for his lost treasure. And because he didn't, I now belonged to someone else. And now Jaden would no longer recognize me, starting with my clothes. Leo took pride in dressing me like a model from his catalog. He surprised me with extravagant reception gowns and visiting dresses, and despite years of living and socializing like royalty, I stopped in my tracks like a wood duck one day when I spotted my lovely green, purple, yellow, red, buff and blue gown in a mirror I was passing by.

Who *was* that woman wearing a huge picture hat piled with flowers, ribbon, and stuffed birds? And look at that excessive jet beading trim on the shoulders, waist and lower half of her skirt! Fancy trim meant one thing: status!

"That can't be you," I muttered beneath my breath, turning to view my new plumage. Ava—the girl who once wore curtains and didn't care about fashion or outer appearance and who had in the past become so meshed in tedious tasks that she swore she was the color gray. It's the male ducks that live the loveliest, most colorful lives. The females are drab. "But not anymore," I said into the mirror. "Look at you, Ava. Your new outer color reflects so well who you are on the inside, a creative being. Try to adapt."

"Talking to yourself, dear?" Leo asked, startling me. "I guess a few words of positive affirmation to one's self is a good thing."

I laughed and felt my face turning red. Then I looked him in the eyes, not sure whether he'd understand. "I guess I still perceive myself as the girl chasing after the turkeys instead of my own dreams," I said.

"How about perceiving yourself as Leo's beautiful wife and as royal-looking as any queen?" he asked. "Ava, you don't notice all the heads turning your way when you walk by, but I do. You don't have to feel guilty for your beauty. You've hidden it long enough."

We both laughed at how silly our conversation had turned, and he took me in his arms and started kissing my neck and whispering into my ears.

"Whistle," I said with a grin.

"Why should I whistle?"

"Just do it," I said, laughing. "It might bring the stuffed birds on my hat back to life again."

He pulled the hat off my head and tossed it on the ground, and we laughed as we often did and then walked hand and hand down through the long halls to our bedroom.

Later that evening I told Leo that I liked the social world he had introduced me to, but that I craved more than biscuits with the ladies, fashion shows, and chit-chatty female gossip. I told him I always wanted to be a writer and that I cared more about inner ideas than I did about outward appearances. It surprised me horribly the next day when he had told me he talked to his creative friends over at one of the women's magazines and they agreed to give me an opportunity to write fashion articles. Leo knew everyone, and he was well liked, and when he wanted something, he had no problem asking, and they had no problem giving.

But fashion articles? I didn't tell Leo how disappointed or uninterested I was in writing about fashion. I didn't want to hurt his feelings or make him look bad in front of the people giving me the opportunity to write in the first place. Still, I wanted nothing to do with it and longed to run and hide within the private corridors of my mind, where maybe I had some ideas lying dormant for a novel.

Instead, I took on the challenge presented and to my astonishment my very first article was published in a local woman's magazine.

A victory for women—ladies, you can kiss good-bye to that hourglass shape of the nineties and say hello to the longer- lined, over-laced corsets that support the spine and abdomen. No more losing your minds! Now women can have both health and curvaceous, decorative fashion at the same time.

Shortly after my first article appeared, I witnessed the power of the wardrobe. The daughter of our neighbors was between plain and outright ugly, but one day she went out wearing the most lavish ball gown, and it converted her into a princess, sparing her from life as a spinster. It had been worth her mother's investment and made my writing about fashion meaningful. Maybe there was more to fashion than I thought.

I went on to write many more articles, including ones about the feminists who were influencing women's dress behind the scenes. Women were starting to wear suits, shirts, hard collars, and ties—typically worn only by men—and these same women were working their way into professions historically belonging to men.

Of course, I wrote articles on the bicycling craze because it was this contraption that turned sport clothing into fashion. No more wearing full wool costumes covering the body in extreme heat just to preserve modesty.

I wrote fast and furiously for the next several years, turning the 1903 opening of the New York Stock Exchange's first building at 10 Broad Street into a fashion story, and the opening of the Manhattan Bridge that same year into a style story, and the 1904 start of the construction on the Grand Central Station into a trend story. And when a woman was arrested for smoking a cigarette while riding in an open automobile in New York City, I was there, jotting down notes concerning everything that woman was wearing, from head to toe. And when the New York subway opened in 1905, I rode along with the 350,000 people on the 9.1-mile tracks, all the while taking notes about what people were wearing.

When I received news that my grandmother Dahlia was on her deathbed with pneumonia, I immediately made arrangements to return to Kentucky. I couldn't imagine the world without her. She was like a horseshoe crab, living on this earth for what seemed like centuries, way before dinosaurs even. She had always been in my life.

But when I saw her lying there in the bed with her eyes open but not seeing anything, I knew it was her time, and I feared I had arrived too late. But then she started to talk, and the things she told me made me wish I had missed my train and arrived a day late so I wouldn't have to hear it.

"That boy, rather, that man from the island showed up here in search of you."

"What man?"

"Jaden, his name was. He showed up at our door six months after you left for New York with Leo."

"No!"

"Yes. I told him you fell in love and got married and moved off to the East Coast. I didn't say where exactly. I figured if a man is nervy enough to come hunting you down all the way from Florida, he'd find a way to tear you apart from your marriage."

"No," I said. "No." It was all I could say. But I knew my heart, wherever it was, was kicked by her words, and it probably left a trail, a track like no other on the floor of the sea.

"He probably would have been a nice one to marry," she continued.

"Remember when I once told you to marry a man that loves you more than you love him? Any man who's going to hunt you down in Kentucky surely loves you more. Are you all right? You look pale. Ava . . . Ava?"

I think I felt more like death that day than Dahlia did, and when she passed later that evening I begged the Lord to take me, too. But instead I returned to New York where I poured every ounce of my mind into my work in an effort to bury the pain I felt for Jaden. Hearing news that he had come searching for me was too much to bear. I couldn't release my love for him, and it flourished deep within me, in that most precious of worlds, like the intricately woven interior of a seashell, the inside kingdom that every woman has, near her beating heart or its former site. I regretted marrying a man for money and instead wished I had chosen another route of escape. If I wanted to make changes in my life, why hadn't I done whatever was necessary to pursue a writing career on my own? I didn't see it as an option back then.

I had casually mentioned to Leo weeks later that there had been a childhood sweetheart, but I stopped there, never telling him that my heart still beat off the coast of Sanibel. Then, one summer day, I walked into his office suggesting that the two of us take a mini-trip to Florida where he had never been. He said nothing but flipped open his maroon account book and studied it religiously. He then closed his eyes and muttered calculations under his breath, then opened his eyes, turned the page of his maroon book, looked up at the calendar, and counted days.

I watched him perform his calculated ritual, aware that I had married a devout man, a worshipper of money. It was he who taught me the power of the green gods. "In God we trust," was his favorite prayer, but occasionally he prayed deeper, and to the same God I prayed to. Leo closed the calendar and looked at me. "A trip to Florida is not going to happen right now," he said. "Besides, it's summer. I have no interest in Florida in the summer."

I stared at him but said nothing.

"What's with that pout?"

"Sorry."

"You don't have to apologize," he said.

"Why can't we go to Florida?"

"Florida has too many mosquitoes in the summer. If you want to go somewhere else, we will. How about Paris? San Francisco? How about a place you've never been before, one we can discover together and call our own?"

I threw my arms around him and kissed him on the lips. There were no bugles blowing when I kissed him, but this time I heard a peaceful anthem. I'd never been to Paris before. I'd never left this country.

When Leo and I returned from Paris, I put my mind to work overtime, and I was fast becoming known for my articles on fashion, all the while wearing the latest and the greatest, while my husband was working on advertising campaigns that promoted the fads that I was wearing. We were acquiring more wealth for ourselves, while creating a reputation and social existence beyond my wildest dreams, and working morning, noon, and night. Nothing was going to stop us, not even that first speed law passed in New York State, mandating a maximum speed of ten miles per hour in populated districts.

Lydia

I put Ava's pages away and glanced up at the stone water tower that looked so out of place in the midst of a steel and glass city that was now sparkling in hues of orange and gold from the descending September sun.

I was glad to learn that Ava was surviving. Her spirit was indomitable, and I was glad to hear of her rising forth from a potentially disastrous choice she had made.

A chill in the air sent geese running up and down my arms, leaving behind their bumpy tracks on my skin; so, I got up and walked to the nearest store that sold bicycles. There, a red one caught my eye, and I purchased it on the spot. It was a poorly thought-out purchase and meant I'd be pedaling instead of eating lunch for the next several months. Unless, of course I'd give in one of these days and let Ethan pay for me. But I preferred paying for myself. My old self-perception, of the best-dressed little girl that got everything handed to her, had long since faded away. I now had to work hard for everything, including the clothes on my back and they were nothing like the fashions Ava was wearing.

"I'd prefer you to take a bus to work," Ethan said one morning as I put my backpack on and mounted my bicycle. "It's dangerous for you to be riding in rush-hour traffic. A woman shouldn't risk her life like that and . . ."

I whipped my hand through the air and slapped him across the face. I wasn't just swatting at Ethan, but at all the men throughout history who held women back from biking and voting and working in the careers of their choice and from doing all they wanted to do in life. Still, none of that justified my slapping poor Ethan. He was just one man who didn't want me getting hurt on my bike.

"I am sorry," I said, touching the red area of his cheek. "I can't believe I did that. I didn't mean to hurt you."

"It didn't hurt," he claimed. "But don't ever do it again."

"Of course not," I said, ashamed I did it once and disgusted he thought I'd ever do it again.

"Why'd you slap me?"

"You were trying to tell me I shouldn't ride my bike to work when I think it's a perfectly fine thing for a woman to do."

"Your choice," he said. "I'm sorry I worry about you and care for you and love you like I do."

"You do?" I gasped. "You love me?"

"Yes. I have from the moment you bumped into me and knocked all my papers to the floor. I never told you this, but I could hardly get you off my mind after the Republican convention, and the worst part was, I had a major deadline to meet, and I've never in all my professional years come close to missing a deadline like I did that night."

"But yours was the next day's cover story."

"I know. See what you almost did? Can you imagine the front page of the *Windy City Press* blank?" He smiled. "You turn me reckless, Lydia Isleworth, and I kind of like it."

His words that day flattered me, but I continued riding to and from work each day, and as I pedaled my way through the city, I appreciated for the first time the simpler strides that women of history had made, things that in present times are taken for granted. Who would want to live in a world where bicycling was only for men? If I could say a huge "thank you" to Ava for going against the stares and ridicule and for riding that bicycle anyway, I would, for I enjoyed my own riding time immensely.

But my appreciation for Ava didn't pardon her from being a criminal in my eyes. And as I rode along Lakeshore Boulevard one Sunday afternoon, my stomach growling from not being able to afford any lunch, I resented her. She had married for money. We were nothing alike, I decided. We were both writers now, but I had done it on my own. I didn't have a wealthy husband to get me what I wanted. And I wasn't the type to need such a man. Neither was she. She was the girl who once vowed to never marry a man. And when she fell in love with Jaden, I forgave her and fell in love myself, but now, to have married for money, it was an act that defied gravity and all that was natural for a woman like her.

I was doing everything myself. I didn't want any man paying or paving my way, and I forgave my father for leaving me nothing. I was stronger for doing it all on my own. Ethan and I were dating, but I never asked him for any help in advancing me at the paper and he never offered. And suddenly, as I was pedaling down Delaware, the revelation that Ethan never offered me any help turned me suspicious. Maybe he was one of them—one of those men who didn't want his woman rising in her career. Maybe he wanted me staying put where I was in the obituaries. And come to think of it, even marriage would be better. He did say he loved me, and when a man says those three words, it usually means he wants to marry a woman, and typically that means she must quit work and stay home. I had questions for Ethan. I had to figure out what he was thinking.

Then, again, I didn't want him knowing what I was thinking, which was nothing close to marriage. Marrying him when my heart was still dancing with someone else would be a crime, and that would put me in prison with Ava.

I knew it was illogical, sad, crazy maybe, to be harboring desires for someone I hadn't seen in so long, but I couldn't help it. As I pedaled alongside Lake Michigan, I tried figuring how I might slowly end things with Ethan. I did care for him. But I loved someone else. I can't help that, can I? Besides, it was getting dangerous for me to view marriage as a place I prefer over the obituary department. And then I knew what I had to do so I reached deep down into my jar of wisdom and pulled out some words my father once spoke.

"It is time to accelerate my career," I said. "Yes, that's what I need to focus on right now—my career!"

XXXIV

CHICAGO
1963
THREE YEARS LATER

Lydia

SOUTHWEST FLORIDA RECOVERED AFTER Hurricane Donna, winds averaging nearly one hundred and thirty-five miles per hour, passed directly over Fort Myers Beach and Fort Myers, and life went on.

The next three years were fascinating ones for me, a female journalist writing her way out of obituaries and into the land of the living. When I accepted the position covering womens' issues, I feared I'd become meshed in recipes or rounded shoes versus pointed shoes, like Ava, but that was not the case.

My first assignment was covering a controversial historical milestone for women taking control of their own fertility. It came in 1960, and the headline for my story was as follows:

U.S. FOOD AND DRUG ADMINISTRATION APPROVES FIRST ORAL CONTRACEPTIVES FOR MARKETING IN THE UNITED STATES

My story, which ran on the front page, described how women had been taking substances by mouth to prevent pregnancy as far back as four thousand years!

And three years later, in 1963, I was still the journalist following the topic when another monumental moment arrived. The headline for that story read:

MAJOR PHARMACEUTICAL COMPANY INTRODUCES ITS
FIRST BIRTH CONTROL PILL

I liked writing about the smaller issues, but kept getting assigned to larger ones.

EQUAL PAY ACT MAKES IT ILLEGAL FOR COMPAINES TO PAY
DIFFERENT RATES TO WOMEN AND MEN WHO DO THE
SAME WORK

That story got me a pay raise and motivated me to work longer and harder than I ever had before. I was driven, and each story I was assigned to cover made me feel like I was pedaling my way over mountains, sweating profusely as I went but getting stronger and more informed and better at mastering my craft. My mind had never trained so hard for anything before.

And when the government took its first steps toward addressing the issue of inequality of the sexes, I was the one to cover it. When President Kennedy formed a Commission on the Status of Women chaired by Eleanor Roosevelt, who was in her seventies, I was the one to interview her.

And when Kennedy issued a presidential order demanding that the civil service make hiring decisions "solely on the basis of ability" and "without regard to sex," I threw my arms up and shouted a personal "hooray" for everyone in the office to hear, and then I wrote and submitted my story.

Maybe it was the jumping jacks I did and the cheering, or not having used a single vacation day in three years, but after turning it in, I felt exhausted and weak, as if I had just tumbled down the side of a mountain and was dying from having overexerted myself on the way up.

I sat crouched over my desk one August morning, hardly able to lift the coffee mug to my mouth. I now drank five strong cups a day, and anything less gave me a pounding headache. Today was the day I upped my dose to six cups, and as the mug touched my lips, I felt my heart double step within me. My heart was something I hadn't felt in a long time.

I laid my head down on my desk and tried to rest a minute, but from that angle I spotted the seashell I had brought to work back on my first day in obits. It was lying buried under a year's worth of papers, with only its tip sticking out. I reached for it and pulled out the rolled-up obituary I had written for Abigail and stuffed inside. Then I put the shell to my ear.

There were all sorts of noises in the office, phones ringing and meetings going on, but I listened deeply as if trying to hear my own soul, and then I heard the sea and in it the words of Abigail, tidbits of wisdom bobbing up and down in the water like buoys for me to grab onto. I remembered her saying a woman is made up of a heart, soul, and mind. I no longer felt my heart, and I was trying to get in tune with my soul. It was my mind working overtime that was drowning out the other elements, but I didn't know what to do about it. And now, due to overexertion, I feared my mind might be shutting down.

"Lydia," said my friend Jane. She covers women and politics. "Hearing anything good in there?"

I jumped in my seat, dropping the shell onto the floor. "I need to get away, Jane. I desperately need a vacation."

"Maybe if you hadn't given all your vacation days away as holiday presents last year, you could take one for yourself."

It was true. I had been like jolly old Saint Nicholas, handing over my vacation days one by one, and now I felt regret for having put intensity and showmanship into where I was now. "I do have a couple of days left. I could take a long weekend. That should be enough."

"Where will you go?" she asked.

"Florida."

"Sun and beach?"

"Yeah," I lied. In truth, I had to release my heart at last from Josh's lu-

dicrous grip. It wasn't fair. It was weird and eerie and psycho and basical-
ly abnormal and not at all grounded in reality that some guy from long ago
still had a hold on it today, and worse, he probably didn't even know or
want to be holding onto it. I was an intelligent woman and aware of all of
these things, which is why I cringed at the thought of my pathetic heart,
with its valves and muscles stubbornly holding onto Josh for dear life, re-
fusing in an annoying way to let go of him.

I stooped over and picked the seashell up off the floor and tossed it
back onto my cluttered desk, fully aware that I was as obsessed over Josh
as I once had been over finding a Junonia shell. It was time to surrender. I
shuffled into my boss's office and told him my plans and that if I didn't do
this now, I'd soon be taking all sorts of sick days, mental ones. He gave me
a solid nod, and I was free to go.

XXXV

SANIBEL ISLAND
A FEW DAYS LATER

Lydia

Whoever claims there are no seasons in Florida is inaccurate. There are, but evidence of them is subtle, and it takes a sensitive eye to appreciate them. It was indeed summer when I arrived, the season when the mangrove cuckoos nest and sing to defend their territory. The beaches might not be chock full of shells this time of year, but there were horse conchs and mammoth whelks waiting by the bay side. It was a good time to visit Sanibel. And loving historical and newsworthy moments as I do, it happened to be just a few weeks after the opening of the causeway bridge linking Sanibel to the mainland.

"It's just a causeway," I told myself as I drove past Punta Rasa, where in the past I had stood waiting for the ferry. "And a beautiful three-mile drive."

As I paid my toll, I thought about Marlena and all the letters she had written me while the bridge was under construction. She was grief-stricken and dreading the completion of it, saying that it was going to be the end of an era for Sanibel as we knew it. She was dramatic, and I tried calming her, reassuring her in my letters that causeways are good. They make getting to where we're going simpler and quicker.

I glanced at my face in the rearview mirror and noticed dark circles under my eyes. Getting to where I was at the paper had been an arduously long journey, one gone alone, without help from anyone. And it had been hard counting my pennies, eating all my dinners at happy hours in the city, living in a dangerous part of town, not dressing anything like Ava, the fashion queen. But now, as I paid my toll and drove onto the causeway bridge, I no longer wanted isolation or independence, and I decided I would loosen up a bit when I returned to Chicago and let people know how I struggled and if I ever needed help. And maybe I'd give Ethan a call. It had been awhile.

I drove slowly, not minding the line of cars behind me, and I unrolled my window to consume the balmy, intoxicating air. The bridge represented the end of an era for Sanibel just as this trip for me would mean the end of the piracy era in which Josh captivated my heart. When it came to matters of love, I didn't want to be like Ava and commit any crime of the heart. And if I didn't set mine free once and for all, I would go on hurting myself, and one day, someone else.

The door of Bougainvillea was open a crack, so I walked in. "Hello, anyone home?" I called out, standing in the entry. "Marlena, it's me."

She had just returned to Sanibel a couple of months ago after finishing work on her fourth independent film in London. Two of those films never made it to box offices in America, but two did, and I had gone to see them at the little theatre not far from where I lived. They were artistic and in-depth, and I liked them both.

"Marlena?" I called again and then peeked around the room. There were no diamond chandeliers or upgraded curtains, and everything looked as it had the last time I was there. But then I spotted Marlena lying on the couch under a blanket pulled up to her chin.

"You're sick," I stated, not knowing whether to kiss her on the cheek or take hold of her hand instead.

"I guess," she said.

"What do you mean, you guess? Either you're sick or you're not."

"I'm glad you're here. Sit down."

I set my two simple bags down and pulled the large armchair closer to her and then sat down. "It's good to see you," I said.

"Be my journalist," she said. "Report to me what it's like out there on the island now that the bridge is opened. I'm imagining pollution and exhaust fumes and noisy engines damaging the delicate ecosystem out there. Am I right?"

"No, not at all. Haven't you been out to see for yourself since the bridge opened?"

"Nope."

"It opened weeks ago. You've been inside that long?"

"I'm scared to go out there. Shouldn't I be?" she asked. "What if I get run over by developers?"

I laughed. "Marlena," I said. "Let me assure you that Sanibel is as charming as ever, and people and ordinances will protect it."

"You sound like one of them."

"One of who?"

"The ones who pushed for the causeway—the people I've battled with for years. I've had screaming matches with them, and I've lost. What's it like out there? Are there hundreds? Thousands?"

"Of what?"

"People arriving on the island."

"There was a line of cars, but nothing ridiculous. Has fame got to your head?"

I regretted it the moment I said it; so, I stood up and walked over to her window and opened the shutters to let light in. "I didn't mean that. I know that would never happen," I said, looking around the room for clues as to what might be going on. There were dirty coffee mugs on the floor and opened boxes of crackers, with crumbs on the floor. There was a steady stream of ants making their way across the lime green walls toward a cracker, and if we didn't pick the food up soon every ant on the island would be marching over to Marlena's house.

I returned to where she was lying on the couch and kneeled down on the hardwood floor beside her. "I'm concerned for you. What's going on? You've got to tell me," I said.

"Don't ask me how I'm feeling unless you want to know."

"I want to know."

"Can you get me a glass of water?" she asked.

"Of course."

When I returned with her water she was sitting up on the couch. "Lydia," she said. "I've known you for years. I'm just going to say it, dear."

"Please do."

"I can't sleep. I can't focus. I try making decisions, small ones, like do I want to wear my Capri pants or my walking pants, but I can't decide. I've been lying around in this playsuit and skirt for days, but I've done no playing, and the polka dots are starting to make me dizzy. Yet, I don't feel like getting up to change. It's effort."

"Everything will be all right," I said.

"But it's not. Look at me! And I could hardly finish that last film. You saw it, right?"

"Yes. You were great."

"Good thing I played a saddened, desolate woman because I don't think I could have played a happy role. There was talk of me winning an award for that part, you know."

"It's wonderful."

"But I wasn't acting. I was being myself. I could hardly get out of bed and to the set in time. I get like this from time to time."

"What do you think it is?"

"I don't know."

"I'm here for you. I'm here to help. What can I do?"

"I don't know. Anything to cheer me up, but I don't know what. Nothing works. Flowers, maybe. I know I'm reaching, but are there any flowers out there?"

I don't know whether she meant to do it or not, but her asking for flowers reminded me strangely of Abigail's craving for flowers a long time ago, and suddenly it double-clicked that Marlena was indeed suffering from the same thing Abigail, her grandmother, had experienced in her lifetime.

Maybe she wasn't seeing the connection. But I was.

"Yes. There are flowers out there," I said as I folded my legs Indian-style on the floor. "Sanibel is infested with flowers, and now the flowers from Fort Myers have a way of getting here. They're creeping across that bridge, curious to mingle for the first time with the Sanibel flowers, for they've heard all about the island for centuries but could never reach it, until now, thanks to that causeway bridge."

I hadn't read Louisa May Alcott in years and my made-up story was nothing like Ava reading *Flower Fables* to her mama, but Marlena's lips were forming a smirk, so I continued my fabricated flower tale.

"As I drove my car onto the island, I overheard out my window a Fort Myers flower telling a Sanibel flower, 'Please don't be threatened by our arrival. We're coming to share in the beauty with you.' Then the Sanibel flower said, 'Welcome to the island. We're protective of our beauty. Will you respect it?' and the newcomer answered, 'We're coming to savor not devour. There's a difference.'

"'Good,' declared the native flower. 'Your arrival is welcomed.'

"'Can we at least thank you by depositing our seeds as we leave?'

"'Oh no,' said the native flower. 'Show your appreciation by leaving the island untouched and exactly as you found it, please.'"

I didn't know where to take the story from there, and I feared my poor fiction imagination might turn it into a horrid news story since I've been trained to find the bad angles in everything, so I ended it there, and Marlena gave me a forced one-syllable laugh.

"Thank you for your story. I'll give you an 'A' for effort," she said. "But do me a favor. Don't ever switch to being a fiction writer. Stay a journalist." We both laughed, but then her face turned solemn again. "I'm sorry to be like this during your visit."

"Don't apologize for how you're feeling," I said. "You weren't put on this earth to entertain me, although you've done a pretty good job with the last two films of yours. But the camera isn't on you right now, Marlena; so, I'm going to ask you. Have you gone to a doctor about any of this?"

"No. Should I?"

"I think so. You know your family history."

"Yeah, more than most people do. I'm not so keen on going to any doctor when my body doesn't hurt. I just feel so lethargic."

"Maybe you need to find the right type of doctor, one who deals with your specific set of symptoms. Let me think about it," I said, not wanting to blurt out that I thought she should see a psychiatrist or psychologist, but that was what I would suggest later in the day, maybe. "We're going to figure it all out and get you help."

I spent the rest of the afternoon freshening Bougainvillea. I pulled boards off the windows, opened curtains, washed the dishes, put in loads of wash, swept the sandy hardwood floors, and emptied all the garbage cans, including the ones out back that raccoons had discovered. I returned with a handful of flowers I had picked and placed them in a vase that I set on the end table next to the couch.

I filled the bath with warm water and added a few drops of lavender, and then I saw to it that she got in safely. Then I went into the kitchen and rummaged through her cabinets in search of something I might make us to eat. And when I found nothing, I knocked on the bathroom door and asked if she minded that I run to the store for groceries.

"Thank you, Lydia," she said. "How can I truly thank you?"

"Just take care of yourself," I said. "I'll be back soon."

I headed out the door looking a sweaty mess from cleaning, convincing myself I wouldn't bump into Josh, not in this quick mini-trip to the store, but then again, I told myself it would be just my luck to bump into him now, after years of not seeing one another.

"A woman is more than outer appearance," I told myself. "She's a heart, soul, and mind as well." Then, a second later, I said, "Bull." Her outer appearance reflects the inner elements; so, I turned around and ran back up the steps into the, house and quickly changed into my three-piece combed-cotton seersucker suit with pearl buttons.

The outfit didn't at all fit my mood, but when I packed, I did so with the expectation of hunting down Josh, and I wanted to look effortlessly good should I find him with a girlfriend, fiancée, wife possibly. I think walking away from the man you once loved while you're looking your best is easier than walking away from him looking a mess, I told myself.

But I didn't bump into Josh at the store. Instead, I saw his father. "Max, is that you?" I asked as I walked out of the store holding four heavy bags of food in my arms.

Max studied me for a moment, and I wondered whether he remembered me at all, and if he didn't, then maybe Josh wouldn't, and maybe my entire love for him had been a puppy crush, the kind that normally sane people forget about with time.

"Linda," he said. "What brings you to Sanibel?"

"Lydia," I corrected. "It's Lydia."

I didn't want to tell him I came to pry my heart free from his son's eternal grip. "My father passed away three years ago," I said, and for a second wondered whether he, like Marlena, had assumed I was the recipient of a three-million-dollar will, which of course I wasn't. I kept it my secret, even from her, that my father chose not to leave me a penny. Being left nothing only fueled me more to pursue all that I wanted for myself, and as I stood there small-talking with Max I wondered what it was that I had been working toward and what it was that my father had been working toward and whether or not that sort of work-like intensity is a trait that runs in families. What an inheritance, I thought.

"I am sorry to hear about your dad," he said.

"Thank you. It feels good being in a place where the two of us once visited together. I'm glad he took me here years ago or I might not know about it today."

"And where are you living now?"

"Chicago, working as a journalist. I cover issues of interest to women."

"Good for you. And you're here for how long?"

"A long weekend. I'm staying with my famous friend," and then I coughed, for how dare I attach that superficial adjective with the word "friend"? Not that she wasn't famous, but just that it had nothing to do with her being my friend, and she herself was uncomfortable with mention of it. "So how'd you fare during Hurricane Donna? You evacuated, I'm sure."

"No. Josh and I stormed it out."

"You didn't," I said, wanting to tell him the truth, that I kneeled beside my bed and prayed a good hour, the first prayer I had sincerely said in all my life, just so the two of them might be safe during that hurricane. "Glad to see the island is fine. Good old Sanibel," I said. "It's a strong island. It'll outlive us all, I'm sure."

The bags were getting heavy in my arms, and I feared that any moment one might tilt too far, and then I'd lose everything onto the sidewalk. "I better get these groceries back to my friend who needs my help," I said.

"I'll tell Josh I bumped into you," he said.

"And remember, my name is Lydia, not Linda."

Just then my groceries all came tumbling out and onto the sidewalk, as I had feared they might. As Max and I both went to gather them up, I noticed my favorite cans of *who, what, when, where* and *why* rolling toward the street and if I didn't ask my questions quick enough, it would be too late.

"*How* is Josh?" I managed to ask.

"Great. Chartering by day, playing his music by night."

"*Where* does he play?"

"The Olive Shell."

"*When*?"

Max stood up and helped me secure the bags in my arms. "Saturday nights."

"Good for him," I said, not needing to ask anything else. "It was good seeing you, Max."

"You too, Lydia. Take care."

"I will. Bye."

I walked back to Bougainvillea, praising myself for changing my outfit before I went and for gathering all the information I needed concerning the topic of Josh. It was only Friday. I set Saturday night as my deadline. That was when I would go see Josh as he played his music. I would wrap it all up tomorrow night.

Marlena was standing in front of a mirror in the great room, dressed in a sheer nylon ruffles 'n lace party dress with a taffeta cummerbund when

I returned.

"Let's go," she said. "I've put so much energy into getting ready that I'm starting to feel fatigued like I want to lie down again and crawl back under that blanket. Let's go now before I don't feel like going anymore."

"Wait a minute" I said as I dropped the bags onto the kitchen counter. "Where are we going?"

"To the show," she replied. "It's starting in about an hour. We can't miss it." I quickly put the food that needed refrigeration away, then left the rest for later.

"Marlena," I said, when I returned to the great room. "What show are you talking about?"

She was standing in the doorway. "The sunset, honey," she said.

"Oh." I took her hand. "I'd love to see a sunset."

I didn't want to suggest that maybe her polka-dot playsuit would have been more appropriate and that her outfit was making me feel under-dressed. But I didn't think it mattered. It was a big occasion for her going out, and my guess was she hadn't been to any shows in a long time.

"Give me a minute," I said, running back up the steps and into the house. "I've got sunset snacks," I called out.

When we arrived at Blind Pass, her favorite spot for sunsets, I had hardly put the car in park, and she was already stepping out. "Didn't your mother ever teach you not to get out of a car until it stops?" I asked.

"Watch it, young lady," she said, rolling her eyes at me. "She and I once watched a sunset on this beach together, you know."

"No, I didn't know that. When?"

"You'll read about it one of these days." She headed for the beach, and I grabbed the blanket and the snacks and caught up with her.

"Here. Let's take these seats, right here," she said, bending over to pat the sand. "It's amazing to think that tickets to a show like this are free. And we've got the best seats in the house."

"We do," I said, dropping onto my buttocks in my form-fitting skirt. I should have taken an extra second to change into my culottes.

"I've missed this," she said. "To think, I used to come to the shows twice a day. The morning show takes place on the eastern stage, you know.

It's the most sizzling performance of all."

I enjoyed the drama returning to her voice. It was like the old Marlena was trying to come out again.

"I'm aware that at times my mind feels down and that my mother's did too and that her mother's did as well," Marlena said.

"I've never told anyone this before," I said. "But my mother experienced something similar shortly after I was born."

"Yours?"

"Yes, only I don't know much about it. I wish I knew more because it haunts me. She took her own life. I can hardly speak of it. You're so fortunate to know about your ancestors and what they were thinking and feeling."

"I've learned from them."

"What have you learned?"

"See where the water is glistening from the sun?"

I looked out at the Gulf of Mexico and saw a perfect pathway on the surface of the water. I nodded.

"It's there at night, too, from the moon. There are always steps we can take, no matter how down we feel or how bad things become, steps that will lead us to survival. After you left for the store, I called a doctor over in Fort Myers today. I made myself an appointment. I'm going to find help," she said. "Making that call was my first glistening step. Getting out of the house to watch this sunset was my second."

"I'm proud of you," I said. "And I believe in you. I believe you'll find the help you need. And I think I'll store what you just said about that glistening pathway in my own jar of wisdom so if ever I need to, I can pull it out and apply it."

She smiled, and so did I.

XXXVI

THE NEXT MORNING, IT felt good to be sipping my coffee with Coke can-sized rollers still in my hair. Rushing off to work every morning back home never allowed me time to primp and pamper myself, and besides, no one cares what a newspaperwoman looks like.

I walked outside Bougainvillea and sat down on the front steps where nearby birds were singing and ruffling their feathers ready to mate. Their chirps were like nourishment to my soul, and I regretted having been so mentally focused at work that I never had time but to swear at the pigeons that pooped on me back in Chicago.

Allowing Josh to dig his claws into my heart all these years wasn't good, either, and I could hardly wait to pry him loose and get on with my life. There had been men whistling at me back home and maybe after this trip I'd start paying them attention. They were many.

"You rolled your hair last night," Marlena said when she joined me with her coffee on the steps.

"I want to look good tonight," I said. "Josh plays over at the Olive Shell, and I'm going there for closure."

"Why do you care how you look if you're going for closure?"

"So I feel better when I walk away."

There was silence but for the birds singing, and then, "Do you still love him?"

"After all this time? Of course not," I said, ashamed that I had loved someone for so long without seeing him.

"I still love someone I haven't seen in decades," she said. "But I only love him a little bit. I've mostly moved on."

"Who? You've never told me. I never wanted to pry, but I've wondered."

"I'll tell you one of these days," she said. "But not now."

If she wanted to revisit that time and the man she once loved, she would have shared her story, and I would have given her center stage, listening attentively, knowing she wasn't preaching or telling me what to do about Josh, but relating maybe, by telling me a story from her own life, a moment she felt like reliving. But she wasn't ready or didn't feel the need. I didn't know which.

Shortly after breakfast I changed into my new hip-riding baby-doll bikini and walked to the beach, quickly learning from the humidity that rolling my hair the night before had been illogical thinking.

I spent a couple of hours sitting by the shore, allowing the sun to lighten the dark circles under my eyes and add color to my skin. I walked a little, watching for shells, and then down where the water could touch my toes. And when I returned to the blanket, I fell asleep, I think, or at least I entered a relaxed state. When I woke, I reminded myself why I came and what I had yet to accomplish on this trip. Closure.

Marlena helped me wash and roll my hair again, and then I sat for one hour under her dryer trying to relax my nerves. I had brought along a book, *Feminine Mystique*, and tried reading it. Shortly after my trip, I was scheduled to interview author Betty Friedan about what her book had done. Overnight, it had lassoed women into action, questioning why society had them giving up their dreams and quitting jobs they didn't want, but jobs men allowed them to take, and once they got married, giving up all ambition outside of the home. Reading it now before seeing Josh, I figured, might keep me from giving in to his handsome charm. I knew it was important for me to read as much of it as I could before seeing him. But reading was difficult under the dryer. I had to hold my head upright, which meant I had to hold the book smack up to my face. I tried watching television, but couldn't hear a thing. The monster dryer was loud as a freight train.

"Do you happen to have any electric rollers?" I shouted to Marlena.

"No, they don't give the poof you get from wet rolled and dried. To-night is too important, babe."

It had been some time since I last paid any attention to putting make-up on and styling my hair, and I had forgotten that I could look anything other than exhausted, overworked, and stressed. Marlena insisted on nothing but big curvy curls, so she criss-crossed my hair in front, pulled it behind my ears, and pinned it at my nape into flatteringly saucy, open curls and so on.

"Remember, I'm going for closure and not to get closer," I reminded her.

"Of course," she said. "But you're going to walk away feeling like a million-dollar star. That's all I'm trying to do here. Now what are you planning to wear?"

"I don't know. I hate my wardrobe. It's conservative and professional and boxy like a man's."

"Go look through mine. A movie star always has something to wear."

And she did. Her closet was sufficient for Marilyn Monroe. I chose a daring dress with cutouts and vinyl, one that displayed the stilt-like legs I'd forgotten I had.

A couple of hours later I sat down at a small round table in the back corner of the Olive Shell, alone but confident, like a journalist surrounded in her mind by the questions she wanted to ask and the information she was collecting. I sat there with purpose. Purpose does keep one company. The lights were dim, and the waiter said the band had been on a ten-minute break and was just about to start back up again.

And, when it did, I sipped my martini and recognized features of the boy whose cheeks once puffed awkwardly out while practicing that day under the coconut tree a long time ago. A journalist is trained to see details. So I noticed his sun-drenched face. Oh, and the cleft in his chin.

A journalist also sees the story behind the appearance. His years of fish and song had aged him well. He was handsome in a rugged way, softened

by that cleft in his chin. I ordered another martini and then placed my
hand over my chest. My heart was dancing within me.

"Stay objective. Don't be moved by anything you see up there," I scolded myself under my breath, then sipped my drink. "You're a journalist, not
a romance writer."

The band asked if anyone in the audience had any requests. I could stay
in my chair no longer. I had to do something. I came to get closer, I reminded myself. No, Ding Dong, I corrected myself. You came to get *closure*. But it was turning out to be harder than I imagined.

I walked around tables that were in my way, rummaging through my
mind as I went, trying to think of a song I might request by the time I got
up there. A woman should always think up a song first and then walk up
to the stage. I stood at the foot of the stage with the band waiting and the
audience staring, yet I could think of not a single song. It was as if all the
music of the world had died from my mind and never existed in the first
place. A song? Music? What's that?

There was a deadly silence. My stubborn heart didn't care. I could feel
it twirling and leaping inside. And finally my mind started returning to
me, conjuring up the names of musical artists. Elvis. Ritchie Valens—he
died in a plane crash in 1959. It had been a sad obituary. I wanted to kick
myself. But instead I looked Josh directly in his eyes and whispered, "Hi.
I just came to say 'hi.' Remember me?"

"Of course I do, Lydia," he said. And a moment later, "Have you got a
request?"

"'Raining in My Heart'?"

"We can do that."

Josh nodded at the band and I returned to my seat where I ordered one
more martini for the night. After six more songs, the band started putting
their instruments away, and Josh joined me at the table. We talked. He
was sorry to hear of my father's death. I told him all about my first job
writing obituaries. We talked about the weather in Chicago. I asked him
what it was like surviving Hurricane Donna. Neither of us mentioned why
our letters had ended. I started breezing over things that had happened in
the news and things making headlines now. It was a topic I was comfort-

able with, even after three martinis, I discovered. I hoped I didn't sound like a rambling headline:

PRESIDENTIAL DEBATES FOCUSING ON ANTI-COMMUNISM. SECRET INVASIONS. THE BAY OF PIGS AND AMERICA BECOMING CUBA'S ARCHENEMY. EVIDENCE OF SOVIET MISSLE SITES IN CUBA. AMERICA AND THE SOVIET UNION ON BRINK OF WAR. ESCALATION IN VIETNAM. ANTI-GOVERNMENT DEMONSTRATIONS BY BUDDHIST MONKS PROVOKE VIOLENT REPRISALS AND IN PROTEST, NUMEROUS MONKS COMMIT SUICIDE BY SETTING THEMSELVES AFIRE.

He talked about the news along with me, but I ended the conversation when I remembered why I had come, to scrape my heart clean of Josh so I might return to my life in the city with no remnants of him within me.

"You're doing exactly what you wanted to do with your life," Josh said when I stopped bringing up current affairs. "It's impressive, Lydia. You're like a real, living, breathing, talking newspaper."

"Thank you," I said, covering my mouth with my hands. Then I laughed. "I'm not usually. I mean . . ." I shook my head. I felt foolish. I didn't want him thinking that news was my life, my passion, all that I focused on over the last several years. But it was. "I am entrenched in all of this stuff at work," I said with a chuckle. "It's hard to turn it off in a short weekend away."

"What a world to be living in," he said.

"I know I've rambled on about mine. Tell me about yours," I said.

"No complaints."

"You live in a quiet world. Quiet and beautiful, don't you?"

He smirked and looked away. It was then that I saw him as the boy I once loved and the man I wanted to get to know.

"Josh," I said. "I could use a good dose of your world. Share it with me, will you? Show me a piece of your world tonight."

His eyes searched mine.

"That is, if you don't have any other plans," I added.

"What do you have in mind, Lydia?"

"How about fishing. I'd love to go fishing."

As we left the Olive Shell together, I feared that maybe my plan for closure wasn't going the way I intended it to, and I wondered, as he took hold of my hand in the parking lot, if maybe there might be a chapter in *Feminine Mystique* outlining what a mixed-up woman like myself should do next in regard to a man. Or what she ought to do when that rare and wonderful sort of man comes around. Maybe there is an alternative set of rules to follow when a man like Josh shows up, or maybe a chapter I hadn't read yet.

He wasn't like the typical man out there. He was impressed by my career aspirations. He always had been, way back on the boat that day when I told him I planned to become a journalist. And still, tonight, he asked with interest about my work and, then, he complimented how far I had gone.

As the boat made its way across the black vastness of water, we talked enough to fill the pages of a newspaper for an entire week, but not about news; we talked about life and nature and things I hadn't talked about with anyone, ever. And when the boat stopped out in the black depths, somewhere near Boca Grande, there was a comfortable silence as we listened for tarpon.

"Shhh. Over there," Josh said some time later and pointed to the water in front of the boat. "You hear it? You hear that tarpon breathing?"

I listened. "No," I answered, only paying attention to his breath close beside me.

I put my arm around him and he then turned and put his hands around my waist and pulled me close for the first time this night, and now I could feel him breathing. He slowly pulled the white gloves I had borrowed from Marlena off my fingers. "Forget the tarpon," he said, grinning. "How do I go about securing a woman like you?"

I know I should have been able to retrieve somewhere in my mind a quote, a chapter from *Feminine Mystique*, anything that might help me turn from him or slap him across the face, but instead, I simply laughed. "Show me your fishing pole and bait," I said, well aware that the author of that book would probably cancel the interview I had set with her had she heard that coming from my mouth.

"I thought you didn't like bait," he continued.

And he was right. He didn't need anything to lure me closer. I was already there within his reach. And I liked it. There was no battle, no acrobats, and the only silver soon to be thrashing about was the chain on his neck. He had secured a silver queen!

As the boat approached Sanibel about an hour before the sun would rise, I knew our time was coming to an end. It was Saturday night, and come Sunday, I'd be flying back to Chicago.

"I've got piles of work waiting for me on my desk. Monday is going to be a bad day," I said. "And I've got a big interview with the author of this book called *Feminine Mystique*. Have you heard of it?"

"Nope." He turned quiet and serious.

"What's wrong?" I asked him. "What are you thinking?"

He stared straight ahead, not turning to look at me and said, "You know damn well that tarpons are released after the capture, right?"

"Yes," I said. "But why are you bringing that up now?"

"Do you regret fishing?" he asked.

"Of course not," I answered. "I haven't had a night like this in a long time." He was quiet as he tied the boat to the dock. "I needed a night where I wasn't thinking about headlines and deadlines and things I had to do come morning, a night so quiet I could hear a fish breathing."

"Yeah," he said. "I wouldn't want to live in a noisy world like yours."

"Josh," I said, disturbed. "Why do you say that? It's not all bad."

He shook his head and looked at his watch. "We're back later than I planned. I've got a lot of minutia to take care of this morning," he said, not bothering to offer me a hand as I hopped off the boat behind him.

"You no longer offer ladies a hand getting off a boat?" I asked.

"Sorry. Didn't want to offend you."

"That's not fair," I said. "Because I make my own money and pay my own bills you assume I don't want physical help getting off a boat?"

"You're looking way too into it," he said. "That's not the case."

"Then what is the case?" I asked following him up to his truck.

"I think we're both tired," he said. "You should try to get sleep. I've got to get going. Like I said, we're getting back later than I had wanted, and I've got a lot of things going on." He opened the passenger door of his truck for me.

"No, thanks," I said. "I'd rather walk."

"Fine by me. That's your choice." He walked around to the other side and got in. "Look," he said. "I know the sun will be out in about five minutes, but I don't feel good letting you walk back."

"Trust me," I said. "It's what I want right now. I'll be fine." "Whatever suits you," he said, then kissed me on the cheek.

He climbed into his truck and drove away. As I walked in the direction of Bougainvillea, I tried figuring out what had gone wrong. Maybe it was because I was returning to Chicago and work on Monday. The thought of it, mixed with the martinis from the night before, churned in my stomach as I rerouted myself to the beach instead. I sat in the sand, watching the sunrise while feeling unsettled.

What is it about the reliable sunrise? A morning watching it paint the sky into a masterpiece brings my desires back to one thing: wanting beauty in my life. I jumped up from the sand and let my head hang as far back as it would go on my neck, like a flower bent from its stem. I could feel the tension from my chin to my chest as I took a deep breath. "I know exactly what I must do," I muttered under my breath as I lifted my head upright again and smiled out at the water.

"Marlena," I called out as I ran through her door. "I've got some news for you."

"It better be good because I was worried out of my wits about you. I know I'm not old enough to be your mother, or am I? Oh, let's not do the calculations. Where were you all night, young lady?"

"I am so sorry," I said. "I should have called."

"Yes, you should have. But did you get the closure you came for?"

"No," I said. "The other one."

"Closer? Oh, Lydia, you've got to be kidding me. I don't know what to say."

"Maybe you can help."

"How?"

"I'm thinking of staying. But I don't know. I've got my career back there, which I could also have here. And if I return there, feeling the way I feel about him now, how am I ever going to date anyone else? The last thing I want to do is one day finding myself married to one person while I love another. I don't want to do what Ava did."

"Have you told Josh how you feel?"

"He has no idea."

She stared at me like I was a ding-a-ling. "Then go!" she said. "Go tell him. What are you waiting for? Learn from her, dear. Learn from Ava before it's too late. Tell that guy you love him!"

I started for the door, and then stopped. "I thought you said stories aren't passed on from one generation to the next with the intent of telling the younger ones what to do."

"True, but if the younger ones are at all wise, they'll pick up on a lesson or two here or there."

XXXVII

THE MORNING HAD TURNED humid and sticky by the time I drove up to the marina and parked my car at a sloppy angle. Max was hosing down his dock when I walked up and said hello.

"Look who's here," he said, turning the water off to shake my hand. "Josh said he bumped into you last night at the club."

"Yes," I said, looking around at the empty boat behind Max and the buckets and fishing gear lined up. "Where is he now?"

"You just missed him. He left about fifteen minutes ago, if that."

"Oh," I said, disappointed. "Are you expecting him back soon?"

He looked at me, perplexed. "He didn't tell you?"

"Tell me what?"

"That he joined the Peace Corps, and he left this morning."

"*What?*"

"The Peace Corps, you know, this generation's answer to Communism. No more of that fifties 'containment' talk. Promote democracy and technology in these developing nations."

"I know all about the Peace Corps. *Where?* Where did he get assigned to?"

"Latin America."

"*Why* there?"

"He'll be working on fishing techniques and putting together gear and boats in one of the villages there . . . Lydia . . . you don't look good. Are you all right?"

I stared at him. Often in journalism we need to further ask the same questions to get the answers we're looking for. "Where exactly in Latin America?"

"Colombia. They say it's green there. I don't know much about it, just that it's a major exporter of emeralds. Oh, and it touches both the Atlantic and Pacific Oceans. Josh loves his water. He'll love it, I'm sure."

"He didn't mention any of it to me. *How* long is he there for?"

"Two years."

"A long time."

"Yeah. I miss him already. I'm trying to see this as being an adventure for him, fishing in new waters and catching weird things. But I'm surprised he didn't mention it to you."

"Yeah, I am too. *Where* is he flying out from?"

"Miami. A friend is driving him there."

"*When* did he leave?"

"About ten minutes ago."

"It was nice seeing you, Max."

"You take care of yourself, young lady, in that big city, you hear?"

"Of course I will. I better get hurrying." I turned and started for my car. "Lydia," he called after me.

"Yes?"

"He's in a silver van."

I glanced back at him and nodded. I got into my car and drove away.

I turned right at the four-way stop and found a line of waiting cars on the causeway. A tall boat was heading leisurely across the bay, and the bridge had slowly started to lift as the boat approached. I put my car in park, opened my door, and stepped out. My eyes followed the line of stopped cars—a station wagon. Taxi. Yellow van. Black Chrysler. Green car. Blue car and another green one after that. And then I saw it, seven cars ahead of me—a silver van.

Josh had his arm hanging outside the window on the passenger side, and I took a few steps, ready to run up alongside the line of vehicles and take hold of his hand forever. But then my heart started pounding fierce-ly, and it didn't feel right. I got back into my car and pulled it over to the sandy area, where cars can park and people can picnic or watch the sun do its thing.

I sat forward in the driver's seat, leaning on the wheel for support, try-ing to figure out what I should do. When the sailboat entered the water directly under the bridge, I had to make my mind up quickly because the bridge would soon lift and the cars would start up again.

Josh never told me he was joining the Peace Corps. Never mentioned he was leaving today. I thought our night together meant something. It did to me. I was about to quit the life I had created for myself back home and stay here forever with him. I assumed he'd be waiting there at the ma-rina with open arms to receive my news, but now I could see he had dif-ferent plans, dreams. I of all people could only support the dreams a per-son has for his life.

When the sailboat appeared on the other side of the bridge, I stepped out of my car once more. I stood there watching the silver van get away.

"I love you," I whispered as I looked out across the bay. After all my chasing and capturing and loving, I let him get away. But those are the rules of the sport, I told myself matter-of-factly. It hurts but you've got to let the silver king go.

When I could no longer see the van, I walked into the water, not car-ing that I still had on my best pair of shoes as I stood there a moment. I rummaged through my memory of the night before. Had I given him any verbal indication of how I cared for him? No. Had I mentioned the possi-bility of my staying longer in order to continue our relationship? No. It wasn't until sunrise that I made the decision to tell him how I loved the beautiful world in which he lived.

Instead, I had left him with the notion that I was a catch and release, returning to Chicago, on my own again, maybe for years, maybe forever. I made a mistake. And now it was too late. It wasn't like I could just print an editor's note in the next day's paper with the correction.

As I stood there ankle-high in the water, I reached deep down into my innermost being and pulled out my heart. I squeezed it tightly in my fist, and then hung my head back and vowed, "I will never marry any other man." I extended my arm out and threw my heart like a skipping stone across the surface of the bay. It landed hard and made a splash.

He was gone, and so was my heart. I didn't want to stick around watching it sink as Ava had once done; so, I got back into my car and drove toward the island.

XXXVIII

CHICAGO
1964
MONTHS LATER

Lydia

I SPENT THE NEXT nine months working sunrise to sunset and then into overtime, despite the laws forbidding a woman to work overtime, beneath the fluorescent lights of the newsroom, trying to forget how I'd rather be outdoors beneath the sky and the moon as it glistens across the waters off Sanibel. But like a swimmer pushing off the edge of the pool, I kicked away from all my "should haves" and moved quicker and stronger toward my deadlines at work, taking on more challenges as I went. That's what happens when a woman's heart is missing. Her mind works overtime to push her through.

But one fall day in particular, two months after returning home from my weekend trip to Sanibel, I noticed my mind distraught and unable to focus on the stories it had to write. I laid my head down on my desk and felt like crying.

"You're in shock," my friend and coworker Jane said from one desk over. "You and the entire country."

Maybe she was right, for how could anyone be heartless and soulless enough to assassinate the president? I had fainted when the news first came into the newsroom, and Jane was there to help me, but I never told her I fainted three more times later that week. I feared something else might be going on inside me. I also knew I had been working crazy hours and taking hardly any care of myself for weeks.

But when I looked at my calendar and did some personal counting of days, turned into weeks, turned into two months, I went to the doctor. He confirmed what I had suspected. I was no longer a heartless woman, for there was a tiny new heart beating and developing deep within my corridors.

Despite nonchalantly puking into a trashcan from time to time, I did all I could to keep the baby growing inside me a secret from the world. It was a frightening world, and the headlines summed it up.

RIOTS. ASSASINATIONS. DEADLY HOT SUMMERS.
ROCK STAR OBITUARIES ETCHED IN ACID. CONGRESS
GIVES PRESIDENT JOHNSON POWERS TO "TAKE ALL
NECESSARY MEASURES TO REPEL ANY ARMED ATTACK
AGAINST THE FORCES OF THE UNITED STATES AND TO
PREVENT FURTHER AGGRESSION."

The baby safely flourishing within me was my own private news, and I didn't want it breaking into any scandalous story. As my nine-month deadline grew on, I panicked that someone at work might find out. I ate healthy and only gained those absolute pounds the baby needed. I also started dressing in ways to hide the belly. And because I had been too thin to begin with, the additional weight filled my cheeks and brought me compliments. I couldn't let anyone know the truth, not even Jane. I couldn't take that risk.

Despite women celebrating a new sense of security in the workforce, thanks to receiving federal protection from discrimination, there were still many inequalities left. The world did not treat pregnant women the same way they treated others. They weren't getting hired because of their pregnancies, and many were getting fired. They had no sense of job security. And they weren't being treated in the same manner as other applicants or employees.

As I wrote stories pertaining to females, I silently appreciated more than ever the efforts women across the nation were making. They were filing more discrimination complaints with the Equal Employment Opportunities Commission than any other single group. Still, I wasn't about to announce my pregnancy to anyone at work and then complain about unfair benefits. When a married woman in this field got pregnant, she was considered halfway on the payroll unless she then took no time off after the birth.

I was a single woman with no one to rely on but myself, and since I never had a baby before, I didn't know whether or not I would need a week off to recover after giving birth, and if I did, I planned on putting in for no more than five vacation days. I didn't like keeping my pregnancy a secret, but I couldn't afford the consequences of making it public. I needed my job now more than ever.

"You're looking good, Lydia," a familiar voice said from behind me one day as I was heating up water for a cup of tea in the break room. "I was just thinking about you the other day, wondering how things were going for you."

It was Ethan. He and I hadn't seen each other but in passing since I broke it off with him some time ago, but his name was everywhere in the papers. "Hey there," I said, as I turned to see him pouring himself coffee.

"What I'm about to say," he said, "is all compliment. So don't take it the wrong way."

"Lay it on me."

"You've added pounds, but it looks great."

I laughed, thinking back to my last doctor appointment when I got scolded for not putting on more weight this far along. I ate a huge feast after that appointment, fearful from what the doctor told me could happen if I didn't gain more. It was early December so at least I was able to hide my growing basketball of a tummy beneath thick sweaters and coats.

"Still covering women's issues?" Ethan asked, and then watched me from the corner of his eye as he sipped his coffee.

"I am," I said. "And you, you're all over the place—from the Democratic National Convention to Dallas." I could imagine everyone asking him about his witnessing Kennedy's assassination, so I decided to end the topic quickly. "I'm sorry you had to be there that day, to be close and to see it all."

"I was in the wrong place at the right time, that's for sure," he said. "Great for a journalist's career, some have said, but horrible for any person to have to see and then try to process. I try keeping things from getting under my skin, but you know, it's hard in this field, especially something like this. This world is a sick place, Lydia."

"I know," I said. "But you're doing a great job covering it. I read your articles all the time. They're always good."

"I'm faced now, this week in fact, with deciding whether to stick with follow-ups of who killed the president or switch to covering Vietnam. They're letting me choose between the two."

"My God," I said. "What a choice to be given."

"I know. It's weighing heavily on my mind. Lydia," he said, his voice softening. "There's nearly 23,300 American military advisers in Vietnam. Can you fathom that?"

"No, but knowing you, you'll interview them all." I laughed. "You've got more bylines than anyone, I think."

He looked troubled, and I knew he could care less about a byline. He was the type who cared about the facts and getting it all one hundred percent correct. People talked about him. He was a man of integrity and had a reputation for working up to the last second of his deadlines for the sake of getting his stories to near-perfect levels and, then, arguing if need be with a tired editor, insisting in the final minute that something be added to a headline or that a story be arranged differently. He followed his stories through to their exact placement in the paper. He owned his stories and held on to them too tightly.

"What brings you to the second floor?" he asked me.

"I was searching for decaf tea. We're out of it on my floor, and some-one suggested I try this floor."

"Tea? How boring. I thought you only drank coffee."

"I made the switch," I said. "I know it's dull and gives me no lift what-soever, but it has nothing to do with wavering ambition. I just needed a change." I laughed, and so did he. "My stories take me three times as long to write since I gave up caffeine, and I'm on a deadline now; so, I better get going." He looked me in the eyes, and I knew he wasn't ready to say good-bye.

"Would you like to have dinner with me tonight?"

I took a sip of my hot water. I drank ten glasses a day for my baby. "Thanks for asking," I replied. "But the honest answer is, I am exhausted."

"What about tomorrow night?"

Tomorrow night I had off at last and there was nothing I wanted more than to sit on my sofa feeling for my baby's hiccups deep within me. "I'm busy tomorrow night."

"And the next?"

The next night I planned to walk down to the local movie theatre alone.

I didn't mind going to a movie alone. The last couple of years Marlena had been playing smaller roles while directing for that independent film company based out of London. She greatly enjoyed it and her latest film would be releasing the day after tomorrow. I couldn't miss it.

"And six months from now?" Ethan asked, fully aware that I was turn-ing him down.

"Busy beyond belief," I blurted out, for just thinking of what lay ahead, an overwhelming triangle: a newborn, a single mom, and a fast-paced, stressful career.

But then I saw a look of rejection on his face, and I felt bad for how I had responded. "I didn't mean it as harsh as it sounded," I said. "I'm just not up for any sort of social engagements right now. I just need time."

He sipped his coffee. "More time," he said. "I've got to respect that. It's what you want. But tell me the truth, Lydia. You're not turning into one of those women's libbers, are you?"

I felt my baby inside kick me in the gut. "Ouch," I said.

"Thank God," he said. "I hoped not."

"They're not so bad, Ethan. If there weren't any assertive, aggressive, ambitious women in the world, I today might not be allowed to ride my bicycle."

He raised an eyebrow at me, and I agreed how goofy I just sounded. And although what I said was the truth, we both laughed, and I knew he was thinking back to the day he tried stopping me from riding my bike to work, and I battled him on it, and then took off—arriving to work before him, I might add. He took a bus.

I sipped my tea and patted him on the shoulder. "You take care of yourself, Ethan. I know you'll make the right decision as to which direction to go—whether it be the follow-up on President Kennedy's assassination or Vietnam. I'll be watching for your bylines. They always let me know where you're at."

"After talking with you, I'm leaning more toward Vietnam," he said, looking like a hurt puppy dog.

"I didn't suggest that, did I?"

"No."

"Then why?"

"It'll give me someplace to go. It's not like there's any personal interests keeping me here at the moment."

"You just be safe, whatever you do," I said, not wanting to take responsibility for his decisions.

"I will. It was good seeing you as always. Bye, Lydia."

"Bye, Ethan."

Had I not sworn that day on the Causeway Bridge that I'd never marry any other man, maybe I would have said "yes" to getting together with Ethan. Just as he made a good journalist, he would have made a fine husband, for any man of integrity is a man worth marrying. But as long as I loved Josh and as long as he had no intentions with me, I would never ever marry any other man, and I held firm to that.

I did my best not to think of him all the time. At first, I could kick the thoughts out of my mind, but lately I let him stay there in my mind like a handsome bird.

It was only fantasy, for the real Josh was off doing volunteer work with the Peace Corps, having no idea at all that I was carrying his baby. I couldn't let myself dwell on it, for doing what was necessary to support my baby without losing my job was all I had to care about for the time being. And that was a lot!

And then, four weeks before my due date, I tried standing up from the chair I had been sitting on and noticed parts of my body aching that I never knew I had. Time was running out, and I had no one to help me once the baby was born. It was something I kept pushing to the bottom of my to-do pile. The people I occasionally socialized with, I also worked with, and I couldn't trust. Friends I grew up with were long since married and living in the suburbs. I didn't feel like calling on them. I needed someone to help me, and I had to think fast.

But thinking fast was something I no longer did. Maybe it was the leg cramps that interrupted my sleep every night, or the hormones, or the secret I was harboring inside me. I had to find a nanny fast, and it was a daunting task for someone like me, someone reaching her wit's end. There was no reaching deep down into my innermost being, not this time. When a woman reaches her wit's end, there's only one thing to do, so I reached out and asked for help.

I knew nothing about babies or mothering. I hardly played with but one doll when I was younger. I never had little siblings to care for. And I had no mother to mimic. I thought about the last role Marlena played— mother of ten opera- singing boys who formed a theatre in their neighborhood, and soon attracted an audience the size of London lining up on the sidewalk outside their home to buy tickets to see the beautifully well-behaved and talented boys perform. Damn, Marlena's acting was superb. Her role as their mother grabbed me and pulled me in, and I forgot she was acting. I wrote her a letter immediately after seeing the movie and explained my circumstances and then invited her to come stay with me for the birth of the baby. I included a roundtrip ticket arriving before my due date and staying for one month.

I had everything perfectly calculated. I'd use five vacations days from work after giving birth and then add a couple of sick days onto that if needed. Then, on the seventh or eighth day I'd return to work, leaving my baby in the matronly arms of Marlena and hire a nanny to take over once she left. It was the perfect plan. I just hoped Marlena was still resting on Sanibel before flying off to London to direct another film. And that she wouldn't be too disappointed by my pregnancy.

When I still didn't hear back from her one week later, I started calling nannies just in case, and when I narrowed my list, I asked them to stay flexible with me until I knew more and that it all depended on what and when I heard back from Marlena. I didn't want to call her. I wasn't good at asking for help and the letter, although it made me wait for a reply, was my most comfortable way of asking.

But then, as I was quietly talking to one of the prospective nannies on the phone at work, I got a sharp spasm across my lower back. My stomach had been tightening in bursts since I first woke, but I assumed my body was just rehearsing for the big day.

"Hola?" the nanny said in the phone. "Que pasa?"

"I don't know," I managed to say five seconds later. "I just had a spasm in my back."

"Oh dear," she said. "You're in labor."

"I can't be, not today."

"Si, si."

"No, no. I've got another week yet. I've got a ton to do. I was planning on shopping this week—diapers, bottles, baby clothes," I whispered into the phone, my words coming out choppy.

"You need to get to the hospital," she said. "Dear? Are you there?"

"No," I said. "Yes, I'm here, but it's coming back again. My back . . ."

"Another contraction. Start counting! Uno . . . dos . . . tres . . . How far apart they are, dear, and then get some help."

Help? I didn't have anyone to help me. As I fought the excruciating wave of pain darting across my back, the piles of work on my desk looked taller than ever, and I had to close my eyes. I told myself, "Stay calm and collected. You can do this. No problem. Just breathe." I imagined the white sands of Sanibel and the turquoise waters. The contraction subsided.

"I don't have time to talk," I said. "Thanks for your time, and I'll be in touch if I decide to further pursue a nanny. You are most certainly my first choice."

"Gracias muchacha. Gracias." I hung up the phone. There were more questions I wanted to ask her, but time was running out and I felt all kinds of troublesome deadlines hitting me from every direction. First and foremost, I had to finish the story I was working on for the paper.

Between contractions, I typed as fast as I could, a story about the new generation of women preparing to push down doors that a former generation of women had been pounding on with regard to womens' rights.

When another contraction came, I stopped typing, closed my eyes once more, and there I was, rolling around in the warm white sand with the birds overhead chirping, "This is why we lay eggs. It's simpler," I think I heard one of the birds whistle down to me. "You ladies should try it."

I opened my eyes and made a phone call to a woman I had been meaning to include in this story. "Now that women have received federal protection from discrimination, are they content?" I asked her.

"Hell no," she shouted. "There's more worth fighting for."

I could feel a contraction coming on. I thought contractions started light, then progressed. It wasn't fair that I was getting hit hard, like a major earthquake. Then again, I had done my best since five o'clock this morning to ignore the simpler tremors I had felt within me. I had been in denial that this might be the day.

"What about benefits for working pregnant women?" I blurted out as I bent over in my seat.

"It's criminal," she said. "That they should lose their jobs or not get hired or be told their careers are over because they're pregnant."

My contraction had reached its strong point, and I was sliding down my chair, almost to the floor. I tried returning to the beach in my mind, but it turned into a dangerous place, with stingrays whipping and jellyfish stinging. "Damn!" I shouted into the phone.

"Exactly," said the woman on the phone. "The majority of men in this country have no regard for women's rights."

"Damn," I shouted again. "They have no idea what we go through. I hate them all!" I could hardly bear the pain across my back. Maybe if the contractions would switch to the front it might be okay. "I'll tell you what I'd like to do to those men," I said, taking a deep breath in. "I'd like to make them stay home all day and bake the meatloaf and scrub the toilets and beg us for a little extra money so they might be able to buy a new lamp for the house. But most importantly, let them give birth! I wonder if there's a way for that to happen! Male seahorses do it. They're the ones to carry the eggs."

"You are good," she said. "Have you thought of helping us kick start our movement? Organized feminism has practically been nonexistent, but now we're . . ."

"Dang!" I cried, feeling something starting up again. "I could be president of your cause, but I've got a lot on my plate right now. I've got to get back to work. Thanks for the . . ."

I hung up just before the next wave of pain reached its peak. And when my phone rang, I didn't know whether I should answer it, but I did. It was Marlena.

"I can't talk now," I said in broken breaths. "I've got to turn a story in and get to the hospital. Call me later. I should be back to work in a couple of days."

I staggered through the newsroom, one time dropping to my knees pretending to tie my shoelace while waiting for the contraction to subside, then I continued onward toward the editor's desk. When I saw him, I was out of my mind and yelled, "Catch," and then, like a kite, I sent my story gliding through the air, apologizing and then racing out of the room. "I'll explain later, but I'm in a hurry," I said before the next contraction.

I longed to be invisible, not wanting to talk to anyone as I made my way through the halls, to the elevator and out the front door into the city streets. From there, I flagged down a taxi and went to the hospital.

XXXIX

JUST AS A MOTHER DOLPHIN has a nursemaid dolphin there at her side to assist her at birth and protect her from predators, I had Marlena.

She had arrived earlier that morning to surprise me and, after our interrupted phone call, she headed directly to the hospital mentioned in my letter. The labor was short for a first-timer like me, but that didn't surprise me. It fit my nature of always being in a hurry.

But no one had prepared me for two hours of pushing. I imagined three maybe four pushes and out with the baby. I've never feared death before, but as I pushed for two agonizing hours, I wondered whether my baby might be without a mother, just like I was as a baby. And in those two hours, I didn't want to think about anything beautiful or relaxing, and once I wondered whether my boss was upset with the headline I included with the story I tossed his way:

WHY WOMEN HATE MEN

Maybe he'd find it comical. It wasn't my job to write headlines, anyway, so he would know I was only kidding. Someone else wrote the headlines. I just wrote the stories. But as I pushed again and again, feeling the veins under my eyes nearly bursting and wrinkles forming on my face, I couldn't stop myself from hating Josh more than I hated pointy shoes, sleeping in rollers, making meatloaf, and poking slimy raw bait on a hook. How dare him love me like that, then leave me the next morning, having no idea of the pain he was causing me, or what I was going through because of our night together.

"I vow I will never go near another man again," I yelled to Marlena between pushes and breaths.

"That's what we all say," said the nurse. "Give it time. You will."

Between pushes, I considered joining that newly organized woman's movement. I'd give them a call next week. I was angry with Josh for making me feel pain and with men in general for making me work on the day I gave birth, so I wanted to be one of those women to push the door down.

Instead, I pushed a baby into the world and suddenly my anger vanished. When the nurses handed me Jack, he was wrapped snuggly in a blanket like a burrito, and I was filled with a kind of love I had never felt before. As I touched his cheek to mine, I would do anything for this little person, anything to make his world good. I cried my eyes out because I loved him. And I loved his father too.

"Oh, Lydia," Marlena said as she held Jack for the first time. "He looks like a newborn pelican with the thin white fuzz atop his head."

And several weeks later, Jack started eating like a baby pelican. Just as parent pelicans take turns collecting and regurgitating food for their little ones, Marlena and I took shifts feeding him at night. I needed her help with the nighttime feedings. I had returned to work as planned, just a few days after getting home from the hospital, and I was exhausted, drinking way too much coffee to get me through my days.

I felt bad being Jack's mommy and leaving him every day like I was. It wasn't my dream situation. I wanted to be the one to hear him crying when he first woke and to bathe him and rock him to sleep for his late morning and afternoon naps.

I fought back tears as I kissed him good-bye each morning. And I reminded myself that I wasn't abandoning him. Rather, like a mother turtle headed out to sea, I was doing what I had to so I could make the money for us to live and eat. My heart beat wildly for my son, and I was happy to have a heart again, but along with a heart comes pain, and I ached for my son every hour I was at work.

Marlena had extended the roundtrip tickets I sent her and stayed with us through the summer. "You're good with him," I marveled one day as she held him a special way on her arms, the only way that would calm his colicky tummy. "How do you know what to do all the time?"

"I don't," she said, her eyes widening. "I'm acting."

I laughed. "Then can you teach him to sing like you did those twelve boys of yours in the movie?"

"I can try," she said, smiling and pacing around the room with his tummy resting on her outstretched arm.

We never talked about how long she planned on staying. I think we were both taking it one day at a time, but one evening, when I got home from work, I peeked at Jack who was sleeping, then I noticed enough packages of diapers to last Jack until potty training. And lying on the floor, since I had no closet in this apartment, was a new wardrobe of clothes to fit him until he was a two-year-old toddler.

"Marlena," I whispered with tears in my eyes. "What is all of this?"

"Look in the freezer," she said. "I stocked you up with meat. It should be enough for six months."

"You didn't have to do all of that. You've done too much already."

"There's something else," she said. "I looked at apartments today. You and Jack need more space. It's insane that you're in this one-room place with a baby."

"I know," I said. "And I'm ashamed. I was embarrassed to have you see it, especially since I have no guest room."

"No, it's not about me. The cot has been fine. But it's time you move."

I walked over to the crib and watched little Jack sleeping on his tummy with his little behind sticking up in the air. As usual, he was lying in his favorite top right corner of the crib.

The apartment I was living in wasn't the sort of place I'd ever imagine bringing a baby home to. But I had never imagined having a baby. I remembered the look of shock in Marlena's eyes the moment she first arrived and saw the place, but I hadn't wanted to discuss it. I was embarrassed that I had invited her here to help me, and then had only a cot for her to sleep on.

For me, the place was fine. I had grown used to it and learned that I could add beauty to the most ugly of rooms simply by putting up a border of paper and then gluing seashells to it. And the walls were decorated with torn-out pictures from last year's calendar, framed. Jack saw blue skies, oceans, boats, and sandy beaches on the walls around his crib.

Except for the lack of space and of closets for my work clothes, I had forgotten how bad the place truly was. And Jack was too young to care. He didn't need a fancy nursery, I told myself. Those are for the mothers, mostly. He only needed my love and his basic needs: feedings, diaper changes, a clean environment, and secure arms around him.

I was doing fine at work, but I was still working to put food on our plates, and until I started bringing home more money I couldn't think about moving into a bigger place. There were many things I wanted to put my money toward, like a nanny and Jack's education. And I could tell by the way Marlena had stocked up my apartment with essentials that it was soon time for her to leave and get on with her own life.

I closed the freezer and turned to look at her. "I will move into a bigger place, but now is not the time," I said. "I'm planning to move out of the women's department soon, and I'll be getting a salary increase."

"I can help you," she said. "I can lend you money in the meantime."

"Thank you," I said. "But no. You've already helped me by being here all this time. I know you've got your own life, and movies to make."

"I'm going to miss you and Jack horribly," she said. "I'm not leaving until you find someone to stay with him during the days. I'll stay however long it takes you. And then I'll visit regularly."

"I don't think I can ever thank you enough," I said.

"You don't have to. You have given me a precious gift. I never had any children of my own. You are a daughter to me, and now I love Jack as my grandson. I've been wondering how I could thank you for all you've done for me."

I hugged her, and we both wiped the tears from our eyes. "Did you ever want children?" I asked.

"Yes and no. I guess I believed that the dreams a girl has for her life are more valuable than anything else in life. I guess there's good and bad to that. I put so much into pursuing my dreams that one day I woke up and it was too late to ever have a child of my own. But God has blessed me with you. I'm so glad you had him."

I felt just as blessed. "What have you got planned for yourself?" I asked her.

"I'm headed back to Sanibel for awhile, and then I'm off to London again. They're starting another film, and I've found that directing is what I love to do. I'll be directing the next two films and playing a supporting role in the third. It's a big lineup, so it'll be a busy few years."

"You'll do great, I'm sure."

And then there was an awkward look in Marlena's eyes, and she looked uncomfortable with what she was about to say. "Lydia."

"Yes?"

"Have you thought about telling Jack's father?"

I shook my head. "Don't go there, Marlena. I can do this on my own. I may not be like Ava, with her rich husband to rely on, but I can manage just fine." I felt bad not telling him, but it had been his choice that morning to leave without telling me his plans with the Peace Corps. And now, if he knew all of this, he might marry me out of obligation, not love.

"Okay, dear. It's your choice," she said. "Did I tell you that I brought more of Ava's journal?"

"No."

"I did, and I'll leave you with it when I go."

"How is she?" I asked. "How is Ava enjoying her life of glamour?"

"I'll let you read for yourself and find out."

XL

I MISSED MARLENA THE moment she left and couldn't wait to see her in the next film. It was early morning, and the sun was rising over the city as she closed the door behind her, waking Jack without knowing. She didn't want his eyes watching her as she said farewell and walked through the door. I watched through the window as she stepped into a taxi and it took off for the airport, and then I walked over to Jack's crib and lifted him into my arms.

It was my day off and I was thrilled to spend it doing nothing but loving and holding Jack. I kissed him on his cheek, then his nose, and then his chin. I laid him on my bed and changed his diaper, kissing him on the tummy. His tiny toes kicked with joy as he looked up at me. I pulled a cozy, dry sleeper over his head, and then kissed him again.

I held him in my arms, walking around the room, stopping to look at the pictures on our walls. He especially liked staring at the one of the boat on the blue sea. Once the sun rose above the building next to ours, I pulled the shade up on a window facing the east and spread a baby blanket down on the spot where a sunbeam had landed. It was Jack's favorite spot and Marlena used to rest him there every morning at this time. He cooed with delight when I turned on classical music.

I then pulled Ava's journal out from the drawer and sat on the warm floor next to Jack and began to read. I was surprised to see that nearly nine years had passed since her last entry. It was like not hearing from a good friend in a long, long time, and there were things I wanted to know.

NEW YORK CITY
1914, nine years later

Ava

A woman's life follows a course as elaborate as the intricate interior kingdom of a seashell. At times she finds herself living, working, or spending her energy in a darkened area not to her liking, but soon she backs out of it or turns herself around and heads for another. There are many corridors to explore and experience and a woman doesn't dwell her entire life in just one. But there will always be that one corridor that she remembers, the one with the glimpse of the sea, and it was the most beautiful of places to be, the one she'd return to if she could.

My life took a busy turn, and I set all personal writing in my journal aside for many years. People always told me God never gives a woman more than she can handle, but three sons had me questioning everything anyone said. It could have been worse—He could have given me three daughters.

The baby-making assembly line within me produced sons as quickly as Henry Ford cranked out automobiles, and, then, after churning out the third, it shut down for a reason unbeknownst to me. And just as it was with the automobiles, it was love at first sight with each of my sons, arriving at the rate of one every twenty-one months.

Where did the years go? I don't know. But now that the boys are six, eight, and ten, I can only look back and smile, for raising them were the best years of my life.

"Thank you, sweetie," I said as my youngest skipped into my bedroom like a gust of wind, handed me a red carnation, and blew me a kiss, and then skipped out as quickly as he had come in. It was the second Sunday in May, and President Woodrow Wilson had signed a proclamation designating it as Mother's Day.

"One from you too," I exclaimed as my middle son walked in, teasingly holding the carnation up. I think he wanted me chasing him through the house and tackling him on the couch until the flower was mine. But I hadn't done anything fun or silly like that in some time, so, instead, I sat up in bed and reached my arm out and took the flower from his hand. I smiled and gave him a wink. "You boys have a nice day out there today."

He nodded, and a second later I could hear him jogging down the long hall toward the front door. They were handsome boys, and charming, turning the heads of girls way too old for them. One day soon they'd be giving flowers to wives of their own, and I would miss them dearly. I wasn't at all ready for any of that. I was clinging to walls of the corridor I had cherished all these years. And I still had more time there.

Leo and I had done a fine job at raising them this far. Whenever I spent too much time with the boys practicing piano or reading poetry or pointing out the beautiful varieties of leaves and flowers and trees, their father stepped in and taught them to be men. He had them work hard, helping in his office with financial calculations, budgets, and dimensions of ad spaces. And where I instilled in the boys an appreciation and a sense of thankfulness for any gifts ever given to them, Leo made them work hard for everything they wanted. We didn't want our boys growing up believing that the luxuries of the world were going to be handed to them and that they didn't have to do their share.

It would have been easy to give them everything they wanted. My writing slowed but continued after the first baby and Leo continued rising through the ranks of his career. He was good at the financial and creative aspects of both catalog and magazine publishing, and by the time I took our third son home from the hospital, my husband had already become associate publisher of a publication boasting the nation's highest circulation.

I was fully engaged being the mommy of three boys. and I no longer had time as I once did to care about, let alone set up, interviews and work toward deadlines. In 1903 I did start writing articles about a womens' suffrage society and continued for seven years until they resorted to acts of defiance to gain attention and further their causes for the rights and advancement of women. It was then that Leo insisted my coverage of it end.

"I believe women should have the right to vote," he said one evening. "But I don't like these extremists."

"If it weren't for groups of aggressive women, I might still be wearing a corset. I'm grateful to these women, Leo."

"I respect the milestones, dear, but the tactics they're using are getting out of control. I don't want my wife writing articles about women who chain themselves to railings and set fire to the content of mailboxes."

"I agree, but maybe if the country would give them a respectable venue to voice their opinions, they'd no longer resort to such measures to get heard."

Around the same time in 1910 I heard word from a business associate who had relatives living in Florida that a storm hit Sanibel, the worst in the history of that island. I tried not to start thinking about Jaden again, but it was hard. I prayed and was later relieved to hear no one was killed.

Soon after respecting my husband's wishes, I switched to writing about more carefree topics, like the changing bathing suit styles. Despite having had three boys, I myself wore them at the lake over the summer and was proud of women doing away with the yards of extra fabric and bloomers. I took pride in bicycling daily and keeping myself trim, and Leo loved watching me lounge around our summer cottage in the new styles. It was the first time ever that I felt the warmth of the sun shining on the curvaceous parts of my body, parts that had never been exposed to outdoor elements before.

The fun and sporadic articles that I wrote in my spare time reflected my fun years of being mommy to three wonderful boys, of spending every July on the lake, of going to the opera regularly with my husband and friends, and of shopping to my heart's content, dressing in all the top fashions. Life to me was simply the best and happiness wasn't something that took any effort. Never for a moment had I ever imagined I was in any danger of coming down with the same spells of sadness my mama once suffered.

There were times when I didn't write articles for months on end and it was okay because I preferred paying attention to my boys and to being their mother. But then one day, when my youngest started school, I felt an emptiness and heard a growling noise in the pit of my stomach. My craving to write something bigger and more meaningful had returned, as always, nagging me here and there throughout my life.

"You haven't written any articles in a while," Leo said when I told him that evening about my need to write. "Would you like me to make a few phone calls, pull strings and get you an important assignment at one of the magazines?" He had poured us both a glass of liquor and we were about to settle down for the evening on the patio off our bedroom.

"And write about necklines lowered for the first time in decades, or something really exciting like rayon?" I responded sarcastically.

"Rayon? What's that?"

I took a sip of the liquor, then set it down on my bureau so I could finish taking my earrings, necklace and remaining jewelry off. "Rayon is a new artificial-silk invention. I'm surprised you haven't heard of it yet," I said as I put my earrings in the gold-plated musical heart box Leo had once bought for me. "I don't want to write any more about that kind of stuff. Besides, I no longer want to write for any magazine that uses semi-nude images to sell products marketed to women. I don't like it. Why are they starting to do that?"

Leo was sitting on the bed, pulling his socks off. "It sells. It especially seems to work with selling soap."

"It's degrading, don't you think?"

"Doesn't matter what I think," he said. "It matters to your sons. It's up to us to raise them to respect the minds of women and not view them as purely physical objects."

"With a mother as intelligent as you, our boys already know a woman is more than a pretty body. They know she's got a mind."

"And a heart and a soul, too, Leo," I said, smiling. I ran the brush through my long, dark hair and watched Leo in the mirror. "I can't figure out if my desire to write comes from my mind or my soul."

"What is it that you want so desperately to write?"

"A novel," I answered. "I've always wanted to."

"You'll never make any money writing fiction," he said. "Unless, of course, you go on to write hundreds of books and you don't have time for, that is. Who wants to sit around waiting that long to make any money?"

"Leo," I said, rolling my eyes. "It's not about money. You know that. We've got all the money in the world. It's about me wanting to do something I've felt passionate about ever since I was a little girl."

"You're a talented writer," he said to me. "I just think you ought to put that into an area that pays and they were paying you, darling, top dollars for your freelance articles."

I stood up and walked over to Leo on the bed and took hold of his hands, pulling him up. For a moment, we stared eye-to-eye and I recognized his look. It was one I had seen a long time ago in my own father's eyes, a look that most people might not catch, but I did. I had never seen it in Leo before, but it was a look of financial concern.

I kissed him on the lips. "Is there anything you want to tell me, dear?" I asked.

"With regard to what?"

"I don't know," I said, noticing him look away. "Anything on your mind. Are you concerned about the security of our savings in any way?" I liked being direct with Leo. Life was too short to beat around the bush.

He laughed, but it wasn't his usual laugh, the one that added an extra ounce of happiness to my supply. "A man is always thinking about security," he said, pulling me toward the patio. "What if something happened to me? I've got to make sure you and the boys are fine." He sat down and I quickly went back into our room for the tray with our cocktails.

When I returned, I noticed the full moon shining down on the rose bushes I had planted and the night was too beautiful to think of morbid things. I set the tray down and sat closely beside him. "Life is too short to worry about money," I said, confident we would never run out. "Besides, I could make a fortune off my wardrobe alone, you know."

"I'd never want you selling your gowns," he said, seriously.

"Why not? Once I sold all my gowns I could then pose semi-nude for those awful magazine ads."

"Don't you ever," he said. "I would flip over in my grave." He pulled me closer and kissed my neck. "But a body like yours would sure sell a lot of soap."

I nudged him with my arm. "I would never," I said with a laugh. "I'd turn curtains into dresses before walking around semi-nude."

That night money, or lack thereof, was the last thing on my mind. We had a mini-fortune saved up, and being poor was a self-perception I had gotten rid of long ago. I dropped it the day I brought our first baby home from the hospital, feeling richer than I had ever imagined being. It was the day I was no longer just Leo's wife but I was also the mother of his child— one of the world's most noble titles. And I no longer felt like I was sharing Leo's money, but rather, that it had become our money the day I became the mother of his child.

It was also the day I truly started loving Leo. And the love grew with each baby I carried inside me, and I believe those boys got bored in my womb and went to work crafting and constructing a new heart for their mommy. Children want for their mommy's heart to beat wildly for their daddy. And so mine did. Leo was the father of my boys and a good one!

"You look more and more like your father every day," I told my oldest son when he slowly walked into my room carrying a red carnation. "Thank you for the flower."

He sat down on the side of my bed and looked me in the eyes. "I miss him," he said. "Will the pain ever go away?"

"I don't know," I said. "I can't answer that."

It hadn't been that long. The day Leo suffered a heart attack and died hours later in the hospital still felt like yesterday to us all, but it wasn't yesterday. Months had gone by since his death, and the boys were doing their best at continuing their lives, going out to play golf today as they always did with their father on Sundays.

I reached over to the bedside table and placed the carnation in the glass of water beside the two carnations my other sons had brought in, and then settled myself back against the headboard of the bed.

"Are you going to stay in bed again today, Mother?" my son asked.

"No," I answered, not believing my own word. "I'll be getting up today. How could I not? It's the first Mother's Day—a good day to get up. I'll be up by the time you boys return from golf."

He slowly left my room. Of the three, he was the most like his father, too mature for his age and ambitious as ever. Surely he'd be the first to fly from the nest and into a world of success and opportunity, but then again, this happened with their father, and I wondered how it might affect my sons long-term.

When I heard the front door close and the house grow quiet, I had to get up. I felt like a hen doing nothing but sitting around on its egg all day. But today was the day. It was officially declared a holiday for mothers, and what sort of mother was I to be hiding away in my bed all day? I couldn't stand to go through another week with my boys walking one-by-one into my bedroom to kiss me good-bye as they left for school. I had seen the looks of fear and disappointment on their faces each morning and again after school when they came to find me still in bed. Over the last three months I had only gotten out for the funeral, financial meetings including the reading of the will, and for a doctor appointment. But after each event, I returned home sinking lower than before.

I tried not to let my mind compare myself to my mama. She had something wrong with her mind. My problem was situational. It had to be. Leo had been keeping secrets from me in the years leading up to his death. At the reading of the will I discovered we no longer had our savings. I did some investigating only to unravel a series of lies about the man I thought I knew. Leo was a gambler and had been for many years, exactly how many, I do not know. Blackjack was his thing, and when gambling was outlawed, he went underground. I was irate for not following up with that look I had seen in his eyes that night, the look of financial concern. And I spent many sleepless nights fantasizing about the conversations and confrontations I wished I could have had with him, had I known. I was mad that the man I loved had hidden this part of himself from me. If only he had told me about it, maybe I'd have been angry at first, but then I could have gotten help for him. His gambling problem flipped back and forth from blackjack to high-risk stock investments, and that was where he lost most of it, I learned.

I took my pillow in my hand and flung it across the room, angry at the thought that this might be my punishment for the crime I once committed. I too had kept a secret from Leo. I never told him that I married him for his wealth and because I needed an escape from my life and my emotions at that time. If he were alive today I'd tell him he was my hero for taking me away like he did and how lucky I was that it turned out as it did, that I fell madly in love with him as the years went by. It could have been bad. I was young and not thinking wisely at the time I married him. I don't know why I thought a man was the only thing that could rescue me from my life and those three young girls who disliked me. Why didn't I know back then that I was strong enough and smart enough to leave on my own? Maybe I was too young to realize the options a woman has for herself in life. And I was grieving for my mother. A person ought not to make major life-changing decisions while still in mourning.

I reached over and picked up the small picture of Leo and me on our wedding day and held it tightly. I did love Leo. I grew to love him immensely. But now I was left to question everything, even the love he had for me. I let the picture drop to the floor, for I had to think of other things now. The financial stability of the family was now my problem, and a big one! By the time I had done the calculations, I knew we couldn't continue living in our mini-mansion, dressing as we all did, socializing and gallivanting around the city and the opera and the restaurants if I planned on sending the boys to university. And I was astounded to discover the money that went into the upkeep of our estate and to pay the nannies, domestic servants, groundsmen, and chefs. Life as we were accustomed to living couldn't go on without Leo's salary.

But worse, I didn't know how the boys would go on without their father. He had been a good father, and that is what I wanted to remember, the role that would define his life. Just thinking of it all, of how badly I wanted to throw my arms around Leo and tell him that I loved him despite the problem and secret he had been keeping from me, made me want to lie back down again in my bed. But I had promised the boys that today would be the day, and I had thrown my pillow across the room, so I couldn't lay my head back down comfortably.

I had to get up, not only for my sons but also for the new life that was growing within me. I was pregnant with Leo's fourth child, the one he would never get to know about. That is what troubled me most. I could think of nothing worse than a father not knowing the existence of one of his children. And, oh, how Leo always wanted a daughter. It had to be a girl. Just two months after his death, I began waking up in the wee hours of the night with wretched growls coming from deep within my stomach. I spent my mornings heaving—a symptom I never experienced with my first three pregnancies.

"Why me?" was my first question. "How could you do this to me, Lord?" was my second. My sons were already manageable ages, but I was a widow in my late thirties—a bit late for the baby-making plant to re-open. But apparently there was one more model to be made, and I wanted as much fanfare to accompany the arrival of this baby as that of the others or it wouldn't be fair.

I picked up the teacup setting on my bedside table and sipped it. It was cold, so I put it down and leaned over to sniff the three carnations. They weren't the most fragrant of flowers, but it didn't matter. They were from my boys.

I focused on the flowers as I slowly stood up. I didn't want to get up. I wanted to lie back down again and arrange the pillows around my face and burrow for one more day. I thought about my mama and wondered whether this was how she felt in her down times. I could understand now. I couldn't then. And I remembered my grandmother telling me that whenever a person feels down, all they must do is thank the Lord for all that is good. That felt like an impossible task, for I was a widow with no savings, three sons, and a daughter on the way, and I could hardly muster the strength to leave my own bedroom. But it was either fall back into bed or drop to my knees and thank God. One was simple and the other difficult. I chose the more difficult of the two.

"Dear Lord," I prayed with one hand on my belly. "Thank you . . . thank you for all that you have given . . . for my three sons . . . for mothers . . . for sunshine . . . flowers and . . . for the new life within me."

It was easier than I thought to conjure up a few things I felt grateful for, and by the end of my prayer, I felt at peace, and I had a new, yet ancient perspective that maybe God had a purpose and a plan in giving me a daughter at a time like this. Surely he must have thought I could handle it—what woman, after having three sons, couldn't—or He wouldn't have allowed it to happen.

I looked around the room I had lived in for weeks on end, and then I glanced down the long hallway with the sun shining through the window and beaming down against the hardwood floor. I didn't know how the sun or the moon did it, how they made everything from a mud puddle to a wooden floor to a sea look more beautiful. I wondered whether it looked like that every morning. Maybe it was God who made things glisten when we really needed them to or helped us take notice of beauty that is always there whether we see it or not. Today, I would walk down that glistening hallway.

I got dressed, not caring about fashion. Solids or small figured prints, beading, a hem that fluctuated between a few inches above the ankle and the instep, medium to heavy fabrics like serge and gabardine—none of that mattered to me now or, come to think of it, ever.

"Can you find me a white carnation?" I asked my assistant when she came in the room, surprised to see me up and dressed.

She pointed toward the flowers the boys had given me.

"Those are for me," I said. "It was nice of the boys. But I also want to honor my mama today, and the custom is that if your mother is alive, wear a colored carnation. If she has passed away, then wear a white one."

"Ah, si, si," said Nora, nodding her head, and then leaving my room.

I stood there waiting for her to return, and when she did, she was carrying a white carnation and helped me pin it to my blouse.

"Thank you," I said and headed out my door and down the long glistening hallway with the morning sun coming through. I didn't go far, just to Leo's office to figure out what it was that I was going to do as provider of this family. My options were slim. I certainly wasn't going to pose semi-nude in any soap advertisements. Writing a novel would take too long, a year, two maybe three being that it was my first, and even then, there was no guarantee that it would get acquired by a publisher, or sell. There was just one thing to do: write more articles—write more articles than I had ever written before!

I drank three strong cups of Nora's espresso and then skimmed through the stack of unread papers and publications that had been delivered to our house and piled up since Leo's death. I took notes as I perused, then looked up addresses in Leo's files, those of people we had socialized with and those he had talked about from work and even those I didn't know but who attended his funeral.

And despite it being Sunday and a new nationally declared holiday, I wrote letters to them all. I told them I needed work and suggested all kinds of ideas I thought would make interesting stories such as: How have mothers traditionally been honored and the efforts leading up to today being declared a national holiday? And what about fathers? There were more stories I thought of. With war in Europe looming, what were women doing to prepare should their men have to leave? Then I mentioned that Teddy Roosevelt, it was rumored, was heading to Captiva Island, Florida to trophy fish. I could go there, bump into him and interview him, the former president on his views concerning the likeliness of America entering the war. And my God, while there, I could look up Jaden. But I doubt they would like the former president story, and come to think of it, Jaden probably wouldn't like me anymore. I was the mother of three boys and pregnant with a daughter.

And in just two hours of writing letters, I felt confident I would have at least five different articles to write and five different deadlines, all from different publications. I had created for myself a lot of work to do, work that would have to wait until Monday, for the boys were due back any time. Today I would spend with them. Monday I would start my interviews. Tuesday, write the stories. Wednesday, I'd edit those stories, and as soon as I heard back from the publications, I would submit them. Friday, I would determine whom I had to let go first. It wouldn't be Nora. I would hold on to her until my last penny, for she had been by my side during the delivery of each of my sons, and I was fond of her, despite her speaking mostly Spanish and my not understanding seventy-five percent of what she said.

But all of that could wait, I decided as I walked back down the hall, out the front door, and around back to our shed. That is where we kept my bicycle. I walked it out into the light and stood there holding onto the handlebars for a moment. It had been awhile since I last rode.

"It should be easy," I told myself. "Once you learn, you never forget how. And if you fall, you just get back up again."

I took off in the direction of where the boys were playing golf. I wanted to surprise them.

XLI

LYDIA

JACK WAS NAPPING CONTENTEDLY on the blanket beside me when I finished reading and closed the journal. The sun was too high now to beam through the window, so I scooped him up and placed him in his crib. He was an easy baby, still napping three times a day, but I couldn't imagine three of him. I didn't know how Ava would manage with three sons and a daughter on the way and no husband to help and support her. Then again, she was a strong woman and she was on her way. I found it inspiring the way she got out of bed like that and forced herself into that office, then outside where she would ride her bicycle to the course where her boys were golfing.

As I walked over to my own bicycle propped against the wall behind the bathroom door, I thought about my own situation—a single working mother—and wondered how I might make it all work. I wondered whether I was still as bold and courageous as I once was—the girl who applied to college against my father's resistance and who stood up in class and disagreed not just with the teacher, but with an entire decade of people who believed a proper woman has no other options but to marry and keep a clean house. I was the girl who insisted on riding the bus not the limousine and that hopped off the bus because she saw flowers and wanted beauty in her life. I was the girl working at the paper after school making the best coffee she could make because she knew that the tiny steps would get her where she wanted to go. I was a girl with hopes and dreams.

I picked up a towel laying on the bathroom floor and started wiping the spokes of my bike. I was still that girl. Once a girl rides toward dreams and goals, she never forgets how. She may fall down from time to time, but all she must do is get back up. And when she does, she might find she's stronger than she once was.

If I could push a baby into the world, I could do most anything, for what female sport is more strenuous and incredible than that? Raising the baby maybe, but it was too soon to think about that. I had to push, push myself harder at work and ride with more strength than ever in the direction of my goals.

XLII

CHICAGO
1968
FOUR YEARS LATER

Lydia

The next four years were turbulent ones for our world, and I wondered often whether writing about a new freedom in hemlines and bolder-colored dresses would have been the more pleasant career choice. But I worked my way out of issues pertaining to women and into news of interest to men, women, and our nation as a whole.

When President Johnson ordered air raids against North Vietnam in early 1965, I started paying closer attention to the war that had been under way for some time already. And I went to Washington in April to cover a large anti-war rally. It was my first major news story, and I was assigned to interviewing university students from all over the country as to why they were protesting the war.

Jack stayed home with Rosie, his nanny. She was a young woman, in her mid-twenties, and plain without makeup or style in her hair, and she refused to wear any hemlines above her knee. Jack didn't need a fashion-savvy girl watching after him. He needed, or so I thought, someone like Rosie. She loved babies and children and desperately longed for a boyfriend so she might marry and move to the suburbs, but I didn't have the heart to tell her that maybe men might notice her more if she let her hair down and put lipstick on those tiny lips of hers. I also felt like giving her a friendly nudge into the sixties, for she was still wearing button-down sweaters daily.

But she was good with Jack, and she was reliable. She knew my work schedule and never showed up late and stayed until whenever I came home, whether that was around Jack's evening bath or later. She made me believe that Jack and I were her only life. Occasionally, when I came home extra late, she'd sleep on the cot, but usually she insisted on returning home. She lived with her parents in an apartment three blocks away. I still lived in the tiny shoebox, but I swore as soon as the world and my job slowed, I'd start scouting around for a bigger and better place.

During the day, she'd walk Jack over to her parents' house in his stroller, or to the parks or around the city so they wouldn't have to be confined to the four walls of the tiny apartment. I saw it as good for Jack. Boys are meant to be outdoors, weather permitting. They're like puppy dogs. They need to be walked daily, and a few times a day is better than just once and it doesn't matter that they were out the day before. They've got to get out every single day!

It hurt me to think that I wasn't the one walking him every day, pointing out the pigeons and the clouds in the sky, but I had to provide for us. At times I envied Rosie for spending time with him.

By Christmas of that same year American troop strength was at nearly 200,000 and growing, combat losses totaled 636 Americans killed, and, here at home, draft quotas had been doubled. I had written a few stories pertaining to the draft and struggled personally with the news of casualties. Maybe if I weren't a mother, it would be simpler to write such stories, for all I could think of when I heard about the men being drafted was that they were just grownup baby boys. Shame on me, for I know a journalist is supposed to remain objective, but does that mean nonaffected?

Every night I came home from work and picked Jack up in my arms, whether he was awake or not. I cradled him and rocked him, unable to imagine my own son ever being drafted off to war. I wanted time to go by slowly. I didn't want Jack growing up in time for any war.

Men. They've had rights all along, rights that women haven't always had, including working overtime and the night shift. But men—they've had to do things no woman would envy. I would never want to do what those men were over there doing, and I could no longer relate to the feminists wanting to be treated in every single way like men. That movement had become a bit too extreme for me to identify with fully, not to say I wasn't grateful for the strides they were making.

Thanks to them, I was glad to be a woman in this world, now more than ever. In 1966, women had federal protection from discrimination in the workplace, and I felt more secure at my job than ever. I was part of a small group of women covering the Vietnam War. Hardly any women were actually sent there, so I covered angles from here at home. About ninety-nine percent of desks in the newsroom still belonged to men, and women were still mostly section writers in the features department, or they covered education and medicine, but more and more, women like myself were marching into hard news.

There were, however, unspoken rules that existed in the newspaper business at this time and I lived accordingly.

"Sorry, but I'm divorced," I'd say anytime a man—and there were many— around the office gave me the look or asked me out. It was a lie, but a woman who was married or searching for a man was labeled a short-timer with regard to her career. I, on the other hand, never had a husband but played the part of being divorced. It worked for me. Divorced women were considered "serious" journalists.

Even sources I interviewed for stories asked me out "off the record," and again I'd reply, "I'm flattered. But you better try someone else. I'm bitter and divorced and not the least bit interested in any relationship."

I became known as the woman married to her work, and that was exactly what I wanted. I had no intentions of becoming anyone's wife and of letting any man ground my career after working hard to get to where I was. The only male I thought I needed in my life was little Jack. But the bigger he got, the more he talked. At first, things were simple. "Clouds. Clouds. Clouds," he'd squeal on my days off when I walked him to the city parks. But soon it turned to, "Birdies. Birds. Pigeons. Poopy."

"Jack," I'd scold. "Don't say 'poopy' so loud. It's a word meant to be whispered."

"Pigeons. Mommy pigeon. Nanny pigeon. Baby pigeon."

"That's right," I answered aware that one of these days Jack might ask where all the daddy pigeons are, including his own. But as the number of American troops was increasing and the draft quotas doubled, I feared that Jack's daddy might become a statistic. I thought of Josh daily. It was hard not to. As Jack grew bigger, he looked more and more like his father, and it was hard for me not to think about him. Jack had his daddy's eyes and his love for nature, something so strong that even a baby brought up in downtown Chicago couldn't hide. When I took Jack to the park just two blocks away, it would take us an hour to get there because he stopped to observe worms or dried-up leaves or green things growing from the sidewalk cracks. I know he didn't get those outdoorsy fetishes from me!

Josh's two years of volunteer work in the Peace Corps had ended, and he was probably back in Florida, where I wanted him to be. However, I feared the father of my child might get away once more. I thought about what Ava had said in her last entry, that she could think of nothing worse than a father not knowing of the existence of his own child.

One morning I decided I had to catch Jack's daddy before he got drafted, before he got away once more. I had to tell him I loved him and that another little person in the world would too and that we were willing to pick up and relocate and do anything necessary to make it work—that is, if he was interested.

There are perks to being a journalist. I spent that entire morning at work making investigative phone calls until I learned all I needed to know about Josh's whereabouts. My worst fear had already come true. He finished his assignment in the Peace Corps and went straight to getting drafted. He was already in the midst of the war and had been for several months. I put my head down on my desk and cried. I cried because he wasn't at all a fighter. He was a peaceful man, wanting to fish and boat and play music. And then, I walked into my boss's office and begged to go there to Vietnam.

My boss refused to send me there, saying he already had enough journalists assigned to that region. I knew the truth. He didn't want to send any more women there. He only wanted male journalists to cover horrific things. And it was probably a good thing, for Jack needed me more than the war needed my coverage of it. But for the next several months I followed the horrific events and the casualty reports as they came into the newsroom, and I started praying for the poor men out there, especially Josh, as I had never prayed before. It felt good to pray. I had hardly ever asked anyone for help with anything, but now, I was asking help from God, and it felt okay to be doing so. I always assumed I'd save my prayer requests for a time when I might be starving, homeless, or dying, but it dawned on me that two of those three things—starving and homeless— might never happen and the third— dying—would surely come but might come all of a sudden, leaving me no time for prayer, so I started now and I thoroughly enjoyed it.

And like Ava, I found it easy to thank God, and soon I prayed so consistently that I started feeling as if the Lord was living beside me like a constant companion. I found comfort in praying and began to realize why it was that people did it in the first place. Any time the slightest fear crossed my mind, I muttered, "Please, Jesus, hold Josh in your arms, wherever he might be and keep him safe. I pray for a miracle. May Josh hear music in the midst of the chaos he's in."

And as I held Jack in my arms and sang to him at night, I wanted for him to have the chance to meet his father. I was no longer an immature woman selfishly obsessing over the guy she once loved. I was now a mother longing more than anything for the father of her son to be alive and well. I felt guilty and ashamed for having kept the baby a secret from him all this time. I felt like a thief, one who robbed a good man of the right to know he has a son. I felt haunted by what I had done and considered picking up my life and moving to Sanibel, where I could at least let Jack's grandfather know so he could begin a relationship with Jack in the meantime. But, no, I couldn't do that to Josh. He would have to be the first to know the news of his son, and I would just have to pay the consequences of my crime and wait. Wait and pray until the war ended or Josh got sent home. I had resources, and I would check on his status and whereabouts daily.

In the meantime, I would have to focus on my career and trust that Jack was in good hands with his nanny. I surrendered him the best I could to her, but then one December day in 1967, I learned that nanny wasn't who I wanted Jack spending another day with. I was working on anti-war stories, one in particular that sent me to New York City. Rosie had never been to any city other than Chicago, and Jack had never been outside Illinois. I was making a fine salary and decided to take them along with me, treat them to a new city. As I conducted interviews during the day, I assumed they were lounging around the lavish hotel, waiting for me to return so we could have dinner. But when I returned from my assignments, I could find them nowhere.

At first, I didn't think much of it so I took a long, hot bath in an effort to unwind. It was then that the phone in our hotel room rang and I quickly hopped out of the bath and answered it, dripping wet and coated in bubbles.

"Rosie, is that you? Where are you?"

"Jail. I need your help."

"Jail? What on earth for?"

"I've been arrested. Me and five hundred and eighty-five other anti-war protestors."

"My God! That's the story I was working on today. Where's Jack?"

"He's fine. He's here. They've got him and want to talk with you."

"You took a child to an anti-war rally? My child? My Jack? I didn't even know you were opposed to the war."

"I am. Can you please get me out of here?"

It was late at night by the time I held Jack in my arms. I took him straight to the hotel room where I wrapped him in a blanket and held him securely as I did when he was first born. At first, he was delighted to play the role of mommy's baby again, and he did a good job, his fingertips softly reaching up for my lips and nose and his own lips smiling with delight over all of mommy's gooey words of affection. But then, he returned to being a big boy in search of independence, and he fought his way free from the blanket.

"I want more candy canes," he said, glancing over at Rosie. "How many did you have today, Jack?" I asked.

"One, two, three, four, five, six . . ."

I glared over at Rosie, not looking happy as his counting continued.

"You need something healthy in your tummy now, Jack," I said after he counted to twelve. "I'll order you a grilled cheese sandwich and soup. We'll eat right here in the room."

"I rode in police car today," he said. "I went to jail with monsters and bad guys."

Ever since I picked them up at the jail, I had been giving Rosie the silent treatment, not because I didn't have a million things to yell and scream at her, but because I was worried about Jack and I wanted to make him my number-one concern. I hardly looked at Rosie as I listened to Jack's long, detailed account of going to jail.

At three and a half, he was already taking interest in the newspaper. He liked pointing to a story, any story, and then he would ask me to read it to him. Of course I didn't read it, but rather, made up something wonderful. I subjectively skewed the objective truth, so he would think the world he lived in was a good place to be. I didn't want him knowing about jail and rapes and political scandals and robberies and car thefts and all the darker sides to living in this world. I especially didn't want him knowing about war. There were nearly half a million U.S. troops involved in the war now and a little boy didn't need to know that grownups are unable to resolve things peacefully and diplomatically, and that they engage in war and people get killed. Jack knew about monsters. They were scary enough.

"Rosie," I said once I turned on cartoons. "He must have been terrified in all those crowds today."

"At least those crowds were antiwar. Until the end, they were peaceful and pleasant, or I wouldn't have taken him. Can you imagine Jack going off to war one day?"

"That's not the point."

"Maybe it is. Things that happen in the world today are going to affect the world Jack lives in tomorrow. You realize our children do inherit the world the way we left it, don't you? I know you're a journalist and you're supposed to play objective, but do you agree with the war in Vietnam, Lydia? Do you? Because there's a danger in shutting off your opinions for the sake of doing your job."

I wanted to grab hold of her and wring her neck. "Look," I said. "The issue right now isn't whether I agree with the war or those anti-war protestors. The only perspective I'm claiming at this moment is that of a mother. Jack doesn't need to worry about how bad the world is. He's too young. You shouldn't have taken him there. End of story, Rosie."

"But . . ." she dared to continue.

"Rosie, pack your bags. You're going home. And you better start looking for a new job. I can no longer trust you with my son."

I didn't like firing her so abruptly, but as a mother, my son was more important. And I didn't want to leave him another day with her, not after this. Suddenly, I didn't want to leave him with anyone. But I had to. When we returned to Chicago, I called around and relied here and there on anyone who was available out of desperation. I had done my best to provide for Jack and for me, and I was tired. I was tired of doing it on my own and of being unbreakably strong and tough and not needing the help of anyone, especially any man. And now that all the good men were off to war, I suddenly appreciated them and feared for them, and prayed for the men, the grown-up little boys, as I had never done before.

And in the weeks following, I continued relying on interim nannies, working my way up to the next level at work and was covering the horrific facts concerning the war, something that in the past would have only been assigned to male journalists, but now it was I who got to write about the gory details. I was working ten- to fourteen-hour days, coming home drained, trying to be a mommy to Jack and doing the best I could to gather enough energy, so he wouldn't think his mommy was a zombie. And then I'd collapse into bed and begin it all again just a few hours later.

I had no energy left at night to do anything but fall fast asleep, and even then I'd wake a couple hours later with scary headlines running through my mind.

CASUALTY STATISTICS ON THE RISE
MORE ANTIWAR PROTESTORS FILL THE STREETS

My mind went from one headline to the next, and every so often it stopped long enough to think about my life and how hectic it had become. In the mornings, when I touched my feet to the floor, I was becoming aware that I had no time to listen to the birds outside my window. And, yes, there are birds and things that are beautiful-sounding even in a city. The sounds of beauty are everywhere, not just on some island. The problem is that I was too busy and stressed to ever listen for them. I was even getting too busy to listen fully to my own son's voice.

One particular morning, after only getting a couple of hours of sleep due to worrying about deadlines and appointments and nannies getting sick, I sat up in bed when the alarm went off and asked, "Is this it, Lord? Is this rat race all there is to my life?" I then heard my son turning on the television all by himself in the other room. "Please help me. I need help, Lord. I'm desperate."

I poured Jack his cereal, showered, dressed and rushed to work.

Later that week I received a letter in the mail from Marlena. She was back on Sanibel in between films and wanted to let me know that she saw Josh at the store. It was major news, and she did a superb job reporting it to me.

JOSH IS BACK FROM THE WAR WITH A CAST ON HIS LEG

That night, after Jack was asleep, I poured myself a cup of coffee and sat down to read. Along with the letter, Marlena had sent me another of Ava's journal entries. I was stunned to discover that many more years had passed since the last entry. It was odd, as if my best friend was aging ahead of me.

XLIII

1928

Ava

China breaks. A wedding dress dulls. Money gets spent. But the prayers a woman utters in her lifetime flutter back and forth throughout the generations like eternal butterflies landing ever-so-lightly on the shoulder of a daughter, granddaughter, great granddaughter, or any old girl, often without her ever knowing.

IT WAS A COLD New York morning, and I knew the coldness had something it wanted to say to me. I could tell by the way it howled outside my window and then knocked on my bones. At first I tried not to pay it any attention, but then, when my knees started creaking, I knew the cold was following me and that it wasn't going to give up.

"I don't have time for you," I said rubbing the goose bumps on my arms.

"Why don't you come back in a couple of weeks?"

I put my robe on and walked over to the table in my room, the one near the window in the spring, and the one where I drank my tea under the rays of morning light. This time of year the table is dark and I place a blanket over my legs when I sit there.

The cold doesn't bother my daughter as it does me, so I try not to complain of it, and we go on drinking our tea in the cups I inherited from my mama. They were part of the set that I was given after her death, and they reminded me of our moments long ago when she, Grandmalia, and I would drink the comfort tea together. But it wasn't the tea or the china or even the brandy that meant anything. It was the ritual and those have a way of continuing throughout generations if someone takes on the sacred responsibility of declaring them rituals in the first place.

I glanced at the clock behind me. It was seven-thirty in the morning. Where was she? My daughter usually came wandering into my room by now to lazily plant a good-morning kiss on my cheek before sliding down into the chair across from me. I loved having tea with her each morning before she left for school and, occasionally, if the boys weren't in a hurry for work, they would wander in, preferring coffee to tea and only having time for a quick sip, if that. I call them boys, but that's because I'm their mother. Ask any woman, and she'd say they're men! Their days of living here with me at the estate were numbered, but I wasn't counting. They could stay as long as they wanted, but my oldest son would soon be engaged, and my middle son was thinking of buying his own place—twice as big as this—and my youngest was making plans to move downtown.

The boys grew up too fast, which is why I'm grateful God blessed me with a daughter. I still had her home with me for many years yet, and I was glad. I wasn't at all ready for a childless house and life.

I enjoyed having tea in the morning with my children. But once they all left and the house was mine, I switched to coffee so I could write. I drank three cups spread throughout the day. The room was cold, so I stood up and paced back and forth a few times, leaning my hands over the tray with the hot tea and rubbing my fingers over the rising steam as one does over a campfire. I thought about which story I might tell my daughter today. She enjoys hearing one story before school, but a short one, and she prefers nonfiction to fiction and her favorite genre, simply put, is true stories having to do with me—her mother—at around her age. But now that I've entered my fifties, I forget things that happened when I was fourteen or fifteen, so I have to think awhile before coming up with a good story to tell her. I tell her whatever I remember. Or what I want to remember. Or what I want to relive. Or what might reunite me with the girl I once was. According to recent statistics, the average life expectancy for a man or woman is under fifty-five years old. I refused to become a statistic. My stories and my daughter would keep me young and full of life, I decided.

I looked at the clock once more, then picked up the tray with the tea and slowly started walking down the long hallway toward Marlena's room. The cold always kept me in bed a couple of minutes later than usual and maybe it was starting to do the same to her. I understood.

"Wake up, coconut. Time for tea with your mama," I said as I tapped the door of her bedroom open with my foot and walked in carrying the tray. "Did I ever tell you about the time my crab crossed the line before some boy's crab?"

"Yes, Mama, and it was the first time his crab ever lost to any other crab," said her lazy voice from beneath a lump of blankets. Her eyes peered out from a hole as she watched me turn for her desk. "Look out for my . . ."

Her warning came too late. I tripped over the radio that she kept on her floor so she could listen in bed at night and my feet came out from under me, sending the tray with my mother's china flying through the air. When it crashed down onto the hardwood floor, it looked like hundreds of shattered seashell pieces, not a single one big or whole enough to keep.

As I lay in the puddles of hot water, with sharp fragments of china cutting into my knees, I fought back tears, for more than china was lost—moments upon moments with Mama and Grandmalia and their fingers holding this very china and their lips sipping from it, then telling me a story or a tidbit or a grumble. It didn't matter what. We always sat around talking about interesting stuff as we drank tea together. Nothing could replace the broken china.

"How many times have I told you, Marlena," I scolded, "not to leave that radio in the middle of the floor. Were you up all night listening to it again?"

"No," she said jumping up from the bed and taking hold of my arm. "I was listening to dramas and commercials for a little while and you know how hard it is to hear from the speakers. I had to move it closer to my bed." She pulled me up to my knees. "Are you cut?" she asked. "I think you are, right there, on your knee just a little."

"I'm fine," I insisted. "But no more radio at night, you hear?"

"Yes. I'm sorry," she said, helping me stand up. "Would you like me to gather up and save the broken china pieces? We can make it all into a beautiful mirror."

"I like that idea," I said and felt a smile set across my face. "Will you do that for me?"

"Yes."

I was devastated over the broken china, but I had to be careful not to blame or make Marlena feel at fault. I didn't want her feeling responsible for my unhappiness. That wasn't her problem. It was mine. I'll never forget my feelings of failure when my reading and stories no longer kept my own mother happy.

"Mother," Marlena said to me as I sat on her bed and held a cloth to my knee. "Are you sad because the china belonged to your mama?"

"Yes," I said. "And to her mama, your great grandmother Dahlia. And I planned on giving it to you."

"I wouldn't want it," she said sharply. "I would never want to drink tea from it without you."

She got me to thinking. After I died, my spirit wouldn't be floating in a cup of tea. So maybe the tea set wasn't the one special item that I wanted to pass on to my daughter after all. Of course there was the money. She and her brothers would get plenty of that. The boys were already making their own money, but they were going to get mine as well because I had a lot to give.

My writing had carried us through and brought in more money than I ever imagined it could. Thanks to my articles and later my columns being published in major magazines here and in Paris, Italy, and England, I made more steady and consistent money throughout the years than Leo ever lost in gambling. My children had everything they ever asked for. I sent them all to the best schools and paid for tutors to teach them whatever it was they weren't learning at those schools. They played piano and golf and tennis and attended every suitable social event.

None of it had been easy. After letting all our staff but Nora go, I worked my tail off writing by day and tending to a family and household chores by night. It was then that I missed my mother the most and the days when we did the household chores side-by-side. I realize she worked hard back then not because she didn't believe in having fun. She worked that hard because she had to. A mother does much that goes unnoticed until she is gone, and then the cobwebs form and the dirt piles up and the house falls down. It did that when she was in her saddened mode, and it did it again when I'd get into mine, but then I'd snap out of it and clean things up. There were times when money was so scarce I could hardly afford eggs, so one by one I sold the garments Leo had bought me. I was savvy in doing so, for just as with real estate, a woman needs to know when to sell. I sold in time, just before the fashions changed.

Those were the years when my children were young and I had no time to primp or powder my nose or care the least bit what I looked like, the times when there wasn't enough sunlight in the day to get done all that I had to do, the days when I'd walk into the kitchen and forget why I had gone there in the first place, and the days when each of my four children had on average six requests per hour, so I ran around in circles like a turkey with its head cut off responding to and handling twenty-four requests per hour, making it an awfully long day, to the point of begging and pleading with the sun to go down soon, just so the kids would go to bed and all would be quiet and I could hear my own thoughts. Those were the sleep-deprived days that put a few wrinkles around my eyes and the days that brought me as much joy as one gets from spending a playful afternoon at the beach and swimming and leaping over waves and floating waist-high in that portion of the sea that is crowded with people and activity and lovely noise. If anyone asked, I'd have to say those were the days—my favorite portion of the sea!

"So, Mother," Marlena said, putting her arm around me. "Did you win anything when your crab crossed the line first? Did you place a bet?"

I laughed. "Of course not," I said, "Placing bets of any kind is wrong. Don't you ever think about placing any bets with anyone, you hear?"

I tried in my mind remembering why I kissed Jaden that night when it was my crab that crossed the line first, or at least I think it was. Regardless of whose crab won or lost that night, I fell in love with him the moment I saw him helping that wounded pelican. And by the end of that night at the shack, I could hardly keep myself from kissing him, so when his crab lost, which I think it may have, I gave him a kiss anyway.

"What happened next? What happened after your crab won?"

"Nothing. End of story," I said with a smile and stood up. "Now get ready for school. We'll have tea together when you get home. I still have a couple of cups left."

When the kids were gone and the house belonged to me, I sipped my coffee in the office that once belonged to Leo but over the years became mine. My nationally syndicated column that dealt with whatever it was women were talking about over tea or coffee was due by the end of the day, but I wasn't flustered. I knew exactly what I wanted to write about.

Today it would be about mothers passing things on to their daughters. Recipes, rituals, lullabies, stories, a crooked nose, voluptuous hips or no hips, ladylike manners or no manners, a dainty way of walking or a sporty way of walking, a disgust or a respect for men, a critical way of viewing others and the world or a loving way, a china set that breaks— But what can they pass down that might truly say who they were or where they had been or how they had felt or what all they loved or experienced during their escapade called life?

And do their daughters really care? I proudly preserved for years, then handed my daughter my own copy of *Flower Fables* by Louisa May Alcott, assuming she'd delight in it as I once did, reading it over and over a hundred times. But instead she let me know how much she prefers a good mystery, like one of the "Hardy Boys" books. A book about talking flowers with personalities didn't enthrall her as it once did me.

It had me thinking that maybe there are other things I should hand down to her. I thought about my mama teaching me the word of God. I still remember today the scripture verses she had me memorize, and I'm glad I can reach into my memory and grab onto those when I need something to cling to. And Dahlia instilled in me the notion of giving thanks to the Lord even in times of despair. I've handed those things on to my own children, and I pray for them daily, but I know there's only so much you can actually hand your children. For instance, I can't hand them salvation itself. It's up to them individually to accept the Lord, as it was with me to do that and God knows, at times it looked as if I was throwing that gift out the door. But each generation is responsible for its own salvation, and that is not to say that the generation before doesn't have to do anything with regard to it. I do think a mother must equip and instruct and teach them everything leading up to it, then pray like crazy that her children will accept it. Praying for the souls of her children may be the most powerful gift a mother can give.

I stopped typing and sipped coffee, knowing full well that my mother's prayers followed me through life like butterflies, and, still, I felt them landing on my shoulder, making me tingle from time to time. I am eternally indebted to my mother for her gift of prayer.

I started to type. I also believe declaring blessings upon children is a good thing to give them. I've told each of my children I believe in them and know they will accomplish great things in life. I am confident they will then tell their own children the same one day. This sort of gift definitely makes its way through the generations.

I continued my typing. But there is an age a woman reaches in which she starts to wonder about her own mother in terms of who she was as a person, heart, soul, and mind. And she longs for something that might help put an intimate character description on her mother and what she loved and felt passionate about in life.

I stopped typing, this time pushing my chair away from the desk a moment, recalling the day we stepped foot on Sanibel for the first time. "It's paradise," my mother had said. And in her eyes, I did, indeed, see a sparkling I had never seen in her before. I saw her passion for the first time that day.

I quickly rolled my chair back up to my desk and started to type again. So why can't a mother hand down a special place to her children? I looked up from the typewriter and thought about what it might mean to show my own children the place their great-grandmother Dahlia loved and their grandmother described as "heavenly" and where their own mother first fell in love. I continued typing fast and furiously. Yes, a mother can most certainly pass on a place to her children. And just as a tea set can break, there are the geologists out there warning that sea islands shouldn't be considered permanent and immutable objects, but natural phenomena such as storms and tides and currents and evolution are too much for me to worry about. Those are the negatives that go along with heavens on earth, I suppose. I stopped typing, pulling the paper out, for I had overdone it a bit. I could redo that page.

Hmmm—maybe this particular column should finish in an open-ended manner in the form of a question, and maybe I should invite my readers to submit what they believe a mother can pass on to her children, grandchildren, great grandchildren. For each mother has her own wonderful ideas of things she wants to pass on.

I finished typing the rest of the column, ending it with the following question:

> *What sort of meaningful, eternal gift can a mother pass on to her children, grandchildren, great grandchildren and so on?*

I stood up, personally giving further thought to it. If I died today and I never took my children to see the place where I once lived and loved and left my heart, then they would never have truly known their mother and that wouldn't be fair for them or me. I think there comes a time when a grown child should really know who their parent is.

"Florida," I announced when Nora came into my office with fresh coffee. "I'm taking the children to see a place called Sanibel Island."

"But you just got back from San Francisco a few weeks ago."

"That's okay. It's been a prosperous and roaring year for us. We can afford another trip. And the boys are getting so independent that soon they'll be taking trips with girlfriends or wives of their own. I've got to take them now before it's too late."

"Why Florida? I thought you planned on taking them to Paris again," said Nora.

"They've been to Paris a half dozen times. But they've never been to Florida, and I've talked about it so many times through the years. I don't know why I've never taken them. It's crazy. I'd like to leave right away. I'll call the boys so they can make arrangements and take vacation time at work."

"I'll start your packing," said Nora.

I walked over to the globe in the corner of the room and gave it a hearty spin. Florida had been hit with heavy hurricanes in recent years and its state economy was in a recession, but our taking a quick trip there now was like tossing pennies into a fountain. We could easily afford it. And my showing the island to my children was priceless. I could think of nothing better to pass on to them then a place they could go to if they ever needed to see beauty in the world. It was the perfect thing to pass on and one that couldn't be broken, except by way of a hurricane, I guess. But I can't worry about the weather.

And I can't worry about my age, although it's hard not to when the average life expectancy is under fifty-five years old. Maybe this is the reason I'm suddenly obsessed with passing something on to them. I had always wanted to pass on a novel to them, but that hasn't happened and might never at this pace. Of course there's always my journal, in which I sporadically wrote throughout the years, but who knows if they'd ever be interested in that. Besides, I've surrendered that to the Lord.

"Heavenly Father," I prayed recently after writing in it. "I hope one day this journal falls into the hands of a young girl who may relate to it. Who might that girl be? I haven't a clue. It might not even be my own daughter. I know my columns reach thousands of readers, but my columns don't mean nearly as much to me as my personal journal has. I once promised my Grandmalia that I'd turn her into a character in a novel and grant her eternal life on earth. I know she's in a better eternity and doesn't need me granting her anything. And so I pray that one day this journal lands in the hands of a girl somewhere out there who needs, if nothing else, a friend or a mother or a family of sorts. Thank you, Lord. I trust that you'll answer my prayers as you see fit. Amen."

I walked over to the window and stared out. I hoped this trip to Florida might touch my children. I'd show them where their grandmother once skinny-dipped. They'll get a kick out of that. And while there I'll get to retrace the footprints of a young girl madly in love for the first time, and I'll watch as she went from believing that anything is possible to believing everything is impossible back to everything is possible with God. A girl like that leaves deep tracks, and I'm sure they're still embedded. But I'll try not to judge too harshly the direction those tracks went or why they slowed. A woman must accept the choices she's made and the ones she's left behind. And focus on where her tracks might go next.

Lydia

I closed the journal, wanting more than anything to throw my arms around Ava and tell her what her journal has meant to me throughout the years and, most importantly, how it was about to change the course of my life. I wanted to thank her, for the journal was more valuable than any million-dollar inheritance and it had been passed on to the right person, one who viewed it as priceless.

She got me to thinking about my own future, something I hardly had time to think about. I didn't want to one day look back and regret the man I left behind, so I walked over to the phone and booked roundtrip airline tickets for Jack and me to fly to Florida. The time was now. If I waited any longer, it would be too late. It might already be too late. Still, I had to tell Josh he had a son, and then I'd have to face the consequences and accept whether he loved or hated me for the secret I had kept from him.

I still felt like a criminal, for I was the one who went after men for withholding rights such as equal jobs and pay from women, yet I had withheld a father's right to know he has a son. Josh had no idea there was a little boy in the world with features of his own.

There were already a lifetime of should-haves racing through my mind, and I feared there might be more soon. I might arrive only to find him in love or married to someone else—those were his rights and the consequences I would have to face. Besides, I wasn't going in hopes of selfishly starting a relationship. I was going so that my son might have a chance at knowing his father and because his father had a right to know about him.

That night I climbed into bed with Jack and opened a wildlife book and started reading it to him.

"Parent pelicans must teach fledglings the necessary skill for dive-bombing fish," I explained as we looked at the picture.

"Why?" asked Jack.

I was glad for Jack's curiosity toward life, and I knew he got it from me, so I did my best to answer every one of his 'why' questions. "So the children can learn basic survival, Jack," I said, and then continued reading. "And the parents take this very seriously and have been known to interrupt a youngster's diving practice in mid-flight if the form is badly off."

"Why?"

"Because it's a parent's job to correct when they see their children going wrong, Jack."

"Why?"

"Well, the watery impact could possibly damage or break a wing while a young bird is learning."

"Do pelicans live in the city?" Jack asked.

"No, they don't," I said. "But they do live on Sanibel Island."

"But I saw them. I saw pelicans."

"No, honey. Those were pigeons."

"Why?"

"That's a good question, Jack, but I'm not sure why they were pigeons," I said, starting to tire. "They just were. God made them that way."

"Where is Sand-a-ball Island?" he asked.

I closed the book and tossed it onto the floor and laid my head next to Jack's on his pillow. "How about I show you in a few weeks? Would you like that? In just a few weeks I'll show you where Sanibel is."

"Why?"

"That's another good question, Jack. Let me think about that one and I'll get back to you on it."

"Why?"

"Because sometimes a mommy doesn't know everything, Jack."

XLIV

LYDIA

IF JACK ASKED THE same questions three weeks later as our plane headed south for Florida, I would have given him the same answer—let me think about it. But I knew why I was going. What I didn't know was whether Josh would want anything to do with us.

Jack was coloring with crayons and nibbling on an endless supply of snacks I had packed him for the flight when I pulled out Ava's latest journal entry. Marlena had sent it to me just after I had called to tell her we were coming. She insisted we stay with her, and I was glad to have a comfortable place to run to should the outcome of my trip not turn out as I prayed it might.

I smiled at Jack as he yawned and then laid his head on my shoulder. He had woken up way before his normal time to catch our flight, and it was a matter of seconds before he'd fall fast asleep. I opened the journal and began to read:

Ava

A strong woman knows what to do. She must pick up the paddles and with all her courage row way out there, to her very own portion of the sea. She may have to row around in circles a bit, or dive down some, but soon she will spot them either bobbing in the water or resting on the floor of the sea, the treasures she thought she had lost for good.

Whether a heart full of love, or a soul that once prayed or a mind that loved learning, or the body that felt better, they are still her treasures and are waiting to be reclaimed.

We arrived in Fort Myers by way of train. But it wasn't until the captain on the ferry came around collecting fares from the passengers that I knew for real we were on our way to Sanibel Island. And when that ferry named "Best" left the mainland at Punta Rassa, steaming its way toward the island, I felt like one of those birds returning after time away. I thanked God for my kids, for my life, and for returning me here, to the island I once swore was the Promised Land.

Our Christmas in New York was lavish, and we all received all the items on our lists. But I didn't tell the kids that the pennies that went to pay for this trip were buying something money couldn't afford—my sanity. This trip was another of my glistening steps.

With my arms tightly around my oldest and youngest sons, I looked out at the aqua water surrounding us and knew I should have taken this trip sooner. Since the early twenties everyone I knew had been vacationing in Florida, and even Thomas Edison and Henry Ford were spending time in Fort Myers.

"Boys," I said, fighting back the tears in my eyes. "I agree with what my mother, your grandmother, once said. Sanibel is probably the closest glimpse of what heaven might look like if there was such a place on earth."

My youngest laughed. "Maybe to you, Mom. But to me, heaven is a room filled with money."

I gave him a scolding look and shook my head in disappointment. "Oh, come on, I didn't raise you, or any of you for that matter, to worship money."

"I'm just kidding," Jonathon said, planting a kiss on my cheek. He was doing well as a young stockbroker. All three of the boys inherited Leo's ambition and watched their mother work like a fool for everything she had. Each of them in their young careers was now making more money than their father ever imagined. They had also remained living at home and close to me all this time, and I knew and wanted for that to reach its end. No, I didn't want it to, but I knew it had to. They were more than ready. They were men. It wasn't that I kept them close selfishly. It was that we were living comfortably on a large estate, and they were fully meshed in their careers. Careers came before women, or at least, lasted longer, I might say. And they had never been in any hurry to marry. I knew that was all naturally changing, and it would be good and healthy for them to fly the nest completely.

"I'd love to sell it all—the estate, the cars, my clothes, furniture—and move out here one day. Maybe I will," I said, looking over the railing at the water below. "I think I could manage fine without all that stuff. It's all just clutter if you think good and hard about it. Yes," I continued. "I think I might do that. Your sister and I will move here once you three get places of your own. Of course we'd visit several times a year. Maybe every other month."

"You're not serious, Mother," said Charles, twenty-four. "No one in their right mind would live in Florida year-round. It's a state without seasons. Don't you like your seasons, Mother?"

"There are seasons. They're just more subtle," I said. "Don't judge it yet."

"Then, if you like it that much," he said. "I'll find out how much it costs to purchase the island for you." Charles worked as a commercial developer and knew a valuable piece of land when he saw one.

"I'd say you could put ten to twenty percent in cash to buy stock in it and get the rest on cheap credit," added Jonathon. "It's that simple."

"Not Sanibel stock, idiot." Charles fake-punched his younger brother. "Land. I might be able to buy the island and develop it for Mom. Land in Florida has been selling and reselling with profits reaching inflated levels."

"Not a bad point, Charley," said Jonathon.

"Boys," I said. "I don't want any of you buying me anything, you hear?"

And I meant it. The purchase had been my idea first, and it was something I wanted them to one day inherit from me, not give to me. It was the perfect thing to pass on. People have been exchanging land and sea as gifts for centuries. Spain once gave Florida to England, and in exchange England gave Havana, Cuba, to Spain. This sort of gift-exchanging continued throughout history, so there is no reason why I couldn't buy a little piece of Florida, with a portion of the sea, for my children to inherit one day.

"Mom, if you really want to buy in Florida, now might not be a bad time to do so and sit on it," Jonathon said, disrupting my thoughts.

"That's right," added Charley. "The bubble burst with the hurricanes and tourism from what I heard has been virtually non-existent up until now, thanks to this auto ferry."

While waiting for the ferry, we had talked with several people and learned that the island had been hit with severe storms in recent years. A 1926 hurricane with a fourteen-foot storm surge covered all the low-lying areas of both Sanibel and Captiva islands, and the saltwater ruined the fertile soil, burying any hopes of further large-scale farming. Who knows whether it was still the sort of place I'd want to spend time at. And who knows what I'd find once I went searching for Jaden.

Maybe he wasn't there any more. According to Dahlia, his family had started back up again growing eggplants and peppers after the freeze, but who knows whether the hurricanes chased them away for good. Island agriculture hadn't recovered, and the man I was talking to said it might never. I tried not to think about Jaden. If he were married and still living there, then maybe this would be just a one-time trip for me. But if he were there and he wasn't married and he was the same person I once loved, then who knows? Anything is possible with God, I suppose. I only knew I no longer wanted to talk about money and investments with my sons.

"We'll talk about it later," I said. The only green I wanted to be thinking about was the island looming before us. "I'd like for us all to relax. And speaking of that, where's Henry and your little sister? I haven't seen them since the ferry left the dock."

My middle son, Henry, was as ambitious as his brothers, but in a different way. He had also worked as a stockbroker, but recently put his mini-fortune into stocks and securities. His brothers lately call him "dewdrop-per" for spending his days sleeping and not having a job. He enjoys telling people he doesn't have to work because his money is working for him. In a sense, he's right. When General Motors issued stock, I also pulled my own savings from the bank and put it all into stock. Everyone was doing it. But then I remembered what my mother once told me, that just because all the other kids are jumping off a cliff, it doesn't mean you should too. So just before this trip, I pulled my savings out of the stock market. That way, if I chose to purchase land on Sanibel, I had money to play with.

"I'll go find them, Mother," said Charles.

"I'll go with him," said Jonathon.

"Thanks," I said, watching the way the women were looking at my grown boys as they disappeared to the other side of the ferry. They kept in good shape, dressed fashionably, and spoke properly to women. And they were handsome—each one of them. I was thrilled when Henry inherited his great-grandfather Milton's hazel eyes. I hadn't ever seen those eyes, but Grandmalia described them in her stories, saying they were a spar-kling brown. When Henry was little I told him where he got his eyes and, horrified, he asked, "Is Milton going to want them back?"

Henry had eyes for one thing, and it wasn't writing poetry like his great-granddaddy, but rather music. He loved playing the trumpet. He also loved drinking while doing so, and I could always tell by the way those eyes flickered with green that he had been drinking. I hoped no one else noticed. I didn't want my son getting into any trouble, but those eyes of his worried me.

"Mom, we found her," Jonathon called out to me.

"Was she with Henry?"

"Sort of. I think you should come see for yourself."

As I made my way to the other side of the ferry, I could hear music above the sound of the engine, and I heard people laughing and clapping, and when I saw they were doing so for Marlena, I stopped in my tracks. There she was, fourteen years old, dancing the Charleston, with her hair bobbing about her shoulders, wearing a skirt her brothers thought was too short but she thought was not short enough. And Henry was playing his trumpet passionately with his eyes closed.

"She looks like a miniature version of you," Charles said as I joined him and Marlena's crowd of admirers. "Only you never laugh or dance anymore, Mother."

"I'm too old for any of that," I said. But I knew that wasn't true. If I was young enough to have a fourteen year-old daughter, I also had to be young enough to still live life to the fullest and have fun.

My eyes followed my daughter dancing the Charleston. How did she do that after only taking ballet? I did take her to see *The Jazz Singer* and she insisted on seeing it fourteen times more after that. I glanced away from her and out over the railing of the ferry, where I thought I spotted a shiny object bobbing up and down in the water. If only I were thirty years younger, I would dive overboard and swim over to it to be sure it was really mine. And then I'd grab onto my heart and swim with it to shore. There I'd find the first man it ever belonged to.

My eyes returned to Marlena. She was every bit beautiful, from her wide, oval blue eyes to the charismatic and charming nose she inherited from her great-grandmother, Dahlia. I guess Grandmalia had been right about that nose and how it skips around the family, showing up on the fourth babies. It pained me horribly when Marlena grumbled about her nose because to me it represented where she came from and the ancestors she was connected to. She was so beautiful that heads turned and watched her, and that nose of hers only added charisma to her face—and it softened her piercing eyes.

Maybe I'm not that old, I thought as I watched her dance. If Jaden is still around, he'd be two years older than me. And I had aged gracefully over the years, with just four wrinkles big enough to count and they were worth it, for my children gave them to me as gifts. Jaden would have a few lines, but knowing him, or the boy he once was, he'd try telling me that wrinkles on a woman's face are the tracks of where she has been and that they're beautiful in a natural sort of way and purposeful too, reminders of the life she has lived. He had been the sort of person to make anyone feel better, even a wounded pelican. He had to be married. I'd find out soon enough.

"I can hardly look at her without smiling," Jonathon said as he marveled at his baby sister. "Look at her. She's a natural entertainer."

Just then Marlena stopped the Charleston, and a beautiful woman in her thirties, smoking a cigarette in a long, decorative holder, reached out from the crowd and pulled her close.

When Henry, who was putting his trumpet away right beside his little sister, didn't notice, I feared he had been sipping from his secret stash of liquor again. I started for where the stranger was whispering in my daughter's ear, but Charles held me back. "She's fine, Mother. She's a small bird with big wings. We're watching her closely," he said.

Then the woman kissed Marlena on the forehead and continued talking to her.

"Marlena," I called out.

She looked around, disoriented, and when she spotted me in the crowd, she said, "Just a minute, Mama. This lady is telling me something important."

"Go get her, Charles," I said. "What's that woman saying to her?"

Charles walked over, and Jonathon followed, but Marlena turned her back to them as if she didn't want them butting in. I laughed when Charles swept her petite body up in his arms and carried her over to me. She was mad, but her dramatic side continued to flare as she swung her head back while in the arms of her brother and blew a kiss to the woman who was still smiling.

The woman held her finger up to her lips as if to say, "Shhh, don't tell," then she waved to my daughter.

When the ferry touched the dock and people started rushing about with anticipation, I nearly did the Charleston myself. Charles put Marlena down, and she and I held playful hands as we joined a line of people exiting the ferry. We bumped into the woman who had been whispering into Marlena's ear and she winked at my daughter.

"What was that woman whispering to you about?" I asked.

"It's a secret," she answered coyly.

I shook my head and looked her straight in the eyes. "I'm your mother," I said. "And that woman was a stranger. You will tell me what she said."

"I can't tell you."

"Why not?" I asked.

"It's none of your beeswax," she said, sounding way too old for her age and making me feel too old to deal with her.

"Marlena," I scolded. "A young lady respects her mother."

She rolled her eyes and said, "If I tell you, it will ruin my destiny. If I tell you, I won't be famous."

"What on God's Earth are you talking about?" I asked.

"I don't know."

"Fine," I snapped. "If you don't tell me everything right this moment, you won't get to search for shells or walk the beach or do anything with us as a family, do you hear?"

By this time we were stepping foot off the ferry, and I was questioning God for giving me a daughter so late in life. I did that from time to time, whenever she acted up. Most of the time, though, she didn't act like this and I thanked God for giving me a daughter so late in life.

When I noticed her eyes moving about in a creative way, as if she were thinking about the seashell mirror she wanted to make, I knew she was about to give in and tell me what the woman had said to her.

"The lady told me that one day I would be famous."

"Famous?" asked Jonathon, walking close behind us and listening unbeknownst to us. "For what?"

Marlena stopped at the end of the dock, just before stepping foot onto the east end of Ferry Road. "The lady on the ferry liked the way I danced. And when I finished, she said that I would be famous, more than Lucky Lindy himself, and she said that I would be rich, not from the stock market, but from my fame. Do you think I could be richer than all three of my brothers?" She looked at me for the answer. "I don't doubt, Marlena, that you're just as adventurous and invincible as Lindbergh," said Charles. "But tell us, what would you be famous for?"

"She said I would be a famous actress in Hollywood."

We all raised an eyebrow. "It's a promising industry," said Henry. "Hollywood's been mounting multimillion-dollar productions to meet insatiable demand for movies."

"Yep, and I'm going there," said Marlena. "As soon as I turn eighteen."

"You along with a bunch of lonely, bored, discontented housewives in America. I hear so many have been up and leaving their lives that there's charity funds set up to support these women once they get there," said Jonathon.

"You hear that, Marlena?" said Charles. "Hollywood is just a far-off patch of California. Go for the sure thing when you get big. Go for where the money is. Marry a rich man like Jonathon or me. Don't marry a Henry who drinks away all his money."

"Bushwa," Henry said.

"Watch your language," I scolded.

"Sorry, Mom," Henry said, patting me on the back, and then he turned to his brothers and said in a lowered voice, "Cut the crap. You're both bootleggers and you know it. And regarding Hollywood, Marlena, it's not all bad. I enjoy what I've seen so far."

"Marlena," I said, squeezing her hand. "First and foremost, don't listen to your brothers. Don't marry a man for his money. Marry the man you love. And secondly, dear, Hollywood is too far away. I'd miss you horribly. The only entertaining you need to do is for your family. You stick by me and keep me smiling, you hear?"

"Okay," she answered, her eyes moving on to something else. "Can we go into that store over there and see if they've got any chocolate?" She was used to getting what she wanted so, before I could answer, she took off running ahead toward Bailey's General Store.

"They didn't have stores like this back when I lived here," I noted. "And we certainly didn't have anything like that," I added as we stopped to check out the 1926 Model-T Ford delivery truck parked in front.

I don't think any of my children could survive an hour without spending money, so inside the store they bought English Herb Soap, Mrs. Stevens' Candies, and Hershey's Chocolate before I pulled each one of them out the door.

I felt eager, but I couldn't tell the kids why. I couldn't tell them about the boy I once loved and the man I wanted to find. They wouldn't understand. Kids want their mommy loving no one but their daddy, I think, even years after their daddy has passed.

Lydia

That was all that Marlena sent me, and it was fine. Our plane was about to land, and now I knew who the stranger was that long ago had planted powerful seeds in the ears of a little girl.

I closed the journal and closed my eyes, wondering whether Ava met up with Jaden and whether he still loved her and whether the two of them spent the rest of their lives happily ever after together on the island. I would soon find out.

XLV

JACK AND I WERE happy to see Marlena. She looked more beautiful at fifty-three than ever, and she claimed it was because she was doing what she wanted to be doing. After directing her last film, she returned home and started working diligently on ideas for writing a screenplay.

"Lydia, if you stay here to live, you can write the novel, and I'll write the screenplay."

"I don't know if I can write a novel."

"Oh, come on!" she said. "Am I going to have to go out and have you build another snowwoman in the sand?" We both laughed. "Of course you can, and, besides, it would be easy. We can base it on my mother's journals.

She would have loved the idea. I just know it."

"Let's just see how my encounter with Josh goes tomorrow," I said. "One thing at a time."

"Grandmarlena," Jack called as he came running into the room. "Can I have some ice cream now?"

"Grandmarlena?" I asked, looking over at Marlena, and then I laughed for a good five minutes.

But that night in bed, I wasn't laughing at all, and I could hardly sleep. Come morning I'd be facing Josh, and thoughts of it kept me awake as if I had downed gallons of caffeine. Maybe it was all a big mistake, one I would regret.

Jack was sound asleep in the bed beside me as I sat up and looked around the yellow room where we were sleeping. Then I walked over to the desk and opened the left drawer and pulled out matches I had seen in there before. I lit a candle and opened Ava's journal. I didn't think Marlena would mind my reading forward. I needed to know whether or not Ava met up with Jaden and how it all went.

Ava

We stayed at an inn located on the Gulf of Mexico where each night we fell asleep to the whisper of the sea, and in the early mornings we sat on the verandah drinking java and looking out at the sea we had heard the night before. I wanted our time on the island to go by slowly as a manatee roaming up the Florida peninsula, but of course it did the opposite. It sped by like a dolphin riding the bow waves of a ship.

The boys woke late and spent their time fishing in the bay or golfing at a nine-hole miniature-style course while Marlena, and I rode bicycles, attended events at the Community House, walked the beach, and went for tea over at Miss Charlotta's Tea Room near the ferry landing. The menu was simple, and the room was filled with residents and visitors alike, and it was a cozy place for the two of us to talk.

"When you were my age," Marlena said as she poured a bee's hive worth of honey into her tea, "what did you want to be when you grew up?"

I waited for the server to pour hot water into my cup. "A fiction writer," I said once the waitress left for another table. "Like Louisa May Alcott. Remember I gave you that book of hers? She was my favorite author when I was around your age. My mother liked her too."

"Is that why you get sad?"

"What do you mean?" I asked, aware that she saw my spells as a mystery she wanted to solve.

"That you've never become a fiction writer like her. Is that why you get sad?"

"Oh," I said, sipping my tea, unaware until now that she had noticed my extended naps and quieter periods in recent months. I took two more sips, and then searched her eyes, hoping she had moved on.

"I don't like when you get sad, Mama."

I still did not know what to say. I didn't know myself why I got sad at times, just that I remember my own mother also getting sad, and as I looked my daughter in the eyes, I could only hope her eyes would never grow sad like ours.

"Am I really sad all that often?"

"Sometimes," she said. "Especially in the winter. I hate when you're sad."

I blew on my tea, then took a long, slow sip, put my cup down on its dainty matching plate, then picked it up again and took another sip. "It has nothing to do with me not becoming a fiction writer." I laughed at her simple innocence. "Writing my columns and magazine articles has been just as rewarding to me," I said. "And so has keeping a journal. I've kept one since I first learned to write, you know. It's long enough to be a novel by now. Three, probably."

"Yeah, but no one ever reads journals. They just sit around in some hiding spot, like under your bed, and even then, when someone finds one, there's usually a lock on it."

I looked at her suspiciously. "You haven't, have you?"

"What?"

"You know, been trying to read my journals, young lady."

"No, Mama," she insisted. "I would never do such a thing. You tell me all your good stories anyway."

Thank Heavens, I thought, for I wouldn't want my daughter knowing how I once snuck out and how I married as an escape and as the only option I thought I had but then grew to love her father later and how he had a secret gambling problem and how even on this very vacation I had, every chance I got, been secretly sitting out on that verandah or lying on the hammock in the grass until wee hours talking and reuniting with someone from my past. How could she possibly understand that my love for Jaden felt as old and precious as the Caloosahatchee River? These were things my children didn't know about me, things they wouldn't understand. But some day Marlena might, and, then, if she ever went through anything remotely similar, I'd want her to know that she was not alone in the world, that there was someone who understood.

"Do me a favor," I said after giving it thought. "One day, a long, long time from today, if you and I are ever far away from each other, break open my journals and read them, okay?" She stared at me as if I were a ghost. "I mean it," I continued. "But not until you're at least twenty-one, promise me?"

She nodded. "Do you want me to lock them up after I read them?"

"No," I said. "Share them with someone, maybe a nice girl like yourself who you think might appreciate them as you did, but only after I'm gone someday, okay?"

"I don't like to think about you being gone," she said.

I rolled my eyes. "I'm talking about when I'm one hundred and fifty, and, believe me, by then, you'll want me gone. Don't worry. I won't go before that." We laughed and talked more that day and the next few about her dreams of becoming a Hollywood movie star and inviting me to the premiers and making more money than all her brothers combined.

There were things my children didn't know about me, and as we went to watch the sunset one night at an area of beach located between the two islands, I considered telling them what I had been up to.

It all began our second afternoon on the island with a little white lie. I told them I had enough of the sun for one day and that I was going to run to the store for something, and insisted they all stay on the beach and have fun without worrying about me. And then I did my probing and found him. We didn't talk long, but I invited him over to the inn that night, way past any hours that might interfere with my family, and he accepted. We spent that night sitting on the verandah overlooking the water, reminiscing and sharing stories and gaps in our lives until sunrise.

But now wasn't the time to tell my children about it. As the sky turned a deep pink, the color of a more mature Roseate Spoonbill, I knew I first had a decision to make before telling them anything. I glanced down the beach at my grown sons, who had been getting antsy to return to their lives back home. They were wrestling in the sand like little boys.

Good, I thought, just as I did when they were babies. Tire them out so they'll fall fast asleep early tonight and I'll have some time to myself. And I knew exactly what I'd be doing with my time. Jaden would show, and we'd pick up where we left off in conversation from the night before and from the five nights before that, and we'd talk and laugh until the morning sun came peeking through, urging us to say good-bye. It was yesterday's sun that meant something special. Our night of getting to know one another all over again had been so pleasant that we weren't expecting the sun so soon, and when we saw it, we quickly kissed, our first kiss in how many years?

I couldn't possibly tell my kids. I was still surprised myself by the way things progressed so quickly in just one week of meeting up and spending the entire night talking to the sound of the waves gently reaching the shore before us. But I shouldn't be surprised. Like my mother once said, a boy who helps hurting animals turns into a kind and gentle man. A boy who prays as a child grows into a God-fearing and respectable adult. And a boy with wide-set, clear eyes and a square jaw only gets better with age. I was surprised that a boy who wanted to marry me some thirty years before still wanted to today. It made me tingle back then and tremble now. And I was glad when Marlena put her little arm around me. Without her knowing, it comforted me. As the sun sank into the horizon I knew I had a decision to make and that I'd have to make it soon.

"Don't you love it here?" I asked her. "Couldn't you stay here forever?"

"Yes, but not with them," she said, pointing to her brothers who were still wrestling in the sand. "I don't think men and women should be on the same island. They belong on an island all their own," she said. "Especially when they drink giggle water. They're drinking it now, aren't they?"

"I don't know," I said. "What's giggle water?"

Marlena looked around the beach, and then whispered in my ear. "Booze."

"Of course not," I insisted. But I knew they were. I knew it this morning when Jaden and I were sitting on the verandah and Henry came sauntering across the lawn, carrying a bucket and not noticing us, that he had been toting more than bait in there. And later that morning, I overheard his brothers ask him where he got the "bait" and he told them it came from deep within the mangroves and that he paid an arm and a leg for it. Then he snapped his fingers together, which I've come to learn over the years means, "you two owe me big time for this one."

Jaden had assured me that the Coast Guard cutter patrols all night in search of rumrunners but seldom do they catch any. I didn't want them catching my sons, just as I didn't want my sons catching me. We all had our secrets, I suppose. But soon I might have to tell them, for we were set to be leaving the island in the morning, and tonight would be my last night of reuniting with Jaden. The decision as to what to do next was up to me, just as it had been many years ago. Together we cried in each other's arms with regret over the decision I made back then. He had the hardest time understanding why I took off and married someone without first returning to Florida to hunt him down. I tried telling him that hunting a man down isn't something a proper lady does.

"Don't give me that crap," he had said to me our first night together, when we were revisiting the details of that time. "You've never had a lady-like bone in your body."

At first I was offended, but then I laughed, and so did he. But now I wondered whether marrying a man and moving my daughter to a new place is something a proper mother does, especially one of my age.

"Couldn't you see a sunset like this every night?" I asked Marlena.

"Yes. I like it better than any shows you've ever taken me to back in New York."

It was the answer I wanted to hear. I had just started her with drama and voice coaches back home because she loved theater, but now she was showing signs of loving something else. Maybe theater was a silly little stage she was going through, one that would pass. Maybe she wouldn't hate me if I told her I was in love with a man from long ago and we were going to get married, and she and I were going to stay here forever and she would grow up right here, not in New York where she had her brand-new drama and voice coaches and Broadway and all that she loved. They loved her too. They said she was a natural, born to be on stage, destined to go far. I've tried to forget that. I don't like anyone telling my daughter what she is destined to do. Destiny is her choice.

I had choices too. I could choose matters of my heart and stay put right here, where there would be new things for Marlena to love. "Why don't you go find one special seashell to bring home with you," I said to her. "That way, even when you're away, you'll have a part of the sea with you."

She jumped up in her jersey bathing suit, one that I would have loved to wear at her age and one that would have my mother gasping, and she walked toward the shore. It's hard being a mother. One moment I feel I should announce that we are staying, that a woman loving a man is more important than ambition. The next moment I wonder whether we should return so I can teach her that nothing is more important than the dreams a girl has for her life. Then again, maybe I'm giving it too much thought and looking too deeply into it. Maybe a mother doesn't have such an impact on her daughter's life and it's no big deal what I choose to do. Maybe I ought to teach her that there comes a time in life when a mother must do something for herself because if a mother sacrifices everything, including romantic love, for her children, they might grow up thinking that adult relationships aren't important, that nothing is as important as a woman pursuing her dreams or a career.

"Lord," I prayed. "What do I teach my children? Tell me what to do, I beg for you to show me what to do!"

The boys, they'd be fine going back without us. They had their careers waiting for them. Of course we'd visit regularly. Then again, New York was far away. Jaden's boys were also grown but living just across the bay in Fort Myers, where the construction of homes was reaching nauseating proportions. Still, my boys would be able to afford whatever they wanted in the "City of Palms" if they chose to stay. It wouldn't hurt to suggest it.

But I know they wouldn't consider it, and I would miss them horribly. But I would be with Jaden. He lost his wife five years ago. He had married her two years after searching for me in Kentucky, and they enjoyed a happy and peaceful marriage. He had always wanted a daughter but never had one. He and the boys farmed the land here as long as they could but when storms and hurricanes ruined conditions for good, they switched gears and lost a ton of money but got by fishing and selling their fish. They did all they could to keep their land, the same land Jaden's father home-steaded back when we were here. And today he takes tourists out fishing and has high hopes for the future of tourism on the island. He swears that the future of Sanibel lies with its sun, sand, and shells, and no longer its soil.

I told him the story of my life, even the sad spells that overtook my mother's life and the ones that I had also been suffering through, especial-ly in the dark winter months. He told me that living in a sunny place might be good, and maybe he was right. I had already felt better being here. And, besides, there comes a time when a mother must return to her own likings and all the things she set aside when her children consumed her, the things she'd like to revisit now that they're grown. I wondered whether that was selfish, but Jaden assured me it was natural instinct to think that way, and he went on to tell me something I never knew about those mother sea turtles.

"Did you know," he asked, "that after wintering hundreds of miles from her nesting beach, a mother sea turtle finds her way back to the exact beach and spot where she laid her eggs in the previous year?"

"No. Impossible," I said.

"It's true. She finds her way back to this exact spot season after season as long as she lives. And did you know that songbirds travel to far-off plac-es seasonally, only to return to the same nest year after year?"

I laughed. "You're using every scrap of nature facts you can think of just to keep me here, aren't you?" I asked him.

"Nature is wise," he said. "We can learn a thing or two from it."

When we returned to the inn for dinner, I knew I had a decision to make, and I wanted to make it decisively, to never look back and never re-gret. I listened through the door as my sons were busy getting all dollied up to go out. I touched the door with my fingers, ready to push it open and tell them my secret. But then I got mad at what they were saying in front of their little sister. Hanging out with them always gave her an earful.

"And you saw the bubs on her. I think she'll be there tonight," Jonathon whispered and they all laughed, including Marlena.

"Boys!" I said, barging in. "You've got to stop chatting idly about females in front of your little sister."

"Sorry, Mom," they all said, still laughing.

I was mad, and it wasn't the time to tell them. Besides, I hadn't yet made up my own mind as to what to do. If I chose what my heart was telling me, the boys would tell me I was crazy and try to stop Marlena and me from staying, but we could run from them, hide in the Everglades like some of the Seminoles did when they didn't want to leave Florida during the third Seminole War. I was being illogical, I knew. I needed time to sort things out.

I was glad when the boys went out and Marlena fell asleep, and I still had an hour before Jaden would come walking up the steps to the verandah. And he would have the same look on his face as he had years ago, when he proposed to me at the lighthouse and didn't know whether I'd show up to marry him the next day or leave the island forever.

I walked over to a bookshelf that covered the entire wall and pulled the history book I had been skimming all week off the shelf.

History has a way of repeating itself. I wondered how cycles get broken.

Lydia

I wanted to wake Marlena up. I had to know. I couldn't wait until sunrise to find out whether Ava stayed on the island for the sake of her heart or returned to New York for the sake of her children. But I had to wait. There were no more pages. I sat in the armchair of the great room thinking about life and praying like I had never prayed before until the sun rose before me, brighter than ever.

"Where'd you grow up?" I blurted out as Marlena walked out of her bedroom.

"Good morning to you, too."

"Did your mother take you back to New York or did the two of you stay here?"

"Lydia," she said. "My mother arranged for me to have the best of both worlds. Birds aren't the only ones that fly back and forth, you know."

XLVI

LYDIA

AN HOUR LATER JACK and I sat down on the dock waiting for a boat to appear. I had done basic investigative work and learned from a few different sources that Josh had taken a couple fishing, dropped them off on Captiva and was now headed back alone.

The sky in some areas looked dark, and the weatherman had said it would rain, but I didn't believe him. I couldn't think about rain. Two dolphins playfully burst forth from the water, but that thrill didn't compare to the one I felt moments later when I spotted his boat coming toward us. I no longer watched the dolphins and instead studied the tall, broad-shouldered man wearing a baseball hat backward. I took Jack's hand in mine and squeezed it tightly.

"Is that the man?"

"Yes, pumpkin," I said, standing up. "That's the man I need to talk to."

Jack went back to counting the dolphins, and I returned in my mind to the fears I had last night. I didn't know whether he would want to see me, or if he'd accept what I had to say. It didn't matter. I had to tell him.

As he grew nearer, I wondered whether he was the same man; after all he had experienced the Peace Corp and then the war. Did he still play his music? Did he view the world as a good place? And I thought about how

I had prayed for him and how praying for him brought me closer to God and made me a better person and how it only made me love him more.

"Now you be a good boy," I said to Jack. "And let me do all the talking, okay? I'll get you a lollipop if you're good and quiet while I talk to the man."

Jack nodded his head and took hold of my hand, and we stood there as the boat docked, unsure whether he noticed us, and then we watched as he tied the rope around the posts.

"Thief, thief," I thought I heard him or the birds overhead cry out to me as they did the day I finally returned the journal to Marlena.

"Lydia Isleworth," he announced a second later as he retied one of the ropes. "It has been a long time. What's kept you away for so long?" He glanced over at me. "I'll bet you hardly get any vacation days with the sort of work you do. The news just doesn't end, does it? It keeps going on day after day after day." He walked away from the post and I noticed a slight limp as he walked up to us, and then kneeled down to look Jack in the eye.

"Hello there, young mate."

Jack nestled his face in my thigh, and I laughed. "He's shy at first, but once he warms up, look out!"

Josh stood up and looked at me as if deciphering how I had aged, and I assumed he was noticing the dark sleep-deprivation circles under my eyes. I had already sized him up and decided he was gorgeous. The sun had aged him handsomely, and he wore an extra fifteen pounds solidly. His face, commonly unshaven in the past, was now clean-shaven. But none of his looks mattered, I convinced myself. I came bearing news, important news. Good or bad? I didn't know. That would be for him to decipher.

"Looks like your life has really changed in the last few years," he said, patting Jack on the head, then letting his eyes wander over to my ring finger.

"No husband," I stated matter-of-factly as I waved my left hand through the air. This wasn't the time to play games. I had to present the facts one by one up front. "I'm not married. Never have been, not to a man anyway."

"Oh?" he raised an eyebrow at me.

"I mean, just to my career, that is."

"Sorry to hear that."

"No, it hasn't been bad. I get to come home to Jack. It's the best part of my day. He's incredible."

"I don't doubt that! So what brings you to Florida? Vacationing or doing a story on men returning home from the war?"

I laughed and shook my head, and Jack laughed too, just for the joy of laughing. He had no idea what we were saying.

"I came here just to get away from it all, reevaluate what's best for our son." I wanted to kick myself in the behind for having slipped and said "our," but he didn't notice at all, and I questioned who had the higher intelligence, him or the dolphin still leaping in the background.

"So, tell me, how old are you little fellow?"

Jack peeked out from my thigh and gave an impish smile. "I'm not little," he stated.

"You're not? What are you then?"

"I'm a big boy!" He pushed his face once more into my thigh and I rubbed my hands through his wavy hair.

"You certainly are a big boy!" said Josh. "I'll bet you're big enough to capture a shark."

"Tell him how old you are, Jack," I hinted. "Four," he whispered, looking up at me.

"Come on, kiddo. Tell him louder. He didn't hear you."

"Four," shouted Jack.

I studied Josh's face, waiting for something to click. The speech I had written, edited, and then rehearsed until I was blue in the face was not surfacing. It was drowning in my nerves. My mind was blank but for the simple number hints I kept tossing his way.

"That's right. Jack, you are four years old. And it has been four years since mommy has been to Sanibel."

Suddenly the world went still—the breeze, my son, and the man standing before us on the dock. It was an eerie still, like when Jack gets quiet in the backseat of the car and I fear he's choking on a lollipop.

But Jack was fine, I noticed, as he wandered off to the edge of the dock and peered down at the water below. Josh looked at me, then over at Jack as if looking at a ghost. But it wasn't a ghost, just more like a shadow, his shadow. They looked a lot alike.

"Jack, want a lollipop now?" I asked, hoping to lure him away from the edge, yet keep him good and quiet a bit longer.

"No, not now, Mom. I don't want a lollipop. I want to capture a shark. The man said I was big enough to capture a shark. I want to fish."

"I'll take you fishing later," I said.

"I want to fish now," he insisted. "Take me fishing now. I don't want to go later."

My plan of Jack being perfectly good was quickly going overboard, and the last thing I wanted at a moment like this was any sort of temper tantrum, especially because he was too old for those and I didn't want to scare Josh away.

"Nothing can stop a boy from wanting to fish," Josh said, studying my eyes. "I think I might understand this little fellow."

Tears were welling up in my eyes, and I tried hard to fight them back. "You can? Why is that?" I asked.

"I was just like him as a kid."

"You were? What do you mean?"

"Lydia, it's hard to hide. Jack is so much like his father it's not funny."

"You think?"

"Yeah, and I'm starting to think you've come for more than just a vacation."

"You're right. We've come to talk with you."

"I'm big enough to catch a shark," Jack interrupted. "Hey, man," he called out to Josh. "Will you take me fishing?"

"Sir, Jack. It's sir, not 'man' and 'excuse me' not 'hey.' " I snickered nervously at Josh. "I told you he warms up."

"Four years old," stated Josh. "Has it really been that long since I saw you last, Lydia? Since you and I went fishing?"

"Yes," I said again. "It has been. You're exactly right."

Josh shook his head and looked down at the dock, then back up at me again and into my eyes, then over at his son, then up at the sky and back down at his feet again.

"I wanted you to meet him. I'm sorry I've kept this from you."

"Why now? Why after four years have you finally decided to introduce us? Looks like you've been doing a fine job on your own, without me knowing."

"I don't know," I said, grabbing hold of the words Ava had used on Jaden. "I'm a woman, not a man-chaser."

"What the . . . ?"

"I didn't feel right hunting you down. That's not what a lady does. It's not proper."

"Maybe for most ladies it isn't, but you? 'Proper' isn't exactly the word I'd ever use to describe you, Lydia."

"Thanks," I said, trying to take it as a compliment. "Maybe it had more to do with me wanting to do everything on my own. But not anymore! I was hurt that morning when I learned you had left. I regretted horribly what we had done, and I questioned whether I meant anything at all to you."

"You meant something. You meant more than you'll ever know, but what was I to do? You yourself were talking all about the life you were returning to and never mentioned a word about any relationship or feelings for me whatsoever. I wasn't going to complicate your ambition, and since you were leaving yourself that day, I never got around to telling you that I was too. Part of it was that I was still thinking of calling off the entire Peace Corps thing. I had wanted to do something, but as it got closer, I didn't want to leave the life I loved. It's like, what was I trying to prove? I considered not going that day, but I'd have to live with that sense of 'should have' all my life, so I went. And finally, after my two years were up, I returned home only to go to war a couple of months later. I'm back now, and I live a good life here, simple. I never told you this, but since we're both telling all, I'll let you know that my mother walked out on my father when I was a boy. I'm looking at you now wondering whether you're leaving in an hour. Tell me, Lydia, what are your intentions, exactly?"

"I'm not your mother," I said. "But I am the mother of your son, and it's

PORTION of the SEA

not about me anymore and it's not about you. It's about him now. How do you want to go about this? He could come visit once a year, more if you like, or not at all. I'll do as you like."

He lowered his voice. "You're just laying this all on me. I haven't absorbed any of this yet."

I reached into the flap of my purse and pulled out a lollipop. "Here, Jack, catch," I said, then tossed it onto the dock. "Sit down while you eat it and keep quiet so you don't choke."

I knew I had exactly seven minutes. That was the time it took Jack to lick, then bite and chew that particular kind of lollipop—the things a mother knows. I stepped closer to Josh and lowered my voice. "I'm sorry," I said. "I didn't mean to dump it all on you like this, but that day you left, I tried catching up with you on the causeway. I had planned on telling you that I'd stay in Florida, write for the paper here, and see if maybe you and I could pursue a relationship. I made that decision before ever knowing I was pregnant with your child. I made it because my feelings for you were strong and I didn't want to let a good thing slip by. And now, the only reason I'm back to tell you all of this is for Jack's sake. You are his father, and it wouldn't be fair to him if I didn't at least try to pursue you, or investigate the possibility of you and me maybe getting back . . ."

"Lydia," he said, placing his finger softly over my lip to stop my speech. "I'm engaged."

The words hit me like the rain that was now starting to fall. The thought of him dating someone else or being engaged or married had crossed my mind, but I ignored it and failed to prepare myself for both that and the rain, and so now I stood there in front of him, my insides cold and drenched from the dark news. My outsides were getting wet too, but I didn't mind that as much.

"Oh my God," I said, putting my hand to my face. I closed my eyes a second, and when I opened them I wished he were no longer standing close. "I feel like a fool. When? When are you getting married?"

"We haven't set a date yet. I'm letting my fiancée choose that."

I wanted to cry. The word "fiancée" struck me like a bolt of lightning. I could only hope she was a good, strong, loving woman, or marriage would be the end of him. Josh was the type to mate for life, good or bad, like the scrub-jays and the American bald eagles. They all mate for life. I laughed at my own stupidity and at the fantasy world in which I lived for having believed that the man I loved would be anchoring out in a boat waiting all these years for me to return, something that only happens in a movie, not in real life. "You must at least have a month picked out."

"We were thinking July," Josh said and then reached for an umbrella. "No thanks," I said. "Jack loves holding umbrellas. Here, Jack."

As Josh opened it and steadied it in his son's little hands, I thought back to the letters he had sent me way back, the ones in which he described the seasons on Sanibel at a time when I badly wanted to be standing in those seasons with him. "What about the daily afternoon thunderstorms in July? Wouldn't you worry about lightning?"

"I hadn't thought of that. She also mentioned September."

"Florida's lovebug season? They do fly united until parted by death. I guess it could be romantic."

"How about winter?" he asked with a grin.

"Passing cold fronts."

"She prefers a spring wedding anyway."

"Alligator mating season? Don't hold the ceremony near a swamp, unless you want gators bellowing as you walk down the aisle."

"They do have rhythm. Can't take that away from them," he said. "For someone who doesn't live in Florida, you sure know a lot about its seasons."

"I read your letters over and over again. You write beautifully, you know. I think you've got a talent. Those letters read like a novel."

He smirked and looked away. "I think she mentioned spring as when she wants to have it."

"Tell her the water might still be brisk in April and lovebug season returns again in May."

"Good thing you're not her wedding consultant."

"If I were, I'd be sure she gave it serious thought, when to have it, that is."

"And when would you have it?"

"Hmmm," I said, smiling. "I'd go with fall, probably late September or early October, when the bald eagles court up in the sky."

"I didn't know you're a bald eagle fan," he said.

"They pair for life. Who wouldn't be a fan of that?"

Just then Jack handed me his empty stick. I was glad he was done, for now he could better hold the umbrella steady. "Is he a fisherman, Mommy?" he asked, standing on his tiptoes and trying to cover me from the rain. "I want to be a fisherman when I grow up."

Josh looked away and then turned his back to us, and I wondered what he was looking at. "What now, Lydia?" he asked, his back still to me. "What do you want from me? You think you can just show up here like this after four years and . . ."

"Please stand over there," I told Jack. "So you don't poke us with that umbrella."

I then lowered my voice and walked up close to Josh. "I understand if you want us to leave. We'll return to our life and you can return to yours. You can forget about us if you'd like to. I certainly didn't come here to ruin your life, and I don't regret telling you, or at least trying for his sake, but it's up to you now. What do you want us to do?"

"Son," he said a moment later, taking his hat off and putting it on Jack's head. "Would you like to go fishing tomorrow morning? I'm leaving at around eight o'clock and I sure could use help."

The rain moved, I noticed. It was still raining several yards away and I could see it beating down on the bay, but where we were standing it had now stopped. I could see the sun shining down on both my son and his father.

"Hey, Lydia," Josh said to me. "You'll never believe what I found just the other day."

"What?"

"A Junonia shell, of all things."

"You did not! It's not fair," I said. "You know I've been looking for years now and even in downtown Chicago, I'd keep my head down every day as I walked along Michigan Avenue, hoping . . . anything is possible, right?"

"Yeah, and I'm going to get my picture in the paper for it. Tomorrow, maybe."

"I hate you," I said, laughing.

"Too bad," he said. "Because I was about to ask if you wanted to share that Junonia with me, so we could both get our picture in the paper together."

I stopped laughing. "I love you," I said and ran into his arms.

It would be the most newsworthy story I took part in ever!

XLVII

SANIBEL ISLAND
1969
ONE YEAR LATER

Marlena

So many steps a woman takes in her life will not be remembered. And most of her tracks will be erased. But there will always be those certain steps she'll never regret, the ones she'll never forget—those glistening steps she took for herself.

IT WAS THE SEASON in which the bald eagles take to the sky for courting that both weddings took place. And the migrating songbirds were lining the trees and the Roseate Spoonbills were nesting on the island and the sea grape leaves were turning red and falling to the ground.

I had never been to a barefoot wedding before, where the aisle was a sandbar in the Gulf of Mexico and we only had twenty minutes of low tide and then the sea would wash over the patch of sand we were standing on. It was early fall, so the water was still warm from the summer months as

I stepped out of the anchored boat and waded onto the sandbar. And just as I glanced upward I witnessed a pair of eagles catching each other's feet in mid-flight and our small group marveled as the birds then dropped close to the earth, as if they might strike, parting just in time. The enormous sun would soon be setting behind the bride and groom, and it was coloring the sky orange against the turquoise water. It reminded me of my own mother's wedding to Jaden years before, only they got married in a church and held their reception on the beach, not a sandbar.

As the ceremony began, I dug my toes into the sand and felt as grounded as one can standing on a sandbar during low tide. I glanced around at the others, barefoot beside me, and wondered whether they had ever gone as far as I. For there had been times when I soared higher than the eagles and other times when I crashed deep down into the depths of the ocean.

"On this special day I give to you in the presence of God and his creations my sacred promise to stay by your side as your husband," the groom said.

I closed my eyes and quickly said my own prayer to the Lord, thanking him for the life I've lived.

"To love you in the spring as the shorebirds arrive with their crisp colors and feathers freshly molted."

I wanted to focus on the wedding ceremony, but my mind often did its own thing. There had been times in my life when my mind was like a burrowing owl, active both day and night, and when anyone tried stopping me I became agitated and probably bobbed and bowed and made clucking noises like an owl. Other times my thoughts were still and stagnant, like a swamp, and I treated people like Lydia, and others who cared, like floating debris headed my way.

"To love and protect you in the summer as the sea turtles crawl ashore to nest." The bride had tears strolling down her cheeks.

There are things passed on in families that go unrecognized until we really talk and share stories, or research our family trees. The illness the doctor recently diagnosed me with I believe my mother had, and based on what she wrote in her journals, perhaps Abigail had, and poor old wandering Milton also may have had a form of it. There are different types of depression—situational, hormonal, chemical, and seasonal having to do with lack of light.

"To love and cry with you in the fall when the feathers of the birds are tattered and faded and their once-sharp colors diminished from sun and rain."

It was spine-tingling at times to relate to the symptoms my ancestors had as described in the journal, but comforting to know I wasn't alone in my own suffering. None of us are.

"To love and comfort you through passing winter cold fronts."

I am glad I took that simple glistening step long ago. The doctor's appointment I made for myself led to a diagnosis and, eventually, treatment and medicine that made a difference.

"To love and laugh with you year-round like the blooming Florida wildflowers."

I wiped tears of joy from my eyes, thankful that God gave me a daughter, not one I gave birth to myself, but in the form of Lydia, and every bit a daughter in the true definition of the word. She, like my mother had once done, was marrying the man of her dreams, and it was as thrilling to me as the spacecraft Eagle landing on the moon. And it made me realize more than ever that anything is indeed possible—with God.

"I promise to love and cherish you vibrantly as you so deserve, as we live our lives passionately according to the seasons on Sanibel."

The bride and groom were now kissing and behind them the sun had just vanished below the horizon, and the guests were anxious to get back into the boat and sail off before the water washed over the sandbar, but we didn't want to interrupt their kiss.

Just then, little Jack bent down where the water meets the sand and scooped up a handful of water, then splashed it toward his mother and father, and the intimate gathering of guests broke out into laughter and applause.

There was just enough time for us to quickly sip champagne before getting back into the boat. And as I took my seat and looked back, I noticed the water had already rushed over the sand we had been standing on, and the shoes I had slipped off my feet and forgotten back there were gone.

But isn't that what happens to our lives? We look back and before we know it a new generation is washing over us. If they're fortunate, they might find a pair of our old shoes, and without knowing, walk in our tracks from time to time. But mostly they'll make new ones of their own.

THE END

PORTION
of the
SEA

READER'S GUIDE

1. **MARLENA** believes girls should be challenged to look ahead and imagine who it is they want to become and what sort of life they'd like for themselves. She says most girls don't give this any thought until they're grown up and are disliking their lives. Do you agree? She also said if women could look back to when they were younger and recall the things they loved to do, they might get ideas for change. Is this true?

2. **SOCIETY AND ROLES.** Ava and Lydia were from two different historical periods—Ava, the late 1800s and Lydia, the fifties—yet they had much in common and would probably be friends had they the chance. What similar struggles did they both face with regard to society's expectation of women? What pressures did Ava get from her mother? What about Lydia from her father, as well as her civics teacher? Are men still that way today?

Tootie tells Ava's mother that outspokenness will serve Ava well, that girls are trained to be perfect little ladies and then enter the real world and don't know how to stand up for themselves or be rude to a rude person or strong in a bad situation. Do you agree? How did each woman rebel?

3. MARLENA tells the young Lydia that she believes in her and one day she will become a success. How can such words influence a girl's life?

4. GEOGRAPHY AND OUTLOOK ON LIFE. How does living in Kentucky in the winter affect Abigail's internal weather? How does moving to Sanibel affect Abigail's spirits? How can geography influence people's moods, dispositions, and outlooks?

5. WISDOM. Ava wants her own wisdom to pick up where her grandmother's left off, but senility has grown roots around Dahlia's wisdom, strangling it. And her mother always shuts the grandmother up just as she's about to say something wise. Is wisdom something women admire and want for themselves today? Is it something younger women can possess, or is wisdom something that belongs to older women only? What use does wisdom have? Is it recognized and appreciated within families? How does one attain wisdom?

6. TOOTIE TELLS AVA to keep reading and writing because those things can change a girl's world. Ava wants a new world for herself. How does the world that Ava wants compare to that which Lydia wants? What sort of world do women want for themselves today?

7. THE DREAMS A WOMAN HAS FOR HER LIFE. Ava lies in bed thinking maybe there's an oasis of hidden beauty deep within her own self, waiting to be discovered. She then tells her grandmother that she one day wants to be a writer. Dahlia tells her: You sound like your mother. She said that once, too. She also said she wanted to be a ballerina. Look at her now. She married your father and that was the end of that. But Ava's ambitions are gusty strong and they're not going to be blown over by negative

words. How can every day life get in the way of accomplishing our dreams? What does Ava do right after her grandmother discourages her?

8. JOY. Dahlia believes joy is an abundant and limitless natural resource within every woman and that whenever it feels scarce, all she must do is tap into it. Ava believes joy is found outdoors and she hopes to collect some as she leaves behind her chores for the day and voyages out alone. Did she find any? Where do you believe joy is found?

9. THE GLISTENING STEPS A WOMAN TAKES FOR HERSELF. The novel makes frequent references to glistening water and glistening pathways. What do these glistening pathways represent in relation to the character's steps they must take to live their own lives? What sorts of glistening steps have you taken, or are you thinking of taking for yourself?

10. A STRONG WOMAN. If you asked Lydia what it meant to be a strong woman, what do you think she'd say? Does Lydia take the idea of being a strong woman too far when she wouldn't let Ethan know of her financial struggles? Is asking a man or God for help a sign of weakness? Is surrendering the stronger thing to do?

11. HEARTACHE. According to Ava, what happens when a woman loses her heart? What happened to Lydia when she lost her heart?

12. PARALLEL LIVES. How does Lydia's life parallel Ava's? How did you respond to reading the parallel lives? Did you at times get confused between the two characters? Did you like the overlap?

13. LEGACIES. What can mothers pass on to their children? Or women pass on to the next generation?

14. ROWING OUT TO YOUR OWN PORTION OF THE SEA. What do you think it means for a woman to pick up her paddles and row out to her very own portion of the sea?

CHRISTINE LEMMON is author of three inspiring novels —
Sanibel Scribbles, *Portion of the Sea*, *Sand in My Eyes*, and the gift book
Whisper from the Ocean. She has worked as an on-air host for a
National Public Radio affiliate, business magazine editor,
and publicist for a non-fiction publishing house.

She lives with her husband and three children on
Sanibel Island, the setting of her three novels.
VISIT CHRISTINELEMMON.COM

ALSO BY CHRISTINE LEMMON

CHRISTINELEMMON.COM

SAND IN MY EYES
An Older Woman Growing
Flowers, A Younger Woman
Caught up in the Weeds, and
the Seasons of Life.

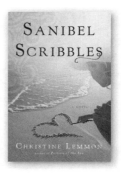

SANIBEL SCRIBBLES
A Story About a Woman's
Journey to an Island, and then
Spain, Facing Mortality and
Embracing Life.

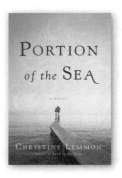

PORTION OF THE SEA
A Tale About the Treasures a
Woman has—Heart, Soul and
Mind—and the Struggle to
Keep Them Afloat.

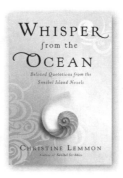

WHISPER FROM THE
OCEAN ~ GIFT BOOK
Treasured Quotations from
Christine Lemmon's first
three novels. Hardcover.